HUNTER OF HEARTS

"Do you have a way with women as you do with animals?" Genevieve asked.

"*Non*, I am afraid I do not. I am a hunter, you see. A *coureur de bois*, as we are called. Sometimes I live with the Indians, sometimes I live on my own in the wilderness. It is as it seems most appropriate at the moment. My women"—he shrugged and his voice took on a faraway tone—"my women have always been of my tribe."

Genevieve sat there silently, not knowing what else to say. There was a strained moment before she had the courage to ask, "You are not here to find a wife?"

He turned toward her, studying her a long moment before he responded, "*Non*. I do not wish to wed again. I came only to see what was for *sale*."

Furious with him, she stood. "You are wrong, Monsieur. Perhaps the other women will sell themselves to the man with the greatest fortune, but I certainly will not!"

SERITA STEVENS

DAUGHTERS OF DESIRE

LEISURE BOOKS ∞ NEW YORK CITY

A LEISURE BOOK

Published by

Dorchester Publishing Co., Inc.
6 East 39th Street
New York, NY 10016

Printed in the United States of America

DEDICATED TO
my own Alexander, the Great, and his brothers
Charlie Dickens and Edgar A. Poe

Sheila and Elizabeth Spiro
for their proofing and suggestions

and finally
The Quebec Government Office
and
my other Canadian friends
for their invaluable assistance

1

Sweat beaded his brow, dampening the edges of his perfectly coiffed wig. It was, the Marquis de Racine thought, an unusually warm evening for early spring. The ballroom doors leading to the gardens were open, and burning incense and melting wax mingled with the scent of early-blooming flowers. Ah, yes—the flowers Louis had ordered replanted on a daily basis, just so he wouldn't be bored with the landscape. In truth, one was seldom bored in the presence of the Sun King.

Racine turned toward the stage. Off to one side the gilt chairs waited for the players. He looked forward to seeing Moliere's new comedy, *Le Bourgeois Gentilhomme*, this night. The playwright was always amusing—even though his subjects were often of a sensitive nature.

A soft cloud of flute music floated through the room as the Marquis stifled a yawn and studied the opulent array of foods before him. He picked up a jellied calf's heart and nibbled a delicate bite. The royal food was supposed to have aphrodisiac qualitites, but not for him.

His private physician told him that his malady was a result of his early years of living too well. Bah! When did one ever live too well? *Mon Dieu!* These quacks knew nothing of what they said.

Racine picked up a sweetmeat. What was needed at these parties was some new blood. Racine knew his problem was due merely to boredom. He glanced at his reflection in one of the many mirrored walls and adjusted his white lace cravat. Perfection! In the candlelight, he looked younger than his sixty-three years; nevertheless, it did not hurt to take pains with one's dress.

Glancing around, Racine smiled at Mademoiselle de Sevinge. Her wasp-like bodice was cut appealing low to reveal creamy white breasts. Her stomacher, of contrasting silk, showed off the glory of her young body. He shook his head as he wet his cracked lips. Ah, it was a shame his problem caused so many difficulties. His gaze traveled across the room, stopping at several other of the bejeweled and silk-swathed women, with their high nests of hair. He didn't want to think how many of these women might have graced his bed, if only he had the power to pleasure them.

Sighing audibly, he turned his attention toward the pastries. He snapped his pudgy fingers and nodded slightly toward where his valet stood. Immediately the man came over to adjust the golden sword belt to a more comfortable position on the Marquis' massive girth. His waistcoat was too tight. He grunted as the valet adjusted that as well. One notch, two notches. What did it matter? Food was his only pleasure now. There was no sense in being uncomfortable. He turned to the rainbow array, studying it with a loving fondness as he wondered which delicacy to sample next.

Heralds proclaimed a new arrival. While Racine seldom paid attention to anyone but his own dear friends, he found himself looking up as the tall, weasel-like Vicomte de Patin and his daughter, Genevieve, were announced. The Marquis' nearly toothless mouth dropped open as he raised his monocle to his eye and squinted. That this man could have such a daughter!

He felt new blood surge through him as his flagging desire revived. Was it merely the shimmering light of the candles? Unconsciously, he took a step forward, scarely aware that his valet had come immediately to his side.

Sacré bleu! The girl was the most delicate morsel he had ever seen. Better than the pastry tray before him. She wore a transparent black dress over a gown of gold brocade. No patches marred the whiteness of her skin—which he was sure could only be natural. Short auburn curls covered her head and trailed down her back, in a popular style of several years ago, but one that suited her to perfection. Even her small feet were delicately covered in black mules molded to her.

The Marquis licked his lips as he took another step forward. His interest did not flag. Ye Gods! He hadn't felt such a stirring in—what? Five years? Not even the court ladies, knowledgeable in the womanly arts though they were, had been able to raise his desire to such a level.

His heart pounded. He could not take his eyes off her. He was scarcely aware of Henri, his valet, wiping the saliva from his chin with a linen handkerchief. He continued to stare.

From the buzz in the room, it seemed he was not the only one to feel such excitement. But he, the Marquis declared, would be the one to possess this girl. She needed someone worldly like him, someone who would be devoted to her, to introduce her to the magnificent arts of love. By the gods, he would have her as his wife!

Yes, as his wife. The thought of owning such a delicate young thing brought forth a still stronger desire. No one, not even Madame de Maintenon before she found favor with the King, had been able to keep his attention this long!

But how was he to win the girl's affections when her father obviously had other plans for her?

He turned to motion Henri to his side, forgetting the valet was there already. Without taking his eyes from Genevieve's curvaceous figure, he said, "Tell the Vicomte de Patin that he is invited to cards in my suite this night."

The valet smiled slightly. "Shall I tell him to bring his daughter?"

The monocle dropped from the Marquis' eye as he turned to stare at the man. "What do you think, ass?" Then he paused. "Perhaps, on second thought, it is better if she does not come. I will not be able to concentrate on my game with her in the room."

Nodding, the valet responded, "Very good, m'lord."

The Marquis turned his attention once more toward the array of sumptuous foods and rejected them—a rare event for him, but he had seen perfection and it was hard to make do with less. He had found the only morsel he wanted to consume.

Heralds once more played—not once but thrice—to announce the entrance of His Majesty Louis XIV.

Racine toyed with a ripe berry and dropped one final morsel of jellied calf heart into his mouth before turning to greet his king. He hoped the added quantity of the aphrodisiac would inspire his body to greater performance. Though with his hardened desire, he doubted he would need it.

The balding little King rolled into the room accompanied by his courtiers and his many mistresses, together with their children and lackeys.

Racine smiled. Later this night he would inform His Majesty that he planned to wed the Vicomte's daughter. He foresaw no problems in winning the girl from her father. He worried only that the King would want the child for himself. Now that could be a problem. Just the thought made his desire flag, but only for a moment. He had only to look at the charming innocence—Venus perfected —with her slender waist and soft green eyes to feel the blood rush through his vital organs again. Perhaps he could even take her to bed this night.

No, he immediately rejected that idea.

While he would love to bed her tonight, if he could have sweetness for life, he would not be satisfied with a mere taste. No, he simply had to make Louis understand how important this was to him.

As Louis nodded to the musicians and made ready to begin the dance, Racine felt the pulsating of his blood. With a slight bow of acknowledgement first to his king, then in the direction of the Vicomte and his innocent beauty, Racine fled through the glass doors into the sweet-scented gardens.

A myriad of waterfalls played over the statues of Venus and Apollo. Racine inhaled the night air and the odor of roses as he walked quickly through the paths to the secret arbors designed for lovers such as he planned to be shortly. How amazing. Even without her presence to inspire him, his desire did not waver. Seated on one of the wrought-iron benches, hidden by groves of flowers and trees, the Marquis closed his eyes. He could almost imagine her with him as gently he touched his treasure, assuring himself that he was not in a dream. Yes, yes. After all these years he would again experience the joy he had once known. He imagined her soft white hands willingly caressing him, touching his precious jewels and stroking his wand of love to fulfillment.

Thinking of her delicate beauty and
fragile features—those large, sparkling
green eyes and long lashes, those firm and
tender breasts just right for nibbling,
made the blood pulse through him even
faster. He ignored the saliva that dripped
from his jowls. Other things were more
important at this moment. How wonderful
it would be when they joined. Oh! Even
now he could hear the voice of her ecstasy.
He wanted her and only her!

Five years of women—acknowledged
as professionals in the supreme art—had
not been able to bring him back to life as
one glimpse of Genevieve had. Genevieve,
what a beautiful name. How it would
sound when he whispered it to her. It took
but a moment more before the smile of
satisfaction came over his face. Even then,
as he once more thought of Genevieve
Simon, the Marquis de Racine knew he
must possess her not only for the moment,
but for life. The joy they would have together would be unbounded!

His long pent-up tension finally
released, the Marquis knew he must not
think of the girl if he was to concentrate on
his strategy to win her, for all the desire in
the world would do him no good if he could
not in reality feel her warm flesh nestled
against his.

His mouth was dry. He licked his lips

as he imagined how she would taste and felt his body once more spring to a life of its own. *Sacré bleu*! He must call the game—and now—before all his energies were spent here.

Dabbing the saliva from his mouth, the Marquis tightened his breeches to proclaim proudly his new-found virility. There was one and only one he wanted. Satisfied, Racine headed back to the dancing and a meeting with Louis.

So confident of his success was he that he was prepared to speak with His Majesty now. Perhaps he could wed Genevieve at the end of the week. He understood women liked to have a moment or two in preparation for their glorious gifts. He could wait a few days to culminate his plans and devour the precious treat which awaited him.

"Ah, Genevieve," he whispered as he walked swiftly back through the gardens. The fountains of Venus were this night overflowing. It was a good sign. Racine gave silent thanks to the goddess of love for the loan of her mortal daughter.

He re-entered the living rooms. His valet whispered that the King could not see him until later that night. Well, so be it. He would have already accomplished what he sought by then. Together with his servant he hurried toward the private suite where the card table was being prepared. It would be necessary to make a minor adjustment to the deck before they began. He knew the King would approve. All was fair in love and war.

2

The fire in the hearth of the ornate gaming room had already burned low, casting ghostly shadows on the rich wood walls, but neither of the players at the green baize table heeded anything but the cards in front of him. No one spoke a word as Racine's man silently refilled the glasses of fine brandy and backed off. The huge hall clock chimed loudly, twice.

Silence continued to reign as the Vicomte defiantly laid down his jack of clubs. His face held a mixture of fear and hope, but lifelong passions for cards and drink had clearly left their marks on him.

Across the table, the Marquis looked at the card, and then looked at Patin, now holding his breath. He smiled slightly, his thin lips curling.

"Well, have you nothing to say?" Patin said, impatient now.

The Marquis smiled again and studied his cards. He was becoming weary of this game and weary of the man across the table, and he knew that very soon he would put an end to everything. With a flourish, Racine laid down the ace and king of spades.

One could hear only the crackling fire and the sharp intake of the Vicomte's breath. His haggard features were etched deeply in the light of the dying fire and the pulses in his temple jumped like a captured hare.

"*Sacré bleu*, you cannot have won this round, too!"

Racine shrugged. "But I have, Patin. You see that I have. Even you, great gamesman that you are, must occasionally lose." Racine grinned.

The Vicomte frowned as his brows knelt together into one dark line. "You are either an excellent player or . . ."

"Or what?" Racine stood abruptly, exploding in self-righteous anger. The fat around his eyes narrowed the orbs to mere slits.

"Or nothing." The Vicomte sighed and motioned for his man to bring him quill, ink and parchment. "I am done for the night. You will take my paper?" He dipped the quill into the ink well without waiting for the answer.

Racine's heavier hand covered Patin's thin one. "*Non, mon cher,* I cannot. You have lost too heavily to me this night."

As the Vicomte looked up at Racine, the gold of his buttons reflected the dying rays of the fire and sparkled on the embroidered burgundy velvet of his doublet. Sweat beaded his brow. "Well, then, what is it you will have of me? A rematch?"

Racine shook his head.

"My lands then? You already own half of them as it stands." Patin forced a smile to his lips, but it did not light his eyes; his jaw continued to work tensely as he rose and paced the floor. The servants had quietly disappeared through the nearby door after clearing the table of the remains of the feast the men had consumed.

Racine's valet rushed to button the silver fastenings of his master's black coat, especially tailored to make him look thinner. Within a moment he had joined Patin by the fire. "You play a good game, my friend." The white, pasty hand touched the shoulder of the defeated man.

"So what is it you want?" The Vicomte looked up into the pig's eyes of the man beside him and knew a moment of despair as he saw Racine motion to his man for more brandy. The devil himself could not have drawn out the torture any longer.

"What do you have? Besides your lands, I mean, for which I have no use at the moment." Racine sipped the liquor and watched the other man squirming like a caught fish.

"Nothing. Except . . . my daughter."

"Oh?" Racine's thick white brow rose as if in surprise. "Your daughter? She wouldn't be that delectable piece I saw you with earlier this evening?"

"*Oui.*" Patin paused a moment. "*Cor bleu!* But you are not serious!"

"And why not?" Racine shrugged. "She is of value."

"To me she is of value because she is my daughter, and I love her."

"And you also hope to marry her off to some wealthy man here at court who will give her a title better than yours, and who will take care of her—and you—for the rest of your days." Racine cracked his thick knuckles as he extended his arms. "What better prize could you give me?"

"*Mon Dieu!* You are serious!" The Vicomte shook his head, unable to believe that this was happening. "But my daughter—!"

"—Will be in good hands." Racine smiled and cracked his knuckles again.

"But the King . . ."

"Already knows of my desire for her. *Diable!* I will be marry her, man! She will be a marquise. Think of the jewels, of the clothes, of the manors and servants she'll have. She'll be welcome at any court, not just that of our dear Sun King. I will wed her by the end of the week."

The Vicomte's mouth dropped open.

"That is, as long as you agree." Racine indicated the parchment and ink still on the table.

"You planned this?"

"*Moi?*" Racine shook his head. "*Non*, my friend, you are wrong. I only talked to the King, telling him of my desire, but since you have no other choice . . ."

"What would you have done if I had won?"

Racine shrugged. "I tell you. My hopes were only speculation. I supposed, had you won, that I would have then had to woo her in the traditional way; but I am not a young man." He leered as his hand brushed his member, engorged as it was with the mere thought of Genevieve. "I cannot wait a long time for my pleasures." His chubby fingers tapped on the table as he idly surveyed the fallen cards.

Patin paced. "You are right. It is time she wed. But I had thought . . ."

"Who could be better for her than me, hmm?" The cat-like smile crossed Racine's face as he picked up a sweetcake, licking the frosting with his pig-pink tongue. "She is one of the most beautiful women

I've ever seen."

Patin's eyes, blearly from drink and defeat, focused on some faraway memory. "Yes, her mother was, too." The Vicomte sighed. "Very well. My Genevieve will be yours."

Racine rubbed his hands together gleefully as he pushed the parchment closer to the other man. "Write it, my friend. Sign it and the game will be closed."

The Vicomte took up the quill and stared a moment at the ink, then at the cards.

"Do you still doubt, my friend? We can play yet another game, but I will ask for more than just your daughter."

"No, I do not doubt you have won fairly." The scratch of the sharpened nib against the stiff paper was the only other sound in the room.

"You will tell your daughter to prepare herself," Racine said, as he folded the paper and handed it back to his man. "I will make the arrangements for our wedding at the end of the week."

The Vicomte de Patin stood and nodded. "Till the end of the week, Racine." He touched the cards one last time and stiffly left the room.

Patin climbed the stairs to their poor quarters off the *rue Dauphine* and smelled the breakfast cooking of onions, wrinkling his nose at the stink. In many ways, he thought, this was the only choice that was available to him and Genevieve, considering their lack of funds.

There was no reason for him to complain. After all, Racine was marrying her, was he not? He rationalized that in some ways the game last night was by far the best that could have happened to him and his daughter. What else did they have to sell besides the ancient lands? It was not his fault. *Hélas*, he had tried his best to be a good father.

By rights they should have been housed in the one of the three royal pavillions where many noblemen, as well as the actors and other entertainers, were accommodated. But Patin had been out of court circles so long, struggling as he had to save the estate in Joigny, that his petition had been forgotten and he had been forced to make do with whatever hangers-on such as he could find. At least the King had remembered to place him on the list for the ball.

He rested on the landing and looked out of the open window in the direction of the palace, spread out before him like the miniature city it was. From here the scent of the orange trees obliterated that of the onions, and he could see the blossoms of the gardens as the workers planted and replanted for the King's outrageous tastes. He wondered if he could appeal to

Louis, but recalled that Racine was a royal cousin of sorts. He grimaced and hurried up the remaining stairs.

His key squeaked in the lock, and as he opened the door he wondered how he could break the news to his Genny. He sighed as he recalled how she had cried and carried on when he'd forbidden her to see Alexandre, that peasant boy, and he winced as he prepared himself for a similar scene. He stepped into her boudoir and saw the golden-red curls framing her face on the pillow. She slept like an angel with that stupid cat, also named Alexandre, curled up at her side. Feeling the master staring at them, Alexandre opened one blue eye and then the other before deciding it was safe to awaken his mistress. More gentle than a man might have been, Alexandre used his paw to push Genevieve's hair from her eyes and caress her lids with his rough tongue as he nuzzled his head next to hers.

Genevieve's eyes fluttered open. She reached out to pet the cat and saw her father standing in front of the bed. "Was it a good game, Papa? Did you win everything from that senile creature?" She smiled as she swung her slender legs off the bed and pushed the cat aside so she could put on her robe. "Shall I ring for breakfast or have you already eaten?"

"Later, my pet." The Vicomte took his

daughter's hands in his and urged her back on the bed. "We must talk."

"No, we must eat. Even if you are not hungry, I am starved. There will be muffins and chocolate downstairs. No?" She smiled at her father and kissed his brow as she went to the washstand. The water was left from yesterday and Genny sighed. "I am not used to having to do things for myself. Well, you will soon be able to afford me my maid." She gave her father a tender smile. "After all, that is why we came to court, is it not, Papa? To fleece these rich nobles of money they do not need?" She dipped her hands in the lukewarm water, washing her face and then, turning to dry herself, she saw her father's face.

Slowly, she put the towel down. "So you did not win. Well, there are other nights."

" 'Tis more than that, my little love."

"What then?" she asked, slipping her feet into embroidered silk mules and purposefully choosing a light chemise of lawn, several petticoats, and an open skirt and matching bodice of sea-green silk. Disappearing behind the screen in the room, she waited for her father to continue. When he said nothing, she peeked out. "Truly, Papa, nothing could be that bad as long as we still have the land."

Slowly he nodded. "That we still have."

"Well then"—she bounded out from behind the dressing partition—"what could be worse?" She hugged him to her and kissed his worried brow as she turned for him to fasten her. With a sigh, she said again, "I shall be so glad to have my maid back. And if you've not won tonight, then you will tomorrow, or the next day."

Silently, the Vicomte assisted his daughter; then, with his hands on her shoulders, he turned her around to face him. "You must listen to me, Genevieve." He paused and tears appeared briefly in his eyes. "You are to be wed."

"Wed?" Her green eyes widened larger than the cat's. "To whom?" She picked up the animal which, having sensed her tension, was rubbing at her feet.

"Whom do you think? The Marquis de Racine. He bested me in the game last night, my Genny, and when I had nothing more to give, he asked for your hand."

"Surely, Papa, you did not give it to him. I. mean, that man is old enough—older than grandpère." She shook her head, unable to believe what her father was saying.

"It is true, my precious." The Vicomte took a linen from his jacket and dabbed at his eyes. "I am sorry, my Genny. I could do nothing else." He shook his head. "But you'll see, it will work out fine. He will give you all that you want. You'll have your maids back, the coachman, the servants, the manor. You will have everything you can possibly desire."

"Everything but love, Papa."

"*Hélas*, child! What marriage has love in it? You will do your duty by the Marquis and you will be free to"—the Vicomte waved his lace-covered wrist—"to do as you please."

"But Papa, if I marry, then I want to love the man I marry. I want to be true to him."

"Such foolish notions you get from your books. I knew I should have forbidden them. If only your mother had not interfered."

"But you see, you loved my mother. You were faithful to her." She saw the look in her father's eyes. "Well, at least, she was faithful to you."

He shrugged. "Most marriages, especially most court marriages, are not like that. You will learn. My pet, the Marquis is old—"

"Too old."

The Vicomte shook his powdered head. "He will soon die, and you will be a widow, my love. A wealthy widow with the choice of any courtier you choose."

Stunned, Genevieve sank back down on the bed and heard the springs creak.

The cat at her side rolled over, begging for his tummy to be scratched. "Papa! How could you do this? How could you sell me like—like a piece of property?"

"Racine adores you. He told me so himself."

"Adores me! How can he adore me when he has only seen me once?" She picked up the volume of poetry she had been reading the night before and threw it against the already stained walls, startling the cat into scurrying under the bed.

Genevieve sighed and closed her eyes. "Papa, please, you cannot ask me to marry. . . ." Her voice trailed off and she shuddered, recalling her nightmares. "You know I was planning to take the vows."

"Pshaw! You do not belong in a convent, my love."

"Papa, I do. 'Tis the only place for me. I have sinned."

"And how have you sinned?" His brow rose slightly in disbelief that his perfect daughter could have sinned. "Not with that peasant fellow?"

She looked at him wide-eyed. "Alexandre! Heavens, no." She shook her head sadly. "We but talked. Though I confess, he did seem gentle and kind." She stared at her father a moment more, then shook her head. How could she tell her father that it was his brother, her uncle, who had caused her to fear men?

The way he had looked at her, the way he had tried to touch her. Even now her stomach cramped as she thought of it. 'Twas true she was quite young then, and she did not think any bodily harm had come to her, but the thought of being with a man, any man, had forever been soured for her. Only Alexandre knew. Only he had been able to encourage her to talk of her fears. And once she had allowed her friend to take her hand, but no more than that.

"Genevieve, my sweet, you must marry him. You have no choice. Not unless you can find the 500 ecus I owe the man."

Her eyes widened again. "Why did you let it get so high? Why did you not stop?" She shook her head and, sighing, she answered her own question. "Never mind. I know. You thought your luck would turn momentarily." She picked up the squirming cat and placed him back on her lap. "And what of Alexandre? May I take him?"

"But of course."

Pleased that she was giving in without a fuss, her father leaned over and kissed her daughter's cheek. He took her by the elbow and assisted her up. "Come. We will breakfast now and you may attend the chapel as you desire. I, for one, will sleep."

Genevieve nodded and stood, still holding the cat. As her father started out the room, she stroked the warm, furry body. "Don't worry, Alex. It will work out." She looked at the hunched-over back of her father waiting in the hall. "I hope."

The cat meowed his response and blinked his eyes, as if he understood. Then, spying a ball of yarn, he jumped from her arms and proceeded to play as Genevieve followed her father out.

3

The clock struck twelve and Patin
yawned.

"You had best get some rest, Papa, if
you are to play again tonight."

"*Non*, my child." His hand touched
hers. "I do not have to use my skills any
longer. Racine has promised to pay all the
debts owed for the estate once you are wed
to him. I may relax in luxury as our
ancestors did"—his eyes grew dreamy as
he thought of the past—"hunting,
gaming, and . . ."

She shook her head. "I do hope you're
not going to say wenching?" She placed
her breakfast roll on the table. "Papa,
sometimes you disgust me. You have no
feeling for anyone but yourself."

"*Mon Dieu*! Is that my daughter

talking?''

She took a deep breath. "Papa, I am not at all pleased about this proposed marriage. I . . ."

"But you will go ahead with it, nonetheless." The Vicomte's eyes narrowed. "You must think of our home. Think of our ancestral lands. Think of . . ."

"Why must I think of them when you did not? When you risked everything with your gaming? No wonder *Maman* cried herself to sleep so many nights." She stood as the bells echoed through the small town surrounding the palace, telling all it was time for mass. "I must go now or I shall be late, and no one must enter the church after the King."

The Vicomte nodded. He watched his daughter hurry from the room and into the street where the carriage waited to take her to the small chapel that Louis had built at the palace for the spiritual needs of its community.

A few of the noblemen were already seated in the pews, but for the most part, the group waiting to receive mass were the wives and daughters of those members of the nobility who had not spent the night in gaming and revelry and on whom the salvation of their families fell. Genevieve slipped into an empty seat next to Louise de La Vallière.

It was impossible not to notice how

sunken the eyes of the King's former mistress had become and how haggard she now looked. That she had been ill was well known; that she had been poisoned by the Marquise de Montespan, the King's current mistress, was suspected by many. Rumor also had it that Louise had, upon her recovery, spent quite a few months at the Carmelite convent and that she had now petitioned His Majesty to allow her to join the nuns in a holy life.

For a very brief moment, Genevieve thought of her own religious inclinations but decided that she could never tolerate being shut away from the world as a nun. True, she disliked much of what she saw in the world, but her dreams were—she allowed a sigh to come forth just as the herald announced the king—her dreams were, as her father had said, very romantic. Perhaps too romantic.

As Louis entered, the congregation stood with their backs to the altar, facing the King, who knelt down on a velvet cushion in the royal tribune. To Genevieve, this was a farce, for it appeared that the people were adoring the King and that only Louis had the right to adore the Savior. The priest came down the aisle swinging the incense lamp and all watched as the King took of the blessed blood and body of Christ.

Only after His Majesty had left did

the many nobles and ministers who had come in the King's entourage follow the King's act of communion. Then they too left, and Genevieve once again felt the peace that being in a church was supposed to bring. She continued to wait silently in her seat as the others present took of the body and the blood, and waited still more until the chapel was relatively empty.

Finally, she approached the altar and genuflected before the cross, feeling tears in her eyes. At this very moment, she was sure she knew what Christ had felt like when, betrayed by his former friends, he was led to his death at the hands of the Romans. Even the names fit: Romans and Racine. But no, if was not Racine who had betrayed her—it was Papa.

She opened her mouth to receive the offering. Her eyes closed as she tried to think of the holy moment she was experiencing, but all she could do was gag at the thought of Racine's fleshy, pampered body sweating all over her.

For a horrified moment, her nightmare returned and her heart pounded. How could she allow a man like Racine to take her? She had to find a way to escape. She had to! The act itself was as vile and disgusting as her uncle had been. Even the holy father said so, although he knew nothing of her private pain, or that her uncle was killed in a duel and she considered it her fault. But if the act were not evil, why would priests and nuns not be allowed this so-called pleasure? Genevieve knew that she herself would hate being with a man—especially a man as decrepit as Racine. Her thoughts went to her friend Alexandre, whom her father had sent away, and the tears again came to her eyes. It was true he was a peasant, and it was true the Patin ancestors would have turned over in their graves if she had run off with him. But he had been the only man, other than her father, for whom she'd had any affection. Only to him had she been able to confess her torment, but he was gone from her life now. And she felt that her peasant friend had betrayed her, in his own way, much as her father had. If he wanted to stay with her, a way would have been found.

"Mistress? Is something wrong?" The priest asked her.

Genevieve opened her eyes and realized that he was still standing in front of her, and that indeed, save for him, she was alone in the chapel. Flushing, Genevieve shook her head. "*Non, Monsieur, 'abbé.*"

The priest, a man not much older than herself, frowned. "But you are crying."

Genevieve took a deep breath. "I cry for the pain Our Lord Jesus must have suffered on the cross and before."

He thought a moment. "Very well. But if you wish to talk, I would be happy to hear your confession."

"I have little to confess but my own fears, Monsieur."

He shrugged and moved on and she was totally alone in the chapel, alone with her thoughts and the statue of Christ on the wall.

Only then did Genevieve allow her tears to flow. "Why have you done this to me, God? Why could you not give me a calling? Why could you not have Papa lose to some other man who would be good to me, someone I could love and respect? Why—?"

A noise at her side startled her and Genevieve looked around to see Claudine, her former maid, who had been taken in one of Papa's losing games by the Duc de Saint-Simon.

"Oh." Genevieve breathed a sigh of relief. " 'Tis you, Claudine."

"*Oui*, Mademoiselle, 'tis I." The little maid approached the altar and genuflected as she sank to her knees. "I have heard of your misfortune."

"So soon?" The taste was sour in Genny's mouth.

"The Marquis is boasting all over court of how wonderful your wedding will be and how he will make you the happiest girl on earth."

"I doubt that!"

"No, 'tis true. I mean, that is what he says. Though you are right, for I have heard from many of the maids he has taken that he pushes and tugs and pulls and often releases himself much too quickly, with no care for the woman."

Disgusted, Genevieve made a face. This was the last thing she wanted to hear.

"Socrates' hemlock would be preferable! I do not want to marry the man, Claudine. It makes me ill to think of his hands touching me and yet . . . Papa needs me." She turned to her former maid with tears in her eyes. "What can I do?"

The maid shook her head. "I do not know, Mistress. I know only that I have come to say good-bye to you."

"Why? Where do you go?"

"To the colonies. New France."

"The colonies?"

"*Oui*, I will be one of the King's Daughters, as we will be called. Several of us from my village have been chosen and asked if we would do the King the honor of going across the waters to marry his soldiers and make children for the wilderness land there."

"Oh." Genevieve sighed. "I shall miss you then, Claudine. I had always hoped that Papa could win you back or that—I don't know, perhaps I could have gotten the Marquis to buy you for me."

"*Non*, I have already received the Duc's permission to leave his service and I go this night."

"So soon?"

"It takes a good week to travel to Normandy and it is from there that the ship will leave."

Genevieve stood to hug her former maid. "Then I shall miss you even more than I missed you when you left my service."

"And I, you." The other girl responded to the hug. She paused a moment and, contemplating, removed a sou from her pocket, placing it in the box before she lit a candle. Her eyes closed as she prayed.

Finally, she spoke. "Perhaps you would go as well? You could escape Racine that way."

Genevieve shook her head. "How can I? I am not made for the dangers of the wilderness. I have barely been able to take care of Papa and me since you and the other servants left. *Non*, it is tempting, but it is not for me. Besides, I do not even wish to marry."

"My cousin wrote me from Quebec. She has gone over already and said life there is not as hard as you think. True, it is a cold hell and there are Indians to worry on, but for the most part they dance, they sing and they make merry." Claudine smiled. "That is, when they are not making babies."

Genevieve shook her head, disgusted. "Papa believes I will do all that he asks, for the sake of our ancestral home, but Claudine, truly, there are some things one cannot do."

The maid smiled sympathetically at her former mistress and took a deep breath. "It is not always as crass as the scene you saw with Marie and the groom."

Genevieve shuddered. "I want no man in my life." She sighed. "But I cannot see it in my heart to have a calling."

"Well, if you went with me to the colonies, and did not find a big strapping soldier to pleasure you . . ." She paused, seeing the color leave her mistress's face. "You have a choice of domestic service or the convent there."

"Not much better than the choices I have here."

"*Non.* But do you think, after all his announcements and rooster strutting, Racine would allow you to take up the holy life?"

Genevieve shook her head.

"Well, at least there, you would have a choice."

"And how will I get to Normandy? And how will I get approved? Surely, when they find out who I am, I will be rejected."

A smile crossed Claudine's lips. "Then they must not find out. You will go as me."

Puzzled, Genevieve responded. "And what of you?"

"I will stay behind and pretend to be you until we are sure the boat has left. Then . . ." She gave a shrug. "There is a man here whom I wish to wed but cannot. If you could but provide me with a few sous . . ."

Genevieve pressed her lips together in thought as she looked to the statue of the Virgin Mary. The Mother's crown sparkled in the candles' glow. "I can not see myself in domestic service, though by God's body, I have certainly done enough for Papa and myself since we were forced to let you and the other servants go." She paused. "Though I do not think I have a calling, anything would be better than marrying that disgusting creature. However, if I were to reject the Marquis, he would no doubt take all of Papa's lands and leave him in despair. So, as you say, the convent life here is out of the question for me."

"Then you must be content to wed the man and take what you will."

Genevieve stared up at the statue of Christ and felt sure she saw his tears mirroring those in her own eyes.

"What will you do to prepare?"

"Me? Nothing. I have been accepted by Pére Marc because I am of good peasant stock and healthy. He says I have good hips, right for childbearing."

Genevieve studied herself doubtfully and thought of the pain she had seen. "And I? Are my hips good enough for childbearing?" She looked to her maid, almost hoping for a negative answer.

Claudine shrugged. "Who knows what will happen until it does?"

"I do. My mother died bearing my brother, who was still-born. My aunt also died in the same way. I fear that for me it will be the same. But as you say, I can refuse all the men and join the convent there. 'Tis the Ursalines, is it not?"

"*Oui*. Do you wish to go? You must leave this night if you are to reach the coast in time."

"This night!" Genevieve's eyes opened slightly as she looked to the statue for guidance. "And you would truly be willing to change places with me?"

Claudine shrugged.

"Truly, I have not much money to pay you with, but I can give you many of my gowns and what few coins I have."

"The purple silk with the ribboned petticoats?"

Genevieve nodded as the idea formed in her mind. "I will tell Papa and the

Marquis that because of the great honor being bestowed upon me, I need to have a few days of meditation and prayer to prepare myself to be his wife. That will please the old goat, I'm sure." She paused and looked again at the Mother. "I will make arrangements to go to Paris—to the Carmelites—this night."

Claudine nodded, smiling.

"Then we will change places."

"And when the Marquis and your father find out?"

"I will"— she hesitated—"I will be sailing to New France."

Claudine hugged her former mistress. "Until tonight, then. I will assist you on your way."

Genevieve nodded and took one more look at the statue of the Lord Jesus looking down upon them. She fancied that he was smiling at her, and she could only pray that her decision to leave was the right one.

4

SOMEWHERE IN THE CANADIAN WILDERNESS

Morning Flower, squatting in front of the tent, angrily pounded the maize. She tried to forget that the men would be returning from their hunt soon, that after the victory ceremonies she would be wed to Grey Cloud. If only the Evil Spirit would heed her petition; if only she could be free of Grey Cloud.

Thunder rumbled. She glanced up quickly, shivering. Her dark eyes scanned the tribal area—the longhouses and the council lodge. No one else appeared to have heard the noise. The children still played in front of the lodge, while the old men talked; the squaws still hurried about, preparing for the evening meal.

She looked to the forest where her youngest brother, Four Winds, practiced with his bow. Beyond him, toward the west, the white tassels of the young corn swayed. If the hunting party found no meat—but of course they would find meat. The Huron might be reduced in number since the days of their glory, but they were still the fiercest of warriors.

The thunder rumbled again but the sky was clear. This time Morning Flower was sure. HA NAE GO ATE GEH, the Evil One, was speaking; he was angry with her for her petition. But she could not marry Grey Cloud, his scarred features twisted like some horrid mask. She pressed her lips tight—the Evil One would demand a sacrifice if he did what she asked, but what had she to offer him? Her gaze again went to her young brother. No! That could not be! Four Winds had nothing to do with her dislike of Grey Cloud. The Evil One would not take him. He couldn't.

Disturbed, she lay her grinding tools aside. Already the maize was ground finer than her mother required. She had crushed the yellow corn as she wished to crush Grey Cloud's desire for her. She could not be his wife!

The baby's hand darted forth, forcing Morning Flower's attention back to the maize. She slapped her sister's fist away. "That's for our dinner!" Dream Child began to cry and Morning Flower took the child into her arms. It was true that she dreaded the return of the men, but knowing that their return meant meat relieved her worry about her sister's welfare.

Placing Dream Child beneath the thick foliage of an oak, Morning Flower swiftly turned her attention toward the forest; her heart began to thud as her keen ears picked up yet another sound. Could it be the men?

The war cry came again. Louder now. The men were returning!

All the camp stopped what they were doing and listened for the repeated cry, listening to learn how many prisoners had been captured. Morning Flower's heart lifted. She didn't care about the prisoners; she cared about the meat that would feed Four Winds and Dream Child.

The village sprang to life as women and old men arranged themselves in two lines down the length of the path. Each tried to catch a glimpse of the triumphant braves. Morning Flower stood on her tiptoes; she could see them advancing, slowly. Where was Standing Pine, her older brother? Where was Grey Cloud?

The warriors were closer now; Iroquois scalps swung from their pole. The rhythmic chant of praise was taken up by the women as the braves neared the village. Not only did the hunting party have meat but they had engaged two enemy tribes. The Hurons and their Black-Robe friends were surely the best of the earth, just as the Iroquois and their English friends were the scum. Morning Flower's heart swelled with pride for her men; surely her brother had killed many of them. But where was he?

At length, the warriors emerged from the forest into the bright sun.

It was then that Morning Flower saw the two bodies carried behind the horses. She froze. An Indian woman did not betray her emotions, but Morning Flower could not restrain her wail as she ran toward the dead—Grey Cloud and Standing Pine.

Tears shimmered in her eyes as she touched her brother's hand. He had been her sacrifice. She bit her lip. It would have been better to have married Grey Cloud than to lose her brother; it would have been better to have taken her own life. If only she had known what price the Evil One would extract.

Numb, Morning Flower glanced toward the prisoners now grouped together; they were being prepared for the gauntlet. Her attention was drawn to the one who stood near the Black-Robe.

Dressed as an Iroquois and swarthy as an Indian, his oddly light eyes seemed to regard her with a burning intensity. Morning Flower knew instinctively that he was not an Iroquois, not an Indian, yet the proud lift of his head, the sensuous mouth, made it difficult for her to look away from those mysterious grey eyes. He acted like the son of a chieftain, not like a humble Iroquois dog of a prisoner.

Morning Flower's heart beat uncomfortably. The Iroquois, or whatever he was, looked older and wiser, but something told her that he was about her age—surely not much more than twenty-and-five summers. He stood as if aware of the beauty of his body, of the rippling of his bear-greased muscles. She knew then, without being told, that this—this imposter was the one who had felled Grey Cloud and Standing Pine. For the former, she thanked him. For the later, she vowed revenge.

With trembling hands, she retreated to join the women, to take up the stick.

Forcing herself to look upon the other prisoners, she stared at the two Black-Robes. Did the Black-Robe befriend and give their magic to the Iroquois as well as the Hurons? She looked at the older man. His pale face was scarred and bruised; clotted blood still disfigured his wounded features; his hands were bound behind

him. A Huron warrior approached to sever
the cord. Even from the distance where
she stood, she could see that the flesh
about his hand had swollen under the
tight band almost concealing the rope.
The knife gashed the right hand of the
Black-Robe as, released from their
bondage, his arms fell heavily to his side,
immobilized. She knew then that she was
right. He was one of the priests who had
betrayed her people, who had gone to help
the Iroquois with the magic of his god. He
would suffer, she thought; they would all
suffer from her brother's death.

Father Raoul glanced at the younger
man beside him, Philippe St. Clair.
Already a well-known fur trapper, Philippe
had ventured farther than any of his
friends had dared. His knowledge of the
forest ways seemed almost instinctive, yet
Father Raoul pitied him. Philippe's father,
the Seigneur St. Clair, had entrusted
Philippe's soul to him, but he had failed to
win the boy over. The priest studied the
Indians near him. It was not for himself
that he feared these agonies, which would
most assuredly join him with the beloved
Virgin; it was for the man at his side. Until
Philippe fully accepted the Church as
savior, he would never find the peace he
continually sought.

As Father Raoul felt the blood creep

slowly into his veins, the numbness was succeeded by acute pain. The rope about his neck was loosened. "My son . . ."

"Save your energy for praying, Father," Philippe responded quickly. "We shall all need your prayers before long."

The older man gave a brief nod as he was pushed into the hands of the next warrior and his robe was stripped from him. Now he wore only his hair shirt, stained with blood. His naked feet and legs were torn and bleeding, festering with thorns and briars. He stared heavenward, waiting for some sign of his coming martyrdom.

The Indians soon completed their work. The young novice, Pierre, stood beside Father Raoul now. His delicate white skin was crusted with blood; his swollen limbs hung helplessly at his side. In contrast, Philippe stood apart, strong and unwavering, like a mighty statue of bronze despite the red gashes about his body.

Philippe was thankful now that his mother had raised him among her people. He would show these Huron dogs how a warrior died; he would show the other Iroquois with them, as well, that despite his white blood, he was as much of man as they. For just that moment, he closed his eyes and thought of his mother resting with the Great Spirit and of his father and his father's current wife, that woman from Paris. Yes, he would show them all that he was a man.

Leaning toward the priest a moment, he said, *"Père . . ."*

The mild blue eyes turned toward Philippe. "My son, God is—"

Philippe cut him off. "Father, you must make for the war post, by the council lodge. You'll be safe if you can reach it."

The curé searched the field ahead of him. The post seemed to loom above the heads of the yelling women, anxious for their vengeance. Grimacing, he touched the young man's hand. "I will trust in Our Lord, my boy. Let us place ourselves under the protection of Jesus. It is the eve of the Assumption of the Blessed Virgin. She will intercede for us or, if it is God's will, she will obtain us strength to win the crown of martyrdom. Mayhap our triumphant assumption into heaven will move her to grant us her patronage."

Philippe turned away from the old man. It was one thing to give up, but it was quite another to believe that some man and his mother, long dead, could now save them, or even help them. The Great Spirit was the only one who could help them. The crowd about them was growing restless. Philippe placed his arms across his body; he knew his proud stance made the Hurons angrier, but if he was to die, he would die as an Iroquois should.

Behind the other priest, Brother Pierre looked faint.

"Bear up, my son," Father Raoul whispered. "Thou art a soldier of Jesus; thou art scourged as he was scourged. My son, it is a glorious privilege to die in his service."

"Heaven is the reward of a happy martyr," Brother Pierre responded weakly, swaying as he clutched the older priest.

Philippe clenched his fist. He might survive because he had a wish to avenge his mother's death. Father Raoul might survive because of his faith. But he doubted Brother Pierre would last the ordeal.

A restless Huron approached the young priest, grinning as he pricked the bleeding novice with his knife.

Groaning, Brother Pierre fell forward, unable to rise. The Huron grasped his tomahawk, lifting it above the blonde head of his captive. Reading murder in the Indian's eyes, Philippe sprang forward, catching the descending blow on his left arm. It gashed into his brawny muscles as he bent over the novice, lifting him up.

There was a murmur of approval among the Hurons. Phillippe's deed had been bold. No one interrupted him as he carried the unconscious novice to the

grassy knoll beyond the post. Returning
to his place next to Father Raoul, he heard
an old woman whispering, "He is worthy
of the stake. He is a warrior above the
Iroquois." Philippe held his head higher;
yes, perhaps he was better than the
Iroquois.

Too soon, it was time to begin the
gauntlet. Phillipe would go first; behind
him waited Father Raoul, then Brother
Pierre, who had regained consciousness.
The two Iroquis captured with them
followed.

With the swinging of the first club,
Philippe started off, pulling forward at a
trot that puzzled Father Raoul. From side
to side Philippe darted, trying to open the
lines for the two priests, trying to avoid
the hundred upraised arms with their
glistening knives. The noise was as he
imagined the Devil Dogs of Hell would
sound, but he did not give in to his fear.
Pausing for a moment, he waited until the
Jesuits had come up behind him, then
once again he bounded forward, dashing
into the midst of the crowd, feeling their
blows rain on his head, but numb to the
pain as he overturned many in his path.

Blood now streamed from his
wounded body. For a moment, the whole
rage of the whippers was turned against
him. Forgetting the French priests, they
pursued Philippe.

Moring Flower joined the mob, wanting to strike him with her club, hating him for her brother's sake—yet when, in that fraction of time, his eyes met hers, the club slipped from her hand; her chance was lost as the others attacked him, trying to cut off his escape.

Then, like a cornered wolf, he turned on them—bursting forth with all his strength. A group of squaws greeted him with their jagged stones and pointed sticks. Dashing into their midst, he struck out and several of them overturned as they tumbled to the ground.

The living pile struggled, striking, beating each other in confusion; a shout of laughter burst from several of the Huron warriors as Philippe snaked out from the human mass and sprang to his feet. Starting off, he left more than half his pursuers fighting among themselves.

Seeing the younger priest falter, Philippe hurried toward him.

"The post, Brother Pierre. Reach the post and you'll be safe."

"Dearest Christ, grant me strength. I shall never again see my dear France." He sank to the ground as the blows fell on the pair with the rhythm of a waterwheel in a frantic storm.

Already numb to his own pain, Philippe grabbed Brother Pierre by the arms. Hoisting him up, he swung the novice over his broad shoulders and made toward the post.

Father Raoul had already reached the sanctuary. Gently, he touched Philippe, helping to relieve him of his burden. "You are blessed, my son. Christ will bless you in his glory when you join him."

"That may be true, Père Raoul, but I have no intention of entering your heaven yet." He turned toward the Hurons, who were advancing again.

Upset that Philippe had escaped them, the women yelled, "When you are bound to the post, you half-Iroquois dog, when the fires are kindled about you, we will torture you until you scream with pain!"

Philippe kept his head high; he graced them with a smile that chilled Morning Flower's blood. This man would not die as easily as the others, she thought.

Raising her fist with the others, she cried, "We will make you yell with torment, Iroquois warrior!"

Ignoring her as he ignored the others, Philippe watched as the Huron elders now entered their lodge.

"What will happen now, my son?" Father Raoul whispered, his voice barely audible.

"Now? We will be given time to rest while they decide our fate in council."

"You mean our deaths are not

assured?" Brother Pierre asked.

Philippe shrugged as an elder of the tribe came toward them and motioned them to follow. "Nothing is ever assured with the Hurons."

Once again bound, they were placed in a tent next to the lodge with two Huron guards to attend them. The two Iroquois prisoners immediately lay down to sleep, but the priests refused to do so.

Philippe stretched out as best he could. "Father," he said to the kneeling priest, "I suggest you try resting. You'll need your strength more than your prayers."

"I gather strength from my prayers, my son, as would you, if you would pray."

Philippe shook his head. "Your Jesus has done nothing for me thus far. I doubt he will do much for me in the future, either."

"My son, if we beseech our heavenly Father to accept our suffering here in atonement for our sins past—"

Philippe turned toward the novice, whose eys were already closed in pain. "You can't tell me that he has sinned enough to merit this."

"Only God knows how we have sinned and what we must suffer before we attain the peace of heaven."

"I'm sorry, Father, but I shall continue in the ways my mother taught me. If your god was so good, so just, why did he make society shun my mother, why did he not allow my mother and father to marry?"

"She would not accept the Church."

"Well, neither shall I." Philippe leaned against the rough back wall. He closed his eyes for a moment, thinking of his mother. "Father, you're a good man. But for you, I wouldn't even have known about my father. But the Great Spirit teaches we must make our own choices. I have made mine. I am now part of the Iroquois as my mother was, as her father was, and when I die, that is how I shall die. For now, I will rest."

Father Raoul smiled sadly and said, "*Ave Maria.* May the Lord bless your soul, Philippe Jean St. Clair."

Sounds of activity outside the tent woke Phillipe. The guard looked in and gave a grunt; Philippe's stomach tightened. Was the time now? A girl entered the tent bearing gourds of water and maize cakes. It was the girl who had run toward the men, the one who had cried. Philippe wondered then if it was her beloved he had killed. Well, if it had been, he was sorry, but his own survival came first.

"Well, dog, aren't you going to eat?"

"Why are you feeding us?" Brother

Pierre struggling to sit up. "If I am to die . . ."

Morning Flower glanced at the young Black-Robe, then at the old Black-Robe before turning her eyes toward Philippe again. "It is our custom." She kicked Philippe. "The dog will tell you. He seems to know our laws well enough." She waited, hoping he would cry out, but in Indian fashion, he remained silent.

"Has the council decided then?"

"The council has met. Already they are talking who will get your heart. I hope you suffer much, dog." She spat at him and left the tent as the guard entered to unbind their hands. Brother Pierre leaned forward, his eyes wide. Philippe knew he was thinking of escape, but the Hurons were wise. There could be no escape—not from the center of the village, surrounded as they. Even if they reached the forest, wounded and ill they would have little chance of survival. Philippe shook his head and the young priest sank back in despair.

Taking a cake, Philippe offered one to Father Raoul and then to Brother Pierre. Both refused.

"If I am to die, let me not eat their poison," Brother Pierre said.

"I hardly think they would poison us, Brother. That would take away all their fun. They rest us and feed us in hopes that we will withstand more tortures."

"Then why do you eat?" Pierre asked.

Philippe shrugged. "I am hungry."

"It is better to greet one's maker with a pure heart and soul, my son," Father Raoul said. "You may have my portion if you wish. I will fast. Mayhap I will thus join my Lord sooner, but I shall trust in him."

Again, Phillipe shrugged as he bit off a piece of the cake. His stomach growled. He would survive, if only to spite the Huron girl, if only to show her that he was not a dog. Indeed, it was the Hurons who were the dogs.

Outside, the noises were growing louder. Philippe could hear the crackle of the fires as the hair on his neck seemed to rise. The Hurons would be drinking the sacrificial wine now, from the cask the Jesuits had been carrying. Then they would have brandy obtained from the French, and rum from the English or Dutch traders. It didn't matter who had sold it to them: the effect was the same—disgusting.

Now and then, a Huron would approach the tent where the prisoners were being held, only to reel away.

The front of their tent open, Philippe could now see the blazing fire and the shadows of the longhouses behind it. It reminded him of his village; he allowed himself a moment of heartbreak for what he would never again see.

Hearing the cackle of a very drunk old woman asking for more firewater, Philippe knew he would survive.

Brother Pierre learned over toward Philippe. "Tonight?" His voice was hoarse with effort.

Philippe shrugged. "Perhaps. If it is, it will not be the plan. In my village"—he saw Father Raoul grimace—"in the Iroquois way, it is only when the warriors are too drunk to control themselves that the prisoners are tortured the night of the victory celebration. If they are to die the honorable way, it is proper for them to appear before the council, to state their case when all are sober, but. . . ." the noise from the dancing grew more frenzied.

Philippe took a deep breath, as suddenly a group detached itself from the center. One warrior, wearing a collar of wild bear claws about his neck and snake skins on his arms, swayed as he came toward them. Streaks of black and red were drawn from his ears to his mouth, while a broad band of green extended across his forehead and around his eyes. Speaking to the guards, he gestured wildly toward the prisoners.

Brother Pierre clutched Philippe's arms; his nails dug into the other man's skin.

"The Black-Robes have turned the Iroquois into dogs. Let them die. Let the Iroquois prove they are men, fit to walk the earth as brothers of the Hurons."

The two guards tried to push the red-streaked warriors away, to calm them down. But the fire-water had inflamed them.

The prisoners were pulled roughly to their feet. Above the noise, Philippe said, "If you do not think Iroquois are brave men, then let me show you. I will die first."

The leader shook his head, grabbing one of the full-blooded Iroquois prisoners. "You will die last, dog. You will see your friends perish and you will cry out in agony for them and for yourself."

Father Raoul made a hasty cross as the five men were led to the stakes. "My son," he whispered to Philippe, "you must accept the Lord Jesus. Now. Before it's too late."

"It's already too late, Father."

"Not while your soul still resides within you."

Philippe shook his head sadly, watching powerless as the Jesuits were tied to the poles alongside him.

The two Iroquois died quickly, unable to withstand the torture. Philippe was sorry that they had cried out, that their souls had not been of the true Indian spirit. He hoped his would be.

A tomahawk sliced the air above him, hitting the post only a quarter inch from his head. His heart pounded fast. At least they would kill him first, before the old priest. He didn't want to witness Father Raoul's death.

Another tomahawk spun forth. Philippe felt pain in his legs but he refused to scream. He was an Iroquois, even if his father was French. He would die as a proud Indian so his mother's warm arms would welcome him.

He looked up then, aware that all noise had stopped, that there was silence in the camp. His stomach tightened. What had happened? What had he missed? He looked down at the blood already pooling at his feet.

Philippe glanced to Father Raoul, then to Brother Pierre. Both were still alive—barely. Both were still tied, as was he.

Then the rumble of thunder rolled the sky again.

"He No," the leading warrior whispered in awe. "He No is speaking."

In response, the thunder god rumbled again, bringing the rain with him. The flames devouring the bodies of the two Iroquois were quickly quenched in the downpour as deafening peals of thunder and flashes of lightning raged above them.

Morning Flower stood to the side; she had been ready to throw her own stick at the Iroquois, ready to avenge Standing Pine as best she could, but now it was too late. Horrified, she watched as the mother of Grey Cloud walked forward to stand in front of Philippe, her wet hair plastered to her head.

"He No has spoken. The Iroquois is dead. The spirit of my son, Grey Cloud, shall inhabit him."

There was silence. All looked to the chief. The only sounds were the wind in the leaves, the rain beating against their skins, the rolling of the thunder.

Finally, the chief nodded. "It is good. The man is above; he is brave. His name will be Kio Diego—Settler of Disputes." All looked toward Philippe. "Does the Iroquois accept?"

Philippe looked at the woman, at the chief, then at the girl. He knew the custom. He knew that if she had been Grey Cloud's wife, she would now be his.

Slowly, Philippe nodded. "I accept."

5

Still in a state of turmoil, Genevieve
returned to the rooms on the rue Dauphine
to find her father pacing the carpet and
mumbling to himself.

"Papa? What is it?" Genevieve went
to him, putting her arms around him.

"He wants to see you."

Puzzled, she pulled back. "Who wants
to see me?"

"Racine!" Her father snapped.

"Why? I thought everything was
settled."

"He wants to see you. We are to meet
him for refreshment at the palace at half
past three."

"Oh." Genevieve pressed her lips
together and shrugged. "Does he think
that I am not who I am? Does he think

that you will cheat him?"

"*Hélas* I do not know what the man thinks. I only know we have received a summons."

"And we must go because you have lost to him, because of the ancestral lands." She sighed. "Very well. But first I must take my constitutional with Alexandre and then I must rest. You may tell my future bridegroom that we will see him at a quarter to four, no earlier."

"Genevieve!" Her father's voice was a mousey whine.

"Papa, I am doing this for you. Surely, I can be allowed a few moments of my own?"

"You are doing it for yourself as well, for our ancestors, your children to come, and for all that he will give you."

"*Ma foi*, Papa! If you think that I am concerned about the riches I will have as a marquise, then you do not know me as well as I thought you did."

The Vicomte flushed. "You would swear at your father?"

Genevieve's green eyes snapped. "If necessary, yes!" She scooped up the cat and hurried back down the steps.

Her heart was pounding when she reached the ground floor, and for a moment she allowed herself to look up in the direction of their rooms. Indeed, if her father thought her as mercenary as he, then he knew nothing of her and she did not owe him the loyalty of staying to wed the Marquis. Or did she? With a sigh, she stroked Alexandre's fluffy fur and heard his contented purr as she hurried toward the Place d'Armes. Quickening her step, she avoided the eyes of the others walking with their chaperones and their maids. The poverty that her father's gambling had thrown them into stung her, and while she knew that it was not the proper thing for a young woman of her standing to be on the street alone, she had no choice at the moment. At least she had Alexandre for company, she thought, cuddling the cat closer to her as she turned down one of the less populated streets. She was not, as she had told her father, walking just for fresh air. Indeed, she had a purpose in mind. She only prayed that La Voisin, the fortune teller who had assisted Mademoiselle de Montespan, would also be able to help her.

The house off Place Saint-Louis was small and not easy to find. Hidden in the shadow of the Ursaline convent, where, if Genevieve went through with the plan, she would hide that night, the house exuded a personality all its own—a personality of evil.

Clinging to her cat, who was now squirming in her arms, Genevieve took a deep breath and then stepped down into the low-ceilinged room. A shiver took hold of her almost immediately, and although it was hot outside, Genevieve felt very cold in here.

"Hello? Is anyone at home?"

No one answered, and she looked around the room to see various bottles—some filled with liquid, some with other things which Genevieve imagined were herbs. A spider's web stretched in one corner of the room glistened with dew-drops and with something else which Genevieve dared not think about. Her stomach turned and she hung on to Alexandre, fearing that if he got loose in this dreadful place she'd never see him again.

"It's all right, *mon petit*," she told the cat, trying to calm herself as well as him. "It's all right. We'll get the answers we seek." Her throat was dry but she forced herself to call out again. "Hello. Please. Is anyone at home? The door was open and I—"

Curtains from the back room parted as a well-dressed woman in a low-cut chestnut silk gown rustled forth. On her white cheek were a star and a moon, attachments much favored by the court ladies; a musk scent filled the room. Everything about her, except the room, spoke of wealth.

"Mademoiselle Simon, daughter of the

Vicomte de Patin, you wish to see me?"

"How did you know my name?"

Catherine Monvoisin, otherwise known as La Voisin, gave a mysterious smile. "I have my ways. Come." She beckoned Genevieve into the interior of the house. Alexandre mewed loudly as if to warn his mistress and La Voisin frowned. "I am afraid I cannot have animals disrupting my talks with the spirits. If he cannot be quiet, you will have to leave him out here."

"No!" Genevieve was horrified. She looked around, hugging the cat closer to her and stroking him. "He will be silent. I promise." The cat looked up at her, his green eyes wide, and she silently pleaded with her pet to obey. He butted his head gently against her as if to say he loved her and that he would do as she asked.

" 'Tis not a very pleasant place, is it?"

"No. 'Tis not," Genevieve agreed as she looked around. This room was even gloomier than the other; there was no window here, no door except the curtained entrance. Three candles had been lit on the mantel and a gruesome skull of someone Genevieve hoped was long dead stood in the center of the table.

La Voisin indicated that Genevieve was to take a seat, and so she did, gingerly perched on the edge of the chair, ready to flee if anything unusual should happen.

The fortune teller smiled at her and reached out to pat Genevieve's hand. "Don't worry, my pet, nothing will harm you. I have control of all the influences here." She paused. "Have you coins?"

Genevieve nodded. From her pocket she removed a gold piece, one of the few she had rescued from her father's fever. If he had known of it, it would have gone to his gaming.

The woman took the coin and bit it. Then, satisfied, she tossed it into the bucket at the side. It clinked in, mingling with the other coins. Genevieve couldn't help but wonder how many other people had sought out La Voisin's help that day.

"Do you live here?"

"*Non, ma petite,*" the woman smiled. "But it provides atmosphere, does it not?"

Genevieve could only nod.

"Now, what is your desire, my pretty? You want a love potion?"

Genevieve's eyes widened in horror. That this woman could even think such! She clung to her cat, who squealed with the pressure.

"No, I can see that is not what you want. Do you wish to poison someone?" She motioned toward the shelf where a skull and bones were prominently displayed.

Mutely, Genevieve shook her head, feeling her stomach rise within her.

"Well, my dear, potions and poisons are what most of the court ladies come here for. What is it you need?"

"To know—to know if I must marry."

"Ah." The witch's eyes lit up. "You are the delicate morsel that Marquis de Racine has bragged about. Yes, I understand perfectly." She smiled and took out her tarot cards. "Here. You shall shuffle and I will read." She pushed the much-used deck across the uneven table to where Genevieve sat.

In her lap Alexandre gave a low growl. Quickly, she petted him.

"That's all right. He may go after the mouse, if he wishes. Just do not let him stray from this room, for I will not be responsible for him if he does."

A chill swept over Genevieve at the woman's words and, rather than letting the cat go, she petted him instead, trying to calm him, to convince him to stay on her lap. The cat obeyed and Genevieve stared in fascination as La Voisin laid the cards out in a cross-shaped formation.

"Let me see. Racine is . . . prince of pentacles, I believe, and you . . . quick, girl, give me your day of birth."

Startled, Genevieve had to think a moment. "Why it is March the 15th. I will be 18."

"Never mind how old you are. Only the date itself matters." She pushed one card here and placed another there. "I see danger for you. But not here." The witch looked up. "I see danger for you. But not here." The witch looked up. "Do you have family in England, perhaps? Or the Caribbean? The two of pentacles tells me there will be much change for you, and I see a possible trip over the water." Her hand rested on the six of swords. "You are fleeing from"— she smiled and pushed the Racine's card over—"him."

"But will I be successful? I mean—"

The witch held up her hand. "There is love in your life. The ace of cups and the two of cups. And there is also loss from the eight of cups. Someone with black hair"—she pointed to the prince of wands—"will try to steal your happiness." Quickly she laid out the five of pentacles, the eight and nine of pentacles. "You will suffer much hardship as you flee, but you will learn and you will accomplish."

Genevieve swallowed hard. "Is there a man associated with my happiness?" She wanted no man in her life, unless he was the prince of whom she dreamed, the prince her father scorned—someone like Alexandre, her peasant friend, but on a higher scale.

La Voisin laughed like the pealing of the church bell. "That you should even ask, *ma petite*! Here." She pushed the king of cups to her. "He is with blue-hazel eyes and his hair is light to brown, or perhaps he is born in the sign of Cancer, in the months of late June and early July. He will be in his maturity and much set in his ways." She had closed her eyes now and was not reading the cards but had her head cocked as if she was listening to a voice outside her own. "He is a man with much empathy who can provide wise counsel, but he is quiet. He does not readily show his emotions." A smile came over her lips, but even as her tongue tickled the other portions of her mouth, she did not open her eyes. "*Mon Dieu*! But he is a lover!" She gave a laugh and her eyes opened. "For him, I would be willing even to take this trip with you." Her hands stretched over the cards as if trying to pick up any other impressions. "Tell me, my pet, where is it you go?"

"I do not know. I am still considering."

La Voisin's brow arched.

"Well, that is, I am not sure I can—"

"*Hélas*." The witch shrugged. "Then perhaps I will go in your stead. I have had enough of these court fops who think their sticks are all the pleasure we need." Her hand covered Genevieve's as she took note of the shocked expression on the girl's face. "Take my advice, precious, for that is what you are seeking. You should flee and never look back, for if you do, you will regret." She pointed to the nine of swords.

"But what of my papa?"

La Voisin gave one of her mysterious smiles. "Your papa will be fine. He is quite a talent that one. Almost as good as—" her hand fondled the lower part of the king of cups card and even the dim light could not hide the blush on Genevieve's face.

"Where—how and when shall I meet this prince you speak of?"

The witch closed her eyes again. "There is a forest of trees and it is there he shall first take you for his wife, though I do not think you will be truly wed yet."

"Not wed?" The horror of being with a man to whom she was not yet wed, especially after what she had seen with her father, was more than Genevieve could imagine. Men were single-minded in their conquest of the female body, it seemed, and even this princely man whom La Voisin described to her could not take the time to legalize his love for her.

"Ah, but my little one, it will be all right. Believe me. He will give you such pleasures as will send you to heaven and you will wish to be with him, always. No matter what."

"So I should go?"

La Voisin shrugged. "That depends on you. But yes, I see it for the best."

"And Papa will be all right?"

"He will."

Genevieve sighed. "Then I suppose I will leave this night."

"For?"

"The colonies of New France."

"Ah, that explains much. I hear those savages are magnificently endowed and know how to pleasure a woman by just touch."

Genevieve looked at the woman directly. "And I hear the savages are to be feared."

Once again the mysterious smile came. "That all depends on your outlook, my pet." She reached over and stroked the cat who still rested quietly in his mistress's lap. "You will go?"

Still unsure, Genevieve stood. She was more than willing to leave and yet remained fascinated by this woman sitting before her. "You will tell no one of my visit?"

"If I told who came and who went, *ma cherie*, my head would have long ago graced the guillotine."

6

The coach rumbled along the well-trod
country roads leading from Versailles to
Paris, and from beneath her hood,
Genevieve peered out to watch France
passing her by.

Changing places with Claudine had
been easier than she had thought it would
be, but until the last moment she had had
doubts. After all, Papa would surely suffer
when it was learned she had fled. But
Papa could take care of himself; he would
find another game and win money from
some other nobleman. Papa was a
survivor. What bothered her the most was
leaving behind her darling Alexandre. She
sighed. Claudine had promised to love and
take care of him, but no one could possibly
love that cat more than she did. Well, if it

was to be, it was to be, she told herself, and she let the curtains of the carriage drop.

Leaning back, she closed her eyes as she thought of that afternoon. It had been meeting the Marquis up close, seeing his squinty pig's eyes, couched like eggs in a bed of fat, and his protruding stomach that not even a tight stomacher could hide, that had made up her mind. She could not stay. If any chance to escape presented itself, then she was a fool not to take advantage of it. His warm, sweaty fingers had reached out to take her hand, disgusting her, and Genevieve could swear from the way he looked at her that he wanted to devour her on the spot. She had tried to imagine what it would be like being his wife; she had thought of him pushing his repellent object into her and she had thought of the groom and the maid, and she wanted to gag. She watched him as his sausage fingers sizzled with delight while he consumed not one, but four, sweets and two cups of chocolate! She had tried to tell herself all the wonderful things she could have when she was wed to him, but nothing could overcome her revulsion at the man himself.

And so she had requested a few days to compose herself. "After all," she had said, smiling prettily, "the great honor you are bestowing upon me by allowing me to become your wife is not something lightly taken." She wished to meditate at the convent, she said, and indeed she had already spoken to the sisters of the Ursaline order. She wanted to dwell on how she might make him the best possible wife.

Her father thought that idea brilliant, until he saw Racine hesitating. "You are already perfect as you are, my dear, and more than ready to be my wife."

"Non," Genevieve had replied modestly, "I must commune with the Lord Jesus and Mother Mary to best prepare myself. *Monsieur l'abbe* agrees that if more marriages were meditated upon, there would be fewer problems. After all"—she blushed—"you do want our union to be blessed with children, heirs to your name, do you not?"

He had agreed quickly after that, and she had allowed him the privilege of kissing her cheek, though it had taken most of her effort to not show her distaste.

From there, it had been easy. Papa and Claudine had accompanied her to the convent, and after kissing her father goodbye, she had taken Claudine's cloak. The carriage ready to take her former maid to Normandy, to her new life in the colonies, had been supplied by the Duc himself. A gift.

And now she, not Claudine, was on her

way to the new life.

Peeking out the window at the dark forest surrounding them, she wondered what Papa would do when he found out. More important, what would Racine do?

After nearly four grueling days of travel she reached the coastal town of Le Havre. From here the ship would be sailing. Taking her one case, all that she had been allowed to bring, Genevieve stepped down into a mass of humanity such as she had never before experienced. Women of all ages—some older than Genevieve and some very much younger— gathered around, chattering and crying, hugging their families and friends and saying their good-byes. A pang of homesickness swept over her as she thought of her father and the fact that she had not said good-bye to him. But he would understand. He would have to. In any case, she had written a letter and left it with Claudine for the time when the Marquis and the Vicomte would find her gone.

As Genevieve looked around at the bedlam, she wondered how anyone was even going to get on the ship. Who was she to see? Where did she go? She turned from one line to the other feeling very lost, and very much alone.

"Excuse, Mademoiselle."

The coachman, with whom she had

become friendly on the trip, tipped his hat. "I best be headed back now. His lordship has other needs for me."

"Oh, yes. Thank you," Genevieve stammered. "I do appreciate all you've done."

He shrugged. "There is one more thing."

"What?" She cocked her head slightly, noticing the way he was studying her.

"The young mistress asked that I give you this before you depart." Without further ado, he handed her a warm, furry bundle.

"Alexandre!" Tears came to Genevieve's eyes as she hugged the cat and felt his rough tongue lick her face.

"The mistress thought as you should have him."

"But will I be able to take him with me on the ship?"

Smiling, the coachman took the cat from her again and tucked him under his arm. "If you hold him like this, none will be the wiser until you're at sail."

"Thank you again," she said, hugging the short man. "And thank you for my Alexandre." She took the cat and with a sigh, she looked around. "Now, if I only knew where to go from here."

So many women, so many people, gathered in the hold as the ship rolled with the gentle waves. Genevieve looked around at the women. There was the detachment of the "King's Daughters," of which she was a part, the women who could be married to the soldiers and single men of the colonies, who would be given generous dowries by the King's treasuries upon their commmitment to wedded life. There were the older women who had already married Christ and were devoting their lives now to the assistance of the poor in the colonies and to the teaching of the savages and the children. Of the men, there were those going over to make their fortunes in fur and land, and there were those going to make their fortunes in the souls of the heathen.

Wanting to see the last of France as the ship sailed away from the port, Genevieve lifted the raw linen peasant's skirt she wore, and made her way up the rickety ladder.

"*Pardon.*" She moved aside as a young woman, about the same age as she, started down.

"Sea-sick already?" There was a mocking laughter in the other girl's voice. "How will you make the wife of a soldier if you cannot stand a little hardship?"

Genevieve's eyes widened. "*Non*, I am not sick—except with longing. I wish to see the land as it disappears. Her voice caught in her throat. "I believe it is the last I shall see of my beloved home."

"*Oui*," the other girl said, and laughed. "You'd best know that. For this ship I am grateful. I shall be making my fortune in the New World."

"And how is that?" Genevieve's hand was on the ladder as she stepped back down, curious about this large-boned girl with the dark, smoldering eyes.

The other girl shrugged. "Never mind. Go up and watch France or you will miss it." She smiled. "We have a good six weeks, mayhap more, to spend talking, if we wish."

Six weeks! Genevieve started. She had never thought about being in this cramped space, sharing with so many women, for six whole weeks and maybe longer. For a moment, she regretted her decision to leave Versailles, but then she thought of Racine and knew she had done the right thing.

"Well? Are you not going up?"

"*Oui*." Genevieve nodded, her attention brought back as she placed her hand on the ladder and Alexandre wriggled inside the deep pocket where she had been keeping him.

"Ah, you are the girl with the cat."

Genevieve blushed. "No, I—"

"You needn't deny it. I can see him moving. But don't worry, I'll keep your secret—as long as he catches mice."

"Mice?"

The other girl laughed at Genevieve's expression. "But of course! What do you think crawls around at night?"

Genevieve shuddered.

"Just be careful the captain doesn't see him until we're well out to sea, or he'll probably be thrown overboard."

The idea of poor little Alexandre being thrown in the ocean was more than Genevieve could bear. She put her hand into her pocket to stroke him and reassure herself that he was all right. In the day that they'd been on ship, she'd fed him scraps from her own meager portion, but she wondered if that would be enough to feed him.

"You'd better get up above if you want your last sight of France."

Genevieve nodded.

"By the way, my name is Annette."

Genevieve looked down and paused a moment, caught off guard. "Mine is Claudine."

Annette stared at her. "Strange, you do not look like a Claudine." The girl shrugged. "Well, we will have all the time to talk later, Claudine."

Unnerved by Annette's perceptiveness and worried that she'd tell someone about Alexandre, Genevieve hurried up the two levels of ladders, past the quarters of the crew and the captain, and finally felt the cool breeze of the open air as she reached the weathered oak of the top deck.

Several others were above as well, mourning the loss of their homeland, as Genevieve was; yet she couldn't help but think of that girl, Annette, who had seemed glad to be leaving France. Well, she supposed there was no explaining some people. Still, as she looked up at the full billowing sails, taking them by the moment farther and farther away from the port, a sadness enveloped her like the misty fog. Had her father found her gone yet? Had Racine?

Even as the wind sped them across the Atlantic, Genevieve felt the doubts surround her. Would life with the Marquis have been that bad? More important, could she actually survive in the colonies with—with such things as rats? What if she died there, or what if she died on the voyage across? It was not unknown for someone to become ill on the trip and be tossed over into the sea! What would happen to her sweet cat then? Forgetting about wanting to keep him secret, and needing to feel his warmth and love, she took Alexandre from her pocket. He mewed and she silenced him with a piece of beef jerky left over from the night before. "It will be all right, my love. You'll see." She held his warm body close to her and felt his rough tongue against her cheek.

"Beautiful animal there."

Startled, Genevieve looked up to see a handsome young man standing at her side. His smooth cheek tinged pink by the winds told her that he was not much older than she, and even with his earthy blue eyes and dark hair there was a ethereal quality about him. "I . . ." She touched the cat, as if he could protect her from problems. "Yes, he is."

"Siamese stock?"

"Part." She hugged Alexandre closer to her as she edged slightly away.

Noticing her discomfort, the man gave a light laugh. "*Pardon*, Mademoiselle. Let me introduce myself. My name is Emile. Brother Emile."

"Brother?"

"*Oui.*"

She knew then why he looked so untouched by the world.

Emile allowed the cloak he was wearing to fall open and she saw his collar and black robe. "I am going back to the colonies now to be with my papa, and of course to assist where I can with the salvaging of souls."

Her eyes widened. "Back to the colonies? You mean you've been there before and you are returning of your own will?"

He laughed again and his eyes twinkled with the last rays of the dying sun. " 'Tis not as desolate as you think. We do have civilization there. Granted, it is not as grand as Paris or the court at Versailles, but it is nice all the same. My father is a landowner in Ville-Marie."

"I thought Quebec was the only city."

"Non!" His back straightened with momentary anger. "Who has told you that! Quebec is but a drop in the ocean compared to the beauty of our Ville-Marie de Montreal. 'Tis on its own island and we are quite the center of the universe. True, Quebec has the governor's mansion and the courts, but that is"— he waved his hand, dismissing Quebec City as Racine had dismissed his servant—"not worth considering." He paused and sighed. "Though it is true that those who live in Quebec get first choice of the products brought in by the ships, since they are closer to the sea. And you girls will also first be chosen in Quebec. Only then, if you do not find someone to your liking, will you travel to Trois-Rivieres, then to our own lovely land."

"But you are glad to be going back?"

"Oui. My papa is there, as well as Maman, and somewhere"—he gave a mysterious smile—"I have a brother. No, a half-brother. We rarely see Philippe.

Still"—the priest at her side shrugged again—"he is family."

"Yes," she said, hearing the sadness in her own voice as she looked back toward the land, which was fainter than ever now and hidden by the clouds of darkening mist, "family is important." Once again, she hugged the cat closer to her, grateful to have him with her and wondering how she was going to survive.

She was still trying to see the land and still feeling the cool breezes through her hair when she heard a now familiar voice at her side.

"You'd best get back down, Claudine, if you want any supper, for soon the pot will be picked clean and neither you nor your cat will have anything."

Surprised, Genevieve turned to find Annette there. But before she could respond to the other girl, Annette had already turned her attentions on the good brother, smiling at him in a way that turned Genevieve's stomach and caused Emile to blush.

Not knowing what to say, she realized that she had best introduce the pair of them. "Annette—"

"Yes?" The other girl continued to stare at the priest, practically devouring him with her eyes, much as Racine had done to Genevieve.

"Brother Emile's family lives in Ville-

Marie and he is returning there."

'How lovely." Annette's voice took on a distinctly lighter note.

"Yes," the young priest said, finally finding his voice, as he continued meeting Annette's sultry gaze. "I will be part of the Jesuit mission to save the souls of the heathens." He cleared his throat. "I believe you ladies had best go below for your evening meal."

Genevieve nodded and, tucking Alexandre back into her pocket, she started down. But only after Brother Emile had turned away did Annette join her.

"Ah, Claudine, it is too bad he has taken his vows," Annette sighed, "but more than one priest has been known to succumb to the pleasures of the flesh."

At the look on Genevieve's face, Annette laughed and hurried below.

7

It was not long before the land was out of sight and surrounding the boat for miles and miles was water, and more water, and more water. The sun glaring on the water, the moon shining on it.

Once they had left port, the women in the hold—those going to the convent and those scheduled to become brides of the soldiers and other men—separated into sectors of the ship. The hanging, swaying hammocks that provided beds for the women were divided from the others by a sheer curtain of muslin strung up along the beams. Not that there could be any privacy with so many in so tight a space, but the attempt had been made.

And once again, those who belonged

to the "King's Daughters" were divided by their own choice. Country girls, as Genevieve was supposed to be, stayed in one sector, while the female convicts and the prostitutes, such as Annette, were placed in another corner. The crimes of the latter were not so great as to warrant beheading, but they were great enough to warrant banishment. In some cases the women had been given a choice—the colonies or death. Few chose the latter.

Annette was one of those who had been given the choice, or so the government said. But in her own eyes, she had had no choice from the day she had been born into the miserable hovel on the lower side of the river. Not especially pretty, Annette had soon learned to use her charms and her body to advantage, and at the early age of ten had made her way out of the hovel and into the streets of Paris, never again looking back. She knew nothing of her family: the mother who bore her and the father who had died early in drink and in shame, and her older brother who had run off to sea—or so she was told—the first chance he had. No, they were not worthy of her concern.

Several times she had tasted luxury in the homes of the men she serviced, but mostly it was all the same—nights spent curled up wherever she could find a warm spot, clutching her worldly possessions to her, fearful of attack as business came and went; a stick and a poke for a *livre*. It was not a life she enjoyed, especially when the old fops with their fetid breath fumbled all over her and couldn't even get up the power to enter or stay, or the sailors off the ships so desperate for a woman that they wet themselves just looking at her, or the young men who didn't have the ability or perhaps the courage to allow her to hold their charms and fled after one meager attempt. But it was the only life she knew.

One had to better oneself wherever one could, Annette had told herself the day she lifted the purse from the gentleman on the docks. How was she to know that he was part of the King's entourage and had guards surrounding him? How was she to know that he would have her thrown into the stinking, rat-infested hole they called a prison?

Of course, she had protested her innocence. Who would not? And then she had tried to seduce the guard so that she could escape. But while the soldier was more than willing to partake of Annette's offerings, he would not let her leave. The best she could get from him was her own candle and some sour milk.

Her trial was rigged. What trial in France was not? But Annette said nothing and merely laughed when the magistrate listed her heinous crimes. Her head was high when he said that she was a menace to the King's society and would have to be done away with. He had paused then, waiting for the full gravity of her crimes to sink in, then had offered her the colonies.

The possibilities of the situation impressed themselves on Annette immediately. If they were pressing women like her into traveling there, that had to mean the men in New France were desperate for the company of a good woman. She imagined that few of the peasant girls going over, brought up good Catholics as they surely were, would know anything of how to pleasure a man. She could certainly make a good living doing her own business, if not, indeed, setting other girls up for business, too.

As humbly as she could, she accepted the magistrate's offer and found herself not being returned to the prison, but being directed immediately to the docks of Le Havre from where the ship would leave. True, she and the other convicts had been shackled to the boat until it was ready to sail, but once the "pure" girls of the country were ready to board, the irons had been removed. Annette thought that a foolish waste of time, since she certainly had no intention of returning to France. Not when such treasures awaited her across the ocean.

She was, she told herself, a survivor,

and as such she would survive this voyage and anything else they put before her. And that was exactly what she later told Genevieve, who was obviously feeling the motion of the ship.

"Don't worry," Annette said, watching Genevieve's green face as the ship weathered its first Atlantic swell, "you'll get over it."

Unable to think, Genevieve merely shook her head. "I shall die and then my poor Alexandre will have no home."

"God's blood, is that foolish cat all you think of?"

Genevieve caressed Alexandre's furry head for comfort. "He is all I have now." The cat was wise enough to know where his food came from and seldom left his mistress's side, unless it was at night to hunt the rodents that invaded the hold. The captain had long ago discovered the pet, but as Annette had predicted, he'd told Genevieve that the cat could stay only so long as he worked like the others on board. Relieved that she no longer had to hide him, she nevertheless wanted him with her all the time.

"I . . ." Genevieve started to cough. She quickly handed the cat to Annette and grabbed the side of the rail.

"Really, you country girls are too delicate." Annette saw then that Genevieve was indeed ill and, quickly putting the cat down, she took the other girl's head, supporting her as Genevieve heaved over the little food she had eaten that day. Her green face turned pale white instead.

Disgusted at Genevieve's obvious lack of survival skills, Annette assisted the other girl back onto the deck. "You ought to rest below."

Genevieve shook her head. "I cannot. There are too many others sick down there and it only makes me sicker."

"Well then, you will rest in my bed, swing or whatever they call those things. Most of the girls in my sector have been put to work and are up and about."

Genevieve looked up. "And why were you allowed to be free?"

Annette shrugged and smiled. "I am friends with the first mate."

Genevieve stared at her new friend, but did not ask what Annette meant. She didn't want to know.

"Come." Annette took her by the hand and led her down below. Alexandre quickly followed.

"If anything happens to me, will you take care of my cat?"

"Phoo! Nothing will happen to you. Millions of people become ill on voyages and survive to live a long and happy life."

"But I am not like the others. I—" Realizing she was about to give away her secret, Genevieve stopped. "I am grateful for your assistance."

Annette smiled. "I think I will be grateful for yours when we land."

"How so?"

"Why, you are quite beautiful. That is plain to see. I have plans for my future in the colonies and I would like your help."

"I don't understand. We must marry one of the men there...." Genevieve paused, showing her dislike of that prospect. "Or go into the convent."

"*Mon Dieu!*" Annette exclaimed. "There is more to life than those two choices. Besides, marriage, if it is to the right man, is not so bad."

Genevieve sighed and sank back onto the swinging hammock as her stomach once more spoke to her of its discomfort.

"I wish never to marry, not unless I have the promise that the man will not touch me."

Even in the dim light of the hold, Genevieve could see Annette's eyes widen. "*Ma foi!* What do you think marriage is? A man uses a woman and unless one is careful, children are produced."

"But I have no wish to be used. That is why I—"

"Why you what?"

Genevieve shook her head, feeling the pounding of her pulses through her brain, and the pain of feeling as if she'd not see another day alive.

"Please, I cannot talk."

Annette touched the other girl's hand and forced a smile. "Rest, then. I will see about finding you some warm broth."

It was the commotion coming from her side of the curtains that woke Genevieve. The screaming and yelling was more than she could bear, and when she heard Annette's voice crying out her name, she knew she had to go to her. With as much dignity as she could muster, Genevieve swung herself out of the hammock. She waited a moment, steadying herself and steadying her stomach as Annette yelled again for her to come.

Parting the curtains, Genevieve gasped. Annette was being held down by three of the other country girls and in the center of the circle was Genevieve's chest —open for all to see.

Her illness forgotten, she ran to her box and looked in. The screaming stopped and there was only silence in the hold now.

"We caught her going through your things. Thief that she is, I wouldn't be surprised if she stole something," one of the girls holding Annette said.

"I was not stealing anything!"

Alexandre, seeing a soft bed, jumped up onto the open box and cuddled in the warm wool cloak on top. Genevieve stared a moment at Annette, then at the other girls. "Let her go."

"No! We caught her red-handed! She's going to suffer. The captain'll flog her and—"

"I said let her go. Nothing is missing."

"You haven't even looked."

"I can see. Besides"—Genevieve took a deep breath—"she was doing me a favor. Like so many of you, I did not feel well. Annette allowed me to rest in her bunk."

"For a reason, I'll bet," the leader of the three holding Annette snorted.

"For the reason that she is decent and honest and was put upon in a faked trial," Genevieve said, not even knowing if what she spoke was true or not. By the gods, she hardly knew this girl and here she was defending her! Yet Annette had helped her. "I asked her to find something for me. She probably did not see the"— she turned quickly toward her bed—"ribbon I asked for and was looking in the trunk."

"Hmm."

" 'Tis the truth." Genevieve removed her cat from his nesting place and slammed shut the lid of her trunk before walking over to where they held the other girl. Methodically, she lifted each of the girls' hands off Annette and then, looking into the other girl's brown eyes, she said, "I thank you for your kindness and I'm sorry these others thought ill of you for it."

Meeting the smaller girl's eyes, Annette stared back at Genevieve. "You are welcome, Mademoiselle."

A flush came to Genevieve's face.

"You will excuse me," Annette said. "I must get up above and away from this foul air." She looked at each of the women and saw to her satisfaction that they shrank back. "We will talk later, eh, Claudine?"

Genevieve nodded and watched Annette disappear up the ladder.

Feeling the angry atmosphere in the hold, Genevieve decided her best bet was to follow the other and, feeling better, she, too, ascended the ladder.

Once above, it took several minutes for Genevieve to find the tall brunette, but finally she discovered Annette sitting in the corner near the taffrail.

"I suppose you expect me to thank you for sticking up for me."

"*Non*," Genevieve said, sliding down to sit next to her as Alexandre cuddled in her lap. "You do not have to thank me. But I would like to know what you were looking for in my trunk. I have little of value with me.,"

"Is that so?" Annette gave a slight smile. "I would scarely call the string of pearls I found valueless. Nor would I disregard all those books of poetry you carry, Mademoiselle Simon, daughter of the Vicomte de Patin."

Genevieve's mouth dropped slightly and she hugged her knees together. "So you know."

"I know. I taught myself to read because it was the only way I could survive and you, too, must learn to survive. You are not a good liar, little Genevieve. If you are to keep up this ruse, you must learn to answer when the name Claudine is called, and you must learn to be rougher and more like a peasant."

"I am who I am." Genevieve shrugged. "You won't tell, will you?"

Annette turned to her. "I will not tell." The girls sat in silence for a moment. "Why is it you left France? Surely, the daughter of a Vicomte, you would have more than enough wealth to get anything you wanted—even first class voyage to the New World, if you wished."

It was Genevieve's turn to smile as she told her friend the sad truth of her father's financial affairs, of how they had to let their maids go, and how her father gambled for their living. "But it was not enough." She looked out over the water in the direction of France. "When he lost half our lands to the Marquis de Racine, Papa then offered me."

Annette shrugged. "So? I have heard

of worse."

"*Non*." Genevieve shook her head. "You did not know Racine. The man was—" Genevieve shivered, just thinking of those pig-like eyes and fat fingers. "I could not have wed him. I could not even bear him to touch me."

"Pshaw! And you think I adore all those men who touch me? My dearest innocent, most men are crude and unpracticed in the arts of love. Most of them do not know their cock from their ass! And yet I must please them and make them seem as if they are the great ones." Annette stretched and turned her head in the direction they traveled toward their new life. "If you ask me, little one, you were foolish. The old marquis would no doubt have bothered you maybe once or twice before he perished of a disturbed heart, and he would have left you with all that money. Now, you are in a worse situation for someone of your delicate nature. You had best learn to like it, for I guarantee the soldier that you will be married to will want to use you like a battering ram and will want it far more frequently than the ancient." She sighed. "Sex, my sweet Genevieve, is something women must endure to get what they want from men. 'Tis a fact of life. And there are but a few men who truly care enough about the woman they are with to wish her pleasure as well."

"But my poetry books—"

"Are just stories. No man is going to come and rescue you, or me for that matter. We are pawns to be used by the men in our lives however they see fit, and we must learn"—she touched her head—"to use our wits or we will never survive."

Genevieve shrugged. "I do not need a man to help me survive. Claudine had told me that if there was no man in the colonies whom I wished to wed, I had the choice of domestic service."

"Which you could never do."

"Or joining the Ursalines. I shall merely go to them. Perhaps Brother Emile will assist me. He is a pleasant enough fellow and certainly safe."

"Yes, certainly." Annette sighed and shook her head. " 'Tis a waste of a good life. Both his and yours. I think I might have a way to help you that will not mean giving up your freedom."

Genevieve turned to look at her friend. "And how might that be?"

"I intend to have my own house."

Shocked, Genevieve was not even aware of her mouth dropping open. "You mean a—"

"*Oui*. A house of ill repute." Annette gave a laugh. "Do not be such a prude, little Genevieve."

Genevieve straightened her back and quickly looked around. "Please. Do not call me that. I will be sore vexed if you are the cause of my being forced to return to France. I will die before I wed the Marquis. Indeed, I will die before I let any man paw me like that." She shivered as her eyes took on a haunted look.

Annette sighed and shook her head. "You've much to learn, my little friend. I still think you'd be better back home with your marquis and his money."

"*Non!* Do not say that. I will have no man. Certainly no man like him!"

"But just think what you could do with it, what you could buy." Genevieve stared at her. "Very well. I shall keep your secret. and I shall not ask you again to join me." She studied the younger girl again. "You are a beauty, though I doubt you realize it. My vote is that all the most eligible men in the colonies will be vying for your hand and that you will find one who sends your heart pounding and who you will be glad to give yourself to in love."

"*Non.* There was but one boy I did have affection for, but Papa sent him away because he was a peasant and not of my class." She sighed. "And even him I did not truly love."

Annette laughed. "He sent a peasant away and kept you from marrying then, and now most likely you will be marrying a peasant."

"*Non*, I tell you, Annette. I will marry only when my heart calls and I doubt it will call for anyone in the colonies."

"We shall see, *ma chère.*"

Life at sea continued with the same daily dullness. The sailors slept in four-hour shifts, changing rotation and their bunks each time the bells rang. Occasionally, another ship would be sighted and the watchman would call out and name the flag. Sometimes it was French. Often it was English, Dutch, or Spanish. As long as it did not attack them, the captain was pleased just to continue on their voyage and hope for safe passage so that they could drop their cargo off and load up with furs, embarking for home before the early frost.

The captain himself seemed to be a relaxed man who seldom used the cat o'nine tails and, in fact, more often Genevieve and the others spent their days sewing gowns from the fabrics being brought over by Madame Mance, who was in charge of them on this voyage. With each pinprick, Geneieve silently cursed her fate, cursed her father for having "sold" her like a piece of meat to Racine, and cursed the fact that she was being forced to live a lie.

Recalling what Annette had told her, she tried to watch the other girls and imitate their mannerisms and their language, but truly most of what they said was so off-color that Genevieve felt herself blushing just listening to their words as they compared their men back home and commented on how the men would be in the colonies. In light of what Annette had told her, Genevieve wondered even more how these women could want or anticipate those disgusting interactions with men. True, it was the only known way to produce a child, and children were delightful. Genevieve herself would dearly love to have several dozen. But if it meant submitting to a man in such an ungodly fashion as she had seen, as she had heard described, then it was not worth it.

The evenings on deck were often filled with the homemade music of the sailors as they played their harmonicas and fiddles, and some even improvised a dance. Of course, under the watchful eye of Madame Mance, the King's Daughters were prevented from joining any of the activity. The ban did not apply to the convicts, some of whom, like Annette, had already taken up with the sailors to make their lives more comfortable for themselves.

And although the sailors were seldom allowed more than four tankards of beer a day, oft times when the captain was in his own spirits, a keg from the hold would be brought up to be shared with those whose thirst was greater than the recommended amount.

Nearly four weeks out, with little to amuse them besides the willing convict women and the prospect of a longer-than-usual voyage because of poor winds, the sailors once again went below. For the most part, the women of the King's Daughters returned to their own section of the hold when the men took to drink, but on this night, Genevieve did not. The music they played had drawn her attention and had caused her to think of home, to think of her peasant boy who had been taken from her. With a wistful sigh, she had tucked herself into a corner of the bow, not far from one of the guns, hoping to enjoy the balmy night and the music and to attract no notice.

But the cat, having missed his mistress below, ran upstairs and meowed, begging that she stroke him. Uneasy, Genevieve picked up her pet and after a few moments of silence it seemed that those who had noticed her chose to ignore her. Breathing easily, she laid her head back against the gun platform as she rested and listened to the sounds of the sea and of the music.

"Nice night, eh, pretty lady?"

Opening her eyes, Genevieve looked

up to see one of the men looming over her, weaving not only with the motion of the ship, but with the drink he had consumed. He grinned lewdly at her as she sat upright and tried to pull away without appearing afraid.

"Yes," she responded. "It is a very nice night." She turned to look at the ocean surrounding her, ignoring the man as she stroked Alexandre.

"You know, it wouldn't be half bad if you'd touch me like you touch that cat o'yours."

Genevieve continued to stare out into the open sea, feeling her heartbeat quicken with fear as her hand steadied on the cat. There was no way she could escape without running past him and he would surely catch her.

"Why don' you answer when I talk t'ye, girl? Ye too proud? Ye think that being one of the King's Daughters makes you above the likes of me? Huh?" He had bent down to her level, balancing even more unsteadily than before. Any moment now, it appeared he might fall over on her. "Answer me, girl!" He was practically shouting now and close enough that she could smell the onion and garlic and whiskey stink of his breath.

"Please"—she tried to edge backwards—"leave me alone. I haven't done anything to you."

He grinned and his eyes widened. "That's just it, me pretty. You've not done anything to me. But I sure would like it if you did."

"Please, I—"

"Leave the girl alone, sir."

Both of them looked up to see Brother Emile standing a few feet away. In the warmth of the night, he wore only his black cassock, blending his outline with that of the night and the stars.

"Why?" the sailor snickered. " 'Cause you want her, brother?"

"By the word of the Lord . . ."

"Oh, don't you give me that holy shit. I knows all about you folks. Me father used to help supply the *abbe* with willing friends, he called 'em."

Brother Emile tried to put more strength into his voice. "Leave the girl alone."

"I won't," The sailor replied, pulling a knife from his boot. The metal glistened silvery in the light of the moon. "Not unless ye want t'fight me, brother."

"I . . ." Brother Emile looked from the knife to Genevieve's frightened face, and back to the knife. Before he could act, another voice moved in.

"Leave her, *mon cher.*"

"Annette! He has a knife."

"Yes, I know." She moved closer in, despite the warning. "*Mon cher,* give me that knife and leave Claudine alone. She does not like men like you."

"Oh, and you do? Never when I have asked have you had time for me."

"But I didn't know until I saw how strong you were just how much I wanted you." Annette's voice became thick and sultry as she edged for the sailor.

"Keep away," he warned. "Ye didn't want me when I wanted you, 'Netta. Now I want me some nice ripe virgin and I got just what I wanted here with me." He laughed as he saw the look on Genevieve's face.

"Poo! A virgin!" Annette stamped her foot, creating a fuss. "You know as well as me, *cheri*, that no virgin can treat you as well as I can. Now, give me the knife and let's go below." She smiled at him, reaching out her hand.

The sailor stood there staring from one girl to the other. Then he looked to his knife and grinned.

"My son, if you hurt either girl—"

"Ye mean, cuz you want the virgin for yerself, huh, brother? Ye had 'Netta."

Genevieve gasped involuntarily and looked to Annette, who shook her head.

"My son, you are mistaken. You—"

"Quiet!" He brandished the knife toward Brother Emile, who drew back fearfully.

"Really, *mon chou*, I am yours if you

want me." Annette once again tried to edge closer to him.

"That a fact?" he said, glancing at the weapon at his side.

He didn't see her quick approach, but he must have sensed it, for his hand rose and, as Genevieve screamed, the blade came down into Annette's side. Just as quickly, the sailor was overpowered by some of the other men.

"You okay, Annette?" The first mate asked.

She nodded. "See to Claudine there. I think she's more frightened than I am."

"*Non.*" Genevieve stood. "I am fine." She moved quickly to Annette's side as the drunken sailor was taken away. "But you are injured."

"I will be fine after a night's rest," Annette protested.

"Then come. I will help you below." She placed Annette's arm over her shoulder and slowly the girls made their way down into the hold.

8

None of the other King's Daughters could understand why Genevieve was spending so much time with Annette. After all, the girl was a hardened criminal and a whore. Whatever she got, she deserved. Even Madame Mance said that if girls like Annette did not encourage the sailors, such a thing as happened the other night would not occur. Therefore, Madame Mance claimed, Annette had brought the injury on herself.

But Genevieve thought otherwise. Annette had been the only one to befriend her and, convict or not, Annette had been brave to rush in and help the way she had. Not even Brother Emile had had the courage to try to take the knife from the sailor. And now that her friend lay not only injured but with a fever, Genevieve was going to do all she could to help her. Of course, she knew that by doing so she risked the displeasure of the others, of Madame Mance especially, but she cared not. After all, once they had reached the colonies she was sure she would seldom see any of them. The new world was a vast wilderness—or so Brother Emile had told her. If she did wed, she might find herself with a man far away from civilization; she might even find herself in one of the smaller settlements up the Saint Lawrence river. Certainly, from their talk, she doubted that she would find any of the girls in the convent. Many of them seemed ready to marry anyone at all.

Fear for the other girl made her call Brother Emile down to her. Even though Genevieve knew that Annette disdained organized religion and seldom went into the church, she was sure that the girl would want to have her sins released if she were soon to die.

There was another reason she stayed at Annette's side. As she dabbed the wet cloth on her friend's feverish brow, she worried that, in her delirium, Annette would say something that would expose Genevieve and give away her secret.

But Annette did not die. She continued to hang on, tossing and turning as the boat weathered yet one more storm.

And despite her own discomfort, Genevieve remained at her bedside.

Four days after the attack, Annette opened her eyes.

"So you're here."

"Did you think I wouldn't be? You saved my life."

Annette lifted her head slightly and looked at the bandage that covered her side. "And it appeared you've saved mine. Therefore we are even, Mademoiselle." At the worried look on Genevieve's face, Annette corrected herself. "I'm sorry, Claudine. Now that you have done your noble deed, you can leave me."

"Why are you so resistant to being helped? The good brother has talked with you, Sister Marie has spoken with you, yet you refuse to be saved. I believe what Madame Mance said was true. If you had not encouraged the men with your lewd behavior, that sailor would have not expected such behavior of me. He would not have wanted what he knew he could not have, but in his drunken state, it did not occur to him that I was any different from you."

"Are you? Besides your father's title and money, which you cannot lay claim to in the wilderness, and besides the accident of your birth, you are the same as me, Mademoiselle," Annette hissed.

"Please. Drink this potion. 'Tis something I obtained from the surgeon and will make you feel better."

Annette shrugged and sipped the drink, making a face. "There. I have drunk and you may go back to the others."

"Why do you say that?"

"You don't think I haven't heard the talk? I may not have been able to move, but I knew what people were saying. Those girls over there feel that because I am a convict I am not as good as they. Well, if they had been born near the river as I had, if they had had to scrounge for everything, they would have done what I did and perhaps worse. Indeed, I know what Madame says of me, but I have done what I've done only to survive, just like you, my noble friend."

Genevieve sighed. "I will leave you to rest. I will return when dinner is being served."

"Why bother?"

"Because you are my friend." Genevieve paused and her voice tightened. "Besides Alexandre, you are the only friend I've ever had."

Annette closed her eyes, ignoring those last words.

"Here, I will leave Alexandre with you so that you will not feel so alone."

"Fine. Just what I need. A damn cat."

Alexandre cuddled up next to Annette and she reluctantly put a hand out to stroke him as Genevieve disappeared.

It took another week for Annette to heal fully, and yet another passed before land was sighted. After seven-and-a-half weeks everyone was more than happy to smell the first tang of land and see the sea gulls in the distance.

Quebec City was coming closer, and so was Genevieve's future. She wondered once again if she shouldn't tell the truth and return. Annette had told her how wonderful it could be with a man, and she had told her how horrid it could be. Of course, Genevieve had scarely listened to the first part because it was the second that she knew to be true. She was sure her friend was lying to her only to make her feel better about what might come, about what might happen if she could not go to the convent here as she hoped, if she did indeed have to wed someone. And then she thought about Racine. They would surely have discovered her absence by now. What had they done to Claudine? What had Racine done to Papa?

The accidental discovery that one of the King's Daughters was already wed and had lied to escape her brute of a husband did not please the authorities on board, and the action taken subsquently quelled all of Genevieve's doubts. She would remain here in the colonies no matter what happened. With a sigh, she watched along with the others as the girl, one of the leaders who had mocked Genevieve for taking care of Annette, was tied to the mizzenmast, just as the sailor had been. The gown was stripped from her back; she was lashed until the blood came. And then it was announced that she would be sent back with the next returning ship, and she would be escorted in chains to her husband. Genevieve knew that, even though she had not already wed Racine, he had enough power to have her, too, punished for running away and brought back to him in the same humiliating manner. She vowed that would never happen.

Once the ship had passed the mouth of the Saint Lawrence River and was surrounded by land, the attitude of all on board changed radically. The nuns for the first time brought the convicts and the King's Daughters together so that they could all sing to the glory of God for having safely delivered them from the storms and frights of the sea and brought them to their new home. No English had attacked them, nor Spanish either. And the wealth of France ordered for the governor and his men, for the nobles and the seigneurs, was once more ready for dispensing.

Like many of the others who were

heartily glad that their voyage had ended, Genevieve spent most of the remaining fifteen days on deck staring at the greenery around her, smelling the moist earth, and listening to the sounds of the animals at night. Everything was so wonderful, in many ways so much like her darling France, and yet so different. She saw flowers and trees that she knew she would never have seen in the forest outside Joigny, and people, too. Or were they people?

Black cliffs rose perpendicular to the ground and formed a gigantic gateway in the dense forest broken only by the occasional smoke of the curling Indian fires. Once or twice, Genevieve saw the swarthy painted men standing on the banks of the river, watching them, and she clung to Alexandre. But the cat provided little security.

She stared at the deeply tanned—almost red—men with their greased hair and nearly naked bodies; some had their faces painted like animals. Only a few were clearly visible but all were horrifyingly savage. Genevieve shivered just seeing them and, hearing some of the tales of terror the nuns told, she prayed that they would stay far away from the town or city that she lived in.

Yet this was land and the start of the new life she had thought about since the

morning her father had told her of Racine.
They continued to travel upriver. Never
had she imagined the land to be so vast,
but here it was taking nearly a month
from the time they had left the Atlantic
until the time they would reach the
primitive settlement.

The transition from forest to
town—one could scarely call Quebec a
city, although the founding fathers had
declared it such—was almost as sudden as
the transition from sea to land. One
moment there were only trees surrounding
them, but the next Genevieve saw a stone
fortress crowning a tall cliff, like a king
surveying his kingdom. From the tower,
flapping in the wind, the very essence of
France cut the brilliant blue sky with its
deeper blue and the fleur-de-lis. The walls
were surely thicker than those
surrounding Paris, and the battlements
seemed to reach to the very sky. Even the
lower part of the city, where the workers
lived, seemed surrounded by the walls.
True, as they neared the place, there was a
house here and a house there, much as
there had been a bird here and a bird there
as they'd neared the land, but her senses
were overwhelmed all the same. And as
she looked up into the bright blue of the
late August sky, tears came to
Genevieve's eyes. The flag of Louis flew
over the settlement and therefore,

wherever she was, she would not be so very far from her beloved France. Mayhap she and Alexandre would one day go back; mayhap Papa would one day forgive her.

In a daze, she gathered her things and stepped into the small boat that was to row them ashore. Cannon boomed from the heights of Cape Diamond announcing the arrival of the new recruits for the colony, announcing the coming of the new brides-to-be. Like the other women, Genevieve wore her best gown and stomacher—best, that is, for someone of Claudine's standing. In addition, she wore the coat of camlet given to each woman, and the taffeta hood. Holding her lawn handkerchief, which would be given to the man of choice, Genevieve looked to the base of the cliffs, where a cluster of stone houses, sheds, and wooden tenements was set down in the midst of the fir and aspen. Men, both white and red, continued to pour from the streets and village paths. In truth, the swarthy forms of the Huron traders seemed far more numerous to Genevieve than her own people, and she turned back to the ship momentarily, wondering if it were not too late to return home. Then she realized that she could not go home.

No, this would have to be her home.

"If you wed, you will take me along as your servant, eh, Claudine?" Annette smiled at her as she took the seat on the small ferry next to her.

Genevieve looked out over the crowd of cheering men who stood on the shores greeting them as their boat was lowered to be rowed in. "If I wed, which is highly unlikely, I doubt my husband will have the money to purchase you as well."

A short, well-dressed gentleman in scarlet embroidered velvet and a thickly plumed hat, which he wore despite the heat, stepped forward. This could only be Jean Talon, the Intendant, who ruled the colony for France. There was a governor as well, responsible for messages to France, but it was Talon who took care of the civil matters and minor disputes, and it was he who settled the fate of the Indians in New France. Genevieve studied the men, glad she had her hood up as she took a deep breath, recognizing the Marquis de Tracey standing at the Intendant's side. She had met him once at court and prayed that he did not recall her, for if he did her play would be up even before she had acted it.

The man did not look her way and, dressed as she was in one of Claudine's gowns, she only hoped that she would go unnoticed. Realizing that Annette was still speaking to her, she turned again to the other girl.

" 'Tis not money I would worry on."

"You are right," Annette responded, misunderstanding. " 'Tis no purchase they have to make, my prudish friend. 'Tis only to win your heart and, as Brother Emile says, if not here, then we will find them in Three Rivers and Ville-Marie as well."

Genevieve frowned and shrugged as their priestly friend stepped from his own boat to be welcomed by the black-robed Jesuits who ran the seminary here. Many of the nuns, upon touching the solid ground, fell upon the soil to kiss the land and utter praise to God.

Once more Genevieve looked at her friend and wondered at her own vocation. Annette was surely wrong about her heart being won, for none of the men appealed to her in the least. And if, as her father said, she lived a dream, then she would be content to remain with her dreams and marry God.

9

Ten leagues from Ville-Marie, the stone manor house facing the river, yet confined within the wooden walls of the fort-like structure of the estate of the Siegneur St. Clair at the edge of the island, readied itself to welcome the returning son, Brother Emile.

Even the sheep were being sheared in honor of the occasion, so that the newest member of the Jesuit order would be provided with wool for his blankets and his winter robes. Only God knew how much he would need them in the desolate wilderness called New France.

The maids, too, many of whom had been heartily sick at the young man's discovery of his vocation, readied themselves in the hope that Emile would learn, perhaps sooner than later, that not all the clergy kept to their vows and churchly promises, and that none but God, since they often traveled alone in the wilds, would know.

However, despite their fervent desires, the new brother of the Jesuit order was firm in his resolve.

His elder half-brother, Philippe, had never considered, never would consider, such stupidity, and for that the maids were gratified, welcoming him home from the forest with as much hurrah as his younger brother received from his father. Even the savage, Christian that he now was, found solace from the boredom of late summer in the arms of a woman here and there. Four Winds, it seemed, was almost as versatile in pleasuring the women at hand as Philippe, the man he called "brother."

Alas, if what they were hearing was truth, Philippe's days of pleasing the few women on his father's estate would soon come to an end, if Seigneur St. Clair—or rather the Intendant, Talon—had his way.

The maid lifted the bucket of hot foaming milk, fresh from the cow's udder, and winced at the mingled shouts and curses as they floated down from the master's bedroom. She sighed and hurried on. Seeing Four Winds, she waved to the Indian.

"Your friend does not fare well with his Papa."

"Ah, yes," the swarthy man replied in perfect French. "He and the old master do not appreciate the finer points of each other's lives. 'Tis too bad if the new law forces my friend to wed when he does not wish to. A marriage should be one of love."

"But that is the only way he will obtain a license to continue the fur trade. And if he does not continue the fur trade, he would have to stay here." She smiled at the dark man.

He shrugged. "*Non.* He would merely come back with me and continue without this paper which your God so highly esteems. But perhaps"—Four Winds looked toward the open window where the old Seigneur lay on his sick bed—"marriage might be good for Philippe."

"How can you say that?" The little maid was astonished. "To marry him off would be like caging a wild bear. He would die of the captivity."

Four Winds smiled and touched the girl's hand. "He would no longer be able to pleasure you the way your husband cannot, eh?"

"Not so!" The maid flushed. "Jean-Paul and I—"

Seeing her husband waving to her in the distance, she flushed and hurried off.

"I will talk with you soon, Indian."

Four Winds shrugged and made his way up to the house.

"You must marry, Philippe. For the sake of the family."

"And I tell you I am married."

"The Indian?" The elderly man looked as pale as the linens he rested on, his grey hair framed by the massive goose-feather pillows brought from France.

"The Indian women were fine for *you*, my father! After all, I am product of that lust." Philippe walked to the window and looked out over the estate, across the river towards the settlement of Lachine on the other side, and to the forest beyond. By the gods, he wished he was there now! He still was unclear as to why he had come at his father's summons. The old man meant nothing to him; the old man had done nothing for him. And certainly he had no liking for his step-mother, the fair Eugenia.

"My son, please," old Jean-Pierre croaked. "I have not long for this world and I wish to see you with children. Your Indian wife, if you choose to think of her as such, is dead, as is the child she brought into this world."

"Then I tell you to ask Emile."

The shocked look on the old man's face was enough to give him another stroke. He clung to the bed post.

"Your . . . brother . . ."

"My half-brother, Sire."

". . . is of the holy order of the Jesuits. He has a calling. How dare you say . . ."

Philippe shrugged. There was a moment of strained silence. "My son, there is a law now . . ."

Philippe smashed his hand into the table. "My dearest Papa, you should know by now that the only law I live by is the law of my people and the natural law of the forest."

The older man sighed and was suddenly caught with a violent cough.

Concerned, his son rushed to St. Clair's side, holding the old man gently until the spasm had subsided.

"You see? You are French, too."

Philippe pulled back, angry that his father had used that moment of his weakness.

"I am a hunter. I do not live by the man-made laws here."

"Ah, but I do. I must. My son, if you do not wed, you will be the hunted and not the hunter. Your license to capture and sell the beaver furs at the annual fair will be taken away, you will be forbidden to go into the forest."

"No one can forbid me that!"

"And I, too, will suffer, as well as poor little Emile."

Philippe snorted. "Poor little Emile is

being taken under the wing of Laval. I doubt he will suffer much. As to you"—he waved his hand around the richly furnished room, reminiscent of the old man's home in Paris. "You should have thought of the consequences when you forced my mother back to her people, when you wed that whore."

The coughing began again. This time Philippe did not move to the bed.

"Please, my son"—the elder's voice was hoarse—"do not do this to me. I have suffered for this land. Your mother . . ."

"Don't talk to me of my mother!" The vein at Philippe's right temple throbbed in anger.

"But I will lose everything I have striven for here if you do not wed within a month of the new brides coming from the King."

"Brides? Or peasant girls to breed more arrogant French who will drive the Indians even farther into the forest?" Throwing the book that lay near his hand across to the fireplace, he shouted, "Very well! I will go to Quebec. I will see Talon and I will show him that I am Indian, not French, and therefore I do not have to abide by his insane laws. Emile is your only son, and since he is a priest, there is no question of his being forced to marry—is there? *Non!* We will see what happens when the great Intendant sees a man of real worth."

With that Phiulippe stormed from the room. The old man sighed and closed his eyes. His son had a temper, but then, so did he. Only with age had Jean-Pierre managed to control it, but it had been his temper that had kept him alive and fighting all these years. He only prayed to the Holy Lord that Philippe's temper would aid him rather than destroy them all.

As he flew down the stairs, Philippe paused. Standing in the door of the study was Eugenia, wearing a low-cut gown that showed nearly all of her possessions. Seeing him, she smiled, coming forward.

"Philippe." The silk of her skirt rustled as she walked. "I have not properly welcomed you home." She leaned forward, kissing his roughened cheek and pressing her ripe body to him.

Disgusted, Philippe pulled away. "You may save your kisses for my father, Eugenia. I want none of them."

"No?" She smiled and arched a brow, leaning over him again so that could smell her overpowering perfume as she nibbled his ear.

"No!" he thundered and quickly fled the house.

Old Bernard was sitting on the bank of the river whittling a doll for his new grandson, as Philippe approached. One of the original *habitants*, or settlers, of this land, Bernard had come to New France with the first soldiers and had soon fallen in love with the wilderness and freedom, much as Philippe had. But Bernard had attached himself to St. Clair, his former captain in the militia, and had gone no farther. He was content with his lot, with his farming in the summer and his violin in the winter. He was also content with the wife the company had given him and the dozen children—several of whom had died—that roamed the streets of the towns and the pathways of the forests in search of their fortunes.

"So tell me," Philippe asked, "is Claude going to be forced into a marriage, too?"

"*Mon Dieu*! I cannot see anyone forcing Claude into marriage." The old man laughed, showing his toothless grin. "But he has gone to Quebec to look at ze girls and to see if there is any which"—the old man twisted his hand back and forth in Gallic expression, then smiled again—"catch his eye. Perhaps he might indeed settle down. After all, zar is a generous dowry for ze girls who have come over now. Not only do they get their own lands once they wed, but they get horses, cows, linens, and much more, and for each child they produce"—he took out his nearly empty purse and jingled it. "So Claude is thinking that ze marriage might not be so much to his disadvantage. He can hunt, he can fish, he can go into ze woods and find ze beaver, and his woman can till ze soil and raise ze children—as woman are meant to do."

Philippe shrugged. 'I do not think a woman should be doing all of that on her own. If I marry, the woman will be at my side—wherever that is. And we shall do what needs to be done together."

"So? You go to Quebec, too?"

Philippe looked back toward the house where he could see his step-mother framed in the window. "*Oui*. I go to Quebec, but not to look at the girls. I will talk with Talon and make him see how ridiculous this scheme is. You cannot force a man to marry any more than you can force feelings of love, any more than you can make love with a woman you despise."

Bernard shrugged. "Love? What is love? It is working toward a common goal. It is"—he paused as momentary tears came to his eyes. "It is something which grows, and grows, and does not stop. You young people"—he stopped again and shook his head as his hand slipped on the wood. Blood spurted forth and quickly Philippe leaned over to bind the wound for the old man.

"I will go to Quebec and see the

women, my dear friend, but I doubt I will find any to my liking."

Bernard once again gave the younger man a toothless grin. "Just be careful you and Claude do not try for the same. I would hate to see blood shed yet again between you two."

"Yes," Philippe responded, with laughter in his voice. "I would hate to best him again, too."

10

Autumn was coming early. The tilled acres running down to the ancient highway, the great Saint Lawrence, had already turned from green to gold. A hint of frost was in the air, too, and the warehouses beyond the fields were closed against it. There was an unaccustomed stir in the narrow streets this day. More people roamed the streets than usually gathered there even on feast days or when the young men from Upper Town would come of an evening to strut about the cafes and inns where a bottle of wine could be had for six French sous, and forty sous was the price of a pound plug from the tobacco stores. Even the road that climbed up the cliff among the twenty-odd houses that clung there with precarious dignity had its group of people who seemed to be in no hurry to be about any particular business.

Beautiful, if not as well ordered as Ville-Marie, Quebec had a charm about it that reminded many of the inhabitants of Paris.

At the top of the main street and to the right was the Bishop's Palace, and next to it, the seminary, newly built to teach the young men—both white and Indian—in the ways of Christ. Already it was acclaimed to be the finest and largest building in the city—with the exception of the Governor's chateau, of course. To the left, on the brow of the cliff, was the very same Chateau of St. Louis, already growing a bit shabby for having been built nearly forty years ago. Opposite that was the Hospice of the Recollects Order, and not far away, facing the St. Charles River, was the Hotel-Dieu with its magnificent gardens.

This was Upper Town, and there was no comparing it to the crowded and huddled place near the water where the city had first started. There were only fifty lots here and the only street of importance, so Father le Tac said, was where the legal gentlemen lived.

The most important of these legal gentlemen was, of course, the Intendant, who governed the civil events of the colony. It was on this street, also facing the St. Charles, where he conducted the meetings of the Sovereign Council. The Palace, as the Intendant's humble house was fondly called, did not have the same grandeur the Governor's Chateau did, but with its double flights of stairs and beautiful sculpted gardens, it gave the agreeable air of a monied landowner's estate in a Paris suburb. It was too bad the gentleman who lived there was not equally agreeable.

Upper Town was not pretentious, yet the way it climbed the cliff gave it a certain dramatic distinction which caused anyone who saw it for the first time to pause in wonderment.

This day, outlined against the grey rocks and the forest's first crimson and purple, it seemed prepared for some great occasion. And this was an occasion of sorts—the presentation of the year's brides, newly come from Normandy and the provinces beyond.

It was straight to the council houses on the river's edge that Philippe now repaired, followed by his Indian brother, Four Winds, or Lancelot, as was his Christian name.

Polite conversation put aside, Philippe quickly came to the point of his visit. "This law of yours is ridiculous!"

"On the contrary, St. Clair, it is one of

the most sensible—if we are to have children in the colony. Otherwise men like you will run off and beget Indian brats with no manners who will overrun us."

"There are other ways of dealing with this. Let nature take its course."

Talon shrugged. "You will marry like the others or you will lose your license."

"No! I will not." Philippe pounded the heavy oak table in the hallway of the Intendant's office, causing even Lancelot to wince for the sake of the table god. "How can you force marriage on these men, on these women?" He motioned toward the Ursaline convent on the rue Donnacona.

Inserting snuff into his rather large nostril and sniffing, Jean Talon shrugged. His small mustache seemed to collapse against his narrow face as he sneezed. "They have come here knowing what is expected of them and they will do as they must, as loyal subjects to the King. My dear Philippe—"

"I am Kio Diego to you! I am as Indian as my comrades in the woods and even though I have, by accident of birth, been sired by a man of your race, my mother was a full-blooded Iroquois, and my wife is, too."

Once again the Intendant shrugged. "We care not how many Indian women you take to your bed, St. Clair. The church does not recognize any marriage not performed by the holy fathers and under the spirit of Christ." He paused to sneeze delicately into his handkerchief and wipe the tears from his eyes. "As to your birth"—he gave a Gallic shrug. "You are the heir to your father's land. Your brother—"

"Half brother," Philippe said through clenched teeth.

Talon gave a slight smile, acknowledging his mistake. "Your half-brother has taken holy vows and therefore cannot inherit the land. As your father's child, you are responsible for the seigneury, and should you refuse to wed according to the laws of this government, you will be refused a permit to hunt and trade with the Indians."

"Bah! No one can forbid me my life with the Indians."

The Intendant shrugged. "Perhaps not. But we can forbid you from selling your furs at the annual fair."

"Then I will take my catch to the English. They pay twice what the French do, anyway!"

At this the civil governor smiled. "You would trek more than a week through the most dangerous territory to deal with those English in Albany?"

Philippe merely stared at him in response.

"You know, I could have you hanged, or at the very least imprisoned for treason at such words."

"Then do so! 'Twould be better than marriage to a woman I do not love merely to keep the title to my father's lands, which I do not wish to have, and which, when I inherit, if he does not take himself another wife and I do inherit, will be given over to my people—my true people."

Talon's mustache twitched as he sighed. "The lands will be yours to do with as you wish—within reason, of course. Should the present government believe that the harboring of savages there"—he paused and tipped his wide brimmed hat toward Lancelot—"I refer, of course, to those who have not seen the light and taken Our Lord as Savior." Talon wet his lips and sipped at the excellent brandy that had just been given him by the captain of the ship—a gift from the Minister of the Interior himself. "As I was saying, should it be suspected that the presence of Indians on your property was endangering others of the community, I would have no hesitation in urging the Governor to call out the militia. And as you know, the Marquis de Tracy has not been known to deal kindly with our darker neighbors."

"Yes!" Philippe spat. "I know all about the Marquis' forays into our lands."

Talon sighed once more. "My dear boy, you are becoming very tiresome. There is absolutely nothing I can do for you. Either you chose a wench from those who have come over on this ship, or you lose your trading license until the next shipment of women in the spring. And by then, I guarantee, you will wish you had found someone, especially since you must pay 150 livres to the Hotel-Dieu, as well."

"Then I will pay. But I will not wed."

"Your Excellency, you must pardon my humble stupidity." Lancelot stepped forward, speaking in stilted French. "But I do wonder. There are many, many men here without a woman. Certainly the number you have brought over this time is small. I do not think there could be enough to wed all the men in the colony."

"Harump!" Talon's dark eyes narrowed as he eyed the Indian.

"Well?" Lancelot continued his polite onslaught. "Is that not the truth? Should all the women be taken before Philippe can choose . . ." He paused and smiled at the Intendant. "Is it not a fact that the best of the women are snapped up here in Quebec before they are shipped to Three Rivers? Those in Ville-Marie and beyond have the worst of the lot."

"Confound it! Who taught you the law? *Oui*, those who have settled out have less chance of finding a woman of beauty, but then, from what I have seen, these women have very little beauty among them. They are peasant girls, made for withstanding the raging climes that the city beauties could not. They are made for breeding more men for the colony and more soldiers to fight the likes of you." He eyed the Indian, then shrank back when Lancelot did not react.

"If you wish the ruling changed to benefit your desires, St. Clair, then you must take it up with the council next week. In the meanwhile, I highly suggest you be at the convent tonight when the girls are presented. After all, if you are to wed, and you are certainly required to by the government's standards, a Frenchman and subject to rules and laws like all else, you will perhaps want the most becoming of those pigs."

"So you will not help me." The cauldron of Philippe's anger bubbled and boiled. Only Lancelot's hand upon his friend's arm kept the peace for the moment. "Very well, I shall take the matter up with the council, as you say. And I shall gladly renounce my French citizenship. I shall gladly spit on the flag and pledge my loyalty with those who have been my people since birth. And if necessary, I will trade with the English—and perhaps I will trade more than just furs!"

He turned then and stormed out as Lancelot followed him.

The Intendant's words rang after them. "And you will swing from the gallows before you do such!" Talon shouted back, waving his fist in the same angry spirit. "I do what I do for the good of France and you are a selfish, foolish young man."

"Well, do we go this night and look at the women?" Lancelot asked as the pair sat on the riverfront in one of the many little cafes, watching the ship that had brought the women and drinking of the newly imported brandy.

Philippe shrugged and turned his attention toward the ship.

Back in Upper Town, the new convent, only recently built and dedicated by the good Marquis de Tracy for the purpose of educating and training the young women of the colony to become good Catholic wives and mothers, hummed with activity as the girls from the ship ran back and forth to the cloth room, studying bolts of fabric, ribbons and other fripperies frowned upon by the nuns and yet acknowledged as being necessary for those courting the human rather than the spiritual man.

But in the small chapel of Saint Anne, the latest addition to the convent knelt to pray. Mother Mary of the Incarnation, who ran the assembly here, had been more than gracious, inviting those who so wished to meet with her own confessor, Bishop Laval himself. And several of the young women had taken advantage of that opportunity, seeing in it a chance not only to meet one of the great leaders of the French community here in the wilderness, but to further their own lives and the lives of the husbands they might chose. But Genevieve, though she probably had far more to confess than the others, could not step foot into the church with its carved figures of Infant Jesus and the Holy Mother, and its stained glass brought directly from Paris. The place was far too sacred for a sinner such as she.

After all, her uncle had claimed she was the devil incarnate, tempting him the way she had. And hadn't it been her prayers that led to his death on the dueling grounds?

And so she remained, her knees on the cold stone of the chapel floor, repeating softly the Hail Marys she had assigned herself, praying that Jesus would forgive her for her wrongdoing and bless this venture she was about to undertake. If she was lucky, she'd be soon permitted to join the order of the Ursalines here, but for now it was important that she pretend an interest in the men.

Tears came to her eyes and she crossed herself as she heard footsteps behind her.

"I thought I'd find you here." Annette shook her head. "Don't you even want to get ready for tonight?"

Genevieve shrugged and stood up, aware only now of the painful cold in her knees from the stone floor.

"Well, I do. Certainly this color blue is very fetching for me. Do you not think so, Claudie?" Annette smiled.

"Please. Do not tease me so."

"Tease you?" The other girl's eyes twinkled. "*Non*, I would not do that. Though I confess, I cannot see why you cannot allow yourself to be called Genevieve now."

"And how can that be?"

Annette shrugged. "You say that Genevieve Claudine is your full name, that you registered under your common name as you were known in your village, but now you are starting a new life here in the new world, you wish to be called by your complete name."

Genevieve's eyes widened. "Why didn't I think of that?"

"Because, my pet," Annette said, holding the length of clothing up to Genevieve's face, "I am the one who's had to survive and live by my wits these many years. But I am sure, once we are out in the wilds, you will soon learn to use yours as well."

Annette's tone made Genevieve laugh. "If you do not want to wed, then why take such pains with your dress? You do not wish any of the men to court you?"

"Oh, but I do," Annette smiled. "You are right that I do not wish to wed, but to set up my house somewhere"—she waved her hand—"away from this religious nonsense."

"Shh!" Genevieve flushed and looked around, fearing the statue of the Savior had ears, or that someone human might overhear them.

Ignoring the other girl, Annette continued in her amused tone, "but I do wish them to court me, my little Genny. For if they want me, then they will visit me when I establish my business."

Genevieve sighed and shook her head. "I fear then what I have seen of the Bishop and the Mother Superior, that you will not be allowed the liberty of—" She blushed furiously, unable to say what it was her friend planned. "That is, I—"

"I have told you, my pet. That is why I need you. You will wed some handsome soldier who will be away a good part of the time, and you will take me along as a domestic since I have no wish to be tamed by one of these obnoxious creatures. Then when your husband is gone . . ."

Genevieve closed her eyes and uttered

a prayer to sustain her. She did not want to think about tonight. She did not want to think about having to marry anyone or, more simply, she did not want to think about having to bed them.

"Please, Annette, I—"

"Come on." Annette took the younger girl's hand. "We've got to get you ready for tonight so that you'll win the hearts of the most eligible."

"But I—"

"You don't have to accept anyone tonight, my love. In fact, you don't even have to accept them after three visits. By the end of the month we leave for Three Rivers—away from all this hocus-pocus." She made a face. "And if there is no one there, on to Ville-Marie and so forth."

Genevieve's strength was no match for the larger-boned girl, and she found herself being led to the cloth room.

11

Philippe respectfully took off his coonskin cap as he and Lancelot entered the wrought-iron gates leading to the schoolrooms of the Ursaline convent where the newly imported girls were "holding court."

"You see how futile this is!" Philippe told his friend. "There will be no woman there who can match what I found in your sister."

The Indian shrugged. "Perhaps not. Then again, perhaps so. You did not love Morning Flower when you were forced to marry her. Mayhap 'twill again be the same. You will find someone who inspires you, and the love will grow."

Philippe stared at the other man. "Whose side are you on? And what would

I do with a French wife? Drag her into the wilderness? Have her become an Indian squaw? You know that as soon as the trade on the island is completed, I shall return with you to our home."

Lancelot shrugged. "The old man . . ."

"So. My father has won you over despite his autocratic, judgmental attitudes."

"*Mon ami*, I do not think he meant to hurt your mother by his marriage to the French woman. He, too, was proscribed by the laws as you are. Surely you must know that he would have lost all his lands and titles, had he insisted that his marriage to your mother was holy. After all, she did not take up the church as did so many of her people."

Philippe stared at him. "*Mon Dieu*! You are sounding like Emile." He shrugged the other's hand off him as the music floated toward them. "Very well. We go in. But I warn you, we do not stay long. Only enough to make our presence known."

Lancelot looked at the soldiers, farmers and other men, young and old, parading by them in their best velvet coats and plumed hats. Then he looked at his own buckskin clothing and that of his friend, and their unpowdered hair. "If that is all you wish, then I believe we shall not have to stay long, for our presence will surely be noted."

Because of the chill of the autumn season, a fire burned in the grate, for the mists rising from the river had infected the stone of the building and those who were wise positioned themselves near the fireplace as the violinists played their lively music.

"You would think that we could dance, at least," Annette complained. Even with the short time for preparations, she had fashioned an elegant, low-cut gown of the blue cloth she had shown Genevieve earlier that day. So low was the cut of the gown that several of the nuns and good women looked askance. But the men, it seemed, did not mind. The stomacher and skirt she had made of one of Genevieve's old dresses, and her hair she had done in the fashion of the nobility, the short, tight curls framing her face.

At her side, Genevieve wore a plain gown of light indigo. Lacking the frills and decorations, it nevertheless could not hide her beauty.

"I am glad we are not dancing," she responded. "For I do not know the dances the peasant women do."

Annette snorted. "You saw plenty on the ship."

"Well, anyway, I do not think the nuns believe in the dance."

"We're the ones supposed to marry these fellows." Annette jerked her head toward some of the fops who had made their entrance and slowly shook her head. "I have seen many a man in my day, *mon coeur*, but none quite as obnoxious as these." She watched one man trying to court another girl. "What do they think, that we are on the meat stands? Better yet, perhaps we are at an auction."

Her hand reached over to reassure her friend. "But do not worry, my pet, we do not have to take any of these clods. There are but two more towns for us and then—"

Genevieve sighed. "Domestic service or the convent."

" 'Tis a true matter that I would rather work for someone and get paid for my work than work for someone and be paid nothing, merely because I am his wife!"

She smiled at a man who came up to speak with her, but somehow managed to push him away when she saw Genevieve looking fearful.

"Are you feeling well, my dear friend?" Annette said, louder and more solicitous than she needed to be. Turning to the man, she said, "Genevieve Claudine contracted a strange illness while we on ship."

The man courting Genevieve quickly

backed away. "I shall see you anon, Mam'selle. Perhaps in a day or two when you feel better."

"Perhaps she will be better in a day or two," Annette responded for the flabergasted Genevieve. "Truly, by God's wish, I hope so. Though we fear He may take her to His bosom very shortly."

It was hard to keep a straight face as sweat broke out on the man's brow and he quickly disappeared into the crowd of men and women milling around the room.

Annette allowed herself a little laugh.

"Why did you say that?" Genevieve was astonished.

Annette's eyes widened. "*Mon coeur*, you did not want that man. He was a boor. Not of your caliber at all."

"But he—"

Puzzled, Annette sat down next to her friend again. "Tell me, do you or do you not want to find someone here to wed? If you wish, then—" She shrugged her shoulders and waved her hand toward the mass of people in the room which was increasing by the moment. "But if you do not, then we must find a way to discourage them in a way which will not make trouble for you."

"I . . ." Genevieve closed her eyes a moment as she tried to steady herself, to think. What did she really want?

A happy girl walked to a corner with

one of the young men, asking him questions about the size of his farm, his livelihood, and the number of sheep he had. It seemed not to matter to her that he was pockmarked and ungainly. Only that he had money. Genevieve shivered.

"I do not know but I—" She drew in her breath and stared wordlessly toward the door.

"What is it?"

"*Mon Dieu!*" Annette whispered. "What a specimen! So tall, so lean and strong"—she breathed heavily like a woman already in love—"so savage!"

"No. No, I do not mean him. I mean *him.*" Genevieve indicated the white man who had accompanied the Indian and who, despite his obvious racial difference, wore the same kind of buckskin coat and leggings. A hunting knife hung at his side.

Genevieve breathed heavily, as if in a trance as she stared at the man—his hair the color the trees in autumn, his eyes the color of the sky. She was glad that she was sitting near the fire now, for a sudden chill overcame her and she knew not the reason. Perhaps, as Annette had said, she truly was becoming ill. Perhaps . . . she closed her eyes, trying not to look at the man, trying not to think the thoughts that she knew, in this convent, she should not be thinking.

And yet, as Annette had pointed out,

the situation was inevitable, wasn't it? Even if they went to work for some family, no doubt the man would insist on having his way—though perhaps he might pay something for it. Silently, Genevieve uttered a prayer to the Holy Mother to protect and guide her in the right direction.

Opening her eyes, she found that he was looking at her, studying her, with the same intensity with which she had, a moment before, been studying him. Once again that strange chill came over her. She wanted to stand, to rise, to go over to him before another girl did, even though she knew it was not the way things were done. Yet she could not move, for her heart was hammering too rapidly. Suddenly she recalled the words of the witch. Could it be he? No, she was sure not, and yet . . .

A scream from one of the women startled everyone as all turned to look at the commotion.

"A beast! A beast just tried to attack me. Kill it! Kill it!" she screamed hysterically.

The little black "beast," frightened by the noise, ran into a corner. It was Alexandre!

One of the nuns took up the scream and with a broom tried to hit the cat under the chair.

"*Non!*" Genevieve cried out, standing

suddenly and running toward the far end of the room where Alex had hidden, pushing the pistol out of the hands of the man ready to fire. "He is no beast. He is my cat."

"Alexandre! Alexandre!"

The cat mewed in response to his name, but was still frightened to come out of hiding, for there were far too many people for him to be comfortable.

"Allow me." The buckskinned man pushed the others aside.

"But I—My cat—"

Philippe merely smiled at her. " 'Twill be all right, Ma'mselle. Believe me." Then, to the astonishment of all the others in the room, he bent down on all fours so that he could see the cat and began to make strange noises. Certainly this was no language Genevieve had ever before heard.

It took several moments before the cat hesitatingly emerged and allowed Philippe to pick him up.

Startled, Genevieve stared at both the man and her cat. Finally she managed to say, "My thanks, sire. Alexandre is a special cat. He is my protector, but he does not like others—men especially."

Philippe shrugged, as Genevieve cuddled and held the cat to her much like an infant. The cat mewed in response, licking her face in love as if he had not seen her for many a day.

"Aye, 'tis evident there is affection between you. But you must be careful of where he goes. Even in the towns, we are not far from the wilderness, where all manner of beasts roam which could easily destroy your pet."

Genevieve hugged the animal closer to her. 'I don't think I could bear it if I lose my Alexandre. I thank you for your warning, Monsieur, and I will take care that he does not stray out of my sight too often." She looked at the cat. "You are a bad boy. You know I told you to stay on the bed."

Philippe laughed. "Mam'selle, if you are a loving cat owner you should know that felines do not take orders well." His arm touched hers. "Come. Let us talk."

She looked directly at him, feeling her heart's beat and the heat where his skin had touched hers. Yet she could not allow him to think she was easy. "You should know, Monsieur, that women are like cats. They do not take orders well either."

His eyes twinkled in the candlelight. "*Touche*. You are right to call me on that, Mam'selle."

The buzz in the room had died down as the courting continued. Unsure of her next step, Genevieve turned and started back toward her seat near the fireplace only to find Annette deep in conversation with Lancelot. No, it was not conversation; it was laughter.

Jealous of her friend's having found a man she obviously wanted and who, from the looks of things, wanted her as she did him, Genevieve turned away again.

"Would you like to sit with me? Perhaps over here?" Philippe guided her over to a set of chairs near the door leading into the courtyard and the gardens well tended by the nuns. Genevieve could feel the other women's eyes throwing daggers-looks at her, and she knew that it was because this man was so attractive. And yet—she hesitated to go with him.

"We will talk and I will get to know Alexandre," he told her.

She liked the way he included the animal, but apparently the cat did not, for at the sound of his name he again began to struggle in her arms.

"Here. Let me help." He took the animal from her hands and looked into the cat's green eyes. Almost immediately Alexandre calmed down. He made a few noises, scatching the pet under his chin, and then handed the silent cat back to his mistress. "He will obey you now, I believe."

"Oh? Do you have a way with women as you do with animals?"

He laughed once more, and to her ears the sound was like the instruments she had heard playing at the King's balls.

"*Non*, I am afraid I do not. I am a hunter, you see. A *coureur de bois*, as we are called. Sometimes I live with Indians, sometimes I live on my own in the wilderness. It is as it seems most appropriate at the moment. My women"—he shrugged and his voice took on a faraway tone—"my women have always been of my tribe."

"Oh." Genevieve sat there silently, not knowing what else to say. There was a strained moment before she had the courage to ask, "You are not here to find a wife?"

He turned toward her, studying her a long moment before he responded, "*Non*. I do not wish to wed again. Certainly, I do not wish to wed when I am being forced to by the government."

The puzzled expression on her face made him continue. "I see you do not know of the laws pertaining to the brides. 'Tis now declared that men must wed within three weeks of the women coming to their town. If they do not, then they lose their license to trade, or lose their farms, or perhaps both if not enough bribes are paid to the right officials."

"*Ma foi*, that is almost as bad as—" She paused, realizing that she had almost given herself away. "I mean, that is not fair. A marriage should be of love and understanding."

His hand touched her briefly. "My sentiments exactly, Mam'selle." He stood. "And so you see, I must leave now. I came only to see what was here for *sale*."

Furious with him, she stood, too. "You are wrong, Monsieur. Perhaps the other women will sell themselves to the man with the greatest fortune, but I certainly will not. I resent you believing that to be so." She started back into the room.

The cat had other plans, however, and with his powerful hind legs, he sprang out of her arms and past the feet of several screaming women, as Genevieve ran after him into the gardens.

"Alexandre! You naughty boy! Where are you?"

She looked around in the darkness but could not see him, for his black coat made him nearly invisible.

"Allow me, Ma'mselle."

She turned to find the man standing behind her.

"No. I will find my cat myself."

He shrugged and stood there, arms folded across his massive chest as he watched her go along the rows of bushes trying to find her errant pet. "Alex? Alexandre, where are you?"

The noise from the tree above made

her look up to see the cat perched on a perilous branch. "Oh, no."

"Shall I assist?"

Genevieve looked from her darling cat to the arrogant man at her side as the bough seemed to sway in the evening breeze and Alexandre, no longer brave, cried for help. "Yes, please. Please, do not let anything happen to him. He is all I have."

Taking a rope out of his pocket, he used it to slowly make his way up the tree. She watched anxiously, like a mother praying for her child. Carefully, he edged out over the tree until he was in reach of the cat.

"Come on, Alexandre. Come on, boy."

The cat stared at him.

"Please, Alex. Go with him."

As if understanding his mistress, he leaped onto the hunter's back, but the move was so sudden that it caused him to lose his footing and the pair of them, cat and man, tumbled to the ground below.

"Oh!" Genevieve ran to him. "Are you hurt?"

"*Non,*" he responded, shaking his head to clear the cobwebs as he sat up. "And I see that little Alexandre is all right, too." The cat meowed his response and went back to cleaning himself. "But I do think you owe me something for my trouble."

"What is that?" Genevieve was puzzled. "I have very little money, but you are certainly welcome to it as long as the price is fair."

He laughed. "Oh, I believe you will think the price fair."

Before she could protest, he leaned over and kissed her, his lips grazing hers in a way that she had never experienced before, in a way that caused her blood, already coursing quickly through her body because of him, to surge even faster. His tongue parted her lips as his passion claimed her and, feeling helplessly moved along on the waves, much as the boat had been, Genevieve responded.

She was flushed when he pulled away.,

"I am sorry. I do not know what came over me."

He merely shrugged. "Mayhap it would be nice if I knew your name."

"My name is Genevieve."

"Well, Genevieve." He leaned over to kiss her yet a second time, engulfing her in his desire and sweeping her forward. "I am Philippe St. Clair." He looked over his shoulder and saw Lancelot standing in the doorway, Annette with him. "I'd better stop now if I do not want your reputation ruined."

Astonished, she looked back and saw the other couple in the doorway. "No, and you certainly would not want to be forced to marry someone who was for sale, would you now?''

Angry again, she scooped up the cat, who this time meekly obeyed her as she hurried toward the dormitory room she shared with Annette.

12

Running through the schoolroom where the other women and men were gathered, Genevieve paused only a moment to pick up her mantelet and hurried out the other entrance. She heard the buzzing of voices behind her. They were talking about her, she was sure. A flush crept over her as she relived that odious man's kiss. He had ruined her. And soon the authorities would discover her secret and send her back. No, she could not return to the meeting room. She could not deal with the questioning looks of the other women nor the accusing looks of the nuns. And she especially did not want to see the obnoxious fellow again.

Once in the dormitory room, she released the struggling Alexandre.

"Now look what you've done! I hope you are happy!" she scolded the cat.

"Oh, Alexandre." Genevieve shook her head, as she scooped him up into her arms and cuddled him once again. "What shall I do?"

With the cat in her arms, she lay down on the narrow straw cot. The bedding was nearly as bad as that on the ship—nay, worse. But it was private all the same—or almost. She looked over to Annette's bed and wondered at the other girl.

Perhaps her very thoughts had communicated themselves through the air, for moments later Annette floated in. Yes, Genevieve thought, floated. The blissful smile on her face made her look almost as if she had been blessed by the Lord Jesus himself, or certainly one of the minor saints.

"Oh. You are here." Annette seemed startled when she saw Genevieve and crashed to earth.

"Where else do you expect me to be?"

Annette shrugged. "With Philippe."

"Is that his name? I don't even recall him telling me so."

Annette smiled. "Perhaps if you had not been in such a hurry to run, you would have heard him telling you."

"And?"

Once more the older girl shrugged. "I do believe you have won his heart."

Genevieve purposely looked down at the cat seated calmly on her lap, because she knew that if she looked at Annette, her own concern would be clear. "That I would doubt. I do not think the man has a heart. Else why would he had embarrassed me so?"

Annette shrugged. "He saved your cat, did he not?"

"An accident."

This time Genevieve looked up to see Annette smiling. "Perhaps and perhaps not." She paused. "I would not mind if you were to take a walk for a moment or so."

"What? Why?" Genevieve looked strangely at the other girl. "This is my room, too."

Annette looked directly at her friend. "Now why do you think, my innocent one?"

Genevieve's eyes widened. "I do not want to take a walk."

With a deep sigh, Annette shook her head. "Truly, you know nothing, do you?" A smile played on her lips. "Just say that I wish to be alone for a moment."

Looking up, Genevieve saw the tall form of the savage Indian who had been with Philippe lounging near the door.

"Annette! How can you! 'Tis part of the rules of the convent. I mean, 'tis holy ground here and—" Flustered, Genevieve could only stare at the other girl.

"My sweet innocent." Annette stood and placed her hands on Genevieve's shoulders, directing her vision away from the entrance where she, too, had seen the shadow of her Indian friend. "Lancelot and I have much to discuss and we wish to do so in private."

"But I—"

" 'Twill be all right, sweetings. Do not fear for me." She leaned over and quietly added. "I do believe he can provide me with the money I need to set up my house."

"Him!" Genevieve's voice squeaked louder than she meant it to.

"*Oui*," Annette said, her finger touching Genevieve's lips. "Is that not *merveilleux*?"

"But—"

"Go. Please. For one hour only. Surely, you can amuse yourself out in the schoolroom. There are plenty of men still waiting to speak with you."

She sighed. "And Philippe? Is he there?"

Annette shrugged. "You must see for yourself, pet. Though I do believe he left moments after you did."

"Oh." She sighed again and picked up Alexandre, then on second thought placed him back on the bed. She wanted no more scenes like before. "You stay put and give

Annette no trouble."

The cat merely stared at her with his wide-opened eyes, then quickly blinked as if to say he understood. Whether he did or not, Genevieve could not take him out there with her.

"Very well, I will go. But I pray that you have a care and do not do anything that will cause trouble."

Annette merely smiled as she watched Genevieve pick up her cape and leave the room.

Moments later the shadow from the hallway emerged, tanned and strong. "She is gone?"

Annette smiled. She patted the bed.

" 'Tis impossible to talk with the noise in the schoolroom."

Annette merely nodded as she looked into his eyes—his deep brown, caring eyes—and she felt her heart melt. Never in her life had she felt like this. Never in her whole history of being with men had she wanted to give herself to a man the way she wanted to give herself to this Indian. And it was happening so fast! A survivor, cynical of life, she had never been one to believe in love at first sight and yet—the way he looked at her, the way her heart pounded. The instant she had seen him across the room, she had known that she wanted him. There was no question about it. And he seemed to feel the same.

"Lancelot . . ."

The bed sagged as he sat beside her. "I love how you say my name." His hand reached up to touch her skin, stroking her cheek. "Though that is not my name. The translation of my name in French is Four Winds, but the good fathers did not like that and so"—he shrugged—"I am Lancelot."

"Four Winds. I like that." Annette smiled as her lips grazed his hand on her cheek. "But I also like Lancelot, for he was also a hero." She placed her hand over his.

"You are not scared?"

"Of what?" There was a lightness in her voice.

"But I am an Indian. A savage. Most women in that schoolroom would have not let me come near them and yet you openly welcomed me."

Annette shrugged and smiled. "Perhaps I see what you really are."

"Oh?" His brows lifted a moment. "And what is that, *ma cherie*?"

She took his hand into hers again and lifted it to her lips. "A man. A very handsome man."

He laughed. He took his hand from her and began caressing her neck. She closed her lids, enjoying his touch, enjoying his musky smell.

Then abruptly, he pulled back.

Shocked with the release of his touch,

Annette opened her eyes. "*Pardon*! Is something wrong?"

Lancelot pressed his lips together. "The good fathers who taught me the love of Jesus—they would not approve."

Annette narrowed her eyes. "*Mon Dieu*! Do not be such a child."

"But we are in a convent. The nuns . . ." He could only stare at her.

"So? How do you think more nuns are born?" She smiled at him.

"But you are—I mean, do you not wish to be wed as a virgin? Is that not the desire of all the women here?"

"And you told me the men of your tribe like to test the woman first to see her responsiveness." She smiled at him. "So I am responsive."

The bed creaking as he lifted his weight from it. "But I am not one of those who must wed. I came merely with Philippe because—"

"But you came. And you cannot deny that what you feel for me is the same that I feel for you, Indian."

Before he could protest, Annette's lips touched his. With her tongue, she parted his mouth and felt the tension in his body dissolve beneath her massaging fingertips. Breathless, she pulled away and looked in his eyes. "We have but a few moments to enjoy some privacy. Come." She pulled him back to the bed. "There is much I need to ask you."

"About?"

"The way a savage makes love."

He laughed as they fell on the bed together. Their lips joined again as he returned her passion, their hands roaming each other, pausing at delicate spots. His hand slipped beneath her voluminous skirts and then her chemise; he stroked her belly gently and tenderly as she continued her exploration of him.

A tingling that Annette had never before experienced radiated through her whole body as the heel of his hand stopped on her mound, pressed firmly and moved in a small, slow circle until her body answered, rubbing up against his hand.

Quickly shedding what clothes she still had on, Annette felt her knees come up and open, ready to his touch as his hand continued its pressure—unrelenting, insistent, slow circles. Her insides opened further. Never stopping the pressure on her mound, his other hand trailed between her legs and his fingers lightly touched her other lips, trailing along from front to back slowly, just a little inside, slowly outside, around, spreading wetness as she gasped, feeling the pressure on her womanhood increasing and her insides gathering together, shooting her up higher than the highest star.

As her tension increased, as she

moaned softly and he covered her mouth with his, he pressed harder and faster until Annette felt the bed rocking and convulsing with her desire.

She collapsed, but his hand didn't leave her as it lightly continued pressing around and around, literally holding her in the palm of his hand. His buckskin breeches had fallen now and she was able to caress his hard muscles and the softness beneath, to see the tumescent organ glistening in the light of the moon streaming in from that single window.

Lancelot's fingers began to explore every inch of her, outside, around, up, down, slowly in, slowly out, but each time pressing farther in, harder and harder until Annette was once more riveted with pleasure. Never had a man cared about pleasing her the way he did, never had she been so pleased!

Their moans were louder now and, even knowing as she did that she needed to control her voice, so that others would not come, would not find them, she could barely think. And once again, she was gripped with a searing power, hanging onto him as she rode wave after wave of love and continued to feel the desire of him rushing over her. Yet still, he had not entered her.

"Please, I—" she choked.

"You wished to know the way of my

people, *mon coeur*. Then so be it." He smiled and kissed her lips, silencing her and then moved his mouth further down her body.

Slowly his hand slid out of her and he rubbed her belly now with both his hands, his fingers spreading her buttocks and then her lower lips. Annette felt the cool air upon her and she stirred, needing him within her and yet wanting whatever it was he planned to do with equal passion. Holding her open he laid his tongue on the tip of her very essence and she squirmed as, in the same slow circles, he pressed lightly, until her body answered with its own circles.

"Oh, Lance . . ."

"Hush, my love."

His fingers now stroked her breast. He was so gentle, so very gentle, she thought through the haze of yet another mounting wave of desire drawing her higher and higher. His sinuous tongue moved gently and firmly, pushing her onto yet another peak. His fingers slid directly inside, firmly pressing, making her soar so high that she was sure the nuns must have heard her scream. How long could this go on? How much more could she stand of this savage torture?

She pulled at his manhood, crying out, tugging at him, wanting to feel his hardness swell within her, wanting to give him the same pleasure he was giving her.

Finally, he nodded, and smiling, he moved up beside her, and held her until she came back to life. Holding her, kissing her, his hands moving over her lightly, Annette found herself instantly aroused again and wanting him—all of him—inside of her. Unable to wait a moment longer, she pulled him on top of her, his hard manhood finding the way between her legs. But he poised there, teasing her.

"Lance . . ." she begged.

He grinned, then slid up and down slowly, tantalizing her once more. Just when she thought she would surely go crazy, he slid inside her—huge, hot, filling her with his love. And then he held her as they pushed and strained against each other, wanting more.

He held her firmly and whispered in her ear something in his own tongue, but she knew what he was saying as he nibbled her lobe and she clung to him, clasping him so hard she could feel the contours of his probing hardness.

Frozen in ecstasy, neither of them moved as the final tidal wave hit them, gripping them and shaking them. Only when Annette felt she could stand no more were they washed ashore together, released.

Momentarily consciousness faded to nothing as she continued to cling to him.

Then she opened her eyes and looked into his. "Do I pass?"

Lancelot shrugged. "That is only part of the test." He rose from the bed and bent to kiss her lightly on the lips before he quickly replaced his fallen clothes.

"I will see you again. No?"

At the door, he turned and smiled at her. "I do not know. I cannot say. It all depends on Philippe."

"But I—"

"Good night, *ma petite*."

Annette sighed and laid back on the bed. "Good night, my Lancelot." She blew him a kiss. "Until the next time."

13

Not wishing to return to the schoolroom, since despite what Annette had told her, she did not want to risk seeing that—that man again, Genevieve hurried past the entrance, the buzz of voices echoing in her ears, and walked quickly down the long hall leading to the gate and the street.

She was glad that the nun who usually stood at the entrance to lock and unlock the gate for visitors was not around because she truly did not want to explain why it was, when the men were all inside and she should be there coaxing and pleasing them, that she felt the need for a walk.

The moon was brilliant and the air crisp, almost cold for an early fall evening, as she wrapped her mantelet around her and wished she had her fur muff. But alas, that was back in Versailles, as was so much of her life.

Walking down the rue Donnacona, she turned in the direction of the mighty Saint Lawrence and saw the ship that had brought them still bobbing up and down with the tide as it waited for letters, packages, and furs to take back to France.

With a sigh, Genevieve started down one of the narrow cobblestone streets that led toward the harbor and Lower Town. She had thought that perhaps, if she could go and look out upon the water, she would feel calmed; but would feel that France was somehow nearer. And she recalled how being near her pond at home in Joigny had always had a soothing effect on her nerves.

The street was empty, but full of long shadows as she walked. Even though a few of the houses had candles burning in the doorway for the convenience of residents coming from a late drink at the tavern, or perhaps his evening at the convent, the light was still limited, and the full moon, playing hide-and-seek with the clouds, did little to add to the illumination. Not that she needed it, Genevieve told herself. She was safe here within the city. Surely, the Indians would not attack at night—or would they? Turning, she wandered the narrow lanes, thinking of her home and her future.

She inhaled of the night flowers and smelled the spray of the distant sea. Did demons really lurk at night as her father had often warned her? No, she was sure not. And yet . . . Hearing a step fall on the cobblestones behind her, echoing loudly in the narrow passage, Genevieve quickly looked around. She could see no one, but that did not prevent her heart from pounding rapidly. Perhaps it had not been so wise to come out on a night like this, alone. She clutched the cape closer to her, wishing that she had taken Alexandre with her, although she knew the cat could really give her little help.

The footsteps stopped and she told herself that it had just been someone going into his home, that it was nothing to fear. Momentarily relieved, she continued her walk, only to find that the steps started again with her movement. Someone was following her!

At the top of the cliff, on the path leading down to Place Royale, she paused. How much steeper the walk looked during the night than the day! Even though a rail and steps were cut into the rocks for guidance, she thought it would be easy for one to fall into the sea and never be heard of again. She looked over her shoulder to the Chateau Saint-Louis standing upright on the terrace above and saw the flag of

Louis flying. Soldiers were making rounds—she could see them clearly in the moonlight walking the ramparts—but it would take her forever and an age to reach them and God only knew what was behind her. Then, as the footsteps resumed, vibrating behind her and appearing to follow her, Genevieve decided that she would continue down. It would be better than turning back and facing whatever it was who had come after her. And even if there was nothing to fear, well—she wanted to take a walk down to the harbor anyway.

She was halfway down the steps when she saw the tall figure looming over the cliff, looking, with the hood covering his face, like one of the banshees an Irish maid had told her about. Her heartbeat increased. Had he been the one following her—and why?

Genevieve could hear the man above saying something to her, but she knew not what, for the moaning of the wind down the cliffs blotted out the sound of his voice. Frightened, she hurried downwards.

As she glanced briefly back while taking a turn, she saw to her dismay that the darkly cloaked figure was following her, and she had yet a good distance to go before she reached Lower Town and places where she could hide. Wondering briefly if she wouldn't do better just to press herself into the cliff and try to avoid him, she realized that if he was following her, it would do no good to stay put. Once more she wished she had her pet with her, for she knew that should anyone try to come at her, Alexandre would lunge at him with his claws out ready for the attack. But she would have to make the best of things without him.

As she ran down the steps, praying that the clogs she wore would not stick in the stone or cause her to trip, she once more looked behind. The man, or whatever he was, for he wore nothing that she could distinguish as belonging to a French citizen, was closing in on her and still speaking to her, though his voice was still being carried away on the wind.

Telling herself not to worry, she turned and hurried on, only to find herself at the bottom of the path before she even realized it. Breathless, she clung to the rail here and knew she had no time to stand and watch the tide flow in as she might have wished. Indeed, she had to seek shelter, she had to find some protector.

Three young men were coming out one of the taverns. Without thinking, Genevieve ran toward them. "Please, kind sirs. You must help me!"

"Well, what have we here, gentlemen?" the man who obviously led them said. He was the drunkest of the three and put his hand on her shoulder. "I do believe 'tis a lady. Or certainly a good facsimile. Would you not agree, Charles? Georges?"

The other two merely laughed and hooted as Genevieve realized instantly that her choice of protectors was questionable.

"Are you new-come to our fair land, Mademoiselle? Do you wish work?"

The other two guffawed as Genevieve tried to loosen the man's hand from her shoulder.

Recalling that she was supposed to be a peasant girl and not of the nobility, she forced her anger to catch for a moment. "*Oui*, Monsieurs. I am of the King's Daughters and I stay with the good sisters of the Ursalines until such time as I find a husband or go on to Three Rivers."

"Well, there is no need for you to leave, little beauty that you are. All three of us will husband you, eh?" He looked from one to the other, without taking his hand off Genevieve.

"But I—"

"I am afraid, gentlemen, that you are too late. You should have been at the convent this evening and made your choice. This delicate morsel is already spoken for."

Quickly, Genevieve turned her head to

see Philippe St. Clair coming down the stairs after her. She gasped. It had been he following her, had she but known. She saw his buckskin suit nearly hidden by his cloak and realized that was why she had not recognized him. Why had he been after her? Did he yet plan to add to her humiliation? *Mon Dieu!* What had she done? Why had she even left the convent?

"I said"—Philippe moved closer—"you will release her." His voice held a menace to it that she had not heard in their earlier meeting.

"And what are you? A woman dressed in fringes?" the leader taunted, his fingers digging into Genevieve's shoulders, causing her to gasp.

She forced herself to turn and saw now that Philippe had dropped the cape which had helped to disguise him earlier.

"No, I am a hunter," he said, his eyes meeting those of the man before her. His hand drifted toward the knife in his belt and Genevieve held her breath, unable to move, for the strength of the young man gripped her to the spot.

From the corner of her eye, she saw one of the unattached pair also going for his knife.

"Philippe!"

Quicker than a flash of lightning, the hunter had disarmed one attacker and swung his fist into the shoulder of the lad holding her. The arm dropped away.

"Run, *mignonne!*"

"But I—"

"Do not argue with me. Run! Toward the water," Philippe commanded as the three young men now united to attack him.

Paralyzed for only a second longer, Genevieve did run, but not far. Finding a length of rope, probably from one of the fishing boats, she grabbed at it. She had seen how the groomsmen at her father's estate, before they had dismissed them, used the whip on the horses that could not be tamed; she had seen the first mate on the ship use the cat o'nine tails on sailors who would not obey. Why not use the rope now? The thick hemp was heavier than she had expected it would be. Nevertheless, it was her foolishness in running without knowing what she was running from that had caused this mess, and had she not gone up to the men, she was sure they would never have noticed her. Therefore, she could not let Philippe fight her battle. Certainly, she could not let him be beaten by three drunken young men who had the strength of the devil and strength of drink in them.

Shouting out all the curses she had ever heard on the estate and allowing a portion of the rope to swing free, she heard the hiss as the hemp cut the air, singing, as it landed upon the eldest of the three.

Startled, he looked up, giving Philippe just enough leeway to hit him in the lower jaw.

And once again, she swung the rope, feeling her arm nearly pulled out of its socket with the force, directing it to the other man, who was now aiming his punch at Philippe. The brief respite was enough. Philippe raised himself from his fallen position and once more scored a hit as he grabbed his cloak from the ground and hurried toward Genevieve.

"Come, my pet. We've no time to waste."

She wanted to say something about his familiarity but knew now was not the time, as she saw the three men start after them. There was no time to protest as Philippe's arm went around her and he propelled her, almost carried her, down the dark street to the Place Royale and the original town founded by Champlain.

Down one street they ran and onto another, as he urged her along, as they continued to hear the steps of their pursuers following them. Running so fast, Genevieve did not look where she was headed and, falling headlong into the mud, was forced to accept his hand as he rescued her.

"I wish I could laugh," he said, "but there is no time."

She glared at him, angry and upset. True, it was her fault. Nevertheless, she was sure now that she could have talked them out of whatever evil deed they had been planning and been safely back at the convent now—had he not appeared to worsen the situation. And what was that remark about her being taken? Surely, it had been in jest.

Breathless, she told him, "*Non*, I cannot go farther."

Without waiting for her to say any more, he scooped her up and continued to run through the stygian streets with their narrow stone buildings.

Finally, he, too, paused. Not letting her down, he listened a moment. "They are behind us, but they are coming. I suggest we find a place to hide, because I, too, am becoming winded."

"*Pardon*," Genevieve said sarcastically, "I did not know the great St. Clair was mortal."

His eyes narrowed for a moment.

"My little cat, were we not in danger for our lives at this moment, I would show you indeed how very mortal I am. But now is not the time." He pushed her behind one of the huge barrels facing the water. "Can you fit?"

"*Oui*," she responded, looking up at him as the sound of footsteps echoed along the dock. "Must you be so close?"

She hissed, as he moved in next to her.

"I must. Unless you wish them to find me, and then you, my pet."

"Do not call me that! I am not your pet. I am—" She took a deep breath as she remembered nearly too late just who she was and who she was supposed to be. The familiarity of this man would yet drive her to murder! Surely, they would not hang someone of her blood if they knew how he had provoked her. Then once again, she realized that no one was to know of her blood and that she would, if she valued her life, have to keep her temper.

Even in the dark shadows created by the barrels, she could see him staring at her, assessing her.

" 'Tis a lovely scent you wear, my lady, but pray"—he wrinkled his nose—"do not use it again."

Her stomach tightened once more in anger as she realized she was referring to the odor of the mud in which she had fallen—no doubt a deposit for slop and other undesirable things.

"Do not worry, Monsieur St. Clair, you can be assured you will seldom see me again after this night—perfumed or not."

The hearing of the footsteps hushed her voice as she closed her eyes and prayed to the Father, Son and Holy Ghost that they would not be seen, that the three young men would quickly lose interest and return home, and that she could soon return to the convent.

But it was not to be. She started to stand as the men passed the first time and Philippe quickly pulled her back down. "Dunce!" he hissed. "Stay seated. They can easily come back."

He proved to be right, for no more than two minutes later, they returned and once again left.

The couple waited in silence. Finally, Genevieve asked, "Do you think it's safe?"

"*Non*, we must wait a good hour yet, until the moon goes down."

"An hour!"

He shrugged. "Go if you wish, Ma'mselle, but do not expect me to rescue you again."

She sighed and stayed where she was. Closing her eyes, she found herself nestling comfortably against the firm, sturdy shoulder at her side.

It was the clock striking the hour of three that woke them both. The moon had disappeared and the wharf was as silent as it had been earlier. Startled to find herself in this cramped position, with a man's arm around her, Genevieve was horrified to recall all that had happened and even more horrified to realize that she might be locked out of the convent. What if the good sisters had discovered her gone? What if she now truly had to marry this oaf?

"Please," she said, nudging him gently, "I must go back."

Without a word he rose and, adjusting her cloak around her tenderly, led her back toward the stairs which earlier she had practically fallen down in such haste to be away from him. If only she had known then.

Mortified at the height before her, she looked at Philippe. "Is there no other way?"

"I can carry you, if you like."

"*Non.*" She shook her head, feeling her hair falling loose at her side, freed now of many of its pins, "I will walk."

Genevieve did not know why it was, but the walk up took double the time it had to go down and, breathless, she reached the top clinging to the rails as the half-hour rang on the clock.

"Truly, I am worried."

He shrugged. "You can always stay with me, Ma'mselle," he teased her.

She drew in a deep breath, taking all of her effort to keep from hitting him.

"Just show me the way to the convent and I shall be fine."

"Will you now?"

She nodded.

"Very well. As you wish." He took her

by the elbow as one of the court gentlemen might have done, and for a moment she thought he knew who she was; then she realized he was merely teasing her.

At the iron gate of the convent, Genevieve's worst fears were confirmed. She was locked out. She looked around the entrance to see if there was another way in.

"There isn't."

"Isn't what?" she snapped.

"Another way in. 'Tis for the safety of the nuns."

Genevieve frowned. "Well, I cannot stay out here all night and I certainly cannot be seen with you."

"Oh?" He smiled. "Well, the offer of my rooms still stands. No one but you and me need know that you spent the night with me."

"Never! I will die first! Besides, someone is bound to see and I would be forced to wed you."

"Ah, yes, that would be a shame, especially since I have no intention of getting married for any foolish government law." He paused. "Just what do you plan to do?"

Genevieve put her hands on the wall. "If you will help me up over—"

"'Twill not work. You are too short—or rather the wall is too high."

"Well, I must get in."

"Come." He took her by the hand as one might an errant child and walked her around to one of the side streets where a candle still burned in a window. "That is your room, yes?"

She stared at the room. "I do not know. They all look alike."

He shrugged. "It is. Trust me."

Before she could say anything more, he had picked up a single stone and correctly aiming it, hit the top of the glass. As the stone bounced off, the window opened.

"What have you done!" Genevieve cried. "Now, I shall surely be ruined."

He did not answer, for at that moment Annette peeked out. "Genny! Genny," she hissed. "Is that you?"

"*Oui.*"

"Go round to the front. I will come let you in."

The window slammed down and Genevieve looked to the man at her side. Her eyes narrowed. "How is it you knew where my rooms where?"

"Because I knew. In fact, had you not run from me, I was coming to tell you that you could go back."

"What?"

He smiled. "My friend and your friend concluded their—er, discussions. When Lancelot saw that you were no longer among those in the schoolroom, he knew you must have gone out and sent me to find you."

"Why did he send you?"

"Probably he imagined that since I controlled your cat, I could control you."

It took all of Genevieve's will to keep from slapping him; instead she turned and hurried toward the gate where Annette now stood. "Good night, Monsieur. Do not bother to see me to the door. I thank you for a most enlightening evening."

He took off his coonskin cap and bowed low. "And I thank you. May I have the pleasure of calling upon you again?"

She couldn't tell if he was making fun of her or not.

"No," she said crisply, hurrying inside, "you may not." Heedless of the noise she might be making, she slammed the iron latch on.

Philippe waited until her footsteps died away in the darkness. Then, smiling to himself, he hurried to the quarters at the inn that he shared with his Indian brother.

14

"What happened to you, my pet?" Annette questioned her softly as the pair hurried back toward their room.

"Do not ask!" Genevieve snapped. "That man is—is—a *man*."

"I should say so." Annette smiled. "So is his friend."

Genevieve jerked her head sharply. "I am sure you explored all the possibilities. Is the Indian going to help you?"

They had neared their room. Even in the light of the dim candle, Genevieve could see her friend flush. "We did not talk of that yet. I mean, I must woo him. Convince him that I am worthy of his investment."

"What makes you think he has money?"

She shrugged. "I know."

"Then perhaps you should marry him." Genevieve pushed the door open angrily.

"*Mon Dieu*! Do you think I wish to be shackled any more than you? *Non*! Annette looked down the hall and lowered her voice slightly. "Come. We cannot talk out here, and it is late."

Genevieve sighed. "You are right. But look at me." She wrinkled her nose as she stared down at her mud-spattered gown. 'Tis no wonder Philippe made fun of me." Tears came to her green eyes momentarily before she brushed them away.

"Oh?" Annette cocked her head sideways and suppressed a smile. "I thought you did not like the man."

"I don't!" Genevieve responded quickly.

"Then what do you care if he thinks ill of you?"

"I don't." Genevieve blinked back her tears. "Only—oh, you would not understand." She sniffled again and looked around for the basin of water. "I just do not know what to do. Are all men so complicated?"

Annette sighed and came over to put her arm around the smaller girl. "Do not worry, my precious. I will help you and you will win his heart, if that is what you wish."

Genevieve shook her head again and said, "Annette, I am so confused. When he kissed me . . ." Her throat closed off. "I do not know. I felt so . . . strange. I know I should not have allowed him such liberties and yet . . ."

Once more Annette smiled and hugged the other girl. "Rest now. You have had a difficult night. I promise things will be better in the morning."

But despite what her friend said, Genevieve found that the morning did not lessen any of her worries. She was relieved that somehow, while she was asleep, Annette had been able to clean her gown and had gathered enough water for her to bathe the worst of the muck off her. However, her absence the night before had been noticed by the nun in charge of the girls and she was forced to explain, leaving Philippe's role out of it, that she had taken a walk, unwittingly become lost, and been attacked by the young men, whom she escaped, she said, by her own wits. And for the most part, that was true.

Given a reprimand by the nun, Genevieve was told that she must not wander off on her own again, for despite the care taken by the Governor, there were elements in the colony that were rather unsavory. After the lecture, Genevieve was dismissed and sent to the chapel to confess, to purify her soul and ready herself to be a good Catholic wife and mother. Genevieve could only hang her head and nod, ignoring Annette's smirk as she hurried toward the confessor's box.

There was to be another "social" that night, when men could return and reacquaint themselves with the women who had interested them the night before, and to give those who had not been able to attend a chance to meet and court.

Much to Genevieve's surprise, Annette seemed as nervous and anxious over how she looked as she was herself.

"Think you that—that *man* and his savage friend will be there?"

"Genny, that man is Philippe and I do not think you will win his heart, if that is what you wish, by calling him other than his true name. His friend is Lancelot, or Four Winds, whichever you wish. But Indian though he may be, he is not a savage." She smiled slightly to herself, recalling the night before.

Genevieve shrugged and tried not to think of Philippe, of his arms around her, of his kiss on her lips. She had already confessed her sin of desire and done Hail Marys for it. She would not repeat her transgression, certainly not unless the man made a formal proposal, she told herself. "Well, I do not plan to take any more walks on my own. If you wish to be with the—with Lancelot, you will have to find a place other than our room."

"Have no fear, dear heart, I will find a place for us to continue our discussion."

Some of the excitement had subsided by the second day, especially since many of the men from the night before had returned to woo the woman of their choice, or perhaps to talk to one of the others. The room was crowded and filled with the smoke of the evil weed tobacco, imported from the English colonies to the south.

Even from her seat near the window, Genevieve could barely breathe as she listened to conversation floating near her.

"Does the hearth draw well?"

"How many acres do you have cleared?"

"How many rooms are there in your house?"

"Do you have wood floors and windows?"

"Do you have proper beds and blankets? Is your bed made of cypress, sassafrass, or cherry?"

"Do you own horses? Pigs, cows, or sheep?"

"Do you drink?"

"How much money have you saved?"

"Are you of clean habit?"

The questions went on and on until Genevieve thought she surely would be

sick. There was much more to marriage
than how much a man possessed. If she
had thought that, she would have stayed
in France; she'd have wed the old marquis.

It surprised her that many of the
plump girls already had picked out their
men, but perhaps that was because the
men thought that wide-hipped women
would produce children more easily, and
the more children one had in the colony,
the more money one received from the
King. Genevieve wondered if she would
survive childbirth; her mother and aunt
had not.

Shivering from the chill of the
evening, but not wanting to venture
farther into the room in case she should
miss Philippe—not that she truly cared if
he came or not, but she owed it to her
friend to alert her if the Indian came,
especially since Annette was busy talking
with one of the soldiers. Why she would
allow another man to court her when she
claimed to be in love with Lancelot
Genevieve would never understand. But
Annette was—well, she had her reasons.
The smoke continued to bother her and
she blinked her eyes and fought off the
tears. The evening was nearly done, and so
far neither of the men had appeared.

It just proved to her that he was a liar.
He did not intend to call again as he said
he would, and she scolded herself for even

hoping such. He was a hunter. He had told her that he had no intention of getting married, so what good was he to her? If she was to remain in the colonies, she would have to wed or make another choice, and none of this would include him.

With a sigh, she looked toward the door once more and then back to the room, only to find herself being stared at by a distinguished gentleman in a fine green velvet coat, one of the few dressed so. Though all the men were in their Sunday best, most of those here wore blue doublets and immaculate frilled shirts, and had their long-tailed coats tied with scarves of red round their waists, characteristic of Quebec men. One or two wore three-cornered hats, as did this officious-looking man, but none had feathers in their hats, as he did, and none strutted so peacockish. Lace frothed at the sleeves of his coat and a sword sheath hung at his side. From the style of his curled powdered wig and the trim of his narrow mustache, from the way the others in the room stared at him, Genevieve knew this man must be of some importance in the colony, but for the life of her she could not recall who he was. All the officials had been presented to them upon landing, but in her worry to avoid the Marquis de Tracey, she had not listened to the names.

The man continued staring at her, and

Genevieve felt her pulses trembling with fear. What did he want of her? Did he see something different in her than in the other women? Was her secret revealed before her new life had even begun? In desperation, she looked around for Annette, but the other girl was now chatting amiably with one of the farmers.

Once again, Genevieve wondered how Annette could "be in love" and act so. If that was what it meant to love, then she did not want it. Yet, Genevieve, who did not know if she even liked Philippe St. Clair, and certainly knew she did not love him, found that she could think of nothing but the way he had kissed her, and she knew that no other man in this room, at least, would be able to excite her senses the way he had. Therefore, she had discouraged almost all of the would-be suitors who had come to sit with her.

Now, seeing the official approach, she wondered if she had been unwise to push all the other men away.

Modestly lowering her eyes, she waited for the man in the close-fitting boots to approach her.

"Mademoiselle." He bowed low. "Welcome to your new land. I trust you will find it invigorating and enchanting, as have most of us."

"*Oui*, Monsieur, I am sure I will." She forced herself to look up into his eyes and realized that even though she was seated and he was standing, they were nearly the same height. Then she realized that he was staring at her in a way that reminded her almost of how Philippe had looked before he had kissed her. *Ma foi!* She prayed this man was not courting her!

"*Pardon.* You must forgive my lapse of memory, but so much has happened. I do not recall your name."

He grinned, causing his mustache to scrunch together. "The name, Mademoiselle, is Talon. Jean Talon. I am the Intendant here and should you need anything"—he took the empty chair beside her and sat down, making himself an inch shorter than she—"you must feel free to call upon me."

"Oh, most assuredly," Genevieve replied. "But I do not lack anything."

There was an awkward pause before he asked, "Tell me your name, little one."

Genevieve winced at that. If anyone was little, 'twas he. But she dared not say anything about that for fear he would be upset, and then only the Lord knew what would happen. "I am Genevieve Claudine Bopar," she said, using Claudine's surname.

"Ah, Genevieve. That is indeed a lovely name for a lovely young woman. Faith, I do believe that you are the most beautiful at this assembly."

"Oh no, Monsieur Talon. You are quite mistaken. There are many girls here far prettier than I. Take Annette, for example." She directed the man's attention toward her friend, who was now laughing with the farmer she had been talking to, and then towards Veronique, one of the other women, who Genevieve knew was more attractive than she.

His hand reached out to boldly touch hers. "Ah, Ma'mselle, 'tis you who are wrong. There is an air of purity about you, of wholesomeness. You come from Normandy?"

She looked at him strangely for a moment, then realized that yes, that was where Claudine came from. And so she nodded.

"My estate is—that is, was—in Normandy. Tell me, which village?"

She could feel the blood draining from her. She never had known the name of her maid's village, and she knew none that would be suitable. Besides, if he said he knew the town, and did not know of her or her family . . . Holy Mother of Mary, she prayed. What was she to do? "The town is small. You would not know the name, but it is not far from Evreux. 'Tis not even big enough to be a village."

He nodded and seemed satisfied with that answer. But he frowned when she took her hand out of his.

"Tell me, it is but early, but I would like to know if any of our young men have caught your eye."

"You mean, to marry?"

He smiled.

"*Non*. There is none I wish to wed yet," she said, quickly folding her hands so that he would not have a moment to capture her attention again, and looked out upon the crowd, wondering if Philippe had yet come. Though she was sure that even if she could not see him, she would probably know of his presence, just because . . .

She barely heard Talon's response. "You will allow me to court you, then, Ma'mselle? You are by far the one with the most dignity, and I am sure you would make a good wife for the colony's civil governor. My own dear wife has recently died and—"

"No, I cannot," she said abruptly, before she had even time to think, to correct herself. "I mean"—she flushed—"I do not know if it would be fair to these other men. You who are so handsome and so courtly. Undoubtedly you would soon sweep me off my feet."

"Ah, that is the point."

"But then, what about these other men who must wed in order to keep their hunting licenses, or their family homes, or—"

The thick brows of the Intendant meshed together. "To whom have you been talking, Mademoiselle?"

Her eyes widened at his angry response. "Many."

"Would there be one Philippe St. Clair among those you spoke with?"

She tried to hide the blush which came to her face, but she knew by the look in Talon's eyes that she was not successful. "Yes, he was one."

"And he has already won your heart?"

Startled by the question, Genevieve could not speak.

"You may forget him, Mademoiselle, for he is known to seduce women of all breeds." Talon sniffled as he took some snuff in his nostril and snapped the silver container closed. "He will lie with anyone without discrimination. And from what he has told me, he will never marry. So if you have set your cap on him—" The Intendant shrugged. "You had best look elsewhere."

"You misunderstand, sir. I do not have my heart set on Monsieur St. Clair. I only met him but once and I did not like him in the slightest." Even as she spoke it, she felt the jerking of her heart and she knew she was lying, but she continued anyway. "He is arrogant and thinks he is—well, I do not care if I never see him again."

"That is true. St. Clair is a pompous young fool."

A smile came to the Intendant's face. "Then may I court you?"

She shook her head slowly and looked to one of the farmers who had earlier come to talk to her, and whom she had rapidly discouraged. "*Non*, I do not think it would be fair. I cannot decide when there are still so many men to meet."

"Fair or not, Ma'mselle Genevieve, I shall come back to see you on the morrow and again on the morrow, and I trust that you will soon come to your senses, for in two weeks' time the women who have not chosen from here will be sent to Three Rivers to meet the men there. I would not like having to travel all that distance to fetch you. And I do not think you will find their rough country manners to your liking. You are much too delicate for one of them."

"But, sir," she protested, worried that her secret was revealed, "I am a country girl."

"Mayhap—but you do not seem one."

Much to the disappointment of the girls, neither Philippe nor Lancelot came to the schoolroom that night, or the next, or the next.

Days were spent in spinning—something which both Annette and Genevieve had great difficulty mastering, in prayer, and in reading, so that their education would, the nuns hoped, encourage them to raise devout Catholic children, even though they might not have any influence in the matter on their new husbands.

By the last week in Quebec, thirty of the hundred girls had already found men to wed.

Once a pair decided to wed, the man had to deal with the "directress" and make known his possessions and means of livelihood. The girl still had the chance to decline any suitor once she learned these facts, but so far only one of them had. Then the documents were drawn up by the notary and the priest. After the marriage contract was signed, the woman was given to be married in a white gown with ribbons and lace, and usually a fine blue sash. Genevieve thought it would have been nice if they could keep the dresses, but alas, they could not, for the gowns were to be worn over and over by other girls until the material fell apart. Besides, as one nun commented, it was doubtful that in the wilderness where most of them were going, there would be any use of these dresses.

As she listened to the service, Genevieve shuddered, for the name and whole ancestry of each girl marrying was read aloud. If anyone but suspected who she was . . . Once more the visions of the poor girl being stripped and flogged came to her. It was for this other reason, she told herself, that she had avoided any of the men here.

Talon, coming to officiate at one of the weddings, reminded Genevieve that she could keep that dress and much more if she decided to stay in Quebec, if she decided to wed him, but again to his apparent astonishment, she pulled back.

In truth, Genevieve thought as she watched the transactions after each wedding, she and the other King's Daughters were very much on sale. Upon each wedding, the couple was given an ox, two pigs, a cow, a pair of chickens, two barrels of salted meat, and eleven crowns of money. 'Twas no wonder so many of the men were eager, despite the humors of the women, to wed and to bed. Each child would give them a pension of 30 livres. If they had up to twelve children, they received 400 livres a year. Genevieve knew enough, having lived in the poverty of her father's gaming, to know what that money could mean.

And yet she refused all those who wished to court her. To Talon's question again, she again responded, "But, sire, 'twould not be fair to the men in Three Rivers and in Ville-Marie, should I wed before choosing among them as well."

"Go then," Talon sniffed, inhaling more of his tobacco, "and you will see what it is like out there. Then you will come running back. But when the next ship comes in, I will, no doubt, find some precious love more dear than you." Thus saying, he stormed out of the convent and out of the Mother Superior's office where the final meeting had been held.

There were but a few days left to their stay in Quebec and there was to be one more "social." "Do you think they have forgotten us?" Genevieve asked, trying not to show her concern as the girls lay abed.

Annette sighed. "I doubt it. At least, Lancelot will not forget me." She turned over toward the other girl, as her voice softened. "Mayhap they have." But she quickly added, "If they do return for us, and wed us, I will believe in miracles."

"But I thought you did not want to wed."

Annette shrugged. "Mayhap I do. But 'tis only a foolish thought that it would be the Indian." She paused. "And you. Would you wed St. Clair if he asked?"

Afraid of what her heart was saying, Genevieve shook her head. "*Non*, I cannot until I know that he would marry me out of love and not because he would keep his hunter's license."

"Sometimes I think you a fool, my pet."

15

Standing on the very wharf where she and Philippe had hidden from the men only weeks before, Genevieve looked back towards Quebec's Upper Town as the girls who had not chosen husbands there now boarded small crafts that reminded her of tree trunks and were, in fact, made of the bark of trees. Because the canoes were so small—at least compared to the ship they had crossed in—ten of them were needed to carry all the girls and a few men for protection should the Indians attack. Oddly enough, it reminded Genevieve of one of Louis' processions as he made his yearly move from Paris to Versailles and back again. Only they were not royalty and were treated far differently.

As they moved on to their next

destination, and the next market, each girl
had with her the single trunk she had
brought from France. Three Rivers, halfway between Quebec and Ville-Marie, was
farther into the forbidding wilderness. For
a moment, Genevieve considered
declaring herself to have a vocation and
staying with the nuns. Neither Philippe
nor Lancelot had returned to Quebec to
see them, but of course she did not care,
she told herself. He was a liar and an
arrogant fool, just like all the men she had
met.

As she considered what it would mean
to stay, she looked again to see Talon
perched eagle-like on the cliff-top path,
watching as the women loaded on. His
hands were on his hips and he seemed to
be smiling. Did he think that she would
stay for him? Or return because of him?

"In the winter, they say this whole
river is frozen and you can skate on it.
Imagine!" Annette declared, putting up a
cheerful front, which Genevieve was sure
she did not feel.

"I do not skate," she responded dully,
as she allowed the nun who would be
accompanying them as far as Three Rivers
to help her into the boat. She stepped
carefully so as not to tip the delicate craft
and looked toward Annette, who was
already seated.

"Then you shall have to learn. I am

sure there are many things we will be learning anew, my pet."

"Yes." Genevieve sighed as she clutched her cat, trying to calm Alexandre and herself, and gave one more look back as the boat pushed off into the water. "I imagine you are correct."

Once they had passed Cape Diamond, it was possible to see the large stone manors belonging to the landowners, which faced the river. She wondered if Philippe's father lived in one of these or still farther up the river. She wondered, as she stared morosely into the greenish water, if she would ever see Philippe again.

As they floated along, birch sails went up over the canoes to aid them with the wind. Even then, she was told, their journey would take them a good two weeks—perhaps longer—depending on the conditions of the river and the weather. Raising the plain parasol she had been given to keep the sun from scorching her face, Genevieve tried to imagine herself as Cleopatra on the Nile. But if she were a queen, she knew what she would command, and since she could not, what use was there pretending she was queen?

By nightfall, they had stopped. Genevieve's legs were so cramped she could hardly walk, and she and Annette took turns massaging each other so that the circulation would return. "Truly, is it all worth it?'' she asked her friend as she watched Alexandre amuse himself with some disgusting dead creature.

Annette shrugged. "For me, it is. For you—I have told you what I think. But since you are here, I would say yes. You did not want to marry that toad Talon, did you?''

"*Non.*" Genevieve shook her head.

"Well, then, perhaps in Three Rivers you will find someone to your liking."

Genevieve looked up at the full moon and the star-studded sky. "Perhaps."

Now the manor-houses they passed were more like little villages, complete with barricades surrounding them, mills propelled by the wind, and smaller houses belonging to the *habitants* who farmed the land outside the fenced walls. She longed to know how much they really worried about attacks here, but she dared not ask.

She tried to concentrate on the greenery reminiscent of France, of her father's estate of Joigny, but even the trees were different here, taller and more brooding, and the birds were ones she had never seen, not heard, before. Was anything the same here as in France? Certainly the colony had to have more similarities to her homeland than the men, grasping and lying as they did. But so far, she had found none.

The deeper they went inland, the fewer estates they saw and the more the green umbrella of leaves shaded them, so that Genevieve's parasol was not quite as necessary. By week's end, however, she was finding her fair skin becoming first ruddy and aching, then brownish. At first it disgusted and irritated her. Then she realized that perhaps it was just as well, for certainly no one who had known her before would recognize her now. She looked to Annette, whose skin had long since been pigmented by the sun, and realized that despite their differences, they could almost pass for sisters.

Time passed far more slowly here than it had on board the ship crossing the Atlantic. There, at least, they had been able to walk about, to stretch their legs. Here, they were forced to sit and sit and sit. If they dared move too much to one side, they risked upsetting the canoe. The worst was keeping the cat quiet as well. More than once the boatman had glared at her and ordered her to hang onto that "damned animal" before he was thrown overboard. Hugging Alex to her, Genevieve was forced to devise ways to quietly amuse him.

If the women had to relieve themselves, they had to wait until designated stop times, since for safety all the canoes had to stay together. And it was impossible not to notice that the man riding in the back had his pistol ready on his lap, should it be needed.

With relief Genevieve and the other women saw the grey stone houses of the coming settlement. Here they would spend the next few weeks, once again meeting the local men, once again choosing and being chosen, and once again having to decide if they would stay or move on to the final settlement of Ville-Marie.

There was no convent here yet, but several of the nuns from Quebec and some of the sisters of the Congregation in Ville-Marie had come together in a small school-house to teach the local children and those of the friendly Indian tribes who wished to learn the ways of Christ. It was here, in this small, two-room building, which would serve both as a meeting place and dormitory for the King's Daughters, that everything was to take place for the next three weeks.

Even though the men of Three Rivers did not dress as fashionably as those in Quebec, they were as opulent in their velvets, satins, and furs as the other men had been. It surprised Genevieve only slightly that the men of the city, for that was what Three Rivers thought of itself, wore different sashes to distinguish them-selves from residents of other cities. The white-on-red, long-tailed coat meant one was of this land, and she was told that if she went as far as Ville-Marie, she would see that there the men wore blue on their coats.

Genevieve listened patiently and tried not to show her boredom as the men courted her and wooed her.

She learned that there were endless rivalries between Three Rivers and Quebec, mainly because the shipment of girls always landed there first and Three Rivers was given but second-best. She pointed out that those on the Isle of Montreal had the worst of the lot, but the men seemed not to care about problems not their own. In fact, one said, it served them right for choosing to live so very far out in the wilderness. At least in Three Rivers they were small, but they were civilized.

Genevieve smiled and listened and yawned.

And one by one their numbers dwindled, as girl after girl decided that she would make her home in this area.

"Soon," Genevieve told Annette the first evening of the last week, "there will be only us two."

"Would that be so bad? *Helas*, if we can work as domestics and but get enough money together . . ."

Genevieve glared. "I will not join you

in your *home*. 'Tis against all natural devices for a man and woman to be joined without the blessing of Christ."

"You are sounding like the good sisters, Genny. I would bet 30 pistoles that if Philippe would woo you in the right way, you would go to him—marital blessing or not."

Flushing, Genevieve shook her head. "No, I could not. You don't understand, Annette. I—my uncle—" Her throat tightened, and before she could finish speaking the sound of a disturbance from the outside reached the ears of the women. The Directress was arguing with someone on the steps, someone who wanted entrance into the meeting room, and as Genevieve stood, she felt her heart pounding. The voice that echoed through the room was the same one that had echoed in her dreams these weeks past. She rose, and in a dream walked towards the door, despite the curious looks of the others. Annette quickly followed.

"Madam Directress," Philippe was saying, obviously trying to keep his temper, "I tell you I wish to enter."

"But you have not told me what possessions you have, young man, which would qualify you to marry one of these good Christian girls. You have not made me see that you would indeed be a good Christian husband. And furthermore, you are not dressed in a manner befitting—"

"I have already met the qualifications in Quebec."

"Yes?"

"Yes!" Philippe snapped. "You may ask Monsieur Talon."

"Madame Directress, please." Genevieve's voice came from a spirit inside her, urging her. "I do wish, as does my friend, to see these two men. They have assured us of their honorable intentions."

She saw the slight smile on Philippe's face, which quickly faded as the Directress looked toward him again.

"And we have been assured of the piety of these men."

The Directress raised her brow; her disbelief was evident beneath the arched cap of her order.

"Indeed, his brother is a Jesuit."

The nun looked for confirmation to Philippe, who only shrugged. "It is true, Madame."

"The law of marriage does not apply to the Indian subjects of the King. So if Monsieur St. Clair wishes to enter without his companion . . ."

Genevieve felt her heart pounding rapidly as she glanced toward Annette and knew her friend would die if Lancelot could not be with her, as well.

"But, truly, Directress, if he is a

Christian and a member in good faith of the community, then should he not be producing good French citizens as well?"

The nun frowned. "I will have to ask about the matter."

"But if you are not sure," Annette put in, "perhaps I could walk along the river with this good man."

Lancelot smiled.

"Unheard of!" The nun was astounded.

"Oh, but she will be chaperoned," Genevieve quickly put in for her friend's sake. "I will be happy to walk with them."

"And Monsieur St. Clair?"

Philippe shrugged. "I will go inside and acquaint myself with the lovely young women there."

Genevieve darted him a look, but dared not let her surprise show as he smiled at her.

"Very well, then." The nun nodded. "But only a short time."

Quickly, before the nun could change her mind, Annette ran back to fetch shawls for both of them and hurried out front.

"Bless you, Mother."

"And you, my child," the nun responded, watching as Lancelot and Annette began to stroll down towards the river, walking at arm's length, with Genevieve a few steps behind them.

"St. Clair?" The Directress opened the door and shooed away all those others gaping at the single window, as Philippe nodded and, with one long look in Genevieve's direction, entered the meeting room.

16

Genevieve trailed behind the couple, feeling strangely jealous and upset as she watched them. Once out of sight of the schoolhouse, Annette and Lancelot could barely keep their hands off each other. Perhaps it as just as well Philippe had not insisted on walking with them. She did not think she could stand him touching her in the intimate fashion the Indian used with her friend. But surely, the Directress couldn't have frightened him off? She rationalized that Philippe hadn't come walking because he hadn't wanted to. The men had stopped in Three Rivers obviously only because Lancelot wanted to be with Annette.

Well, it was all right, she told herself. Philippe St. Clair was not for her, anyway.

She had already decided to find and wed someone of substance here in the colony, someone—other than Talon—who would not only love her and be gentle with her, but who could protect her should Racine ever find her. Not that she could imagine the doting old man surviving the ocean voyage, but one never knew.

She tried not to look at the Indian and her friend, but it was impossible not to see the joy they felt in each other. Such affection would seem impossible since they barely knew each other, and yet Genevieve wished the same would happen to her, wished that some man would . . . Tears came to her eyes.

"Would you care for a linen, Ma'mselle? 'Tis not fitting to see tears on such a pretty face."

Her heart hammered as she looked up to see the tall hunter walking beside her. "Philippe! But I thought you had gone inside."

He grinned. "When one goes inside, surely there are also ways of getting out again?"

"But how? I mean, the directress—"

He merely smiled. "You forget, Mademoiselle, that I have lived many years with the Indians."

"Oh." She could only stare at him, studying his dark, lined face, the shock of reddish gold curls so like her own, and looking into his blue eyes.

"Would you care to walk along the waterfront?"

She turned to see that Annette and Lancelot had disappeared from sight. She started toward where she thought they would be, but Philippe's muscular arm blocked her path. "I do not think 'twould be wise to come upon them now."

"But . . ." She paused, then flushed, realizing what he was referring to. She heard the sounds of laughter. And then she drew back, recalling that she was supposed to be angry with him. After all, he had promised to call—and he had not. He had not even cared to send a message that he was leaving town or to let her know that he cared about her in any way. And yet, the way he was looking at her now, Genevieve hoped that perhaps he might, a little.

He offered her his arm in a gentlemanly fashion, but she shook her head.

"Ma'mselle Genevieve is upset that I did not call as I promised."

She darted a quick look at him and shrugged.

"I know I would be most perturbed if a promise made me was not kept."

" 'Twas no promise." Her voice was high and nervous. "You merely made a passing comment. It was not something to which you could be held."

"No," he said, his steps now in line with hers, "but you did hold me to it."

"No, I assure you I did not."

His hand touched her shoulder, stopping her in the shade of a large tree. She stiffened slightly as she turned toward him. "Monsieur St. Clair . . ."

"It was Philippe a moment ago."

"That is because I forgot."

"Forgot what? That you were angry with me?"

"I was not angry."

He laughed. "Genevieve, my little cat lady, do not lie to me. I can see it in your eyes. I can see, too, that you missed me."

"*Non*, you are wrong. I never once thought of you."

He leaned over, his lips brushing hers gently, like drops of dew on the morning petals; and like the flower opening up, its petals touched by the sun, her mouth opened as his tongue nudged its way in and he kissed her, exploring her as he held her to him.

It took but a moment for her body to respond to the heightened sensation, for her to recall the ecstasy of his former kiss. She thought the low moan was coming from Annette down by the river, and it surprised her to find out it was not. Her arms went around his neck, and his hands carefully, gently, inched their way from her upper back, caressing her and stroking her, until he casually brushed against her erect nipples.

The touch of his hand in so sensitive an area jolted her. She pulled away from him, flushing. "I am sorry."

"You are sorry? For what, *mignonne*?" He took her hand in his. " 'Tis I who must apologize. I admit my desire for you carried me away."

"Oh." She stiffened, not wanting to look in his eyes. All he had for her was desire. He admitted it. He did not love her; he did not feel about her as she seemed to feel about him. Her breasts tingled and her skin burned where he had made contact.

"I should not have touched you so, but truly you are so beautiful."

She shrugged. "Perhaps we should walk on and find Annette. After all, the Directress expects us back soon."

His hand took hers, and he kissed each of her fingers slowly and sensually, looking into her mesmerized eyes as he did so. "You are right to have been upset with me for not coming, but truly, 'twas not of my doing. My father has been ill, and he called me to him."

"Oh." She was unable to pull her hand from him, unable to think. His touch created strange sensations in her body, feelings that she had only remotely dreamed of and yet, she tried to tell herself it was wrong. This man was not the marrying type. He would not make her his wife. He would use her, as most men wished to, and he would once more disappear.

Finding her voice with difficulty, she asked, "But I thought your father lived near Quebec?"

"No, my sweet." Philippe shook his head. "The St. Clair estate is near Hochelaga." He paused. "Rather, that is the Indian name of what the French now call Ville-Marie de Montreal."

"But you came to the gathering in Quebec. And why do you say *the French*? You are French, are you not?"

He shrugged. His hand stroked her cheek, pushing away hairs that had fallen forward. "I came because I had to. The Intendant insisted."

"*Oui*. I know of your law here. Monsieur Talon has said that he himself is not exempt from it."

"No?" Philippe's eyes widened.

"And he asked me to be his bride."

"No!" The thunder of his response startled her. "That cannot be. You will be ruined. You will be—"

"But I refused him," she cut in. "I did not want such a man."

Philippe calmed immediately. "You made a wise choice, my little cat lady. Talon would not have made you happy."

She forced herself to shrug. "I do not know that. I only know that I would chose another." She stared at him, wanting to know if he would make her happy, or if he even cared to try. But she had her answer; he had told her. He had been looking at the women because he had to—and Genevieve was not going to marry anyone, no matter how much she might feel for him, if he did not love her as she did him. And yet, even as she studied him, she knew from the way her heart pounded that, if he asked, she would have him and would pray to the Lord that she could win his heart.

"I hope you find what you seek, *mignonne*," he said, leaning forward and kissing her, but this time chastely on the cheek. "I must depart now, for there is much to do preparing for the autumn fair, and I have much to sell."

She could still feel the burning of her body from a moment ago. Perhaps he didn't know how he had affected her, and if that was the case, she would not tell him. "Will I see you again?"

He gave her a sad smile. "Perhaps in Ville-Marie. I do not know."

She forced herself to nod. "If God wills it."

His shrug told her all. "*Oui*, if God wills it." He turned then and hurried down the path, leaving her to wonder if Philippe also willed it, leaving her to wonder what had happened to the beautiful moment she had just experienced.

She was still staring at his disappearing figure when a disheveled Annette hurried up the road. "Come. We must return before the Directress seeks us out."

Genevieve sighed and nodded as she helped Annette straighten her gown.

"Did you ask her?" The Indian asked his companion, as they shared drinks in the tavern.

"No."

"*Sang Dieu!* Why not? You told me yourself you thought you were in love with her."

Philippe gave one of his Gallic shrugs. "I am. But marriage? It is not possible. I am away so much. And what will she do, then? Roam the estate alone with Papa, Emile, Claude, Bernard, and the others to keep her company? 'Twould not be right. I cannot do this to her. It is best if I forget her."

"Her friend, Annette, would be with her, too. That is, if I—" The Indian stopped suddenly realizing what he was saying.

"*Merveilleux!* It is true?" Philippe paused. "Have you also lost your heart?"

Imitating his friend, Lancelot shrugged. "But as you say, marriage is out of the question."

"For me, yes. I travel from village to town, trapping and hunting. For you—she can live with your people, with Dream Child and Dancer. They can teach her the Indian ways."

Lancelot shook his head.

"And why not? She would make a good squaw?"

"*Oui*, she would. But I do not marry unless you do."

"Ah! Foolish!" Philippe spat. He looked around the small room, almost wishing for some snuff, for anything to take his mind off the conversation. But there was nothing.

"*Non*, I am your brother in blood, Philippe. I go with you. I trap with you. I will not marry unless you do."

"And what of Annette?"

Lancelot grinned. "She is, as you say, a lusty wench. Well worth being an Indian squaw. But she has a notion of setting up a house of a strange sort. I understand it not."

Philippe shrugged and swallowed his brandy, motioning for the innkeeper to bring him another.

"The Indian, too?"

Philippe glanced at Lancelot and then again at the innkeeper. He nodded and saw the man wink. Philippe felt a sickness rising within him. He prayed that the man would not cheat, for he could not be responsible for his temper if that happened. It was true that many of the French traders got the Indians drunk, then substituted inferior, watered-down liquor for the imported kind and laughed as the Indians, their systems unable to handle the spirits, made fools of themselves, selling bundles of hard-won furs for less than a trader would normally have paid for a single pelt.

Philippe was not of that ilk. He had always paid his Indian brothers their fair share of the gold. This was why, in fact, many of the chiefs sought Philippe out, sometimes at great trouble to their tribesman, hunting him down to sell him their furs rather than dealing with those who treated them less than fairly. Philippe knew that this caused him to have many enemies among the *coureurs de bois*; many would easily slit his throat at night, or see other harm done to him. But he had always remained on his guard, and continued to do so even now.

"I say if we love them, we should wed them. Then your papa would be happy, you would have the estate, the government would be happy, and we would be satisfied."

"Ah, but you forget about the girls. They would be very unhappy living alone on the estate."

Lancelot shrugged as the innkeeper

came over with the drinks. "Then we take them on our travels. Have you never longed for the warmth of a woman when you are out there?"

"*Sang Dieu!* That is out of the question!" Philippe nearly exploded as he crashed the two drinks from the table onto the sawdust-strewn floor. He stood, towering over the owner. "You will bring us two more drinks, Monsieur, and you will make them of equal value." He eyed the man silently; the little man scurried back to the counter for the refills.

Philippe then turned to Lancelot. "I will not do something only to please the governor. I am a man on my own and need no one to tell me who I can hunt with and who I can sell to." Even as the owner prepared the drinks, Philippe stood and, removing the bottle of inferior brandy from the shelf, smashed it on the floor, signifying to him all that the government did to him and to the Indians. As the owner gasped, Philippe took out several coins from his purse and threw them onto the liquor-soaked floor. Then, taking his great coat, he walked quickly from the tavern.

"But Philippe," Lancelot protested, following. "I do not understand why you cannot marry her. If you love her, she will be happy to stay wherever you decide."

Philippe glared at his companion.

"Enough! We have much to prepare for the autumn fair. Do you come or do you linger over the women?"

Lancelot stared a moment, looked at the schoolhouse, then at the canoe. "You are being a fool. As am I."

"Perhaps." Philippe picked up a paddle. "Now, come."

17

"Think you we shall see them again?" Genevieve asked as the girls sat in the back of the canoe, watching the vast wilderness pass by them, stretching out towards infinity as the canoes, far fewer than they had started out with from Quebec, journeyed towards the Isle of Montreal and the settlements near Ville-Marie. She looked back towards the banks of the river, towards the flat plains of Three Rivers' lower town, which they had just left, trying to see within the deep recesses of the forest where perhaps, veiled by the foliage, Philippe and Lancelot might have made camp.

Annette shrugged. "I know not Philippe's mind, but if Lancelot has a say, then I do believe our paths will cross not once but many times more."

She smiled slightly, giving Genevieve a moment's passing jealousy.

"Well, I do not care."

"Then why ask? And why did you not chose someone at Three Rivers?"

Genevieve shrugged. "There was no one there who suited me."

"You mean no one who could match your feelings for Philippe."

"That is not what I said." Genevieve practically overturned the canoe with the vehemence of her words and received a stern look from the boatmaster. For comfort, she picked up Alexandre, who had settled in the bottom of the craft.

Both girls were silent for a moment as the water rushed past the fragile sides of their boat.

"Perhaps if you admitted that you loved him, 'twould be easier."

"But I do not," Genevieve affirmed. "He is not."

"He is not what?" Annette smiled, gently touching the other girl. "Faith, I do believe that if you were to woo him as I have Lancelot, you would have no doubt of seeing him again, and again, until you could be sure that he would wed you for love."

Genevieve flushed. "I cannot."

"Why? 'Tis not a sin if you truly love. And besides, he will wed you."

"How can you be sure?"

Annette shrugged. " 'Tis just a feeling I have. You need not fear he would not be gentle, sweetings. I do think that your marquis would have been concerned for only his own pleasures, but if Philippe is anything like his friend . . ."

Blushing even brighter than before Genevieve once more shook her head. "*Non*, I cannot. Do not talk of such to me!" She put her hands over her ears.

When she saw that Annette remained silent, she lowered her hands. " 'Tis not just being used or the pain I fear."

"What then?"

Genevieve looked now to the land, the untamed cliffs soaring above them like castle walls, forlorn and savage in their ruin, and the noonday sun piercing its sword-like rays through the umbrella of verdure under which they now passed. " 'Tis after. The birth of a child is fatal to many women. To my mother and her sister, both."

"*Hélas*! If that is but all, my pet . . ." Annette shook her head. "There are ways to prevent the settling of the seed."

Genevieve looked at her friend strangely. "No. Do not tell me. I do not wish to know." She sat back against the pillows, indicating that conversation was at an end. On her lap, Alexandre looked up at her, his eyes narrowing as if he did not believe that she wished to end the talk this way. Frowning, Genevieve stroked the cat, trying to ignore his knowing look, trying to ignore her own curiosity.

She looked again toward the shore, and the primitive world beyond, its fallen trunks swarming with creatures and the entrances to the pulpy swamps visible briefly through the foliage. Each dip of the paddles into the water made a music of its own, combining with the song of the land—the chirping of the few birds and the low hum of the insects.

The tall-standing pines cast their huge shadows on the illuminated water, and Genevieve stared at the sun dancing on the small crests. Once more she stared into the depths of the forest wishing that Philippe were with her, wishing that he had, despite her protest, continued to kiss her and love her the way her heart called out to be loved.

Few of the other women talked as the canoes moved ever forward. It would take a good ten days for them to reach their next destination, and all of their strength was required for the consuming effort of just sitting upright in the craft. On the third day out, they had been warned about talking overmuch. It was feared that if the Indians knew of their traveling through the land, with so few men to guard them, with their number down to twenty, they would be easy prey for the savages. This was the land of the disputes between the Huron and Iroquois, and waring parties were no doubt roaming the trails even now. Genevieve vowed she would not ask Annette anything further about the men, about her relationship with Lancelot, for she knew it would only create a hole in her heart. Besides, it was easy for their voices to carry and many of their words, if not whole conversations, could be picked up on the wind and carried back to the others, or even to the shore.

Several times the river opened into little bays where houses, surrounded by barricades, could be seen before the river narrowed again with the overhanging trees shading it.

A serpent slid into the water not far from their boat. Genevieve clung to Alexandre, worried that he would see the menace and try to attack, worried that he would fall overboard and that the Directress, who traveled with them, would allow him to drown.

By evening of the eighth day, they could see open woodland and sparkling lakes in the distance. It was a relief to know that a settlement would soon be in sight.

The St. Clair household was up in arms. Never had it been so divided as it was now. Some agreed with Philippe; some agreed with the Seigneur. And while the individual arguments continued in the mills, in the fields, and on the fishing banks, Philippe's own argument with his father also went on.

" 'Tis no concern of mine if the estate has been threatened. Talon is a pig. *Non*, he is worse than that."

"Whatever the case may be, I, too, would like to see you wed."

"But only to a good French girl, no doubt. Were I to tell you that my chosen wife was from my tribe—"

"You are as much French as you are Indian, my son. Stop this foolish behavior and do as they ask. Do as I ask. 'Tis not much to beg from a son who will have control of this whole land."

"And I tell you I do not want control of your lands. I did not want them when you banished my mother, and I do not want them now. Nor do I care about your title, or the title of my grandfather."

St. Clair shook his grey head and sighed. "Philippe, I did not banish her. She went of her own accord."

"So say you, but I know differently. I know how she cried at night in our lodge and how she begged for the Great Spirit to make you want her again."

Once more the old man sighed. " 'Twas not of my doing, Philippe."

"*Non*, you let the government rule you then as you let them rule you now."

"As to my title, Philippe, like it or not, it will pass to you. I am a good French citizen. My kind wishes to see that our lands are populated and protected."

"Protected from the people you are trying to steal them from, you mean. Protected from the natural desire that anyone would have seeing their animals slaughtered, their lands taken from them, and their children stolen away and raised in a way that is foreign to them, to seek revenge."

"We do not steal the children. They are brought to the convents by those parents who have seen the ways of the good Christian and who wish their infants to know the blessings they have."

Philippe's look told what he thought of that.

"My son, would it be so terrible if you took one of the women to wife? She would be safe and happy here while you went off on your hunts. You would have a guaranteed warm bed to return to when you desired, and I would see that she is happy and well provided for."

"And how would you see her happy? Would you find her someone to warm her bed when I am not here?"

"Philippe!" The old man rose from his bed in a coughing fit of anger.

Irritated, his son hurried over to him and handed him the medication which the Governor's own physician had ordered on St. Clair's last visit to Quebec.

" 'Tis not long that I have for this world. I would like to know, Philippe, that I have a grandchild to carry on my name. We are an old and honorable family with estates and lands in many places."

Philippe snorted. "You need not tell me of grandfather and his wealth, or of what it would mean to him to know the line was carried on. You have lectured me on that since the day I returned home."

"*Oui*, that I have. It is because it is something so dear to my heart. Could you not have pity on an old man and wed, if only for that reason? Think you of all the power your child would have? Of all he would be able to do? If you wish to help free the Indians of their worries, you can do so. So can your child. You could but say the word and buy what lands you wished." St. Clair studied his son and saw the softening of his jawline.

"I should not have to buy lands for my people when these lands already belong to them. I should not have to bow to a foreign king, when I do not accept him."

"Philippe, I promise you, the girl you choose will be made happy here, and you may have as many Indian wives as you wish."

"I need but one wife and one wife only, Father. I'll not do as you."

"My son, I loved your mother. Truly. I did."

Philippe shrugged and stood. Walking to the window, his eyes fixed on the distant flag and fortifications surrounding Ville-Marie and the home of Marquerite Bourgeoys, who led the Sisters of the Congregation, where those of the King's Daughters who had not yet chosen husbands would be housed. Had Genevieve come with them or had she remained behind in Three Rivers? He would not blame her if she had, for he had given her no promises this time that he would return for her. Yet he had been unable to rid himself of the taste of her soft pliant lips or to forget the feel of her warm, supple body as it had pressed against him. There was passion in her kiss, and if she herself would not acknowledge it because of her modest upbringing, Philippe knew that he could bring her to that passion and that the desire he was sure she had for him could be sparked and fully flamed. But was it fair to ask her to wed him when he knew what life awaited her? And yet, were she to wed any one of the men, her life would be difficult at best. She had chosen that life when she came here from France; she knew that the wilderness would not be easy. So why not with him? Even as he thought of her, his hands could feel her touch and he could smell the delicate rose scent in her hair. She was a flower waiting for a touch to blossom into a woman. He would be the one to help her.

His father had not spoken and now Philippe turned to the older man. "Very well. There is a young woman I have met. However, I do not know if she will have me."

"She would be a fool not to."

"That is what I think, but I do not know her mind, and I must be honest and tell her that she will not share my company for long."

"Philippe, do not spoil so soon what joy you might have. Honesty is good, but in good measure."

Philippe glared at his father. "I will tell Genevieve what I must tell her. I will also let her know that I intend to have many Indian women as well, for I do not like a relationship founded on dishonesty."

The old man sighed. "There is a difference between dishonesty and omission."

"So say the French," Philippe snorted. "If you wish me to wed, you will have to put up with my foibles, Father. And if I wish my wife to be housed here, then I suppose I must put up with yours."

He walked back to the window. "Lancelot!" He shouted out.

The Indian appeared from beneath the shade of a tree.

"Prepare our packs. We go the autumn fair and then we go to visit the King's Daughters."

18

The town of Ville-Marie on the Isle of
Montreal was in many ways prettier than
Quebec City, and certainly it was larger
than Three Rivers. Built on the same plan
as the other settlements, of an upper and a
lower town, this city differed in that it had
been planned and laid out so that the
streets were not narrow, irregular lanes,
but airy and well situated, all meeting at
the Place d'Armes in the center of the
town. And while the ground was not quite
as flat as at Three Rivers, the slope up
towards Mount Royal in the center of the
island was gentle, not harsh like Quebec's
mountainous paths. From the little the
King's Daughters had seen, most of the
island appeared to be populated by estates
of various sizes. Genevieve could not help

wondering which one belonged to the St. Clair family.

Genevieve quickly noted other differences. For one, Ville-Marie was warmer than Quebec had been and had a greater variety of foliage; for another, the settlement, though smaller than the governing city, had a greater number of people coming in and out of the sheltered harbor, mainly because the island was the last real settlement where those wishing to trade furs for Quebec and the European ports could do so.

It was hard not to notice the activity in the bustling streets as the girls rode toward the home of Marguerite Bourgeoys, and Genevieve wondered if Philippe was part of the crowd of men shouting and trading in the square. But straining her eyes as best she could, she caught no sight of him.

Since that day of her conversation with Annette she had thought of trying to seduce him, as her friend suggested, but what would happen to her if he really did not intend to wed her? How would she face herself? Certainly no man would have her after that. And could she even allow herself to marry God as a sister of the order if she was soiled so? She decided to pray on it and see what came of her request for help. If she saw Philippe again, if God did indeed will it, then she would take that as a sign He approved. For she could think of no other reason that she would see him again.

It did not take Genevieve and Annette long to realize that Marquerite Bourgeoys, gentle and kind as she was, had taken the vows of the Congregation of Notre Dame and followed the rules of the Sulpicians, an order far stricter and less tolerant than even the Jesuits.

Perhaps it was an effort to escape, or perhaps they really did find men with whom they felt compatible—whatever the reason, by the end of the first week there, five of the young women had found husbands. As Annette and Genevieve shared their plain meals and muted conversation with the other thirteen, both knew that this was not the life for them. At least in the Ursaline convent, some music and some dancing had been allowed for the meetings with the men, but here they were not even given new material for gowns.

"So what shall we do?" Genevieve asked. "Philippe and Lancelot have forgotten us. That much is obvious. And certainly, I shall not join this order."

Annette laughed. "I would hope not. But *ma petite*, there is but one week gone and two weeks to go here. They will come for us. I feel it."

Genevieve sighed. "I wish I felt as certain." She stroked the cat cuddled on her lap and looked up towards the statue of Christ hanging on the wall above their door.

Annette shrugged and walked toward the window. "I am bored with this whole thing. Perhaps we should go out."

As if agreeing with her, Alexandre jumped from Genevieve's arms to the ledge. Genevieve's eyes widened as she stared at the cat and at the nail in the window which he now played with, working it loose.

"Dare we?"

"Why not? 'Tis not our fault that they are busy with their fur trading. Besides, it is a fair, is it not? Therefore there should be some fun."

"But the good sisters said it was dangerous to go out. All the women of the town have been told to stay indoors. Did you not hear the loud noises last night when the savages became drunk on the whiskey?"

Annette nodded. "But if we are careful, everything should be all right. After all, what can they do to us in daylight? Surely, you don't intend to sit and sew all day or read prayers like the others."

Genevieve looked at the material which the sister had given her to make into an altar cloth.

Before she could reply, Alexandre answered for his mistress. He had loosened the nail so that now his trim black body could easily pass through the gap.

"Alex!" She called his name, trying to stop him. With but a backward glance, the cat yawned and jumped from the ledge into the busy street.

"Shall we join him?" Annette asked, pushing the window further open, her skirts now tied between her legs.

"Just hurry, please." Genevieve responded, as she, too, tied up her gown and slid through the window.

The cat was nowhere in sight when the girls emerged from the house, but there was plenty of activity in the streets near the river. "Where can he have gone?" Genevieve moaned. "Alexandre! Alex, come back!"

"I don't know about you, but if I were him, I'd head down there." Annette smiled and pointed toward the action. "Perhaps I can even find a purse or two to pick."

"Annette!" Genevieve was startled by the girl's remark as she hurried along, keeping her eyes open, watching for her pet. The pair made their way down to the stalls.

Breathless, they reached the street without any sign of the cat.

"Oh, Annette, where could he be?"

"Having fun, methinks." Annette smiled and patted Genevieve's arm. "Do not worry, sweetings. Your cat can take care of himself; better, I think, than his mistress can."

"I am fine on my own."

"Oh? Then why do you always do what you are told?"

"I do not."

Annette shrugged as they pressed against the side of a stone building to avoid a very drinken Indian falling into the muddied street.

"In truth, you do. Each time they say to go to mass or to pray, you are the first one there." Annette led the younger girl towards the booths where bright fabrics and beads were displayed.

"That is because I worry about my future."

Annette smiled. "Do not. Once we find Philippe and Lancelot . . ."

Eagerly, Genevieve turned to her friend. "Think you we will find them here?"

Shrugging, Annette moved on to finger another display. Copper-bright pots and pans; wools of various widths, depths and colors; glass beads sewn onto various fashion pieces or loose in containers; booths of all natures lined the streets, ready to entice the Indians to give up their hard-earned furs in exchange for the little trinkets. Several of the counters already had empty bottles of the brandy brought out to induce the Indians to trade.

"Say, what do you girls do here?" One trader asked. "You know 'tis not safe. Go home. Go home with ye now." He shooed them away from his wares, urging them back up one of the quieter streets.

"We will go home in good time, sir," Genevieve responded, "just as soon as we find my cat."

"Your cat? You would risk your life with these roaming savages for a mere cat? Phew!" The man cried, spitting a wad of well-chewed tobacco onto the walk in front of Annette's feet. "If I were you, my little lady, I'd get you home now afore sumthin' bad does happen. 'Taint the place and time to be explorin'."

Annette smiled at the man and, shrugging, pushed Genevieve on. The girls continued walking through the thronging streets filled with men of various colors from white and ruddy to the darker skin tones of the slaves brought up from the English colonies. Even the savages were of different hues and different paintings. Each, it appeared, belonged to a different tribe, for each wore another color on his face, or his hair another fashion.

"God's blood!" Annette held her nose. "This bear grease is worse than the unwashed stink of the many days on the boat."

"Truly," Genevieve responded, not seeming to mind even that Annette had cursed.

"Come." She indicated the landing pier. "There is cheering and yelling there. Let's see if they're playing some games."

"It does not look like games to me. And I want to find Alexandre."

"He will be fine, I promise. Now, come." Grabbing Genevieve by the arm, she pulled her along.

If it was possible, the rue de la Commune, where the river met the land, was even more crowded than the streets had been. Genevieve looked back in the direction they had walked. Every street looked the same and, for an instant, she wondered if they'd find their way back.

But of course they had to. Besides, it was not as if they were in Paris. Sooner or later, they would find the large house on the slope, and she hoped that Alexandre would, too. She prayed the cat wouldn't get into any trouble, for already the Directress had threatened to make her keep him outside; Genevieve knew that Alexandre, as adventuresome as he might appear, would be very upset if he could not cuddle with her at night.

Forgetting the cat for a moment, Genevieve gasped, awed by a huge Indian who had emerged from what appeared to be the main canoe. Wearing eight eagle feathers in a grand crown, he seemed to be one of the leaders of his people, yet he could not have been older than thirty. The sun reflected off the bear grease on his body, and Genevieve was surprised to find that he was staring in her direction.

"He wants you," Annette whispered.

"You are joking, surely."

"Look, he is motioning in your direction and is talking to his men."

"You are dreaming, Annette. He is an Indian."

"So? So is Lancelot."

"But I have found the man I wish—if he wishes to have me. That is, I—" Genevieve stuttered, and flushed, feeling distinctly uncomfortable at the way the young chieftain stared at her. "Come on. I have had enough of this excitement. Let's return to the house."

"*Non*, I am not ready yet."

"Then I will go back on my own."

Annette sighed. "Let us stay just a few more minutes. I want to see those booths. Perhaps they have something of interest."

"Oh, Annette. Very well. And then we shall leave." Genevieve turned once more toward the water. The chieftain, who had now begun talking in a rapid-fire dialect to one of the traders, motioned in her direction.

"I think I'd best leave. I do not like what they are saying."

"How do you know what they're saying?" Annette scoffed. "I *was* only joking when I said he wanted you."

"Perhaps"—Genevieve shrugged—"but I do not like the way he is looking at me. I am going to walk up to the hill."

"Don't be foolish. It's much too crowded back there, and besides, I am sure some fun will start soon."

The sounds of a fight broke into the noise around them as, curious, Annette turned toward the arena. Two of the Indians, both apparently quite drunk, were slugging it out, yelling and cursing each other in their own foreign tongue.

Unable to keep a straight face, Annette began to laugh, as did many of the white men near her. "It is one thing to drink, and quite another, it seems, to hold one's drink, eh?" Annette said, expecting Genevieve to respond.

But as she turned, she found the other girl was gone.

19

Trudging through the streets of the town, taking care to avoid those who made their living by picking others' pockets, Philippe hurried along, the bundle of furs on his naked back. Wearing only his leggings, his skin tanned by constant exposure to sun, only the thick dark hairs on his chest gave away the fact that he was not the Indian like his companion, who also carried furs. Philippe had hoped to trade some of his catch with one of the men going up river to Quebec so that he would not have to carry the load. It would mean less money for him, since undoubtedly the other trader would want a cut, but it would also mean he could more easily return to the forest and would have a few moments, at least, to spend with Genevieve before leaving.

He had not yet been to the Congregational House where the girls were staying. He and Lancelot had planned to walk over that evening, or perhaps even the following day, after most of the Indians had returned to their lands, having traded their furs and drunk most of the proceeds.

As the sun beat upon his back, he shivered. "I shall be glad to get back to the quiet of our forest, eh?" He nudged Lancelot.

The Indian nodded.

It was one thing to need to trade with these people; it was quite another to like doing it. If he could, Philippe would have sent Lancelot to deal with the Frenchmen, but he knew that no matter how well his friend knew the language, nor how well he knew what to expect, the traders would always find a way to cheat him and make the Indian feel foolish. And so, despite his distaste for the task, Philippe led the way.

"Perhaps it would be best for us to wait and see the girls on the morrow. I would not like to have them out walking with all these unsavory fellows about—even with us to protect them."

"Agreed," the taciturn Indian responded.

"On the other hand, I do wish to see her as soon as possible."

"Agreed," Lancelot again responded.

Philippe glanced at him and then realized that his friend was not really in the conversation with him. Most likely his friend was thinking of Annette. He sighed and hoped that the governors would not give Lancelot any difficult about marrying the woman of his choice. After all, although he was a Christian, she had been imported for the express purpose of marriage to the workers and soldiers, for the creation of children to grow into armies against the Indians. Philippe frowned. He would help Lancelot work on that problem if it did, indeed, become a problem.

In the sweltering heat, so unusual for the end of September, and the press of bodies, Philippe edged closer to the water, where the cooling breeze would lend some relief. Philippe's eyes scanned the pier, studying the designs on the more than sixty canoes that had arrived that morning alone. "Looks like the Mohawks have arrived. And our Huron brother, Standing Eagle."

"White Ghost, too," Lancelot added.

Philippe frowned at hearing the name of the Iroquois who, in Philippe's mind, shared responsibility for his mother's death. Had his father not given her up, White Ghost, whose name came from the number of white men he had killed, would not have wooed her. But, feeling loyal to her French husband, Philippe's mother had refused the warrior. When he persisted, she had chosen an honorable death rather than a dishonorable life living with a man who was not her husband. For even though she had left of her own free will and torn up the marriage certificate, it had all been a show. In the eyes of God, she was wed to her Frenchman until her death. Philippe continued to stare at the empty canoe and wondered just how much his father truly understood about his long-dead wife.

"Come. Let us get this business done. I do not want to meet with him, nor do I even want to see Standing Eagle."

Lancelot shrugged. The Indian had started to move on when a familiar cry halted Philippe. He looked down at his feet to see the black cat stretched out, tummy up, begging to be rubbed.

Pleased and somewhat astonished, Philippe laughed. "So, Alexandre, you have survived thus far?" He bent over and stroked the animal's exposed stomach. "And what are you doing all the way down here when your mistress is up there?"

The cat stared at him, blinking, now butting his head against Philippe's leg as he begged to picked up and cuddled. "I see. You don't like this crowd any more than I do."

Alex meowed in response.

"And why are you out here rather than inside the safe house with Genevieve?"

Crying in response, the cat raised a paw to show Philippe that he had been hurt.

"Oh. Well, it's not very bad, fellow. But we'll take care of it when I take you back to your mistress."

"*Mon Dieu*! 'Tis one thing to believe in animal spirits as we do. 'Tis quite another to carry on a whole conversation with them."

Philippe smiled. "You are right, Lancelot. We will get on. I will carry the cat while you take my fur bundle. I wouldn't want Alexandre to get the wrong impression of me. He might get upset and tell Genevieve not to marry me."

Lancelot shook his head. "Do you know, I believe falling in love has made you addle-brained. You'd never catch me talking to a cat like that."

"If this were Annette's rather than Genevieve's, you would." He dug the splinter out of the cat's paw with his knife and, bandaging it with a clean linen, he set the injured cat on his shoulder where Alexandre was more than content to ride.

The deal he made finally with the trader was not to Philippe's satisfaction, but now that he had Alexandre, he was especially in a hurry to see Genevieve.

"I thought you said we would wait until morrow."

Philippe smiled. "You wait if you wish. I cannot. Besides, I do not want to take the chance that someone has already claimed her."

"If she feels about you as you believe, I doubt she would go with anyone else."

Philippe shook his head. "Alas, but I did not tell her that I would come for her, and if she has found anyone remotely interesting—but come." He rubbed his free hands together. "I am in a hurry to speak with her and settle this matter once and for all. Then my father will have his wedding celebration and the Intendant will be satisfied." He paused, recalling what she had told him. "Then again"—he smiled—"perhaps he will not be pleased. But that is all right with me."

The sounds of screams halted the pair as they climbed the hill towards the Congregational House. Philippe led the way back into the crowd. "Perhaps we'd best see what the matter is."

"I know what the matter is," Lancelot responded, "and there is nothing we can do. 'Tis two of the Mohawks fighting for control of a bottle." He frowned and shook his head. "A great nation disgraced."

"*Oui*," Philippe added, feeling the cat clawing into his shoulder, "Only the disgrace is on the French side for their treatment of their fellow man, not on the Indian's. Come. Let us hurry before Alexandre tears my skin apart." He forced a smile.

At the stone house at the edge of the hill, the pair paused. "Mayhap we should have dressed to present ourselves," Lancelot said, glancing at his friend. "I do not think Sister Marguerite will approve of the fashions we wear."

Philippe shrugged. "Why? We are doing them a favor. We are marrying the girls, and besides, if Genevieve does not wish me, then she may reject me dressed as I am as easily as if I dressed the part of the seigneur's son."

"But Philippe, the sisters—"

It was too late, for the huge iron gate was now being opened.

"Go away!" The grey-habited sister cried. "This is a holy place. You are not wanted here. Go back to your drinks."

She began to shut the gate when Philippe placed his foot inside.

"*Pardon*, Sister." He spoke slowly to calm her frantic fears. "We have come to see the women."

"Then you must meet with the Directress, and she will judge if you are fit husbandly material," the woman said suspiciously.

Philippe glanced at Lancelot and then back at the sister. "We already have, in

Three Rivers. She will no doubt recall the son of Jean St. Clair."

"St. Clair?" The nun's eyes were wide with astonishment. "*Non*, you cannot be St. Clair. He is a Jesuit."

"That is my half-brother, Emile. He is not the one called upon to marry for the sake of the estate," Philippe responded, his foot still in the door. "And the girls we wish to see are Mademoiselle Genevieve Bopar, and Mademoiselle Annette L'Che."

The sister's eyes widened in even bigger surprise. "I am sorry, Monsieur St. Clair, but that is not possible."

"Why not? Has she married someone else? Has she already pledged to another?" He felt the cat standing upon his shoulders, hunching and hissing. Not wanting the cat to add to his troubles, he put Alexandre on the ground, but the cat continued to hiss as the nun edged back.

"Get that wicked creature away! 'Tis the devil's work, just like the girl herself."

"No! No, 'tis not the devil's work," came a cry from within the house as Annette ran forward, escaping the grasp of two of the sisters who had been restraining her. "Alexandre is safe. Therefore, Genevieve must be safe, too."

"What do you mean, 'safe'?" Philippe cried, throwing the door open, the small sister's strength no match for his. "What do you mean? What have you done with her?"

"I?" Annette looked at him and then at Lancelot. "Nothing!" She had never thought to see anyone so furious; not even the king's man when she'd picked his purse had been this angry. "'Tis quite simple, Philippe. We were bored with the"—she looked anxiously towards the women of the Congregation who had gathered around—"with all the prayer and wanted to see what the fair was about."

"*Sang Dieu!*" Philippe blew up. "Did no one tell you that it is unsafe for young women out there? That walking out there without an escort makes you fair game?"

"Yes, but I—" Annette looked again over her shoulder, this time at the elderly leader of the group. "We did not think we'd be gone long, and we only wanted to see what the excitement was."

Cursing under his breath, Philippe's eyes narrowed. "And where is Genevieve? What did you do with her? Into what mischief did you lead her?"

"I did nothing!"

His anger was tearing him apart. "Tell me quick, girl, before I—" His hand went to Annette's shoulder just as another hand went to his.

Before Philippe could say or do anything more, Lancelot's fingers dug into his friend's shoulder. "Have a care, my brother, for I will scalp you myself if you

255

dare lay a hand on her."

At the word 'scalp,' one of the older nuns fainted.

The diversion enough to calm him for the moment, Philippe dcropped his arm and Lancelot dropped his as the nun was revived and led back into the house.

"You had best tell me now."

And so Annette related to him how they had climbed from the window and walked through the streets, and how when she had turned to say something to her friend, Genevieve had disappeared.

20

"Tell me again what happened," Philippe prodded Annette as he paced the small room where the three of them now talked.

"Philippe," Lancelot interjected, his hand over Annette's, aware of the watchful eyes of the nun who sat in the corner, "she has told you three times."

"Yes, and each time she recalls something else."

"I am only saying what I remember," Annette defended herself. "How did I know something would happen? We were talking and she disappeared."

"This is more than just a disappearance. If she had been coming back here to the house, she would have been here when you arrived, and even had she gotten lost in the town, she would surely be back by now," Lancelot said, in one of his longest speeches since the incident had occurred.

"Well, I am going out to look for her," Philippe said.

"And I, too," Annette said.

"No, Mademoislle." The sister stood, blocking the door. "You are not. 'Tis bad enough we have one missing. We want nothing to happen to you."

"But she is my friend. I can help find her."

"That is not your purpose on earth," the grey-habited sister said, frowning. "You have been brought here to wed, to make good Christian children."

"No, I was sent here because it was this or the gallows, Sister!"

The fragile nun gasped. "I did not know that we—" she looked to Marguerite Bourgeoys, who had entered the room. The head of the Congregational sisters nodded slowly.

" 'Tis a fact, Sister Elizabeth. We did indeed take on some unfortunates in hopes that they would mend their ways and that in this new world they would build a solid life away from the memory of their crimes."

She stepped forward and eyed the two men, then looked at Annette. "Ma'mselle, the sister is right, however. You have been brought to Ville-Marie for the purpose of marriage. If you do not wish that, then you must make another choice. But we cannot allow you to wander through dangerous crowds such as those." She waved her hand toward the window, from which the noises of the fair still filtered in. "We cannot risk you, too, being lost or kidnapped."

"Kidnapped?" Annette looked to Philippe. He shrugged.

"Possibly. I will have to ask around and see what I can learn. And then, if that is the fact, I will search out the man and make him sorry if he has touched her!"

Annette shook her head. "Kidnapped? Is that what you think happened to her? Then I must be with you to find her! For if it had not been for my prodding, she would not have gone out there. And it was I who wanted to stay out longer." She knelt down to kiss the hem of the Congregational superior. "Mother Marguerite, I must help my friend. Allow me to travel with Lancelot and Philippe, to find Genevieve and bring her safely back to the bosom of—of God," Annette added quickly, hoping that it would convince the holy woman.

There was a moment of silence before the older woman responded. It was to Philippe she turned now, as if the other two were not even in the room. "This is something I must pray on, for I would be derelict in my duty toward the girls and toward the men of this colony if I allowed this young woman to leave my house without proper guidance." She paused. "You go and find out what you can about the missing girl. Then I shall decide if Annette may accompany you or not."

She motioned for Annette to raise herself.

"Come, child. We have much to meditate on."

Mother Marguerite was already at the door and the keys to the chapel were jingling in her hand. With a backward glance at Philippe and Lancelot, who were now being led out of the room, Annette picked up Genevieve's cat and followed her.

"Well," Lancelot asked, as they left the house, "where do we begin?"

"The waterfront. We've already lost much time in discussion. If she has, indeed, been kidnapped as the good mother says, then we shall learn what we need with drinks to loosen some tongues."

Nodding, Lancelot followed his friend's swift strides as they hurried into the noisy street.

At several places they paused and spoke to men in the booths, to traders at the corners, but none knew of Genevieve, they said, and none claimed to know anything of her disappearance.

Halfway to the tavern Philippe halted as, there in front of him, being made a fool of by one of the other traders, was White Ghost.

"Ah, Kio Diego. Greetings, my friend, my son, my brother." The drunken Indian slapped Philippe on the back.

"Greetings to you, White Ghost," Philippe responded, pulling the nearly empty bottle of watered-down rum from the other man. "A warrior does not need this to make him happy."

"Oh, but I do."

The Indian grabbed for the bottle as Philippe turned to the trader. "Did you give him this?"

With a Gallic shrug, the trader acknowledged it. "If they want to buy liquor for their furs, what's it to me."

"There is a law to that effect, Monsieur Edward."

"And who is going to report me? I am getting my furs in the same fashion as the others. There is no difference."

Furious, Philippe stared at the man. "Give me what you have bought from him."

"I shall not. He has the drink. Why do I want to give up what is rightfully mine?" The man's hand slid to his side slowly and carefully until he reached his knife. "If you wish a game for it, my friend, I will oblige you, but I do not play fair.''

Philippe looked at the Indian who, rather than fighting for his drink, had now passed out on the street. "That much I can see."

" 'Tis not my fault they cannot hold their liquor. If they wish to buy, I will sell."

"They wish to buy only because they have been force-fed a taste of it. Because they know nothing of what it does to them." Philippe now went for his knife, too, as his knees bent for the struggle.

The bearded trader looked at him, then at Lancelot poised at the side, ready as his friend to fight.

"Very well, then! Here." He threw a small bundle of beaver pelts at the men. "There are other fools out there more willing and with better furs. I overpaid for this."

Sheathing his knife, he walked away.

Philippe stared in disgust at the great warrior now lying at their feet. "Help me pick him up. We will take him back to his canoe and wait for him to sober up. Perhaps then he will tell me what he knows of Genevieve."

Lancelot nodded and hoisted the dead weight over his shoulder.

It took several hours before the Indian came to and stared up, bleary-eyed, into Philippe's face.

"You are my brother. I thank you. I will owe you a good deed in return, for I do not forget kindness, even from such as you."

"Don't thank me. Just tell me what I need to know and then you may be on your way."

White Ghost shrugged. "I am grateful to you for saving my furs. I will tell you all that you ask." He sat up in the canoe, wincing with the pain in his head.

"There is a young woman . . ."

The Indian held up his hand. "Say no more. Her hair was the color of the red fox and shimmered in the light." He frowned as he shaded his eyes from the sun. "She has left these shores and if you seek her, you'll travel far."

"How far?"

The older man shrugged. "Ask at the camp of Chief No Retreat. He will tell you more."

"Who took her, White Ghost? You know as much as the chief."

The Indian shrugged. "Several admired her beauty, but I believe it was Standing Eagle who wished her the most. She had not a man with her, and if she is your woman . . ."

"She is not my woman—not yet. But I wish to make her mine."

"Then you'll need to set your canoe in the direction of the setting sun and travel quickly before the council has declared her to be his squaw."

Frowning, Philippe edged his way out of the canoe.

"May the spirit of your mother be with you," White Ghost called out as Philippe hurried back toward the street.

"May the spirit of your ancestors protect you," Philippe responded to the blessing.

"And so we go west," Philippe told Annette. "You will stay here with the cat until we return."

"No!" Annette shouted, "I am going with you."

Lancelot shrugged. "You heard the ruling of Mother Marguerite. If you wish to leave this house, it must be as a wife—my wife." He sipped the wine that the sisters had kindly provided and tried not to meet her eyes as the three of them talked.

"But that is not fair." Annette gritted her teeth. "I did not come over here to wed and have no intention of doing so." She stood and paced the small room. "Truly, I do enjoy being with you, Lancelot, but—"

Lancelot shrugged again. "If we want God's blessing for our journey and the safe recovery of your friend—"

"Phoo! What do I care for God! How has He helped me?"

"You are safe from the gallows, are you not?" Philippe responded. "Anyway, we shall be off in the morning. I am not in favor of your coming as it is, but since Lancelot wishes, and since he does believe in this religious nonsense . . ."

"See! You are a man of my own heart!" Annette cried. "The trouble is, I do not love you."

Philippe gave a slight smile. "Nor I you, my dear, but you must wed if you wish to join us, else the good mother will have the militia out in full force."

Annette looked from one man to the other as she paused in her pacing. Finally she held out her hand to Lancelot. "Very well, then. I will wed you. The sisters cannot object since they have given me but these choices." She paused. "I warn you, Lancelot, I am not going to make a good wife, for I fully intend to make my fortune on my own. I do not cook, I sew only what I need to sew and provide only what I need to provide. I'll not be an unpaid domestic. You know of my plans."

"It will be as you wish, Annette," Lancelot replied stoically. "You may warm any bed as long as you warm mine as well."

She stared at him. "In truth, you do not mind?"

He shrugged.

"I am not tricking you, you know. You

can't object, for you knew beforehand what I wished." She sighed. "I am doing this only for my friend's sake." She glanced at Philippe. "I know for a fact that she would be quite upset were I to choose you."

A glimmer of hope showed in Philippe's eyes for just a moment as the candle before them flickered. "She can chose me only if we reach her in time." He paused and looked at the pair. "I will fetch the sister and tell her to bring the priest and the notary."

"And you would leave us alone then?" The tension made her voice high as she looked to Lancelot.

"From you, Annette, that sounds strange. Besides, you are now betrothed and soon to be wed. I see no reason why you cannot be in the same room for a few moments."

"No, I—"

" 'Twill be but a moment," Philippe said, closing the door after him.

The fire burned steadily, and Annette could feel the heat on her cheeks as she knew that Lancelot was watching her as she was watching him.

"Since you do not care if I wed you or not," Lancelot said, "and since you are doing this only for your friend, I do not have to kiss you, do I?"

Annette's eyes focused on his lips and

felt his on hers. "No, you do not." She involuntarily took a step forward. "But you must understand, Lancelot. 'Tis nothing to do with your lack of charms."

He shrugged, unmoving, as she took yet another involuntary step, nearly touching him.

"Well, perhaps to seal our fates, to show that you understand my desires, too . . ."

He cocked his head and smiled slightly. "*Oui*, Ma'mselle. I do know your desires."

"Lancelot, 'tis not you. You must know that."

"Then prove it," he said, as his arms now drew her into his and his kisses ignited the fire within her. He pressed her body to his with a passion beyond what either of them had ever felt before. "If you wish to warm other beds, my Annette, you must first warm mine sufficiently. I will not let you free until I am satisfied." His tongue parted her lips, gently, exploring.

She returned his kisses and touched him delicately. "Then I suppose I will have my work cut out for me. Perhaps I shall like being a wife after all."

"*Oui*," Lancelot responded, kissing her again. "You will."

21

The wedding was simpler than those of most of the King's Daughters and, although Annette dressed in the required white gown, she refused to go through the ritual of the music and the dinner following.

"And what of the cows, the pigs, the sheep and the money which are to be given me?" She asked of the notary who stood in official capacity.

"Those are for the women who wed French citizens."

"And is Lancelot not a French citizen? Certainly, the government assesses taxes on the furs he sells."

"*Oui*, he pays taxes." The man eyed the new bridegroom. "But he is not a citizen of the colony."

Lancelot put his hand on his new wife's arm. "Annette, it does not signify. I do not need all those things for my tribe."

"*Non*, but I do. My house will require the land for building and the seeds and animals for farming. Do you want me to starve?"

He bent over and kissed her cheek in front of the sisters, who blushed hotly. "You will never starve while you are with me, my love." He took her hand. "Come. We have some celebrating to do."

"But my dowry. It is mine!"

He nudged her toward the door.

"Have no fear, Annette," Philippe reassured her. "I will talk with them." He pushed her toward her husband. "Go off now and prepare to leave with the first sun, for I do not want to waste any more time than we have already done."

Seeing it was no good to argue, Annette nodded and, without reluctance, followed her husband into the private room prepared for them. She would see just how much satisfying her Indian needed!

The morning found the couple still locked in each other's arms as Philippe pounded on the door. " 'Tis time to leave."

" 'Tis too soon!" Annette called back. "Leave us be."

Philippe shrugged. "If you want to join me in the search for Genevieve, I leave now." The floor boards vibrated as he stomped away. Moments later, the door of the newlyweds' room was flung open.

Philippe eyed his friend's wife. "Surely, you cannot plan to travel the forest dressed like that?" He motioned to her blue silk gown and voluminous petticoats.

"And what would I be wearing? Nothing at all, like the Indian women?"

Lancelot grinned. " 'Tis not quite as indecent as that, my love, but frankly, I wouldn't mind. Though I fear you'd get bitten up by the bugs unless you put on enough bear grease."

Annette wrinkled her nose in disgust.

"Here. You'll wear this." Philippe threw a pair of leggings and a cambric shirt towards her from his own gear. " 'Twill be big, but it is better than getting your gown caught in the trees as we walk."

Annette could only stare at him and did not move until Lancelot pushed her.

"Go. Change. Philippe is right. If you wish to come with us, then you must wear the proper clothes."

"If I wish to come!" Annette fumed. "Why do you think I married you?" Leggings in hand, she slammed the door to the room behind her.

Genevieve was aware of the motion

beneath her and for a few moments she thought she was still on ship. A drop of water fell on her face and she realized she was outside. Had she fallen asleep on deck? She attempted to move and found her hands were bound.

She opened her eyes. Blue sky was above, but so was the darkly painted face of an Indian. "Who are you?"

The Indian continued to stare at her.

"Who are you?" Genevieve repeated.

"He speaks no French, Ma'mselle. But I do," a voice farther away than her vision carried said.

Struggling to sit up, she felt the rocking of the canoe.

"Please. Do not move so. We are far enough away from shore than I can unbind you," the voice said; then, in another language foreign to her, he gave directions for her hands to be unleashed. She pulled back as far as she could, trying to avoid the stink of the man while the guard over her cut the leathers from her wrists.

"Where am I? And who are you? What has happened to me? And where is my cat?"

The guard spoke rapid-fire and she felt an arm around her shoulders hoist her into a sitting position.

"Yes, it is better you are awake. Then I can get to know my new squaw."

Genevieve stared at the tall Indian before her. "I am no one's squaw—least of all yours." She looked around at the wide expanse of river surrounding them, and in longing at the distant shoreline. "What did you do to me? Where is my cat?"

"The animal is no more."

Her mouth dropped open. "You killed him."

" 'Tis good fur to sell."

"No! No, I don't believe you." She moved forward quickly and was just as quickly taken down as the canoe rocked violently. Only with great effort was the canoe again brought under control. "If you have killed my Alexandre, then you can kill me, too."

"Alexandre? He is a man?"

"He is my cat. What have you done with him?"

Her captor shook his head. "I know no cat."

"But I saw him with you. I saw you pick him up."

The leader smiled. "Ah, yes, the animal. Good fur. Good brandy."

Genevieve could only stare silently at the man in front of her and mourn her poor pet.

Finally, as the oars dipped quietly into the river, she asked again. "Who are you and what do you want of me? Why am I here?"

"I have told you, Ma'mselle. I sell much furs for you."

"You what?"

"Is truth by your god. I sell many wolf, beaver, and buffalo hides for trader's sale of you."

Her mouth dropped open. "Who—which trader sold me?"

"Man who say he own you. Man who say you were his woman."

She could only stare in astonishment at the Indian. Her voice choked as she managed to speak. "No man owns me. No man ever did." Then she went white. Could it have been Philippe? But he did not own her. He hadn't even been to see her since they'd come to Ville-Marie, yet he did live hereabouts. Genevieve didn't want to ask, but she had to know. And how else would she have seen Alexandre in this heathen's hands? "The man who said he owned me, who helped you, was his name St. Clair?"

There was more talk in their foreign tongue, which to her ears sounded like garbled nonsense.

"Yes, yes. We know St. Clair."

Genevieve felt the blood drain from her body as she stared mutely into the water. Not only hadn't he wanted her, but he had sold her into slavery! Tears came to her eyes, and she quickly brushed them away. She cared not so much about losing her freedom as about losing her pet. Alexandre was the only one who had ever really cared for her.

She continued to stare into the water, her head aching from the blow that had obviously been how they had been able to take her into the boat. She forced herself to look up into the eyes of the Indian who was studying her. "And what is to happen to me?"

"Good only," the Indian said. "I tell you, you be my squaw. Council see you make good babies, and they bring you to my tepee."

Genevieve froze at his words. "I don't want to make babies. I don't want to—" She realized that to explain to this creature was useless, for he'd surely not understand. As she returned her attention to the river, she wondered what death was like.

Dressed in Philippe's clothes, Annette emerged a rather comical picture. But as far as the men were concerned, she looked fine.

"We are wasting time," Philippe said as he ordered Lancelot to take one load of supplies and Annette another.

"But I—"

"Do you wish to come?"

She nodded.

"Then you must work alongside us."

Reluctantly, she picked up the roll as Lancelot adjusted it on her shoulder. "We will be in the canoes most of the way, my precious, so have no fear."

"It doesn't bother me," she said. "If I can't carry it, you will."

Despite her snippy remarks, Annette was more than happy to share in the work as she picked up a paddle and moved it the way Lancelot showed her. At least she was free of the convent, the Directress and the sisters constantly watching over her, constantly making her feel unclean and useless. She was sure that if they had had a life like hers, they would not have been so holy, but arguing did no good with people like them. She knew that from experience.

"I hope you know where we're going," she said to Philippe.

"I don't." His paddle dipped in and out of the water. "But your husband does."

Annette glanced at Lancelot. "And how long will it take us to reach there? When will we find Genevieve and be able to return to civilization?"

"Why do you wish to return there?" Philippe stared at her. "I would have thought you'd had enough restrictions."

"*Sang Dieu!*" She cursed. "I hate

their righteous rules as much as you do, Philippe. But I want my money, my dowry."

"Oh, yes. Your dowry."

"You did get it, did you not?"

"*Oui*. I made an arrangement."

Annette's back stiffened. "What kind of arrangement?"

"When I wed Genevieve, she will get a double dowry—"

"But she doesn't need it."

"—to be placed at the use of the good sisters. They have much work to do in taking care of the sick, both the whites and Indians who come to them. I knew you would want your money going to a good cause."

"Good cause! The only good cause I know is myself. I wanted that money!"

"*Oui*. And I know what you want it for. If you wish to have your house, you shall, but not at the expense of the King. You will find, my dear, that there are restrictions applied to that coin, as with anything else the government gives. You would not have been able to use it as you pleased."

Annette settled back in the canoe and glared at Philippe and then at her husband. "Did you know about this?"

Lancelot shrugged and smiled. He touched the hand of his new wife. "Don't worry, my love, it will be some while before you can set up that house—before I am satisfied enough to allow you to pleasure others."

22

Genevieve stared at the endless water and
forest around her. It seemed they had
been in the canoe for a month, but in fact it
had been only five days. Still the Indians
kept moving. Each time they made camp,
she thought about trying to run, looked
for a moment to escape; but none came.
She was guarded as if she were a precious
treasure and, she supposed, to the chief
who had bought her with his hard-earned
furs, she was.

Genevieve couldn't help wondering if
anyone knew where she was, if anyone
cared what had happened to her. What
had Annette told them when she returned
to the house alone? Or perhaps she had not
returned. Perhaps she, too, had been
kidnapped—or worse. Not knowing what

had happened to her friend, Genevieve mourned Annette as well. She thought that the nuns would have questioned the sanity of anyone disappearing, especially one who had crossed the Atlantic for the purpose of marriage for the dowry that the king was providing. Yet the nuns were simple. She doubted they had even questioned closely her being gone. She knew for a fact that Sister Beatrice would be more than happy that Alexandre was no longer making a pest of himself and crying at night.

She wept again for Alexandre, and for her father, knowing more than ever that she'd never see home again. How many times during those few days did she think about Racine, and wonder what would have happened if she had indeed wed him. About Philippe—she would bite her tongue whenever his name came to her mind. He was responsible for her condition now and, wherever he was, she would somehow have her revenge. She still did not understand how or why he had done this to her. But even a second questioning of the Indians had confirmed that St. Clair was the man who had sold her to them.

More than a week after her capture, the canoe pulled into shore. It was still daylight, so she knew that their river trip was over, at least for now. Having learned to hear and understand certain words, she knew that they would be walking the rest of the way to the encampment, wherever that was. She didn't see any signs of settlements or civilization, but then she hadn't expected she would. In God's name, she wondered, what hell had she fallen into?

At least the Indian, whoever he was, had not yet abused her, though she fully expected him to, and every evening as they made camp she was watchful for the moment when he would try to attack her—for as far as Genevieve was concerned that was what it would be. From the way she was guarded, she knew that escape without the help of another was nearly impossible. Even if she did get free of the camp, they would come after her and surely kill her. So she made up her mind—if he touched her in any way, she would kill him first before they killed her, for her own death, she knew, would then be inevitable. Still, it was preferable to die by her own hand, to die perhaps in the struggle to end the life of her captor, than to allow herself to be used. Would not God prefer her sacrifice to living a life of hatred? She was sure He would.

And even as she thought about it, hope somehow continued. The sisters surely had to have sent someone after her. Would the militia try to find her? Would

Talon come after her? She couldn't think that she would be forever swallowed up in the wilderness and that no one at all would even care.

Trudging along, her hands once again bound to one of the guards, she allowed the hem of her skirt, torn as it was, to trail along after her, the threads dropping as she purposely stepped on branches, breaking them so that some sort of a trail would be left. If she didn't have hope, Genevieve thought, then she had nothing.

Occasionally, the overhanging branches with their leaves thinning in anticipation of the coming winter, allowed some sunlight to filter through; but for the most part the colored umbrella of green, gold, and red shaded their path as animals of various types darted back and forth through the forest and the birds cried hauntingly.

Her captors must have been as tired and hungry as she was, for when they next rested, she found them lackadaisical about guarding her. Or perhaps it was that they were so far inland now that no one would ever find her and, even if she did escape, she would never reach civilization alive.

"I will not give up hope," she whispered to the bluejay that perched on the limb above her.

Even as she said that, a glint of metal attracted her attention and she saw the knife lying just inches from her. Sharply she drew in her breath and saw one of the savages glance her way but, deep in conversation, they apparently were paying her no mind. Still, even if she could reach the knife without being noticed, where would she hide it? And wouldn't the warrior know it was gone?

Genevieve hesitated only a moment more as, keeping her eyes on the men, she inched carefully forward, then stopped, and once again moved as they went on talking.

She was within reach of the weapon when the guard turned toward her and, kneeling by the fire, offered her a piece of roast rabbit. Disgusted, Genevieve shook her head. It was true she had eaten very little since her capture, but their food repelled her and besides, starvation, though not a quick way to die, was a sure way. Still, she cautioned herself that she would need energy for her fight. Finally accepting a piece of meat, she nibbled at it, trying not to think about what she was eating or why.

She had to admit that her captor was treating her decently, but that was only because he expected her to work in his lodgings and wanted to keep her alive. From the stories she had been told, Genevieve had few illusions about what would happen to her should she refuse to work.

It was only with the fire burning low, and the blanket thrown over her, that she once again thought about the knife. The weapon had not been noticed, nor had it been missed, and she knew that she'd have no other choice but this one.

An owl hotted as she reached her hand out.

One of the sleeping men moved.

Genevieve watched carefully, her eyes accustomed now to the darkness around her. She was sure they could hear the rapid beating of her heart and knew what she was planning and what she was thinking; she was sure they could see in the darkness far better than she, and yet she had to dare.

Slowly, she reached cautiously forward.

Her fingers felt the cold of the metal as she strained against the bonds that held her feet tied to the guard and prayed he would not notice her changed position.

The owl hooted once again, nearly making her jump out of her skin, but no one else seemed to notice it.

With the greatest of relief, Genevieve felt her fingers go round the object as her aching muscles strained and drew back ever so slowly. Tucking the metal into the waistband of her skirt, she knew that she'd have to find a better hiding place for it later, but for now she was content just to have it.

"How much farther is it?" she asked with the coming of morning.

Her kidnapper shrugged. "Four, maybe five days' walk."

Genevieve nodded.

"You not mind?"

"What's there to mind? What choice do I have?"

He grinned. "You make good squaw. You listen well." He came over and touched her hair, stroking it in a way that she might have stroked Alexandre. "I call you Red Feather for your hair feel like feathers of bird."

She grimaced and steeled herself to the touch. She was sure her hair felt more like a bird's nest than its feathers, but she certainly wasn't going to argue.

It was several hours later before she had a chance to look at her treasure and was disappointed to realize that it was only the handle of a broken knife. No wonder it hadn't been sought after. Still, she felt the sharp edge and decided it was worth keeping. Finding an open section where her hem had come loose, she slipped the metal handle inside. It knocked against her legs as she walked, but as long as the Indians didn't notice anything, she could tolerate it.

* * *

The canoe containing Philippe and the happy couple finally stopped to make camp at the end of the second day.

"How can you take it, sitting all the time like that?" Annette complained as she dragged a bucket of water up from the river to help Lancelot with the cooking.

The Indian shrugged and turned to Philippe, who also shrugged. "You do what you have to do, my dear," Lancelot replied.

"Besides, if we wish to find Genevieve we mustn't let them get too far ahead of us. Once they reach their tribe, it will be much harder to rescue her. From what I've learned, Standing Eagle was traveling with only two other men. I like those odds far better than fighting ten."

Lancelot nodded as he adjusted the sticks heavy with fish that he had killed. He offered one to his wife.

"Perhaps I should let you do all the cooking, sweetings," Annette said with a cajoling smile. "You are certainly far more adept at it than I."

"Oh, and I suppose you wish to go out hunting and bringing back the food for me to cook?"

She smiled. "I'd like to hunt, but not food. Men. 'Tis men who have ruined me, and men who will make my fortune."

Annette took the fish from him and had just laid it on the grass to eat when a blur of dark fur ran in, grabbed the fish, stick and all, and ran back to the shelter of the trees. Eyes wide, Annette stared. "What was that?"

Lancelot, too was puzzled. "I do not know. Never have I seen an animal move like that so fast."

"Come," Philippe said, standing. "I wish to find out. Perhaps it is something new we can trap for furs."

"Perhaps," Lancelot said, standing as well.

"You don't think you're going to leave me over here without protection, do you?" Annette cried, standing too. "If it could run in and take my fish like that, who knows what it would do to me." Her arm laced through her husband's, and she allowed him to move ahead as she kept up behind.

Carefully, Philippe parted the branches, his club ready to strike out as they all saw the black furry body busily gnawing at the fish, tearing it apart as if it hadn't eaten in days.

The trio edged closer as Philippe raised his arm ready to bring the weapon down.

"Wait!" Annette cried out, seeing the animal's face for the first time. "Wait, you can't do that!"

Scared by her voice, the animal ran off into the trees as an irritated Philippe looked up. "You had best tell your wife, Lancelot, that we make our living by killing fur animals and if she is to warn them all off, we will soon have no choice but to live on her meager earnings."

"But you don't understand," Annette said, staring at the torn-apart fish that the animal had left. "That was Alexandre!"

"What!"

" 'Tis true. The animal was Genevieve's cat."

"How can you be sure?"

"Philippe, I have lived with that miserable creature since we left France. I know the animal."

Philippe shook his head, unable to believe it might be true. "Your wife is crazed, my friend. How could the cat have followed us from Ville-Marie? There is water to cross."

"So he paid the ferrier!"

" 'Tis impossible."

" 'Tis true, I say." She knelt down near the ground. "Alexandre! Alex!"

There was a rustling in the bushes, but nothing came forth.

"Alexandre! Alex!" This time it was Philippe who issued the call.

Hesitatingly, the animal moved forward, his golden-green eyes made luminous by the darker forest.

"Alexandre!" Philippe said again.

This time, recognizing the voice, the

cat, much thinner for wear, came forth.

"*Sang Dieu*! I do not believe this." He turned to Annette. "Did you bring him along and decide not to tell me?"

"Where would I hide him if I had?" Annette shook her head. "No, I did not bring the cat. I assumed he would stay back in Ville-Marie and await our return."

"And he assumed not." Philippe held out his hand and, eager for human warmth, Alex quickly presented himself for an affectionate rub.

" 'Tis most likely he knew Genevieve had gone and is following her scent," Lancelot put in. "I have heard that some animals are remarkable in that way."

"*Oui*." Philippe brought Alexandre back over to where the fish remained and nudged the food in front of the cat. "Some animals are indeed remarkable that way. I doubt he would pick up scent if Standing Eagle traveled by water, but I, too, have heard of pets locating their masters. We shall keep the cat with us," he decided. "Perhaps it will help lead us to her."

As if knowing he was safe for the moment, Alexandre licked his lips with his wide pink tongue and proceeded to clean himself.

23

They came to the clearing with the wigwams far sooner than Genevieve had imagined they would. She had felt the constant pounding of the metal of the broken knife hitting her leg as she walked and was sorry that she'd not been able to use it. Of course, she could still defend herself, but now the possibility of dying if she killed the young chief was far greater. Sitting in the small, round wigwam, she waited for her fate to be decided as shouting could be heard throughout the camp. With regret, she removed the metal handle from the hem of her skirt and, leaning back, closed her eyes.

Food was eventually brought her, but other than that, she saw no one except the guard. Several times she peeked out from under the sides of the shelter only to see what appeared to be everyday activity under way—children playing naked as their mothers pounded corn, sewed, or tanned the hides in preparation for winter. She wanted to know what was going to happen to her; she wanted to ask questions. But there was no one to ask except the guard and he spoke no French.

Days passed and, just when she thought she had been totally forgotten, the young chieftain came in.

"Council wish to speak with Red Feather."

Genevieve grimaced. She didn't particularly like that name, nor did she like the idea of seeing these old men, but maybe, if she could convince them that she had been kidnapped and brought here against her will . . .

Her hopes faded when she realized that the man who desired her was heading the council; whatever he wanted probably would be.

"I do not wish to be your squaw," she stated. "I belong to another."

"And who you belong to? Man sold you said you were his."

Sick to her stomach as Philippe's face seemed to loom over her, she closed her eyes a moment. "*Non.* I did not belong to him. He lied. I belong to God." Her voice quivered, for certainly, if she escaped here alive, she would go back to the convent and join the sisters, perhaps the Ursalines in Quebec.

There was a murmur of voices as one of the older men spoke up. "If you belong to your god, why you no work for him? Why you no carry his child?"

Genevieve stared at them and wondered if they understood the concept of marriage as the nuns saw it, but from the looks on their faces she knew that was unlikely. "I do not wish to belong to a man in earthly form," she stated again. "I wish to pray and be with the other women."

The old man shrugged and murmured something again before the chief stood. "You will be my bride in two suns, on feast of corn god."

"But I—"

She was not given any more opportunity to protest or to say anything else as she was led away back to the small wigwam. Food was pushed in through the opening for her and, left alone, she cried.

It was only later that afternoon that she met Dreams Standing Still, a pretty young girl who was, she explained haltingly, supposed to help Genevieve get ready for the honor of becoming the chieftain's bride.

"May I have a bath, at least?"

The girl looked at her strangely.

"Can I wash my hair? My clothes?"

Dreams Standing Still shook her head and produced a brightly beaded outfit and headband that Genevieve would be wearing for the ceremony. "Put on grease. Not water. Water bring many insect bites."

Genevieve sighed and wondered how she was going to survive this. As Dreams Standing Still left, she fingered the metal handle once more and hoped that the edge of blade still left would be enough to fatally wound him as well as herself.

In the twilight hours, the day before the ceremony, Genevieve dreamed of Alexandre—of holding her furry pet and cuddling him to her, of how affecionate and smart he was. She dreamed of his rough, wet tongue licking her face—and opened her eyes.

Gasping, she sat up. The cat stood over her, licking himself with his pink tongue and yawning. She continued to stare. "Alexandre!" She whispered hoarsely.

The cat stretched and yawned again, as if he been with her all along instead of lost, as she had believed.

"Oh, Alexandre! How did you ever find me, sweetings? I thought they had killed you!"

"You thought what?" The back flap of her wigwam was loosened and raised as Philippe slid under.

Once again, she stared in horror, backing away from him as far as she could. "Don't you come near me! Bastard!" Her hand searched frantically for the little bit of weapon she had. "How dare you come to gloat over your handiwork?"

He looked at her, puzzled, as he edged forward.

"Come any closer and I'll scream!" Raising her hand swiftly, she brought the edge of the handle down hard on his face.

The shock of the sight of his blood made her pause long enough for him to wrest the instrument from her hand.

"Kill me now, then, if you must. I'd rather die than be enslaved!" she cried, tears in her eyes now.

Pinning her down so she could not attack him again, he stared at her. "Now explain yourself."

"*Non!* You must explain yourself!" she continued to sob. "I was looking for my Alexandre, and suddenly I am taken by these creatures. They say that 'tis you who sold me to them."

"Sold you! *Sang Dieu!*" He shook his head. "Oh, my Genevieve, I could never have sold you. *Diable!* How could I have done that to you?"

She sniffled and stared at the blood coagulating on his face. "I do not know. All I know is what they have said." Her voice trembled. "He . . . the Indian gave many furs to some trader and said that this trader—" She sniffled again and turned her head toward the flap, not wanting to look into Philippe's eyes. "They said it was you."

"*Ma foi!*" He shook his head. "Look at me, my Genevieve." He released her slowly and turned her head toward him. "I would do nothing to hurt you. I would never have sold you to anyone except myself. My sweet, I was on my way to the Congregational House to ask you to be my wife."

"I do not believe you."

"Believe it." He leaned over and kissed her gently on the brow and wiped her tears.

She sat up and pulled away from him, still staring at the injury she had made on his face. She wanted so to believe him; she wanted to think that he loved her and that he wanted to marry her for that reason alone. But as she looked in his eyes, she didn't dare ask if it were true.

Reaching up to touch the dried blood on his cheek, she said, "I am sorry I hurt you. I was afraid."

Leaning over to kiss her again, he said, "I understand, *ma petite.*" He stroked her cheek. "I will go talk now to Standing Eagle and soon you will be free to return with me."

"Return? Where?"

"Ville-Marie. My father's estate." He took her hand in hers. "You will wed me, will you not?"

Genevieve pressed her lips together and nodded. "But what of—?" she waved her hand toward the camp of Indians.

"I will take care of them, my sweet. Have no fear." He turned and started to slide out of the wigwam.

"No, wait. Don't leave me, Philippe. Please."

He reached over again. "My darling, I shall not leave you again, but I must talk to Standing Eagle and free you. And then we will leave."

"Kiss me, please."

He pulled back into the wigwam and drew her into his arms, kissing her brow, kissing her lids and her cheeks. And then his lips touched hers, parting her lips as he took her into him, showing her the passion and the happiness that he felt at finding her. She clung to him for a moment more, hugging him and crying.

"It will be all right, my sweet. I promise. I will be but a few moments."

She nodded and, releasing him, she watched him slide out from under the flap as he disappeared back into the forest. Picking up her darling Alexandre, she hugged him, stroked him, and continued crying.

It wasn't long before Genevieve heard

the words of Lancelot's French outside the wigwam and, imperfect as it was, it sounded like coming home. Unable to restrain her curiosity, she peeked through the flap, not caring about the guard anymore. Lancelot was soon joined by Philippe and then Annette. Genevieve wanted to laugh at her friend's costume—the other girl looked so comical—but decided she had best not.

There was fire in Philippe's eyes as he called for Standing Eagle to come out of his lodge, and he repeated his command both in Huron and in French as many of the tribe stopped what they were doing to watch.

Slowly, the flap to the other tent opened and the tall chief emerged.

"What is it you want, Frenchman?"

"I want the woman."

"You cannot have her. She is mine. I bought her."

"*Non*, you could not have. She belongs to me."

Anger began to well up in Genevieve's body and at her side, she clenched her fist. She belonged to no one! She realized then that it was only Philippe's way of obtaining her freedom. At least, she hoped he did not believe that she was his possession.

"She was sold to me." Standing Eagle stepped forward, his hand on the knife hanging from his belt.

"By who?"

Genevieve held her breath, not wanting to hear the answer and yet having to know.

"By who?" Philippe repeated. " 'Twas not by me, I'll warrant, because I did not arrive in town until after you left."

Still, Genevieve waited. Finally, Standing Eagle said, "The trader said she belonged to him. I gave him all my furs for her and she is to be my second wife."

"You were cheated, then," Philippe said. Seeing the men gathering behind their chief, he added, "I will give you from my furs what you have paid. But I wish to have the woman back. She is mine."

There was a silence as the chief motioned something to the guard and the flap of her wigwam was lifted.

"Come," the guard said.

Scrambling to her feet, Genevieve grabbed Alexandre and ducked her head under the opening as she emerged from the wigwam for the first time since she'd arrived.

"Red Feather," the chieftain called her name.

She looked in his direction.

"You will answer when I speak to you, squaw."

"I am not yet your squaw."

He grunted. "No, but on the morrow

you will be."

She continued to stare at him a moment before she turned her eyees to Philippe.

"Do you belong to him? Are you his woman?"

There was a moment's pause. Genevieve swallowed her pride and then nodded. "*Oui*. I am."

"You told me you belonged to no one. How can that be? How do you come to be his woman?"

She blushed hotly, not knowing what to say and not wishing to lie. If she said they were already wed, then he would wonder why she had been roaming the streets that day. And how could she have said she did not belong to anyone? The whole assembly of women and men waited, as did Philippe. She glanced at Annette and the answer came to her. "I am his woman because I have shared his bed."

"That is true?"

She blushed again, nodding, unable to look Philippe in the eyes, unable to let him know that she did, indeed, wish to share his bed, and the fact that he had now asked her to marry him made no matter. Her weeks of captivity and these last few moments had taught her that she needed to express her love for him—however it was to be.

The old man from the council now spoke up. He was obviously wiser than the chief. "Does that make you his woman?"

Genevieve looked at Philippe, not knowing what to say. The chief answered for him. "In white man's land, I do not think it does. If the great St. Clair wishes to have Red Feather for his woman then he must fight me. We will fight until first blood."

"No!" Genevieve cried out. "That is not right. You did not buy me fairly."

" 'Tis all right, *mignonne*," Philippe said, soothingly. "We will fight and I will win you and then there can be no excuses." He turned to the chief. "But if I fight and win, I do not have to pay you for her."

"Agreed." Standing Eagle nodded. "If you lose, you must leave and she will be my squaw."

Philippe nodded as slowly he undid his shirt and vest.

"But you are hurt already," she protested, staring at the cut she had given him earlier.

"I am fine, Genevieve. Go inside the tent. You and Annette both."

"No. I will not."

"Then be silent."

Genevieve nodded.

"Think you I wish to miss a good fight?" Annette commented as she hurried over to Genevieve's side.

One of the Indians began pounding on the drums as Philippe now removed his boots and indicated that Standing Eagle must take off his moccasins. Neither had any weapons as they paused, arms extended, ready to fight, and the rhythm of the drum invaded the air and then quieted.

Each silently circled the other, looking for the best moment to breach his defenses.

It was the Indian who kicked out first.

Ducking, Philippe missed his footing, falling forward slightly as Genevieve gasped and held tight to Annette's arm at her side.

"*Ma foi*! Do not kill me as well as him."

Absentmindedly, Genevieve nodded and released her friend's forearm. "Please, dear Lord," Genevieve prayed, unable to take her sight from Philippe, unable to think about anything but his safety. She loved him. She knew that and as long as they were to be married, it didn't matter that he did not love her as much. She would make him love her, make him care for her. 'Twas the only way. But it could not be if he lost, for she knew that if he fell, Philippe would be honorable, as much as it might hurt him. He would go his way and leave her to Standing Eagle.

The men circled again and, this time, Philippe's fist landed squarely on the Indian's jaw, although he received a blow himself at the same time.

"Oh, Annette, I cannot look! I cannot see him hurt."

"Have faith, sweetings. Philippe will be fine." She patted the other girl's arm. "As will you."

"I do not know." Genevieve shook her head.

"You're the one who believes in God. Then believe in Him," Annette scolded as she turned her attention back to the fight.

Genevieve put her hand on the cat at her side, but Alexandre stiffened. He'd been watching the fight as eagerly as she, his eyes darting back and forth as each man moved, ducked, and hit. Then suddenly, he began to hiss as a movement in the bush startled him. His back arched and his claws sprang out.

Before Genevieve could stop the cat, Alexandre had run into the circle and leaped up into the face of Standing Eagle, surprising him into falling to the ground with scratches on his face.

The Indian threw the animal off him, sending him to the ground with a force that might have killed any other, but Alexandre leaped up again, hissing and clawing as Philippe stopped his circling motion and called to the pet.

Calming down, Alexandre walked over to Philippe, rubbing his back against the man's legs.

" 'Twould seem the cat knows more about you than do I, Standing Eagle."

"What do you mean?" The Indian asked, his eyes narrowing as he wiped the blood from his face.

"I could call it a draw now and be gone with the woman, but that would not be fair, would it?"

"*Non.* It would not."

"Then why was your archer waiting for a signal from you? Were you planning on having me hit when you were down and making it seem as if I had fallen from your blows? Or were you planning just to kill us?"

"No, I—" The Indian looked at the cat, hissing again as Standing Eagle made to move, and then he nodded. "Go! Take the woman! Be gone. I never wish to see you again."

Philippe stood up with the cat in his arms and shrugged. "Lancelot, get the small bundle from the canoe."

"But, Philippe—"

"Do as I say, Lancelot. Standing Eagle may not play fairly, but I do. He has paid good fur for Genevieve and it is only right that I reimburse him."

Shrugging, Lancelot disappeared into the grove of trees as Genevieve ran to

Philippe's side, hugging both him and the cat.

"Oh! I love you! I love you both!" She cried as tears of joy streamed down her face. "You are unhurt?"

Philippe nodded. "All but one scratch, on my cheek."

She flushed. "For that I am sorry."

"Come, no regrets." He leaned down, kissing her fully on the lips as many of the tribe around them applauded. Then pulling away from her quickly, he took her hand. "I know, *mignonne*, that you do not like lies. Therefore, we must do something about what you said earlier."

His hand brushed away the hair from her face as he saw the concern in her eyes. "Do not worry. I know where there is a Jesuit at a nearby village. We will get him to marry us, eh?"

She smiled up at him through the tears that still veiled her vision and nodded.

24

As they headed away from the Indian
camp, Genevieve could hardly believe
everything that had happened. She still
did not understand how they had found
her, and the fact that Annette was now,
despite her former protests, wed to
Lancelot surprised her even more.

"I did it for you, sweetings."

"Me?"

Genevieve slipped her big toe into the
river near where they had camped and
quickly pulled back, shivering. But she
needed to wash not only her clothes but
herself as well. The stink of the Indian
camp had appalled her and she wondered
how she must appear to Philippe and the
others.

"*Oui*, my friend, you did not think I
was going to let you come on this

adventure by yourself did you?"

"Some adventure." Genevieve began scrubbing her gown against the rock and was relieved to see the color returning to it as the dirt and grime washed out. "I do not think it was an adventure."

"Well, it was better than staying in that boring place. Imagine no dancing, no singing, no music of any kind except in the chapel!" Annette made a face. "Anyway, the sisters and I did not get along very well, especially after you disappeared."

"What did I have to do with it?"

Annette shrugged. "They thought you a witch because of your cat. Or mayhap they thought him the devil. I do not know. All I do understand is that the sisters seemed heartily glad to see the last of Alexandre and since I was your friend, they believed me tainted, too."

Genevieve turned to her cat, who sat on the water's edge, cleaning himself in his own fashion. "My poor baby," she paused. "But Annette—marriage?"

The other girl shrugged again as she slid into the river. "The foolish sisters said they could not let me leave unless I was wed. As it was, they were not pleased that I choose Lancelot."

"Well, who were you expected to choose?"

"Philippe," Annette said as she dived under the water, her hair floating up above so she could not hear Genevieve's cry of surprise.

Not willing to let Annette escape with such a statement, Genevieve jumped into the river, forgetting the chill, and breathless, swam to the rock where Annette had pulled herself up.

"What did you mean by that?"

"What I said. The sisters wanted me to marry Philippe because he is a Frenchman."

"And what did Philippe say about that?" Genevieve's teeth chattered as she looked back toward the water.

"What do you think he said, *ma coeur*?" There was laughter in Annette's voice.

Genevieve stared into the water. "I do not know. He has said he wants to wed me, but 'twould seem that his problem—I mean, all he needs a wife for is to keep his license." She paused, still not looking in Annette's direction. "I do not think it matters to him who he weds."

"Well you think wrong, *mignonne*." Philippe's deep voice startled Genevieve. She turned, then, gasping, jumped back into the frigid waters.

She emerged sputtering. "What are you doing here? I thought Annette was with me."

"She was."

"But you—"

"*Ma petite*, we are to be man and wife soon. Surely, my seeing you now should not matter."

"But it is too soon. It goes against all ..." Her hands covering her breasts, she sank down, trying to hide her exposed flesh.

"Against all what?" Philippe said, stripping off his breeches.

"Please." Genevieve closed her eyes not wanting to see him. "Go away."

She winced at the sound of the splash as he jumped into the water with her, and she peeked through her half-closed lids to see that he was treading water only a few feet from her. "Can you not wait?"

"Genevieve, I am in the water and I am hidden from sight now, as are you." He touched her hand, drawing it away from her breast. "Come. Let us swim a bit. I need refreshing as much as do you."

Hypnotized by his eyes, made dizzy by the spinning depths to which his gaze led her, she nodded, and for a moment they swam together.

To her own shame, Genevieve found herself looking in his direction, trying to see beneath the surface of the water, wondering what it would be like to touch him, to press herself to him.

"I must rest," she said, pausing by the rock again. "All that walking tired me out."

He shrugged and leaned against the rock with her. "In truth, Genevieve, you are the one I wish to marry. Even had Annette wished me, she is not the one I want."

"Why not? She is pretty and she"—Genevieve lowered her eyes—"she knows how to please a man. Whereas I know nothing."

"Then I will teach you, my little cat. You are the one I want."

Before she could respond, he leaned over and drew her into his arms, kissing her tenderly upon the brow. When he saw that she didn't resist, his lips trailed over her lids, down her cheeks, touching the pulses of her neck. He whispered her name as he nibbled her ear and Genevieve did not know if the chills were from the water or from her response to him, but she found herself clinging closer to him, wanting the warmth from his body as a strange moan seemed to come from some strained creature.

His lips met hers and she could taste the freshness of the water, and the sweetness of him, as her arms went around his neck, massaging the muscles there. She pressed herself even closer so that now she could feel his hardness touching her skin, tantalizing her.

The moan was his this time as he stroked her erect nipples and, placing his mouth gently over one, he sucked delicately while his hand toyed with the other. She shivered again and again, wondering at this strange desire for him that swept over her body like one of the waves and threatened to engulf her.

His hands continued to search, trailing down her body, teasing her senses and, confused, she tried to push away but only succeeded in pulling him closer.

As his hands cupped her bottom, she could feel his manhood touching her very core, stroking her outer lips.

"Philippe . . . I . . ."

"Hush, my love. 'Twill be all right."

"No." Tears were in her eyes now. She wanted him. How badly she wanted him—and how scared she was! If she begot a child, would she die as her mother had, as her aunt had? "No, I cannot."

With all the power she could muster, she dived down, escaping his arms, and swam toward the other shore, crying all the while.

"Genevieve!" he called out to her. "Genevieve, my love, I will not hurt you."

She could only shake her head and run from him.

"So?" Annette asked, sitting beside her in the makeshift tent that Lancelot had devised for the two women. "Did you talk with Philippe?"

Genevieve glared at Annette. She didn't know wether to be angry or glad. A turmoil of confused emotions boiled up within her as she let out the first tears. "Oh, Annette, I am so stupid, and so foolish. I shall never be able to please him. He is probably hoping that we never find the priest, that—" She shook her head. "I cannot wed him, or any man fearing—fearing the night as I do."

"Hush, sweetings," the older girl held Genevieve. " 'Tis not the night you fear, but the act of love and, indeed, it can be love. I can testify to that."

"But what you said before, on the boat . . . ?"

Annette shrugged. "What I said on the boat is still true. There are many men who would poke and stick their thing in you and care nothing of your pleasure. But I do not think your Philippe is like that. Certainly, he cannot be if he is Lancelot's friend."

Still crying, Genevieve shook her head. " 'Tis not only the act I fear, but after. I have told you how my mother died and my aunt. I fear the same will happen to me."

"And if it does?" Annette shrugged. "Life is meant to be lived. Did you not learn anything from yhour kidnapping?"

She was silent a moment and then nodded. "*Oui*, I learned that I was very hurt when I thought Philippe had betrayed me and sold me. And when he came and told me he had not, I realized that I was so hurt because I did love him and wanted to give myself to him. But Annette—"

"There are no buts. I have told you, there are ways to prevent conception. If you wish, I will teach them to you, but you know as well as I do that Philippe would very much like a son."

"Has he told you?"

"*Non*, he has not," Annette shook her head. "But Lancelot has told me that he does wish for my belly to grow round and full with his child, and I am sure that Philippe, if he is a man like his friend, would wish the same."

Genevieve sighed heavily. "Perhaps I would feel differently if we were wed."

"I think not. If you love him, then you love him. Surely, a small paper cannot matter that much."

"But in the eyes of God—"

"In the eyes of God, as I see it, Genevieve, you are wed the moment you become his woman."

"Then you are a bigamist." A smile came to Genevieve's lips.

Annette smiled back. "*Oui*, I suppose I am."

The evening meal cleared away,

Genevieve went to look for Philippe.

"I believe he is gone to the river," Lancelot told her.

"To swim?"

He shrugged. Genevieve made her way through the brush to the river's edge where they had been that afternoon.

Philippe was not swimming, but was seated on the rock, staring into the waters. Silently, she came and sat down beside him.

For a moment neither of them said anything. Then they both spoke at once. "I am sorry," each said.

And they both laughed.

He leaned over and touched her cheek. "Truly, my sweet Genevieve, I am sorry. I did not mean to press you today. It was only seeing you in the water like that. I am a man."

"I know." She hung her head. "And I am sorry, too, for I do not think I am the wife for you."

Startled, he drew away from her, and in the deepening shadows stared into her eyes.

"Philippe, why do you look at me that way?"

"Because I do not believe you."

She averted her gaze and looked at the water swirling beneath her feet. "Why not? It is true. I do not love you."

"Must one love to wed? I do not

believe more than one tenth of the women who came with you now love their new husbands."

"But for me, love is necessary." Her voice was strained as she refused to look at him. "I am sorry. You will find someone else to wed."

He turned away from her for the moment and she wondered if she had hurt him, but when he spoke again, his voice showed no emotion. "What if we wed merely for the sake of it and I let you stay in Ville-Marie? You need not even be with me." He paused. "In truth, you know I do not like this idea of marriage, especially since I will have to leave you much of the time to hunt and trap, but it is these damn laws and these damn nobles who make the laws, who think they are God that they can control our lives. Since I must have my license to sell, and since the authorities insist, I suppose if you will not have me, I must find another."

"Yes," she said, upset that he could cast her off so quickly when she had hoped for some argument. It had to be true, then. He did not love her. He wanted her only, as he said now, to keep his license.

"No, when I wed, I wish it to be for love."

His move was sudden as he took her trembling face into his hand and forced her to look into his eyes. "You cannot say that you have no feeling for me, *ma cherie*, for if you say that, then I know you lie." Taking her hand in his, her eyes unable now to look from him, he began to kiss her fingers one by one, and felt her trembling within.

"You cannot lie to me, my little cat. If what you feel for me is not love, then I know not what it is."

She felt his eyes go into her very soul. "I am afraid, Philippe." She spoke now as if in a trance. "My mother and my aunt . . ."

He leaned over and kissed her cheek gently, tenderly. "I know, my pet. Annette has told me. 'Tis about time you confessed to me. It is not good to have secrets with me." His hand stroked her cheek and her neck, creating in her the same desire as before. "But you need not fear childbirth, *mignonne*. If you wish, we can wait for child. I do not need to have a son."

"But Lancelot—"

"Is Lancelot. And I am me."

She sighed and shook her head. "There is much you do not know about me. There is much I should tell you."

He shrugged. "So, you will tell me, and I will learn. But need that prevent us from getting married on the morrow or whenever it is that we find the priest? Surely, whatever you must tell me cannot be so dreadful."

He picked up her hand again, kissing her palm and keeping her prisoner with his eyes. "As long as you do not lie to me, there will never be a quarrel between us. 'Tis dishonesty, especially the dishonesty of those damned nobles, that I abhor."

She looked deep into his eyes and wondered how he would react when he learned of her lies, when he learned she was part of that damned nobility.

"So, *ma petite*, do you become my wife?"

He leaned over and kissed her and as their lips met, her desire for him overcame her caution, and she nodded.

"Good. Then that is settled."

Genevieve stared at him, surprised that he pulled away so quickly.

"Do you not want—?"

"*Non*, my little cat, I will be content to wait, for each day I want you my desire grows and I know that I shall be more ready and willing to pleasure you when that moment comes. I want your enjoyment, not mine alone. When you are ready, you will show me your love. It was wrong of me to demand it today."

"But I wish to give you my love now." Her hand touched his cheek where the mark of her anger still remained.

"No"—he shook his head—"You do not. You are afraid still, for I can tell from your trembling, and it is not the trembling I felt when I kissed you."

He took her hand and drew her up. "Come. We have left the lovebirds alone long enough. We will return and I will wait until you are truly ready to be my wife."

She stared after him as he headed up the path, and she prayed that she could make him love her before he found out her hidden truths.

25

Lancelot shook his head as he came out of
the little hut in the midst of the clearing.
His eyes were moist from his tears and
Philippe pushed the women gently off to
the side while he joined his friend inside.

"What is it? Why cannot we not go in
and wait for the priest?" Annette asked.
"Surely, 'twould be best to wait inside
than roast out here."

Genevieve sighed. She had heard
enough of what the Indians could do. She
did not need to see for herself what they
had done to the priest who was to marry
them. "I do not think we shall be seeing
the priest, Annette. It would appear, from
what your husband and Philippe say, that
the good father has gone." Turning, she
sought the shade of a nearby tree.

Annette stared after Lancelot who had again disappeared inside and she could hear them working—digging it appeared. She frowned, then shrugged. "Death is part of life. I suppose you will wait till Ville-Marie to be wed then, yes?"

"It is what Philippe wants."

"And will you wait until then to warm his bed?"

Genevieve blushed. "I do not know. Yes, I suppose."

"*Sang Dieu*! How can you enjoy life if you do not live it? Believe me, little one, Philippe loves you."

"He does not say so. He talks only of his need to marry and of his hatred for those in office who have made this silly law."

Annette sighed. "He will be good to you. I am sure."

"Until he finds out who I am."

"Then you do not tell him."

"Annette, I cannot be like that. He has said what he hates worse than the nobility is dishonesty—and I am both."

"*Hélas*! If you are trying to be someone else, then you must forget what you were and who you were."

"How can I?" She stroked the cat at her side, holding back the tears.

"I guarantee, *mon coeur*, when you have made love to a man like Philippe, all other thoughts will leave your head.

Forget your fears and push them from you. He loves you and will continue to love you. But I see the signs. The more you push him away, the more he will wonder, and the more he will question. If you wish him not to think you hide some more terrible secret, you must take him into you and let him know you."

Genevieve's hand on the cat was unsteady as she looked up to her friend. "I do not know what to do."

Annette shook her head. " 'Tis not difficult. I warrant he will show you what you need to do to please him. She looked back to where the men were digging the grave for the dead priest. "Come." Annette stood and started to walk back to the river. "I will tell you all you need to know and then you must promise me that you will give yourself to him. 'Tis evident from your eyes that it is what you want. I see you look at him with longing like a lost soul."

"And do you see him looking at me?"

"Truly, my pet, I do. If he loves you as I believe he does, surely he will forgive you."

Genevieve's voice choked in her as she saw Philippe's shadow outlined in the clearing. "I pray he will." She forced her head up. "Tell me, please, what I need to know and I promise you, I will make him happy."

" 'Tis you and he who should be happy," Annette said. And sitting Genevieve down near the canoe, far away from the scene of death, she began to explain the facts of lovemaking to her friend.

The nights were growing colder, and as they continued to trek north, back to the Isle of Montreal, Genevieve looked toward Philippe's apparently sleeping form many times and once even made a move toward him, but then stopped. She knew what she had promised Annette, yet words were far easier than deeds, and although she wanted to believe that he would love her even when he knew the truth about her, she could not bring herself to the final moment of giving, for fear that in the end he would reject her.

Philippe's coughing began insidiously, as most of those illnesses did.

"You are all right, Philippe?" Genevieve asked, bringing him the hot drink.

"I am fine." He smiled at her and turned toward the fire to get its heat.

"Perhaps you would like me to keep you warm this night?"

He smiled tenderly at her. "Only if you wish to, my little cat. I do admit you would be far better at cuddling than your Alexandre there."

She looked at the cat. "What? Has he been leaving my side at night and coming to you?"

Philippe forced a laugh. "Do not be angry with the animal, my pet. You forget I am sleeping nearest the fire."

"*Oui*. And for that reason, too, I shall sleep with you."

He shrugged and lay back to close his eyes.

"How much farther is it to your home?"

" 'Tis not my home, but my father's." His eyes clouded momentarily. "We have but two days' journey. No more than three, certainly." He closed his eyes once more and rested his head.

Genevieve stared at him a moment, then touched his fevered brow. Her eyes darted to the scar still on his cheek and she knew then that his illness was caused by the cut she gave him. And she knew that if he died, she would never forgive herself for not loving him the way she told herself she would. "Oh, Philippe," she said, resting her head on his chest, knowing that he was already sound asleep. "I do love you and I promise I shall do all in my power to make you happy."

With difficulty the trio managed to carry Philippe to the canoe that morning. They were an odd lot—one Indian, two women, one ill white man and one cat—who docked near the Seigneury de St. Clair on the far side of the Isle of

Montreal.

Immediately, the Honorable Jean-Pierre welcomed the group and took them in as he sent one of the *habitants* to the town for the physician to come bleed his boy.

"*Non*, I will not let that be done," Genevieve said, as she sat guard next to Philipe's fevered body. "I have seen too many people die from the bloodletting. In Joigny—" She blushed and stopped. "I mean, in my town, there were two people that I know of who died of the weakness brought by bloodletting."

The physician turned to the Seigneur, then looked at Genevieve with the air of one who knew much better. "My dear young woman—"

"No, it is fine," said Jean-Pierre. "Do not bleed him, as the girl says. Give us the proper medication for him and be gone. If he is not better in a week's time, then we will reconsider."

"But your excellency, I beg of you. This foolish chit is but a peasant girl and knows not of what she speaks. I have learned at the court of Louis himself."

Genevieve gasped.

The doctor gave her a haughty look, obviously believing that she had been impressed by his statement.

"Then you will allow me to bleed him."

"No." She shook her head slowly. "No, I say." She continued to stare at him and realized that he was indeed the physician who had cared for Madam LeCont before she mysteriously died. There had been an inquest into the woman's death, for she had had many enemies at court, but nothing out of the ordinary could be found. Still, no one had been surprised when the doctor had left for the colonies where, he said, his work would be more appreciated. By no means was she going to let her darling Philippe into this man's hands.

No sooner had the Seigneur and the doctor left the room than Jean-Pierre returned to see her sponging his son's brow with all the tenderness of a woman in love.

"Please, my dearest father-in-law to be, do not let that doctor near Philippe. I beg you."

The Seigneur shrugged. "He is the best in Ville-Marie. But surely you have a reason for saying that."

"*Oui.*" She took a deep breath and looked at her sleeping darling. "In France, my family"—she paused, not knowing how to phrase this without exposing herself—"we lived near the court and I—that is, we—often assisted with affairs there." She blushed. "That is, we served those who did."

Jean-Pierre nodded. "Go on."

"There were several deaths at which Monsieur le Docteur attended and while I cannot say as a certain fact that he is responsible . . ." She looked up at the older man.

"What you say is serious."

"I know. And I pray that I am wrong. But please, let me take care of Philippe in my own way."

"Very well. For one week. But I do not support your suspicion about the physician, my dear. He has cured many in the colony and will, I believe, cure many more."

Genevieve continued throughout the week to sit by Philippe's bed, sponging him, wiping the pus which now appeared on his cheek wound, keeping his linens dry and the room's fire constant. Several times a day she would dab his lips with water and when he swallowed once, she rejoiced. But his eyes did not open.

"Oh, Philippe, please get well. You saved me and I have repaid you only with pulling away from you. If you get well, I will be yours—in every way." She touched his hand, still burning with fever, and leaned over to kiss his brow, feeling his breath hot on her cheek as tears moistened her eyes. He would get well. He had to.

The week was up and he had not yet

improved.

Closing her eyes for just a moment so that she could rest, Genevieve felt the presence of another in the room. It amazed her to open her eyes and see the cat sitting on the bed with Philippe.

"Alexandre! How did you get in here?"

The cat meowed and, jumping off the bed, he ran to the window's ledge. Genevieve stared at the opening. She was sure all the windows in the room had been sealed. Again, she looked at the cat. Was he, as the sisters claimed, part witch?

She had no time to think on the matter for something else drew her attention—the color in Philippe's face was pinkish. Quickly, she crossed the room to him and touched his brow.

His forehead was cool! And as her hand rested on his skin, his hand came up to touch hers.

"Philippe!" She jumped. "You are better!"

He smiled at her, his eyes clear. "I am." His lips touched her hand. "Much thanks to you."

"How do you know? You have been sleeping all this time."

He shrugged. "I heard your voice. I have heard you talking with my father."

She eyed him suspiciously. "What else did you hear?"

Philippe's hand still covered hers. "Do you still wish to wed me?"

Genevieve blushed, then nodded.

"*Merveilleux*! Go fetch Papa then and tell him to get Father Raoul."

"But you are not well yet."

His hand touched her face. "For you, *ma petite*, I am well. But you, you must go tell my father and then you will rest and tomorrow . . ." He smiled up at her, his eyes twinkling in the light of the sun. Forcing her fears down, she smiled back.

The wedding was to be two days later, for not only did the priest have to get ready, but Jean-Pierre wanted not only that all the *habitants* be invited, but all his friends from the city as well.

" 'Tis too bad we cannot get those from Quebec to come."

"*Oui*," Philippe responded, the first time he ate downstairs with the rest of the family, across the table from his step-mother. "I am sure the Intendant would love to come." His gaze flitted to Genevieve's and she blushed. "But I for one do not wish to wait. So we wed this week. And then I return to the forest."

Genevieve's mouth dropped. "To the forest?"

"*Oui*."

"But you cannot trap well in the

winter. Even I know that the animals hibernate."

He shrugged and, ignoring a stare from Eugenia, got to his feet. "I will rest now and I suggest you do the same, Genevieve. Tomorrow will be a long and tiring day."

But unable to sleep, and wanting to convince Philippe that he was not only too ill to leave so soon, but that wherever he was she planned to be, she left her own bed and with the candle in her hand started for his room, only to stop in the chilled hallway when she saw the heavy velvet of his step-mother's robe dusting the edge of his doorway as the oak silently closed.

Heart hammering, Genevieve stood in the cold hall, scarcely feeling herself shivering as she stared numbly at the wooden door, and thought of Philippe, and her, and his step-mother.

26

The traditional, white beribboned dress was brought over from the house of the Congregational sisters; the nuns expressed their happiness that Genevieve was safely returned to the bosom of her friends. Genevieve couldn't help noticing, though, how they eyed Alexandre, perched on the fence and watching with his keen gaze as they passed into the house.

From her bedroom, she could hear the murmur of people gathering outside the house, where the wedding would take place. So pleased was Jean-Pierre that his son was marrying a Frenchwoman that he had spared no expense on this joyous occasion. Not only were all the *habitants* who worked the land invited, along with the famous fiddles and flutes, but so was everyone in Ville-Marie who was willing to travel the few hours to reach the estate.

Genevieve looked out the window as canoes and small boats filled with people pulled up to the riverfront entrance, and she heard the neighing of the horses of those arriving via land.

"Stand still, will you?" Annette cursed. "How can I finish this tuck if you do not co-operate?"

Genevieve sighed and did as her friend requested.

"Is something the matter, pet? You do not look happy. I would think you would be glad for this day. After all, once you are wed here, there is no way that Racine can come for you. And since you will now be Madame St. Clair, anyone trying to trace you will have a far more difficult time."

"Perhaps." Genevieve winced as one of the pins stuck her.

"Surely, you cannot be concerned about this night. You know that Philippe will be gentle."

"I do hope so." Her voice had a faraway quality to it.

"Well, what is wrong then? I have instructed you in all the arts of pleasing a man. You need only follow his lead. I am sure he will tell you what pleasures him as well."

Tears now came to Genevieve's eyes. "Think you that he will?"

"And why should he not?"

"Because he is not pleased with me. Because he is marrying me only to please his father, to keep his license."

"Pshaw! That is the silliest thing I have yet heard. I tell you, Genevieve, I have seen how he looks at you when you do not notice, and I have seen, too, how you look at him. If this night is not filled with glorious passion for you, then I will eat this dress."

Genevieve smiled slightly, but the sadness was still in her tone. "Perhaps he is yet in love with another and the look you see is when he thinks of her."

"Then why does he not marry this other woman?"

"Perhaps she is already taken."

Annette looked at her strangely. "Is there something you have learned that you're not sharing?"

Turning to look out the window again, Genevieve saw Philippe down below walking with Lancelot. She saw Eugenia coming over to join the men, dressed in silks that rivaled anything Genevieve had seen in Versailles. She heard the woman's laughter float up as she conversed animatedly with the men.

"No." Genevieve's heart was heavy as she shook her head. "I only think that perhaps, with another woman, he might be happier."

"Do not act so silly. I tell you, he loves you."

Even as Annette spoke, Philippe looked up towards her. He smiled as she quickly disappeared back into the room, for it was bad luck for the bridegroom to see the bride before the moment of the wedding.

Only as the fiddler began to play and Annette led her friend down the stairs did Genevieve's fears return. But she vowed to forget Eugenia and think only of her love for Philippe.

The wedding ceremony was the same as the one she had heard repeated over and over for the other King's Daughters. Lost in her own worries, she heard her name being called.

"Genevieve Claudine Bopar, where is it you hail from?"

"Joigny," she replied, then seeing Annette looking at her strangely, she flushed. "Rather, I come from Evreux. The family I worked with, sir," she told the notary, "lived in Joigny."

He shrugged and crossed out what he had written as Genevieve once more glanced back toward Annette and found Eugenia watching her as well.

Feeling Philippe's eyes upon her, she forced herself to smile at him, praying that she would please him more than his step-mother, that she would be able to take his mind off this other woman.

As the dancing and the music continued into the night, Genevieve was escorted up to Philippe's room, which had been decorated with flowers for the occasion.

"Now, remember, you must not be the first on the bed," Annette told her.

"*Mon Dieu*! Why not?"

"Because the first into bed will be the first to die. My grandmama told me many times about this."

"That is silly. Besides, I would not want to live if Philippe was dead."

"Just heed my warning," Annette told her, "and let him in bed first. 'Twould relieve your mind, I think, that if he is to die first, then you would not die in birthing."

Genevieve pressed her lips together, trying to forget her fears.

It wasn't long before the clashing cymbals heralded Philippe as he came up the stairs.

"I will depart now." Annette hugged the younger girl. "And do not worry so. 'Twill all be fine in the morning, I promise."

Genevieve could only nod as the door handle turned and Philippe stood framed in the doorway. He carried Alexandre in with him. "I thought you would like some company while I prepare myself," he said, smiling at her as he stripped off his shirt and breeches.

Philippe did care about her. At least, he knew her feelings for the animal.

Taking the cat from him, she cuddled the pet and felt the warm roughness of his tongue. How glad she was that she had been able to take him with her, for if it had not been for him, she would surely have gone crazy these past few months. "Do not mind that I will be with someone else tonight, precious boy. My heart will always belong to you, Alexandre."

"I hope not," Philippe said, leaning over and kissing her on the neck. "That is, you are welcome to love the cat as you wish since, I, too, have a fondness for him. But I hope in time you will come to love me more than you do him."

Giving him a tremulous smile, she looked up, unable to believe what she was hearing. She already did love him, probably more than he would ever know, but how could she tell him so, how could she expose her heart to him until she was sure he really felt the same about her and that his words were more than mere words?

"Come, my lovely little wife, it is time for us to bed."

His arms went around her waist, holding her to him so that she could feel his muscles and his readiness touching her. "Do not worry, my little cat lady," he said, nuzzling her ear, "I will not hurt you." He paused, seeing that she was fighting her fears. "I know of your uncle, *ma petite.*"

She gasped and stepped back as the color drained from her face. "How could you! I told no one."

"*Non*, my sweet, you told Annette."

Her face paled. "Yes. Yes, on the boat, I did. But she should not have told you. She should not have—"

"Hush, my love." He grabbed her hand and kissed her palm. "She did what she thought was best. In truth, my dearest, all men are not such brutes."

Tears sparkled in Genevieve's eyes as Philippe leaned over and kissed her lids, taking her fears away.

"Come. Let me show you how wonderful love can be."

Genevieve could only nod as he drew her hand out and led her toward the bed.

"Wait. Is it not right that I get in first?"

He looked at her strangely. "Is that some custom from your town that I know nothing of?"

"I—yes it is." She started toward the bed. But before she could reach it, a streak of black fur zoomed past her and landed in the very center. "Alexandre! This is not for you tonight. You must be a good boy or you will have to leave."

The cat looked at her with his all-knowing eyes and hopped down, settling himself in a nearby chair to watch the proceedings.

Philippe laughed. "*Non*, my lovely wife, I do not relish the idea of being entertainment for the cat." He picked up the animal and quickly scooted him outside. The door closed, he turned to her once more. "Now, we are truly alone."

She swallowed hard and nodded as she drank more of the homemade wine Annette had brought for her earlier. Taking her into his arms, Philippe now kissed her, this time on the lips. Tasting her sweetness mingling with that of the wine as his tongue explored the delicate structure of her mouth, he gently nibbled at her goodness. Roaming her gown, his hands found the opening. She resisted for a moment as his hands touched her bare skin, but he held her tightly, caressing her and soothing her with his words. "My love, do not feel so skittish. You are like a new-born colt. Truly, I will not harm you."

She looked up at him, believing him and wanting him, yet fearing him all the same. She reached for the wine and drank another glass as her body flushed pink.

Philippe waited a moment, then kissed her once more, his hands exploring her body in the same way his mouth explored hers once more, and this time the wine and the love she felt for him flowed from her as she melted in his arms, responding to his kisses with all the pent-up passion she had been feeling since she first met him. As she clung to him, she knew the nightmares about her uncle's touch would harm her no more.

Philippe pulled back slightly. "That is better." He kissed her again, and again she responded. His expert hands undressed her without her even noticing it. As her nightclothes fell from her, he lifted her into his arms and carried her to the bed. It was only then, as his manhood brushed against her, that she noticed that he, too, had shed his breeches and they were together as they had been that day in the river.

"Philippe," she started to say, "there is something I must tell you."

"Yes, my love," he responded, looking into her eyes.

Losing her nerve, she shook her head. "I . . . I want to please you."

He gave a laugh. "Then I'm sure you will." His kiss was more powerful than it had ever been as his fingers trailed down her body and sent shivers up her spine. "Come, let me help you relax and enjoy our first night." He handed her another glass of the wine and watched as she sipped it slowly.

"Have you put something in this? Why is it I feel so strange?"

He laughed again and drew her to him. "*Non*, my princess, it is nothing but homemade wine, but I'll warrant it is quite potent. I trust it will ease your fears away."

"Just being with you will do that," she said, her voice sounding faraway, not quite her own. She cuddled in his arms, willing herself to think only of him now and forever more.

He smiled and kissed the pulse at the base of her neck. She shivered and then he took her hand, kissing each finger, one at a time, and allowed his tongue to trail up her arm, enchanting her. Firmly and gently, he caressed her neck.

"Philippe . . ." she lay her head against his hairy chest.

"Sh, don't talk. Just enjoy." His fingers began to massage her back and she could feel herself becoming one with him. He moved and, near the foot of the bed, he began to massage her feet, relaxing her. Starting with one hand on each ankle, his hands slid up to her buttocks as just a hint of thumbs trailed down between her legs. She squirmed slightly as he moved his magical hands up and down her legs, one at a time, each time coming closer and closer to the cleft, but not touching.

Wanting to do something for him, she turned over and felt the warmth and her desire for him, combined with the wine she had drunk, spreading through her body, and urgently moved her hands as she tried to reach him.

He smiled but said nothing as he moved out of her reach, tantalizing her, and allowed his mouth to settle for a moment to suckle each breast.

"Philippe!" She gasped.

His fingers now slid down between her breasts to her belly and down to each leg, his thumbs trailing lightly between her thighs, pausing for the briefest of seconds as she moaned with his touch. Tingling feelings radiated out to her fingers and toes. Once more she tried to reach out to him, to try to pleasure him as Annette had told her that men liked, but once more he avoided her as now his one hand slid slowly down across her belly. The heel of his hand stopped now on her mound and, pressing firmly, rotated in small, slow circles as her own body responded, answering his urgent need for her.

On their own, her knees came up and opened now to his touch as his hand continued its pressure—unrelenting, insistent, slow circles. All she wanted at that moment was to feel his touch, to know him as her husband, as the waves of pleasure washed over her like the waves on the ship. Never stopping the pressure on her mound, his other hand trailed between her legs and now his fingers lightly touched her other lips, trailing along from front to back, slowly inside just a little, slowly outside and around. Genevieve could feel her own wetness as he increased his pressure on the center of her core and the water of love continued to wash over her. Instinctively, she raised her hips to his hand, rotating her body against his as he moved faster and faster.

"Philippe," she moaned again, as she felt the waves washing over her quicker and quicker, and she imagined that this had to be what birds felt like when they flew for the first time, the dizzying heights of love.

She collapsed, feeling the warm glow spread over her, but wanting to please him even more. He smiled and evaded her grasp again as he continued to hold her in the palm of his hand, lightly continuing to arouse her. Then he bent his head and his mouth kissed her essence, his tongue dancing slow circles the way his fingers had done, moments ago.

"Please," she whimpered. "I want to . . ."

His only response was his sinuous tongue moving gently and firmly, pushing yet another wave over her as his fingers pressed inside of her and she cried out. She was sure she could be heard over the sounds of the music outside, but she did not care. She wanted him and she loved him and she wanted him to love her. Aching for him, she reached out, but once more, he avoided her grasp.

"How do you feel, my lovely one?" His voice was warm and soft as he now nibbled her ear. "Do you wish me to continue?"

"Please, Philippe."

His tongue licked the sensitive parts of her breasts. "You must learn to tell me what you want, *mon coeur*. I cannot read your mind." His mouth started down toward her belly again.

"No. I mean, yes, Philippe, please."

"Then tell me, my little one," he commanded as his hands moved lightly over her body, tingling her, burning her with his desire.

"I want you inside of me."

"Ah, that is what I wanted to hear." He grinned as he kissed her deeply. On all fours now, he let his hands stroke her thighs once more and gently spread her so that his massive manhood was poised at the entrance of her temple.

"You are sure you want this?"

"Yes. Yes, I am sure," she cried, her hips straining to meet him.

His hands cupped her buttocks as,

holding her, he gently slid in, up and down, filling her. She winced momentarily and he paused, but she shook her head. "I love you, Philippe," she whispered, not even sure if he heard her. "I want you within me." He nodded and as he held her, she pushed toward him, wanting to meet him, wanting to give him all the pleasure that he had given her. The momentary pain quickly eased as his nipples rubbed against hers and he leaned down to kiss her mouth again, holding her firmly to him as he delighted her in a way she had never thought possible. And once again the stormy wave overcame her as she clung to him and he clung to her, and they were both washed overboard together as ecstasy shook them, draining all their energy away.

Finally, he collapsed at her side and held her to him as the moment of intense pleasure faded away to the warmth of their bodies.

They continued to doze in each other's arms as the noise of the wedding celebrations continued outside.

Opening her eyes the next morning, she was surprised to find Philippe in her bed, but then with wonderous recall, she remembered all the pleasure of the night before. Indeed, she had not expected such. Had she known sooner that it would be this good, she would have urged him earlier, yet she did not think that being with Racine would have been the same at all. She realized then that she was truly free of her nightmres.

"You are all right, my dove?" he asked, seeing her eyes open.

"I am fine, but I fear you must not be."

"Why is that?"

"Because," she said, peeking under the covers, "you are flat."

He laughed and hugged her to him. "Come." He guided her hand as she touched the soft skin. "I will show you how to make him come alive again."

"And then?" She looked up into his eyes and strained upward to kiss him. "May we make love again?"

"*Ma foi*, I thought you were without experience."

"I am, but I like the experience I had. I do admit my fears were exaggerated." She teased at his manhood, touching his now hard sex and the soft secrets beneath. His smell was more of an aphrodisiac than the wine had been the night before.

His light blue eyes searched her face. "In truth, my dearest, in many cases the pain is not exaggerated. Not all men want their wives to enjoy the act as they themselves do." He rose up slightly on his elbow to kiss her brow, then pushed her damp curls from her cheek. "You did truly enjoy it, did you not, my Genevieve?"

She could only nod, staring at him.

As he smiled, he nodded, and his mouth tantalized her body once again. She squirmed in exquisite pleasure, wanting him, trying to draw him closer to her. Each sensation, heightened by his touch, made her breathless. With tender roughness he now possessed her breasts, her belly, her inner thighs. Genevieve could think of nothing but her hunger for him and her desire to bring him the same pleasure he brought her.

As his hands moved between her thighs, she inched higher, responding to his touch, feeling the passion in the catch of his breath and seeing it in the blue of his eyes. Softly, he whispered his desire for her. And even though he did not say "love," Genevieve pushed her fears away as she sought his lips. This moment of ecstasy was theirs, her body undulating beneath his, moving in time with his thrusts. Arching higher and higher, she strained to be a part of him, and her lips parted with a gasp as she realized he was as ready as she. She welcomed him as they rode the wave like the dolphins she had seen dancing in the sea.

Floating on a cloud of euphoria she knew that he was hers, and nothing Eugenia could do would destroy that.

27

Furious, the Marquis paced in front of the
window of his study as Antoine Le Bera,
the messenger, talked. From below the
study, sounds of screams could be heard
and the messenger winced as the Marquis
paced, his gold stick pounding out a
rhythm on the floor.

"What do you mean, you found out
nothing?"

"All I know, your excellency, is that
she switched places with the Duc's maid-
servant."

"I knew that, fool! I want more
information. I want to know where she is!
And I want her back. Now."

"But Your Excellency, she cannot be
found."

"Then you will question this servant

more. Give her whatever inducements it takes, even to taking care of her new husband." His eyes narrowed at the frightened servant. "Genevieve is mine and I shall have her back, no matter what."

"But what if she has fled?"

"There is nowhere she can go that I will not find her." He went swiftly to the ornate desk in the study. "Here." He scrawled a cheque for several thousand livres. "You break the information from the servant girl this night, you draw this from my banker on Monday, and wherever Genevieve is, you will find her and bring her back to me. At all costs. If you need more, I shall supply it."

The messenger stared at the paper, stunned at the amount, then nodded as the Marquis slammed his account book closed and dismissed him.

As Racine had predicted, it did not take much longer for Claudine to confess her part in Genevieve's escape. Notifying the Marquis that Genevieve was now in the colonies, Antoine took the coach to LeHavre and there waited for the ship to New France.

Staring at the miniature the Vicomte had given the Marquis and the Marquis had given him, Antoine was as taken with the young girl's beauty as the Marquis had been. The roseate tints on her pale cheeks gave her a delicate, almost goddess-like quality, and the soft auburn curls piled about her head were like clouds of colored sugar. Indeed, Antoine thought he'd never seen one so lovely. "If she is truly this beautiful, 'tis no wonder the Marquis wants her." He stroked the painted picture and wondered if there was a way that he could keep the girl for himself.

The estate of St. Clair was calming down now from the wedding celebrations, which had lasted seven days. And while Genevieve had been with her new husband almost constantly since that first night, she now found him to be aloof and distant.

She had not seen Eugenia near him since the day of the wedding, and she did not think that Philippe's step-mother had had any time to make a play for him; certainly Genevieve had kept her husband more than occupied and had herself enjoyed every minute of it. Why, then, was he acting so strangely?

"I swear," she told Annette as they walked near the river bank, "I still do not know if he loves me or not. He cares for me and he pleases me, as I do him, but—" Her voice broke. "I wonder if there is not someone else he cares more about."

"Oh, poo!" Annette threw a stone into the river and they watched the ever enlarging circles it made as it hit the water. "I tell you there is none he loves more than you."

"Then why has he never said he loves me?—except perhaps for whispers when we make love. 'Tis odd, I tell you. I would readily confess my love to him, if he would to me."

Annette shrugged. "I do not think men act that way. I had to tell Lancelot that I wanted him before he could admit he wanted me."

Genevieve shook her head, "I cannot say that until I know."

"Then you may never know, my pet. I think you should talk to him of your fears now, for I do believe he and Lancelot plan to winter in the Huron village."

"Impossible! He's not said anything to me."

"Then ask."

"Most assuredly I will." She turned back toward the house as the evening grew dark. Frost would soon be on their breaths, she thought, and wondered what this wilderness would look like covered in snow.

As she climbed the steps to the room she shared with Philippe, voices alerted her to there being more than just a friendly chattering going on upstairs. Pausing at the rail a moment, she listened to the words of Eugenia and Philippe, and she flushed. Then, not wanting to hear any more, Genevieve did the foolhardy thing of rushing toward their room rather than away.

Only as she neared the top of the stairs did she see her step-mother-in-law, wearing naught but a skimpy robe, leaving the bedroom. Genevieve stopped a moment and stared at the woman who brazenly stared back. Breaking away from her gaze, Genevieve ran into the bedroom to find Philippe preparing his pack.

"What is this? Are we going away? And why was Eugenia in here?"

The words all came out in such a rush that Philippe had to put his arms around her and get her to repeat what she had said.

Tears sparkled in her eyes as she repeated, "Why was Eugenia here?"

His arms dropped from her side. He turned back to the bed to finish his packing.

"She came to say good-bye to me."

"Good-bye? Why? Where are you going?" She hurried to the bed.

He continued to fold his clothes.

"Look at me. Tell me." Genevieve pulled the leather case away from him.

"I am going, *mignonne*. Back to the forest."

"Then I am going with you."

"*Non*. You will stay here. My father

will take care of you."

"How will he take care of me?" The tears were now streaming down her eyes. "Will he warm my bed at night?"

Philippe turned toward her, anger in his eyes. "I will kill him if he touches you."

"Then take me."

"*Non*, you will not like it."

"How do you know what I'd like?" Her hands went to her hips. "You arrogant, insufferable—" Her eyes narrowed. "I don't even know why I love you."

Philippe paused in what he was doing and looked up at her. "What was that you said?"

Flushing, Genevieve repeated, "I said, I don't even know why I love you."

"But you say you do love me?" As he stared at her, his eyes softened and he crossed the room to take her tenderly in his arms.

She nodded.

"And I love you, my little cat. But you do not understand life in the wilderness, living with the Indians. It is much too harsh for one such as you."

She laid her head on his chest. "If you had not rescued me, I would have had to suffer it."

"That is true."

"And what of Annette? She is married to an Indian. Does she go or stay?"

He sighed. "Lancelot wishes to take her, but I disagree."

"Well, if she goes, why can I not?"

He shook his head. "You will find it difficult, my love. And we cannot take your pet. He would have to stay here."

"So he will stay. Your father likes him well enough. True, I will miss Alexandre, but I would miss you more."

"Indeed?"

"Philippe, do not make me beg. I do not wish to stay here in this house without you."

He kissed her brow and then her lids and then her mouth as they joined in their passion. "There is something about you that every time I see you, I am tantalized." He swung her up into his arms and carried her over to the bed. "You see, if you come with me, I shall get no trapping done. I shall spend the whole time in the warmth of the wigwam cuddled up next to you."

Genevieve shrugged and smiled. "I wouldn't mind that."

"No," he said, laughing, "I am sure you would not. But we cannot live on love alone."

"But your father said—"

"I do not care what my father said," he snapped at her. "I am to make my own life in this world. I refuse to be the land-holder he wishes. Emile can be left the lands." He paused. "If he comes back from the mission he is now on, I believe my father will try to get him posted with the *curé* nearby. Or at the very least in the Huron village not far from Lachine." He leaned over and stroked her brow. "I do not want to talk about my family now. I want to make love to you."

"Yes?" Her eyes opened wide, teasing as she put her arms about him and nibbled at his ear lobe. "And I want to make love to you." Their kisses mingled as their bodies strained toward each other, each wanting to give, each wanting to be a part of the other. Touching and stroking, caring and caressing, they floated up onto the magical cloud of love and let their passions carry them away.

Only when they lay in the bed resting, did she ask, "Tell me, please, what was Eugenia doing here?"

Philippe sighed. "She was, like you, upset that I was leaving and she wanted to convince me to stay."

Genevieve's back stiffened. "And how did she try to convince you?"

He kissed her once more. "It does not matter, for neither her words nor her methods would ever work on me."

Genevieve eyed her husband a moment before she dared asked the question. "Does that mean you don't love her?"

"*Sang Dieu*! Where in God's blood did you ever come up with that idea?"

Genevieve looked away. "She—I saw her coming from your room the night before the wedding."

"So that is why you were upset. Annette told me you cried most of the day and she did not understand why."

She nodded as his arms went around her. "*Mignonne.*" His eyes met hers, as his lips grazed hers. "I tell you now that I know how you feel. I do love you and only you. Never have I been enchanted by another woman except Morning Flower, and never had I planned to wed again."

"Do you mean you would have married me even had you not been forced to do so?"

He shrugged. "I would never have met you had I not been forced into it, *ma petite.*" He hugged her closer to him. "Ah, very well, you may come along. But I warn you, 'twill not be the easy life you'd have here."

"As long as I am with you, nothing matters."

Sighing, he blew out the candle and held her and loved her until morning.

28

The Huron village where Lancelot lived, to the south of Ville-Marie, was indeed primitive compared to the luxuries of the St. Clair estate, yet Genevieve did not mind, for she was away from his stepmother, and more important, so was he.

Despite Philippe's order, however, the cat would not stay behind, and within a week after their arrival, a lean and scrawny Alexandre appeared. Genevieve hugged him like a long-lost child, and like a naughty little boy, he squirmed in her arms, preferring to play with the children and interesting things on the ground rather than with his mistress. Philippe reluctantly gave permission for the cat to stay.

As the cold began to seep into the

days and food gathering was curtailed, Genevieve found herself helping the Indian women with the mending, wood gathering, and scraping of the hides for the new blankets and robes that the men would wear. She soon found herself becoming used to the labor of drawing water from the river and the pungent odor of bear's grease, which was used less and less in the winter months.

From the women, she also learned the various herbs that grew in the valley and along the river banks and their uses in cures, and she learned to appreciate the beauty of nature in a way she never had before.

The easy and natural way the Indians had with their children was also something that she liked. "Look how well behaved they are, and how much fun they have when they play," she said to Annette. "I cannot recall having such fun when I was a girl. There were so many rules I had to follow."

"Do you still think of home?"

"Is it not natural?" she asked, pounding the corn into meal as Annette prepared the flat cakes. "But I am quickly forgetting and concentrating only on my life here. In faith," she said as she struggled over preparation of a stew for their husbands, "who would ever have thought I'd be cooking bear?"

"In more ways then one!" Annette laughed, indicating her friend's new costume.

"Do you not like it?"

Annette shrugged. "For me, it does nothing, but I trust Philippe will appreciate it."

"I hope so. Though I am sure the good father, when he passes through, will object vehemently if I wear this in public like a heathen woman. I wonder sometimes if the missionaries are doing the right thing by converting the Indians."

"Do I hear you?"

"Truly, you do. I mean, with few exceptions, those whom I have met who have been convinced by the Jesuits to become Catholics can no longer appreciate the natural arts the way they once did. They now fear hell and the everlasting fires more than would seem necessary, and they have become very solemn. Indeed, 'twould seem they have become different people than the ones who cling to the old ways."

Annette nodded. "Well, I have never much liked religion and you can see how joyous I am."

Genevieve laughed as her loincloth swung about her hips. "Indeed, Pere Marc would have a fit if he could see me now." She indicated her bare breasts and the simple cloth covering her vital parts.

"I am sure he would." Annette smiled. "But I, for one, prefer the leggings for the warmth. Of course, my legs are not as shapely as yours."

Genevieve looked down at her own legs and shrugged, knowing that her friend must be teasing.

"But do not they often come off when you are with Lancelot?" Genevieve put more dried herbs into the boiling cauldron.

The older woman grinned. "Your mind has become as dirty as mine. Who would have thought prim and proper Genevieve would don this costume?"

The new Madame St. Clair shrugged and smiled. "It's all the easier to seduce my husband when I wear this." Her eyes twinkled.

"You had best have a care or what I told you to prevent conception will soon not work."

Once more Genevieve shrugged. "If a child results, then it shall be. I will have to trust in Philippe, and in God, that everything will be all right."

Annette shook her head. "Indeed, marriage has changed you."

"Only that I know I love Philippe and will give him whatever it is in my power to do."

"And will you tell him who you are?"

"If I can." Genevieve averted her eyes

and began to stir the stew on the fire before them. Breaking the moment, she stood. "Here, let me show you what I just made. 'Tis not quite as expert as the other woman can do, but I think it is good nonetheless." She handed Annette the fur mantel she had, with great effort, sewn together. She had done not only the sewing but the curing of the skins and the drying of the leather. "Do you think Philippe will like it?"

"I think Philippe will love it." The voice from the entrance starlted both women, as cold air entered the warmer wigwam, bringing Philippe with it.

Neither noticed as Annette quickly slipping out.

"Genevieve! Oh, my little Genevieve," he whispered, catching her in his arms and tenderly stroking her exposed breasts. "*Ma foi*, I am glad that you have adapted so well. Indeed, I am even happier that you were not one of those prissy Frenchwoman I hear so many of the girls have become."

Genevieve shrugged. "Perhaps their husbands did not care to please them as you please me."

He leaned over and kissed her neck, his hands tantalizing the hard nubs of her areolae so that she could only groan with delight and, turning to face him, kissed him deeply. "I have missed you, my love."

"And I you."

He guided her down to the furry-matted floor as his hands quickly sought her inner sex, caressing her and driving her to a frenzy.

"Oh, Philippe," she gasped. "Do not torment me so! I would rather be tortured by the Indians than to have you withhold your love."

He laughed. "Mayhap, my lady, I should impale you on my hard pole. 'Twould not be a quick death, though, for I would have to thrust many times before I reached your heart."

"Then I am yours to torment, if you indeed plan to kill me that way." She hugged him, and taking him in her mouth, kissed the hard length of his love and tasted his drops of passion as she turned on him, quickly throwing him to the floor and mounting him as she had heard the other women talk of.

"Genevieve!"

She paused. "Do you not like this? The other women said you would."

He laughed, "Ah, so it is the other women's talk. I feared you had tried out your experience with another man while I was gone."

She touched his cheek tenderly. "There is no other man for me but you."

"And that," he said, stroking her buttocks and gently widening the cleft, is how it should be." Tenderly, he pulled her down upon him, riding together with her, until they both reached the peak of their love and rode the wave till moans of pleasure escaped from each of them.

His hand stroked her exhausted brow. "Do you know, I am glad you wanted to come along. In fact, each day I think I love you more and more."

Genevieve's hand caressed his hairy chest. "And I you."

"Would you be content to live in this village, with my Indian friends, for the rest of our natural lives?"

"If it is your wish, I would."

Philippe kissed the tip of her nose. "That is what I hoped to hear." He reluctantly stood and drew her up with him, rubbing his bare body against hers and kissing her again. "I would love to spend the rest of the night with you, but I came in merely to say that I was called to the chief's lodge, for his daughter is to chose her man this night and I am requested to be present."

"Why? She cannot chose you." Genevieve's breath caught as her old jealousy surfaced.

Gently, he pushed the hair from her brow. "*Non*, she cannot chose me because I have you and you have been made an honorary member of the tribe, as have I. But I wish you to come and see the ceremony, for it will be something you will enjoy."

She nodded. "I enjoy just being with you, my love." And taking the leggings and embroidered shirt that she wore when not alone with him, she quickly dressed.

The lodge was filled with everyone from the tribe, and the women squeezed into the corner watched the men pass the ritual pipe and the Medicine Man perform the elaborate dance to bless the new month and ask for much food for the coming winter. Seated behind her husband, Genevieve laid her head on his shoulder. It had taken a few moments for her to adjust to not only the smoke of the pipes, but to the smell of unwashed bodies pressed into the small area. Even now it did not please her, but if Philippe could stand it, so could she.

"And now," Chief Running Feet said, "we must talk of our future generations." He looked to the girl seated at his right and then toward several of the young warriors.

"Kio Diego, Man who Settles Disputes, who do you think I shall give my daughter to in marriage?"

Surprised, Philippe stood. "Who do you wish to give her to, my chief?"

The old man smiled. "Both men are worthy opponents and both have won many battles."

"But your daughter has one heart only. Where does she wish it to be given?"

"Ah, you are wise and you are right." He motioned his hand upward and the young girl rose to stand in front of her father, her back to the tribe. "White Rabbit Running, is there one here who has called to you and beckoned you to become his wife?" He paused as she looked around the lodge. "Do not be hasty, my child, for marriage is sacred both by our gods and the god of the Black-Robes. You need wed only where your heart agrees, where the longing calls and cannot be denied."

The girl bowed her head and flushed. "Father, there is one, but he is not among those who have asked for my hand."

Genevieve held her breath as the girl looked in Philippe's direction, and for a moment, she feared that the girl wanted her husband. But instead she motioned to another young brave seated at the edge of the lodge. Genevieve stared at him. He could not be much older than sixteen summers, but then the girl was only fifteen summers herself.

The old chief nodded. "Very well, when he has proven himself, he may ask for your hand. Until then, I can promise nothing."

The girl leaned over to kiss her father as yet another young girl was brought up to choose her mate.

With relief, Genevieve leaned back. "And they are supposed to be savages! France, which claims to be civilized, will allow parents to sell their daughters and marry them off without their permission."

Philippe shrugged. "Then you must see how I value my Indian life here and my freedom, and how I hate the civilized French. 'Tis the nobles in particular I dislike, for they try to rule everything and everyone without a care for anyone else." He took her hand. "But my sweet, you did not run into that trouble, did you?" His eyes met hers. "After all, you wed the man who took your heart."

"*Oui*." she discreetly leaned over and kissed him. "That I did. Only . . ."

"Only what, Genevieve?" His eyes narrowed as he studied her.

" 'Tis nothing." She pulled back to enjoy the rest of the ceremony and the dancing. How was she going to tell him who she was? How could she reveal her secret to him when every time they spoke, he made some scathing comment about the nobility? Perhaps in a while, perhaps after she knew him better, she'd be able to tell him without the fear and worry that he would leave her.

His arm went around hers lovingly, as if to warm her and she, comforted by his touch, leaned her head against his shoulder in a brazen manner. "If you are tired, my pet, we can return to our wigwam."

She smiled up at him and nodded. No, she wasn't tired, but every moment alone with him was golden, for he was so often gone. Once the winters set in, she knew they'd be moving south to the mountainous valleys which would protect them from the howling winds, but that would also mean that he would have to go farther for trapping and hunting food, and that she would have even less time to spend with him. She knew, despite what he said, that he wanted a child as much as Lancelot, and Genevieve had vowed that before the snows melted, she would have the news he wished to hear.

29

The months passed and even though
Genevieve was enjoying her life with
Philippe and the relative freedom of the
Indian village, Annette was not. Oh, she
liked being away from the authorities and
the strict sisters in the homes they had
been shunted to while waiting for
marriage, and she liked the loose-fitting
clothes, since fashion had never been her
strong point, but what she didn't like was
the idea of forever being a wife, of being
dependent on Lancelot.

"How much longer must we stay
here?" she asked her husband that night
as the pair cuddled beneath their bearskin
rug.

"Why, my precious Love Dancer?"
Lancelot asked, using the name he had

given her, for she almost always danced around him when they made love. "I thought you were happy here?"

Annette sighed. "I am happy with you, that is true, and I am glad that Genevieve and Philippe are happy here as well, but I would rather be back in the cities of the French colony."

"For what? What can you gain there that you cannot here?"

"Money! My house! My plans. You recall, do you not, that Philippe settled my dowry on the St. Clair estate until such time as I could claim it. Well, I wish now to claim it." She turned to her husband, her hands stroking his lean body as she talked. " 'Tis no disgrace on your part, my Lancelot, for you have kept me well satisfied, but do you not see? That is where my talents lie. I have never been able to cook without burning, or to sew without some wrong seam or other mishap. I am not meant to be a wife. I came here to make my fortune. How was I to know that I would fall in love with an Indian?"

"As I recall, he gave your dowry to the sisters. But where is it you would go?"

"Ville-Marie. Not the town directly, but perhaps on the outskirts near the St. Clair estate, so that the prim and proper sisters' ears won't burn upon hearing of the lovemaking, and so I will be far enough away from the authorities in Quebec that I can work without hindrance. Since Philippe gave away my fortune without asking, 'tis the least he can do."

"Love Dancer, from what I have heard of the French governors, they would still give you trouble. The Black-Robes tell me that the bishop, Laval, is quite the man for seeing everything is done according to the holy word. He has even started trying to control the books the people are reading, and he has shut down more than one play for being lewd. Faith, I would not be surprised if the players took to the forests to make their play."

She stared at him, not wanting to believe what he was saying. "But it is so far. It is farther to get to Ville-Marie from Quebec than it was to get from Paris to LeHavre. How can the governors there have control over what the people do at such a distance?"

He shrugged. "It would seem almost a reversal, for I would swear that Quebec is far livelier and gayer, and certainly the women are more up on French fashion than those in Ville-Marie. The sisters of the Congregation are the watchdogs for Laval, and the Récollets, who have just now come, are even worse than the Jesuits."

"You are jesting me?"

He shook his head.

"Well, then, how shall I set up my house? How shall I make my fortune? Lancelot, I have told you, I will not tolerate being poor anymore, and there is no reason why I cannot put my talents to use. If not with me, then I will hire other women."

He shrugged again. "If you can find them. I will have to think about this and talk with Philippe, but I cannot promise anything, for the late winter is the best time to trap. That is when we find the animals in their lairs and unsuspecting of our arrows."

"Is that how you catch them?"

"It is how I caught you." He smiled and leaned over to kiss her, stroking her exposed breasts and sucking on them one at a time. "Meanwhile, you still have me to please."

"*Oui!*" She laughed as she pulled the covers over their heads and directed her mouth downward. "I shall please you, my lord, as you have never been pleased before."

It was several days later, before Lancelot could even talk with Philippe regarding Annette's request, when the pair were summoned to the chief's lodge because a Black-Robe had come to find them.

"What could we have done wrong?" Lancelot asked.

"Must you always think in terms of us having done something? You are a good Christian, my friend, and believe me, the Jesuits are not as perfect as they may wish to appear."

"I know. You are going to say it was they who wooed your mother to the religion and then later refused to acknowledge her marriage to your father. But Philippe, you cannot always carry such a grudge."

Philippe shrugged and took two long strides to reach the chief's tepee. "Emile!" Philippe was taken aback. "What do you here, and how did you know in which village to find me?"

"I did not," the young priest replied. "I have been to many these past few weeks, always seeking out the Frenchmen, until someone said they thought you had taken up here."

"So, what is it you want? Surely, you have not been given a mission to convert me?" Philippe laughed. "For you know that would be next to impossible."

"*Non*, brother. Though I would truly like to have you see the light, I come at the request of our father."

Philippe frowned.

"He is ill and again wishes you at his side."

"I can do nothing for his illness. He has the physician."

"He wishes you."

"Now? 'Tis the best of our season. Soon the animals will be coming out of their caves, just newly waking from their winter slumbers, and we will be able to trap them."

"But he wishes to see you, and he says there are missives for you from Quebec. The Intendant wishes to see you about some matter."

Once more Philippe frowned. "What does Talon wish now?"

"I do not know, brother, only that father has requested I find you as soon as possible and bring you home."

"So you have given up your holy duties to become a messenger for our father."

"*Non*, but this is important."

Philippe shrugged. "Father is of the class, Emile, who thinks that everything he wants is important when he wants it. He does not consider the needs of anyone else." He looked at Lancelot. "I must talk about this with my partner and my wife, and I will let you know."

"I head back day after tomorrow because I must join my mission in Lachine."

"Ah." Philippe lifted his brow. "So Papa did pull the strings for you.

Understandable that he would want his favored son close to him."

"Philippe, do not say that!"

The older man shrugged and turned. "Go to my wigwam. Genevieve will make you comfortable for the evening and I will be back shortly."

"Genevieve! Of the King's Daughters?" Emile was startled. "What is she doing here?"

"She is my wife."

"Oh." Emile flushed. "It's just that marriage to you . . . I did not think that she would. I mean, she had spoken of a desire to take holy vows and I thought perhaps . . . well, never mind."

Philippe stared after his younger brother as the man disappeared down the lane to the wigwam.

The following morning the four of them said their temporary good-byes to their Indian clan and with Philippe at the head of one canoe and Lancelot at the other, they moved off downriver back toward the Isle of Montreal. Pleased, Annette turned to see the village disappearing and, touching her husband's arm lightly, she said laughingly, "You see, God wills it."

They stopped to rest and make camp only once in those five days. Impatient to find out what his father wanted and to return to his trapping and beloved forest as soon as possible, Philippe had insisted that all the men take turns paddling. "But Philippe," Genevieve protested. "Brother Emile is a priest. He should not have to worry about mundane things like keeping the canoe straight on course."

Philippe laughed. "You are right, *ma petite*. He is a man of God. However, he came out here to find me in the canoe. How do you think he paddled then?"

She flushed and remained silent the rest of the trip, knowing that to take her in-law's side would put her in jeopardy with her husband.

Truly, she told herself, she was glad to return to the St. Clair estate, for the comforts of a bed were more welcoming than the hard ground, no matter how many fur rugs were laid on it. But she knew, too, that the closer she was to civilization, the more chances she had of being found out. Not that anyone save Annette knew her secret, but the Marquis would have been more than angered at finding her gone. The more she thought on it, the more she worried that even if he did not come for her, he would surely send someone.

"But there is no way he can take you back," Annette said to calm her. "After all, you are wed to Philippe and, like it or not, his father is one of the most influential men in the colony."

"If he was that influential, why could he not get Philippe freed of the onus of having to wed when he said he did not want to?"

Annette shrugged. "Perhaps because he truly wanted his son to marry, and he certainly is fond of you." She patted the younger girl's hand. "Do not fret so, Genevieve, everything will be all right. If you worry too much, it will be bad for the baby."

Genevieve gasped. "How did you know?"

"I know. I can see it in your eyes, in the glow on your face. And I know the symptoms."

"But Annette," Genevieve whispered, "please, say nothing to anyone else."

"You've not told Philippe yet?"

She shook her head. "I have been waiting for the right moment. I will tell him everything at once."

"You mean you're going to tell him who you are? Now?" Annette's eyes were wide. "Are you sure that's wise?"

Genevieve shook her head. "No, I am not sure, but holding the secret from him hurts." She paused, as her throat tightened and a bird flew by, calling out the coming of spring. "Every night I wake up worried at what might happen if he found out and it was not I who told him. Annette, he is so against the nobility, and so against dishonesty—" Tears flooded her cheeks now. "I fear that he will leave me if he finds out the truth."

Annette sighed. "Then you are right. I suppose you must tell him. Mayhap do so before he leaves for Quebec."

"I cannot. He has promised to take me and I do not want to anger him while we travel, for if he leaves me..." She let sentence hang and Annette shook her head.

"Genevieve, he would be a fool to leave you. I say, tell him this night and be done with it so you can sleep and relax and let the baby be fine."

Pacing by the pier, Genevieve nodded and turned toward the house where she could see from the light in their room that Philippe was already preparing his things. "Yes, let me go to him. We will see you in the morning."

Only as she entered the house and made her way up the stairs did she hear the soft husky voices coming from the bedroom. Eugenia was in there!

Genevieve's hand went to the knob, but before she could move to enter, she heard the moan of lovemaking. She wanted to run, she wanted to hide herself away and not hear this, not face it. But she should have known that if they came back to the estate, Philippe's step-mother would again be after him. Did not his father see anything? Did not the old man understand?

Knowing that it might mean losing him completely gave her the courage to throw open the door, and she gasped at what she saw! 'Twas not Philippe in their room after all, but Eugenia and Claude, the son of old Bernard. As Eugenia darted angry eyes at her, Genevieve shut the door behind her. "What are you doing in here? This is my room. Mine and Philippe's."

"*Non*, my little daughter, you will be in the other wing while your husband is gone. I like this room because it reminds me so of him."

Genevieve stared at the woman, unable to comprehend what she was saying.

"If you are looking for your errant husband, you'll look far, my love. He's left for the capital. To meet with the Governor and find out what he can about you."

"What do you mean, find out about me?" Even as she stared at Eugenia, she realized the woman had drunk more than she ought, and apparently Claude had also, as his bumbling hands tried ineffectually to do up his breeches buttons.

"Think you that you fooled him with your innocence? Evreux is a long way from Joigny, my dear. Even I know that and I was born here. Of course, I told him what little I noticed about you—how you used only the correct spoons, how you dressed quite in fashion for someone who pretended to be a country girl."

Genevieve looked down at her gown, puzzled as she tried to tell the difference between this and the one that Annette wore.

"And of course, your sweet, soft manners and accent. I knew that you had to be one of those runaways. It just takes proof. That's all."

Grabbing her mantle, Genevieve turned toward the door. "He will not be gone long, for he was here with me only at dinner. I will find him and deny everything you said."

"I think not, lovely." Eugenia's laughter rang out. "By now he will have paddled half the way to Three Rivers. You have not the strength in your little arms to move that fast. And when you are out of the way, he will have me."

Unable to think or respond, Genevieve slammed the door to the room and ran down the stairs again, but Eugenia was right. The canoe Philippe had used was gone, as was his satchel from the storage room.

Afraid and tearful, she ran back to find Annette, to find out from her what she might know. Surely, Lancelot would have told have told her if they were planning to leave earlier. Surely, he would have told her if Philippe was unhappy with her—or would he?

30

Annette, when Genevieve found her, was just as puzzled as her friend about what Eugenia had said, and just as furious with her husband for leaving her behind.

"He is such a shadow of Philippe! I swear by God, it seems he can never make a decision on his own without consulting the great Philippe. He cannot even argue like a man!" She paced angrily. "I am sure your husband put him up to leaving me. The question is why?" She continued to pace on the waterfront. "Well, I shall show him I can manage on my own. He does not believe my house shall be, but it shall, I tell you. I shall make more money in this colony than even the King himself! I mean, look at all those men out there, starving for the love and affection of a good woman." She snorted. "Lancelot will see that this will be the last time he ever leaves me."

Genevieve, caught up in her own worry about Eugenia's words, did not respond. "Do you think that Racine has located me already?" She looked anxiously along the river highway that Philippe would have taken. Freed from the winter, the river was dangerous nevertheless: patches of ice broke away without warning and, with the heat of the sun on the water, caused eddies and swirls which could suck an unsuspecting canoe in and over before the rider realized what was happening. But Philippe was an expert and she did not worry about him with the canoe. It was only what he would learn when he reached Quebec, and why he had left in such a hurry, that caused her concern.

"*Non*, my pet." Annette tried to calm her. "If the Marquis had sent spies to find you, more than just my fine Lady Eugenia would have known. Papa St. Clair would have undoubtedly been told."

"Papa St. Clair?"

"*Oui*." Annette smiled. "He has told me that I may call him that, and that I may have one of the empty *habitant* cottages to start my house." Her eyes sparkled with the prospect of her future. "I shall show that—that Christian savage he cannot keep me from my destiny."

"I am glad for you." Genevieve put her hand on Annette's shoulder. Then she sighed. "Do you think he would have protected me?" She blew on her hands to prevent the cold of the evening from forming there as she looked up to see dark clouds forming and wondered how far Philippe was now.

"*Oui.* He would and he will. He is quite fond of you, and of the cat," Annette said, pointing to Alexandre, who had come down to the water's edge with them to play with the sticks floating there.

"No, Alexandre, do not go near that!" she scolded the cat. " 'Twould be easy for you to fall in and I cannot swim to save you."

The cat looked up at the sharpness of her voice and one more put a paw out, as if to test the water, or her.

"I said, no!" She ran up and shooed him back toward the house, toward the barn where he had been having fun earlier with the horses and the mice.

"Oh, Annette, what shall I do?"

"Do?" The other girl was puzzled. "There is not much you can do but help me prepare my house until Philippe returns. Then you will learn what really was said and not said."

"Think you that Eugenia is just talking out of malice?"

"I did see her staring at you when you made the slip at the wedding, but yes, she can have no proof of anything. Not unless she has sources of which we do not know."

Genevieve sighed and looked again toward the river. "I guess you are right. There is nothing I can but wait." She took Annette's hand. "I am chilled and am going inside. Do you wish to help me move my things from that room?" She pointed to where the light had gone out and she assumed that Eugenia had been satisfied with Claude for the night, or else they had both become too drunk to care.

Annette nodded and the girls hurried toward the house.

The following day, Genevieve set up her room in the one adjacent to the old man. He seemed to be getting sicker by the day, yet from all that she could see, he was doing everything that was required of him—both by the physician and by good common sense.

Jean-Pierre was both grateful and glad for her company, and soon the pair developed quite a camaraderie, as Genevieve played him at chess and back-gammon, and even read to him.

" 'Tis not many a country girl who can read as well as you," he remarked one day.

Genevieve flushed. Since Eugenia had made mention of the flaws in her disguise, she had tried to hide her abilities, but not knowing the life of a peasant girl like Claudine, she had remained unsuccessful. "The family I worked for allowed me to learn to read along with their daughter," she told him.

"Indeed, they were good people. You should tell Philippe of them."

"Why?"

"Then perhaps he will not be so against the nobility. He believes we all use people just for our own ends and care nothing for others."

She stiffened. "Yes, I know. He has told me that many times." She looked down at the book in her hands and closed it. "I am tired, Papa St. Clair," she said, calling him by the familiar term which both she and Annette now used. "I think I should rest."

"You haven't a secret you wish to tell me? Eh?"

"A secret!" Startled, she let the book drop from her hands.

St. Clair gave a Gallic shrug. "My son. He is virile, is he not? And he pleases you, yes?"

Genevieve nodded. "*Oui*. He is very virile and he does please me much."

"Then?"

She blushed, realizing now what the secret was. "You are right, Papa St. Clair, only I have not yet told Philippe. I was

going to tell him that night before he left."
Her eyes sought the distant river framed
by the window curtains. "But he
disappeared without me."

"My dear, my dear." The dry hand
patted hers, stroking hers. "Do not judge
my Philippe too harshly. He has had many
troubles in his young life and I know I
have caused more than one myself. But
that he loves you, I do not doubt."

"But he promised to take me with
him."

"If he left without you, you can be
sure his reason was a good one."

Genevieve could only shrug and sigh.

"Go now. Rest. I, too, shall sleep a
bit."

She looked toward the old man, concerned. "Mayhap a visit from the
physician would be in order?"

"*Non*, do not bother your head. I
always feel worse when that old codger
comes. He is, as you say, a charlatan and a
quack."

"Oh, no. I did not say that. I only
said—that is, I only said what I had heard
back in France, and that I wished to take
care of Philippe on my own."

"Nevertheless, *ma petite*, you are
doing a fine job in caring for me, and I will
see that your children are amply rewarded
in my will. Perhaps," he said, smiling,
"perhaps I will even be able to leave you

some little parcel of land back in France, not far from Orleans. You would like to go back, *non*?"

Once more Genevieve looked toward the window and the river leading to the sea, leading to the ocean, and leading back to France. Her voice was sad and in that moment, she felt very far away. "*Oui*, perhaps one day I shall go back." She corrected herself quickly. "But with Philippe, of course."

"Of course." The old man smiled and motioned for her to be gone.

Nodding, Genevieve took her book and her games and slowly closed the door behind her.

She was worried about Papa St. Clair, perhaps more than she should be, but it seemed to her that with all the medication and care he was receiving, he should long ago have recovered. She herself could see no cause for his lack of energy. She shook her head. Perhaps she should have a talk with the cook and see if they could not make some food more palatable to the old man, for what he ate always seemed to make him tired. She looked again to the closed door. At least he did not lack the joy of life. She smiled to herself and hurried away to see what progress Annette was making on the house.

Indeed, with the help of Bernard, Claude, and two of the other men on the estate, Annette's plans were progressing rapidly. The once-small single hut had been turned, with much work, into a three-room cottage. Lean-tos had been added on and built into the framework and there was even a stove brought down from the main house.

"Is this not *merveilleux*!" Annette cried, her arms outstretched as she wandered from room to room, testing the bed here and testing the bed there. "True, it is small and it is not decorated as I would have wished, but it is a start."

"*Oui*," Genevieve admitted. "It is a start." She looked around at the rustic furnishings, the crude table in the corner near the fireplace where Annette would keep her books and records, and the two chairs, both of which had come from the big house. "But from where will your clients come?"

Annette shrugged her big shoulders. "Somewhere. 'Tis word of mouth that an establishment like this needs to succeed. One man tells another, and tells another." She shrugged again. "I will send Claude into town and have him talk of it."

Genevieve's eyes were wide. "Surely, you and Claude have not—"

"*Ma foi*! Indeed no! Do you think I would give away my charms for nothing? He is but a peasant."

"But Annette, that is what most on

the island are."

Once more the new brothel owner shrugged. "Mayhap they are the majority, but there are many like Philippe and his father. Ville-Marie de Montreal is filled with men of quality," she added, becoming somewhat defensive. "And I will take peasants, too. If they can pay."

"But you have no girls yet. And how will you charge?"

"Until I have girls to work for me, I work for myself. I have always done so and will do so again. As to pay, my uppity friend, I will charge 4 livres, just as I did in Paris."

"But Annette," Genevieve said, sitting down on one of the beds and hearing the awful creak of the ropes, "most people here do not seem to have the ready cash. The *habitants*, they barter and trade for what they wish, and many of their needs are taken care of by the seigneurs. Have you not yet learned that?"

Once again, the new madam shrugged. "If they wish me, and they will, no doubt about that, especially once my reputation is around, then they will find a way to pay me. Now leave me to my work, unless you wish to join me in my venture."

"*Non.*" Genevieve shook her head and sighed sadly. "I cannot see myself in the arms of any man but Philippe. and to tell the truth, I cannot see you in the arms of any man other than Lancelot."

"Well, if he meant me to stay in his arms then he should have taken me with him."

Down at the waterfront, Genevieve paused to sit a moment, as she watched old Bernard mend his fishing nets in preparation for the spring.

"Ah, 'tis the young mistress now."

"Greetings, I come merely to enjoy the view of the water."

"*Oui.* 'Tis calming, is it not? Oft times when I quarrel with Sadie, or my Claude, I will come here and the spirit of the water will soothe my wounds."

"But water is what also takes our friends from us."

"*Oui*," the old man acknowledged. "And I can hear in your voice longing for the young master, but he will return soon, no doubt. And with him, all the lovely fashions and news from Quebec that he went to get."

She stared at the old man. "He went to get fashions? I thought he had a missive from the governor." Her heart pounded.

"*Oui*, but he told me that he wanted to bring back something special for his lady-love."

Genevieve looked back up toward the window that had been theirs, where

Eugenia now conducted her affairs. She hoped the old man referred to her, but Philippe could easily have been referring to Eugenia. For all she knew, he loved the woman and hid it because she was his Father's wife. What would happen, Genevieve wondered, if she were out of the way? Indeed, she wondered how Annette's venture would succeed with women like Philippe's step-mother around.

"Bernard." She took a deep breath and steadied herself. "Do you know for a fact that he went only to get news? The Lady Eugenia . . ."

"Bah!" Bernard made a face. "What does she know? 'Tis true. I was with the seigneur when the message came. True, I cannot read overwell, but I do know that the governor summoned Philippe because he worries about the safety of the colony, the Indians and such being what they are, like a keg of powder about to blow sky high!" He waved his arms over his head, dropping the net.

At that moment, the arrow came whooshing through the air, hitting his exposed chest. Bernard's eyes went wide with surprise and pain. "*Sang Dieu*! It is an attack! Get to the house, mistress. Get to the house and ring the bell!"

"No!" Genevieve stood. "I cannot leave you like this, Bernard."

He shook his hoary head. "*Non*, you

must. I shall in a moment be dead," he protested, as his voice faded. "Get to the house and save ... yourself ... the gates ... shut ... they will ..." He closed his eyes then, as yet another arrow was fired from across the river, narrowly missing Genevieve.

Picking up her skirts, she fled the riverbank. "Attack! Attack!" she yelled as loudly as she could, running toward the house. "Indians! Attack!"

From the fields, men dropped their hoes and stopped their horses, as people began running to the main house, to the fortified complex, and prayed for safety.

31

Even as people poured into the yard, Genevieve ordered Claude to watch the gates and close them the moment all the habitants and their families were in. Pulling on the bell with all her might, she summoned all those within hearing distance and told the others to take over. As soon as one of the *habitant* wives came to take over for her, Genevieve ran up the stairs to Papa St. Clair's bedroom.

Why was he lying so still? Why was his head at such an awkward angle?

"Papa St. Clair!" She shook the old man. "Papa St. Clair, the Indians are attacking. What shall we do?"

Slowly the old man opened his eyes. He blinked, then closed them again.

"What is wrong with you, Papa St.

Clair? The Indians are coming. We need to do something.''

"Close . . . gates . . ." he said, his voice distorted with the effort and, straining, he raised his hand, pointing to the corner of the room where, for the first time, Genevieve noticed the matchlock.

Running over to the gun, she saw the old wheel-lock pistol too, but that would do no good. Genevieve recalled her father using them and their range was not that far. Hanging on the wall was also a newer flintlock musket. She picked that up and prayed for guidance. Oft times, back in France, she had gone hunting with her father and held the guns and ammunition while he readied and fired. Sometimes she would reload one gun for him while he was firing the other. But it had been so long. Would she remember now?

She looked back to the bed. The old man's eyes were again closed, his hand still outstretched. She knew that something terrible had happened to him, perhaps another attack, but she couldn't think about him now. There seemed no one else to take charge and so she would have to.

Finding the powder, she carefully measured out enough for a shot and through the window took aim at the Indians now crossing the river. Could she even hit them this far? She doubted it, but hoped that once they heard the guns they would be frightened and run off.

"One, two, three," she said, trying to calm herself, trying to sight the red men as they moved forward through the tall grasses toward the house.

The force of the shot knocked her back and startled many of those downstairs, but she saw it had the desired effect of halting the Indians, at least for the moment.

Guns in hand, she ran down the stairs. Claude and one of the other men met her in the foyer. "Including the old man, we are but ten."

She shook her head sadly. "We are but eight. The old man has had another attack and cannot help us, and your father, Claude, I am sorry to say, has already been killed."

Sorrow flooded Claude's face and he turned his face away. "Then we will kill all those bastards, or be killed ourselves. I will get the other guns from the storeroom. There are enough for all of us." He opened the door with keys from the wall, exposing several muskets, bayonets and pistols.

"You can forget about Lady Eugenia," the second man said, "she is useless and has already fainted."

"Then there are but six of us to fight off over two dozen of them!" Genevieve ran into the yard and turned quickly around, looking and looking. "Where is Annette?"

Claude shrugged.

"Where is Annette?" she asked again.

"Perhaps she did not hear the warning," a woman said.

"*Mon Dieu!*" Genevieve cursed. "She is still in the house down the river. Someone must fetch her."

No one moved.

"All right, then," Genevieve said, taking charge. "You, Claude, you mount that ladder there and watch. Fire as much as you can to scare them off."

"*Non*, I shall fire to kill them." He ran up the ladder as she assigned the others to their positions and ordered the women to get bandages ready from the house linens.

The young priest crossed himself for fear of the battle ahead. Genevieve handed him his gun.

"*Non*, I cannot shoot this. 'Tis against the laws of God."

"Hang the laws of God," Genevieve cursed. "We are fighting for our lives. Go and fetch Annette from the house or fire a gun."

Once more Brother Emile shook his head. "It is her choice to sin and to stay with her sin. I will go and pray for her and for you all." Hands clasped together, he disappeared into the chapel at the side of the main house.

To keep her temper, Genevieve crossed herself and then, ordering Claude to watch her, she slipped out the back of the palisades and ran for all her worth toward Annette's little house.

Even though winter was just now ending, the grasses were long and the wetness from the spring rains, which had only just started, now made the soggy ground damp and hard to run over. Nevertheless, she sped along, tripping more than once, and each time she touched her hand to the dagger she had hidden in her clothes.

Her gown was already torn and muddied as she neared the house. "Annette! Annette!" she called out to her friend.

The girl appeared at the doorway with a gun in her hand.

"Come! Quick!"

"No, I cannot leave my house. I cannot leave all I have built here."

"Don't be a fool, Annette." Genevieve reached the entrance now and began to drag her friend from the house.

"But all my dowry, all that I have hoped for, and worked for. 'Twill be destroyed."

"Idiot. If you don't come with me," Genevieve said, tugging at her, "you will be killed. And me, too."

Even as she said that, a flaming arrow

landed inches from them. The wet grass put it out, but Genevieve's eyes were wide. "Do you wish to kill me and my baby, too?"

"I do not want to leave my little house!" Annette firmly held the pistol she had taken from the house only one day earlier. It had been, she had told Genevieve, for protection from unruly men. "I can and will fend off any Indians that come this way."

"How can you fight the arrows? Bernard is already dead, and the old man—"

Once more an arrow shot through the air and this time it hit its mark as the roof shot up in flames.

"*Sang Dieu*! My house! My fortune!" Annette fought against her friend, as she tried to throw wet grass, tried anything to stop the fire.

"Well, then, kill yourself if you must. I will not be responsible for your life. I have others to consider!" Genevieve cried as she started to make her way back to the estate.

"Yes. Yes, wait," Annette responded. "I am coming. You are right," she sobbed, "My fortune is gone." She began to run after Genevieve, and quickly tripped in the mud. "Oh, Genevieve! Genny! My ankle. I cannot move."

Even knowing that the Indians were close, Genevieve did not hesitate. Annette had helped her many a time and she needed to repay the favor. She prayed only that it would not cost them both their lives.

Quickly, Genevieve tore the hem from her dress and bound her friend's foot. "Lean on me. We will walk as quickly as we can."

"Hurry! Hurry!" Claude called down to them.

Genevieve nodded as she looked back once more to see Annette's little house now consumed in flames. More arrows flew, filled with the same deadly fire, and both women coughed as the smoke invaded their lungs.

No sooner had they reached the back gates of the fortified area than the cry of the warriors echoed around them. Within the walls of the estate, Annette collapsed, crying of all she had lost and of the pain in her leg.

Genevieve felt sorry for her, but there was no chance to minister to her friend now. She had to take control because no one else seemed to be doing it. It surprised her that everyone was looking up to her, but she supposed with Papa St. Clair unable to move, his wife in a faint, and her son in the chapel, Genevieve was the next head of the family.

Ordering all the ammunition to be brought from the house, she watched as

Claude and the two other men loaded their guns, then helped them re-load for a second round, and again for a third. Several flaming arrows hit the grass within the compound and were quickly extinguished.

"We cannot use the water to put out the fire anymore," she told the men. "We must use our feet, our blankets or whatever else is handy, for if we use up all our water, there is no more, and I would not dream of sending anyone else to the river."

Claude nodded as Annette reloaded his gun, balancing as best she could on the ladder next to him. "Madame, they are much closer than before and I do not think the guns are frightening them."

Crossing herself, Genevieve climbed the ladder and peeked out through the hole in the wood. He was right. It would only be a matter of hours before the Indians overcame those in the fort, and then—what? With their skills, she knew the Indians could easily scale the walls and within minutes murder them all. And she could not, she would not die, along with her yet-unborn baby, without Philippe with her, without at least making sure that he knew she loved him. It no longer mattered if he said he loved her, if he meant it or not. She would have to tell him everything and tell him how she loved him, and for that she needed to stay alive.

"We shoot to kill. As you say, Claude, they will have no compunction about killing us. These Iroquois are bloody monsters. Kill who you can and mayhap we can slow them down. Mayhap word can be sent upstream." She turned. "Will anyone volunteer to reach the town? Will anyone risk his life for all of us?"

"I will." A young *habitant* stepped forward. "I am not yet wed and therefore will have few to grieve for me."

Genevieve smiled at him and nodded. "I will write a note."

"There is no need. I will remember all that I need to know and perchance if I do not get through, someone will come across my body and know the story." He slung the gun over his head and tucked a dagger into his pocket just as Eugenia came running out of the house.

"No! Albert, you cannot go. I forbid it."

"My lady, I must. There is no one else."

"No—"

Eugenia's words were cut off as another arrow, sailing through the air, hit her directly in the cleft of her gown. Eyes wide, she sank to the ground.

"Eugenia!" Genevieve ran to her, as did Albert.

Blood pouring from the wound, she

grasped Albert's hand. "I did not want to lose you, my dearest, and now it seems I shall."

"*Sang Dieu!*" he cried. "Do not say that. You are not to die. You will live and be here when I return."

She smiled sadly and strained to look at Genevieve. Her voice was barely audible. "I did not tell him, my little runaway. Your secret is safe with me.,"

"But you said—"

"*Oui.*" Eugenia's smile was weak. "I said what I said because I was angry and jealous that you had someone I wanted so desperately. He is a good man. And a faithful one. Do not worry about him. He will not cheat on you, expect mayhap with his love for trapping."

"Eugenia, do not talk so. Albert says you will be fine." She motioned to one of the men to help carry the other woman inside. "Fetch Emile. He should be with her."

"*Oui*, he must be with me. I wish my last rites." Her hand moved slowly and with great effort over her chest as she made the sign of the cross. "I have much to confess—and not only to you, my daughter-in-law."

Genevieve shook her head and stayed with her until Brother Emile appeared.

"*Maman!*" Emile ran to her, sobbing. "*Maman*, why were you out there? I told you to stay within the house. I told you to stay safe." He knelt at her side as her hand brushed the damp curls from his brow.

She smiled slightly. " 'Tis better this way, my love, I was not happy here and well you know that. Please, Emile, hear my confession and absolve me before the Lord."

Sobbing, he nodded and Genevieve slipped out. Two. Two were dead now and God only knew how many others out there in the fields, those who lived in unguarded settlements, had not reached safety.

"We need more ammunition," Claude called out, "if we are to protect Albert in the canoe."

"*Oui*," Genevieve said, not thinking as she ran towards the table and noticed how little was left. It had seemed like so much before.

She handed what she could to Annette, then went to help the other men reload.

By nightfall, all were exhausted. The second *habitant* had been wounded in the arm, and could no longer shoot, and so now he reloaded as Genevieve fired the guns. Eugenia lingered on, but everyone knew that it would not be long before she joined her maker. A tearful Emile came to Genevieve.

"My mother had much to confess."

Genevieve merely nodded, not wanting to take her sight off the river, off the place where she had last seen the Indians. "I pray Albert has reached the town by now."

"And pray, too, that he can find those brave enough to come to our aid, or we will all soon perish."

"How gloomy you talk, Brother. I would have thought, being a priest, you'd have a more joyous attitude toward life."

He gave a short laugh and shrugged. Then he sighed. "Maman had admitted that 'tis her fault Papa is ill."

"What?" Genevieve turned quickly and, seeing a movement in the dying light, she fired off a shot. The accompanying scream told her that she had hit her target. "Think you they will fight at night?"

Emile shook his head. " 'Tis doubtful. They cannot see, but we best have someone keep guard." He took his place next to her on the narrow wooden rampart. "I will do so."

"And will you fire a gun if you have to?"

Emile looked heavenward a moment and then slowly nodded. "*Oui*, if it does seem necessary, then I shall do so, for I've no more wish to die than you do."

Genevieve nodded, but did not turn away from the view before her.

"Maman did confess to me her sins and asks your forgiveness for her lies and dealings with my half-brother."

"She has it," Genevieve promised, willing herself to be generous toward the dying woman.

"She asks, too, that you let it be known that Papa was poisoned."

"Poisoned!" Genevieve nearly dropped the gun was she holding.

"*Oui,* 'twas her desire to have him die so that Philippe would inherit and she would wed him instead."

Genevieve flushed. "I see."

"But Philippe did not want her, and for that I am glad, that my brother did not sin with the flesh of my flesh."

"Why are you telling me this?"

"Because as I said, she asks your forgiveness. She trusts that you will see that what is proper to be done will be done."

Genevieve nodded and left the ramparts as she gave him the gun. "Watch well, Brother. We will talk later, I am sure."

Little happened during the night, but none of the inhabitants of the estate could sleep, for the Indians outside were dancing and crying, sending their dead to the heavens, and as they cried for their dead, Eugenia faded away. It was nearly dawn before her death was noticed and then there was nothing they could do until this battle was over. There was no time to bury her and no way they could take her to the family plot; and if none of them survived, then all would have to be buried as well by Philippe when he returned.

Genevieve stood guard over the ammunition, watching it carefully and knowing that they barely had enough to last the day. "I pray that Albert got through to the town," she said again. "And I pray that someone will come out with him to help us." Her eyes scanned the distant horizon looking for any movement, either Indian or French.

But there was nothing.

"Think you that we scared them all away?" Annette asked, looking longingly back toward her burned house.

" 'Tis possible," Genevieve admitted, "and I do hope that is the situation, but I doubt it. Philippe has told me many times that the Iroquois are mean-tempered and will not easily give up a battle. They will fight to the last and when they think they are being abused, they will kill whoever is in their sight."

Annette pressed her lips together and for the first time that Genevieve ever knew, she crossed herself. "I did not feel this scared when I was in the docket, for I knew I could charm the judge and mayhap the keyman. But my charms would be of little use to these savages." She cried, "Oh, Lancelot, why did you leave me here?" She pounded on the fence, nearly shaking the logs loose from the rampart, and sobbed.

Genevieve wanted to comfort her, but she could not, for she felt the same anger towards Philippe. If he were here, she would not have this worry, for he would have known what to do; he would have fired the guns properly and not wasted ammunition. Perhaps he would even have been able to talk to the Indians and tell them to hold off. She didn't know.

"Come," she told Annette, "let us go down and have some food to eat. There is only jerky and a bit of water left, but it will serve to keep our stomachs full and our thoughts from food."

Annette nodded and followed her as Claude took up the watch.

Genevieve looked now toward the house and saw her pet in the window, licking himself and watching her. She smiled at him as he showed his pink tongue and yawned, and her heart went out to him. He had been so good these past hours—no, it had been days, she told herself—staying indoors and keeping out of harm's way. After this was over, she would reward him. Mayhap she would catch a fish for him, or some other treat he liked. He jumped off the ledge and laid back his ears as he hunched his back.

"Alexandre, what is wrong, my love?"

Before anyone else could speak or call out a warning, the cat flew like a streak of black lightning, knocking his mistress down with the force of his flight, and taking, high in his heart, the arrow that would have hit her.

"Alexandre!" she sobbed. "Oh, Alex." Genevieve lifted the bloody animal in her arms, cuddling him to her as she sobbed. "Alexandre, please, you cannot die."

Weakly, he licked her face to say that he loved her and moved slightly in her arms, his paw reaching up to her face, touching one of her tears before his open eyes took on a glassy look as his soul ascended to cat heaven.

"Oh, Alexandre." Genevieve continued to sob, until Annette knelt down by her and took the dead cat. Laying the body in the shadow of the house, she led Genevieve inside.

But there was no time to mourn, for the Indians were coming closer again and had renewed their attack.

Taking up another gun, Genevieve resolutely put her anger and grief behind her and brushed away her tears as she climbed the ladder to the rampart. With all her hatred toward the red bastards, she fired the gun.

32

There was no doubt that the Indians were coming closer now, and that none of the defenders was a good enough shot to stop them. Only a few Indians hit the ground, and more seemed to spring up behind them like weeds.

"*Cor bleu!*" Claude exclaimed, "there are more of them than ever. We are all doomed."

"Do not say that." Emile's tone was sanctimonious. "We are in God's hands."

"*Non*," Genevieve sniffled, still feeling the loss of her cat, "we are in our own hands. God can choose to help us if he wishes, but if He doesn't wish—" she didn't finish the sentence.

Annette climbed up the ramparts. "This is the last of the ammunition. After this, we will have to fight them off with the bayonets and daggers."

"If we get that chance," Genevieve said, seeing the flaming arrows coming toward them once more. She turned quickly and threw down her mantle to snuff out the flame. The odor of burnt wool wafted up to them but there was plenty burning this day besides the wool, and more would burn unless they were careful.

Beyond the river, on the other side, they could see smoke rising in the distance—heavy black smoke, the kind that meant a settlement was burning.

Genevieve crossed herself and prayed that they would be spared the pain. Pressing her eyes to the peep hole, she scanned the river, hoping for some sign of French life, for some indication of help on its way. But none was there.

Fire arrows were still flying in, and Genevieve knew that in moments the end would be upon them.

Tearfully, Genevieve stepped down from the palisades and took Annette aside. "I do not know about you, but I wish to write a final note to Philippe and"—her voice broke for a moment—"to tell him my secret, tell him that I love him."

Annette nodded.

"And then I shall ask Emile to confess

me, for I have sinned against the natural order of things by my lie. 'Tis my doing that this is all happening to us."

"What do you mean?"

Genevieve shrugged. "The Book of Job. He tried to run from his destiny, as I did mine. He was punished for it, as I am being punished."

"Do not be so silly." Annette shook her head. "God is not punishing us. Does not the faith preach of a higher good, of a heaven worth going to? Indeed, He is rewarding you for your good work and for your love of Philippe."

With a sigh, Genevieve shook her head. "I do not know anymore what I believe. I only know that my soul will love Philippe always and will think about him, no matter where I am."

"Go, then." Annette pushed her toward the house. "Write your note and write for me, too, that I loved Lancelot with all my heart and soul." She paused. "And write that I would not have even considered the house had he not left me the way he did."

Nodding, Genevieve started inside to fetch paper and pen. Who knew what would happen? If the Indians set the whole estate on fire and burned the main house, whatever letter she wrote would surely be lost in the flames, but it was something she had to do for her own cleansing.

No sooner had she sat down than the cry from outside shook the rafters. Fearing that the Indians were already upon them, Genevieve ran out to find Claude cheering. "They are here! They have come!" He shook his hands in the air. "And look how those Indian cowards run! To the devil with them all, I say. To the devil!"

Unable to believe what she had heard, Genevieve ran up the ladder to look for herself. It was true. The men from Ville-Marie were coming to their rescue and leading the pack were Philippe and Lancelot. With happy tears in her eyes, she hugged Annette, and Annette hugged her back.

Nearly falling as she jumped down the ladder, she hurried to the gate, wanting to open it, wanting to be the first to greet him, wanting to feel his kiss on her lips and hear him say he loved her.

"Do I look all right?" She asked anxiously.

Annette wiped a powder smudge from Genevieve's cheek. "No. And neither do I. But I am sure they will not mind, for I recall that they have seen us in worse states before."

Claude threw open the heavy wooden gates as all cheered and, unable to contain her joy at seeing him alive, and at being alive herself, Genevieve ran into Philippe's open arms, hugging him and kissing him.

"Looks as if we are not needed after all, eh?"

Lancelot laughed as he took Annette within his loving circle.

"Oh, my husband, I have such tales to tell you." Tears of joy and of sorrow ran down Genevieve's cheek. "There are so many dead and almost all have suffered in some way or the other. Your father—" She paused and looked at Emile who had come out to join them, to say his few prayers over the heathen dead.

"Yes, what of my father? Is he dead?"

"*Non.* But he is close to it. He suffered a stroke and cannot now talk. He has lain abed these few days of our fight and has not been able to do anything."

Tears came to Philippe's eyes as he shook his head. "That must have killed him in itself, as he has always been an active man." He placed his arm around his wife. "Come. Let us go to him."

Emile touched her hand. "God gives thanks for forgiveness."

Genevieve looked at him, and realizing he was asking that she not tell Philippe of Eugenia's confessed poisoning, she nodded. It was not for her to say anything.

"Yes, let us see your father." She turned to her husband. "I know he will be heartily glad to find you well and safe, for in truth we feared that with the Indians attacking us, they could have easily attacked and killed anyone on the way."

Philippe shook his head. "They would not hurt me because I know them too well and I am one of them." He stroked her cheek. "But I'm grateful to whatever god there is that you are safe."

She smiled at him and knew that soon she would have to tell him her secrets.

It was only later, when they were again alone, when burial for Eugenia, Bernard, and the others had taken place, that the pair were able to talk.

"Your father will recover, I think. He has a strong spirit."

"Not as strong as yours." Philippe took her into his arms and kissed her brow. "You still have powder smudges on your brow, my love, my brave little cat."

Tears came to Genevieve's eyes as she heard the term and she turned away quickly, not wanting him to see her sorrow. But his arms went around her, encompassing her and soothing her hurt the best he could. "I know. I have heard of your bravery in saving Annette, and I have heard of your taking command and pushing the others even when it appeared hope had gone, and even Albert, before he died of his wounds, spoke of how marvelous you were."

She sniffled.

"And I also heard of your dear Alexandre. I know you will miss him but, as with our human friends, his role on earth was done."

Teary-eyed, she looked up at her husband. "You sound more like Emile than you do the skeptic I knew."

"Perhaps, as I said before, I am not a skeptic now. *Certainement* there is a god, for when I learned of the trouble here, I prayed mightily that I would come back and find you unharmed, and so I did." He paused, still holding her. "Indeed, I am sorry to learn of Eugenia's death for she was, in her own way, good to my father. Still, now I can swear to you that there was nothing ever between us. I know, *mignonne*, that you mistrusted her, but I would never have betrayed you for the likes of her."

"I know." Genevieve looked up into her husband's blue eyes. "Before she died, she confessed to me that many times she had tried to attract you and failed." She shook her head. "But what I do not understand is why you went off without me when you promised you would take me. Annette, too, was angry with Lancelot. Why did you?"

He leaned over and kissed her lips for the answer. "Because I loved you too dearly."

She looked at him strangely.

"I had heard from my sources that there was trouble among the Indians, and I feared that if you and Annette were with us, they would harm the pair of you and that certainly, if we had to flee, your being there would slow us." He shook his head. "I never dreamed they would attack the estate while we were gone."

She walked to the window to look out over the estate yard, the gates now open, the grasses waving tall and readying themselves for spring and summer, and the river ice nearly gone. All seemed so peaceful and for some, she thought, it was. She felt a sudden ache in her heart. She wanted to cuddle her Alexandre, and again she felt the tears form in her eyes as she realized she'd never again feel his rough tongue against her cheek, his paw pushing back her hair, his lovebites on her nose, or the sound of his contented purr as she stroked him.

"Well, we did survive."

"*Oui*, that you did, my love." Philippe stood behind her now, wrapping his arms about her securely and lovingly. "Come. Show me how you missed me. For truly, I did miss you."

Turning, Genevieve welcomed his lips and his arms and hugged him to her, smothering him with her desire as she tried to smother her fears and her sorrows.

Gently, he lifted her into his arms,

carrying her to the bed, stroking the fires within her to prime readiness as he kissed and touched her, his tongue trailing down her neck, licking and sucking at her nubby breasts as she moaned with delight, his teeth nibbling her earlobes and chewing delicately on her lower lip, and indeed kissing her as she had never been kissed before.

In return, Genevieve, too, showed her passions as she heated him, touching him tenderly as her mouth nibbled at his soft treasures and kissing the length of his being with such intense passion as made Philippe thought he would burn.

Their desires on fire, he slowly spread her legs and consummated their lusts and loves, bringing her first to one fulfillment, then a second before he, too, joined her in the waves of happy reunion, and his energy cascaded with her down the water-fall of love only to be ready again with a desire that no water could quench.

Exhausted, they slept and again made love, then slept again.

The sun was high in the sky when the knock on their door startled them.

"Can the pair of you not get enough of each other?" Annette teased from the hall. "Breakfast awaits you outside, if you are ready and willing to get to work."

"Soon," Genevieve called lazily from

the bed. "Soon."

Returning to her own room, cuddled next to her own husband, Annette laid her head on his shoulder. "It is all your fault, you know. Had you not left me without a word, I would never have tried to start up my house, and I would never have insisted on staying in it until the fire, and I would not have hurt my foot when Genevieve came to rescue me." She held out her bandaged ankle.

Lancelot leaned down and kissed it and then, lifting her skirt, continued to kiss her. "You are right, my dove. It was cowardly of me not to tell you of our plans, but Philippe—"

"*Hélas*! Can you not make a move without him? I suppose if he said jump, you would ask how high?"

"No, that is not true. Do I ask him when I may make love to you?"

"Do you?" she challenged.

Laughing, he pushed her down on the bed and began to kiss her deeply, letting his hands roam where a husband's hands might, until Annette was wriggling and squirming with pleasure.

"Truly, my pet," he said, kissing her again now on her exposed nipples, "I feared for your safety and could not tell you, for I knew that, foolhardy as you were, you would still insist on coming."

"Indeed, I do insist on coming!" She

grinned as she pulled him down upon her, arching her hips to meet his and moving in a rhythm not to match either of theirs individually but to make a unique music that was totally for them together. As the pleasure sang through them, she clung to him desperately, wanting him to know how she loved him, wanting him to know how she had missed him.

Lying at his side after, she looked up into his dark, unreadable eyes. "You are going to be a father."

"What? When?" He touched her belly. "You mean now?" Lancelot shook his head. "That is ridiculous. How could you know now? So soon."

"Because I do," she shrugged. " 'Tis a feeling I have. And I know that feeling is true."

"Boy or girl?"

Annette reached up to stroke her husband's smooth cheek. "Boy I think."

Lancelot kissed her belly, his hand gently rubbing. "Then methinks we'd best try for a girl, too. I would not want our boy to be lonely."

Laughing, Annette pulled him back down on her.

33

"Why do you have to return to Quebec again?" Genevieve shook her head, unable to understand what Philippe was saying.

"*Non*, my dearest wife, 'tis not for me, but for thee. Our gracious new governor, Frontenac, has apparently heard not only of my own adventures, which is why I was called in the first place to lead a band of men against the Iroquois who attacked the estate, but he has also heard of your exploits."

"Me? I did nothing."

"You were the one who kept the people fighting here. From what is told about you, my love, you are now a national heroine."

"But that is silly. I only did what was necessary to save my life."

"And the life of Annette, and of my father, and of Emile, and I heard tell that you even helped Eugenia until the very end." He paused. "And thanks to you, my father is quickly recovering."

Genevieve blushed. "Nevertheless, I did not care for Quebec and am not eager to go there."

"The governor also wants to meet the woman who tamed me."

This time she laughed. "I would like to meet her, too!"

Philippe smiled. "Besides, most young women I know would be thrilled with the idea of being invited to the Governor's chateau. I'll grant you that the mansions and the chambers in Quebec won't be as grand as those in Paris or Versailles, but it is interesting if you have nothing else to compare it to."

She flushed, not wanting to tell him that indeed, she had something to compare it to, and just as she did not like her taste of life in the court of King Louis, she was sure she would not like her taste of life in the court of Governor Frontenac.

But Annette was excited about a return trip to the city. "Just think, we can see the new fashions and mayhap I can find some other women to add to my house."

"I thought you gave up that idea."

"Oh, for myself, yes." She shrugged

and pointed to her now slightly enlarged belly. "It is, of course, out of the question for me. That does not mean we cannot find a girl or two for me to manage into a blossoming career." She paused. "Is something the matter? Are you and Philippe"—Annette cleared her throat—"close enough?"

"*Oui*, as close as before."

"And he has noticed nothing about your changing size?"

Genevieve shrugged. "If he has, he's said nothing."

"Should you not tell him?"

"Soon. Perhaps before we leave for Quebec."

But even as they prepared for a return trip to the stone city on the cliff, Genevieve tried and failed to communicate her message, deciding finally to wait until Philippe did notice her expanding size before she said anything. Besides, she knew now that she would never let him go anywhere without her, for she had missed him too much when he was away. She only prayed that they would go and come back quickly, before anyone she knew from her former life reappeared. After all, with new boats arriving almost every month, certainly during the summer months, it was quite possible that someone she had known at Louis' court would suddenly appear, or even more possible that someone who had attended the wedding would, like Eugenia, guess her circumstances.

With the first ship of the year arriving through the jagged edges of floating ice, cheers went up in the city. 'Twas a good sign when a new boat came in, for it meant not only luxuries from France, but news from home and fashion patterns for the women, and perhaps a comedy or two which could be played for a bit until Laval got wind of the action and shut it down.

Still clutching the miniature in his hand, Antoine Le Bera stepped off the ship, heartily glad to be ashore and almost ready to kiss the soil as the nuns were now doing, though he scarely believed in God, certainly not enough to thank Him. He supposed he should, though. The storms they had been through on the Atlantic, not yet free of winter's throes, had been treacherous, and Antoine knew that had he not had the extra incentive of the girl, he would never have taken the ship at this time, but would have been quite content to lounge in LeHavre for another good month, or perhaps two.

Well, he was here now, he told himself, as he took a room in one of the better-looking taverns recently built in Upper Town, and began to make his plans. He would have to start his work. Once again,

he looked at the delicate painted picture
and resisted the urge to kiss the miniature
in public. Indeed, his heart thumped
wildly at the thought of such a catch, that
he could even dare think he might be able
to make her his. He held his breath a
moment, and knew that he could only try.

As with all the other newcomers to
these shores, Antoine was invited that
night to a ball at the Governor's Chateau
in honor of the safe arrival of the new
militia, led by Captain Philippe St. Clair of
Ville-Marie de Montreal, and to toast his
successful mission in subduing the
Iroquois who had been rampaging the
settlements. St. Clair, Antoine was told,
though a half-breed himself, was willing to
take the role only because he would know
which tribes had been on the warpath and
which had not and he feared, as most
Indians did, that without proper guidance,
the militia might kill many innocent red
men, and an all-out war would be started.

And so, deciding that the ball would
be a good place to talk with people, to
show the miniature and see if the girl was
known, he accepted. For all he knew, she
could even have gone south to the English
colonies, though Antoine thought that
unlikely, as the English and French were
again warring with each other, especially
now that William had taken over the
throne of Louis' brother-in-law, James.

And she could have gone into hiding in the forest, though he hoped with her breeding and beauty she had not, for he would hate to have to track her through the wilds, hate to have to deal with these savages, all for the sake of a few coins. Now, if he knew for a fact that he could capture her and take her for himself, escaping the clutches of Racine, he would go anywhere, but he could not know that and was, therefore, reluctant to put out any more effort than was necessary. So, even though he did not truly believe, he made his way toward the church and there lit a candle as he bent his knee and prayed to the Lord that his mission would be accomplished easily and swiftly.

As Genevieve lay in her husband's arms, stretching and feeling as if she never wanted to leave them, she felt his lips on her brow.

"Is there something you wish to tell me, *mignonne*?"

"Tell you?" Genevieve looked up into his blue eyes, slightly startled. She had been thinking about the moment she had arrived here in Quebec, and the moment even longer past when she had left the coast of France behind.

He gently touched her rounding stomach and Genevieve flushed.

"Oh, *oui*." She smiled.

"And when were you going to tell me of this little addition to my life?"

She shrugged. "If you had waited the night before your last trip to Quebec, you would have know then."

"And then I never would have left you alone."

"I would have liked that." She reached up to kiss him and pull his lips down to hers. "I love you, Philippe."

"I know that. And I guess I also knew of our child, but I feared for your safety coming along with me. I did not want to think of it, and since you did not tell me—" He shrugged. "I, too, love you, my cat lady." He brushed her hair from her brow. "Tell me, why do you sound so sad? Is there more you need to say?"

She paused a moment, looking in his eyes, and then shook her head. "*Non*, there is nothing. I am only sad about those who died."

"*Oui*, and so am I. But we all must go at one time or another."

"Yes, I suppose so." And for a moment she thought of her father and wondered if he was still alive. Would the fury of the Marquis have extended that far? Pushing up and away from Philippe, she said, "We ought to dress for this ball now."

"Ah, yes, this foolish ball in which I am being honored for taking the captaincy of a militia troop that would have destroyed innocent lives if I had not chosen to go along. What could I do?"

Genevieve leaned back and kissed him, melting into his arms again for just one moment more. She had a premonition of something evil happening this night and told herself it was nothing but her own worries. "Indeed, how I love you. But if we are to be presented, then we must be presentable."

He laughed and nodded.

The simple gowns she had brought in Claudine's trunk no longer fit her expanding figure, and while she could have, with some difficulty, made something up herself, she was not talented in that way. After all, she had never needed to sew. It had always been done for her. She had been determined to attempt a gown, but Philippe had seen her difficulty, and while he did not know the reason for her clumsiness, he had insisted that one of the dressmakers in Quebec make her gown for the ball.

And so it was. The dress of silk and tafetta rustled as she walked, and the stomacher was cut in such a way that her pregnancy, early as it was yet, did not show. The v-neck of her gown enhanced her long slender neck, and despite the fact that her skin was now almost as brown and tanned as Philippe's, the delicate beauty was still very much there. For just a moment, as she walked into the ornate ballroom with the gilded chandeliers and the sparkling crystal trays filled with tempting sweets, Genevieve was reminded of her moments in Louis' court, of the moments when she had first seen the ungainly Marquis de Racine. Clinging to the arm of her husband, smartly turned out in a uniform he had worn merely for the gathering tonight and planned to use no more, she walked forward to greet the new governor.

"My dear, Madame St. Clair, 'tis indeed an honor to meet you, for I have heard from many that your husband, wild and freedom-loving as he was, would never agree to wed, despite our well-intentioned laws."

Genevieve was forced to smile by the light in the handsome Governor's face. "Indeed, I did nothing, sire."

"But we are nevertheless indebted to you, Madame. Were if not for you, I doubt we would have been able to convince him to take the command."

She looked to Philippe, who was being made distinctly uncomfortably by the talk. "I am glad that my husband's talents are finally being appreciated."

The music started up and the Governor stood. "May I have this dance, Madame?"

Once again she looked to Philippe, who nodded. "Just as long as you aren't doing it just to make me jealous, Monsieur, for I get very perturbed when I think someone is after my wife." His tone was stiff and unnatural—just as he appeared to be in the uniform. It was clear to all that his obedience was reluctant.

The Governor gave a good-natured laugh and extended his beringed hand, much as the King once had done to Genevieve. She took it and, forcing a smile, she felt her heart pound. Was this where her premonition would come to fact? She looked into the eyes of the Governor as they began to dance and felt at ease for the moment, but the sense of fear remained heavy as a stone around her neck.

"Indeed, my dear, for a country girl you dance remarkably well."

Genevieve flushed. Dressed as she was, and in this setting, she had for the moment forgotten that she was Claudine Bopar and not Genevieve Simon, daughter of the Vicomte de Patin.

"You are right, your excellency. I was blessed by good employers when I lived in Evreux. The family had me take lessons at the same time as the daughter of the family so that we might practice together."

"A most pleasant surprise." He

smiled at her, his moustache turning up as he spun her around the room.

She was relieved when the music stopped and Philippe was able to reclaim her.

"*Mignonne*, are you unwell? You are shivering." His arms went around her as he guided her to the seats. "Mayhap you would like a drink?"

She nodded, still unable to speak.

But even as Philippe moved off, she knew that her moment of unveiling was at hand. Her eyes met those of a plump, bewigged man and, as his eyes narrowed, she realized that he had been staring at her all night long. Who was he? Did he know her? Was he someone from the court at home? She feared he might be, but then, why did his name not come to her?

Trembling, she forced herself to look the other way, to watch Philippe as he made his way across the room looking every bit as awkward and uneasy as she felt, although his uneasiness sprang merely from being at a place he did not wish to be.

"Madame?"

"Oh!" She turned as the voice startled her. That man, whoever he was, had come to sit at her side.

"May I sit here?"

"My husband will return in a moment."

"What I have to say will take but a moment. You are Genevieve Simon, are you not?"

She flushed hotly and raised her fan, trying to cool her face and hide her reaction. "Indeed, no, sir. My name is Genevieve St. Clair."

"True, your coloring has changed. You no longer look the delicate rosebud. But, indeed, I would say you are, or were, Genevieve Simon, daughter of the Vicomte de Patin."

"No, sir, you are mistaken." She cut the man short. "My name before marriage was Genevieve Claudine Bopar."

"Ah, yes." His brow lifted. "Bopar. I do see and understand why you would take your maid's name."

Before she could respond, Philippe was upon them. The drinks were no longer in his hands; instead, he held his sword outright. "Sire, I do believe you are annoying my wife."

"Indeed?" Antoine stood, his knees creaking. "I do not mean to do so, Captain St. Clair. 'Tis only that she looked familiar. I thought I might have known her in France."

"That, sir, is highly doubtful, since my dear little wife lived in a small town near Evreux, and would have been nowhere near the court. Therefore you cannot have met her. Ever."

Antoine looked at Genevieve, then back at Philippe. "I am sure that I know her."

Philippe glanced at his wife.

Confused as to who this man was, she shook her head.

"Well, then, sir, since you calling my wife a lair, I shall have to challenge you to a duel."

Antoine's brow raised slightly. "A duel? Very well then. You have a second?"

"I do," Philippe responded. "We will meet tomorrow at dawn. There are some plains outside the city."

Antoine shrugged. "Agreed. And if I win, then you must concede that I am right and your wife is a liar."

Genevieve inhaled sharply as both men turned to stare at her.

34

"But you cannot fight him," Genevieve protested once they were back in their room.

"Why not, *mignonne*? Is he right? Does he know you? How?"

She flushed hotly. "No, he is not right. I do not know this man, but I"—she paused, searching for some reason to stop the duel—"you are so much better than he could ever be. That is obvious."

Philippe gave a low laugh. "*Certainement*, I am in better shape than the toad."

"And you would not want to have his death on your conscience , would you?"

Philippe studied his young wife a long moment. "No, I would not want his death, but then, we are only to duel till first blood." He took her into his arms. "Come, my love, tell me your real worries. Certainly you do not think he will injure me."

She shook her head.

"Then what is the real reason you do not wish us to duel? He has called you a liar. Shall I let this dishonor stand?" He smiled and kissed her gently on the lips. "I might be half-Indian, but I am also half-French, and my French blood boils when I think of how he acted toward you."

Genevieve sighed and turned to the window. Once again she searched her memory, but she could not recall ever meeting any Antoine Le Bera, but what if he did remember her? Or what if he was in the employ of the Marquis? Certainly, as Philippe's wife she was safe here in the colonies. He could not drag her back. But, she did not want her husband to fight. In fact, if she had her way, they would return to Ville-Marie immediately. But Philippe had promised the Governor to meet with him regarding the Indian situation, and those meetings would continue on into the week.

"Well?"

She looked back at him. "Fight if you wish. I just do not like the idea of anyone being hurt."

Philippe came over and put his arms around her waist, pulling her back toward him, kissing her neck. "My love, do not worry. Everything will be fine and this toad, whoever he is, will go back to France and never again worry us savages in the colony." He smiled tenderly and Genevieve could only nod.

The following morning found Philippe facing Antoine on the mist-covered plains outside the city. Lancelot stood several paces behind him and the other man's second, recruited just that evening, stood behind Antoine.

Winter had not yet fully left Quebec, and the morning chill caused both women to shiver, even with their fur muffs and hoods.

"Did you tell him?"

"How could I?" Genevieve anxiously watched as the men chose their weapons—swords. "He would be so upset with me, Annette. I know that he would leave me forever if he knew the truth. You should have heard the unkind words he had for Frontenac and his nobles, and Philippe is supposed to like those men, or at least he is working with them." Tears fell from her eyes, sticking to her cheeks. "Besides, the man is wrong. I do not know him. I do not recall ever having seen him before."

"But how would he know you, and your maid's name, and your father's name? If he does not remember you from court, then there can be only one other way he would have guessed."

Genevieve closed her eyes, not wanting to hear what her friend was saying, and not wanting to see the fight, which was about to start.

"Genny, you must tell Philippe all. He will understand, I assure you. He loves you. Especially now that you carry his child, he will not desert you."

"I have tried, Annette," she wailed. "Truly, I have."

Annette shrugged. "Well, I only hope that it is not too late to make amends."

"What do you mean?"

"I mean that if this Le Bera does not win this round, and he is sent to take you away, he will not rest until you go with him. From what you yourself have told me, and from what I know of the Marquis de Racine, he is not a man to be trifled with."

"You never said you knew of him before."

Again, Annette shrugged. "What was done was done. There was no reason to add to your worry."

Genevieve bit her lower lip as she watched her husband and Le Bera dueling, their swords clashing as they danced around each other, parrying and pointing, slashing sleeves and leaves off the trees.

To her surprise, it took two rounds before her husband had the fatter man at sword point, his back on the ground.

"Do you give up, sire?"

Breathless, Antoine looked toward Genevieve and shrugged.

"Say it!" Philippe edged his sword closer to the man's chest.

"Very well, perhaps I was mistaken. It is possible that I never met your wife."

Philippe grunted and removed his sword as the little man stood, looking in disgust at the dirt on his coat.

"Come, Genevieve." Philippe turned to his wife and nodded to Annette and Lancelot. "Our work here is done."

Antoine stared at the couple as they rode off in their light carriage and rubbed his hands together. Mistress Genevieve would have sorry days after this, for neither he nor the Marquis liked to be bested.

Returning to his rooms, he mulled over his strategy over a cup of chocolate and warmed his extremities by the fire as he searched through his papers.

"Ah!" His tight eyes lit up as he found the marriage document. Faked though it was by the Marquis, should such a thing be necessary, it nevertheless looked quite official and regular. No one, not even Frontenac, would be able to deny the signature of the minister of foreign affairs, Jean Colbert, who had signed as a favor to the Marquis.

Tapping the parchment against his

still cold fingers, the messenger smiled. "Indeed, Mademoiselle Simon, you will be sorry you did not acknowledge your obligations when first given the chance."

The court was abuzz with gossip and rumors, but as Genevieve stepped out of the carriage with her husband, everyone stopped to look at her. She flushed, wondering if she was the topic of conversation or if it was just her imagination.

"But of course everyone will be talking about the duel," Annette reassured her. "After all, it might be illegal, but they all do it."

Genevieve nodded, but her fears were not calmed. Why, after all, would she be summoned to the governor's chambers with her husband, when the meeting regarding the militia had nothing whatsoever to do with her?

As they walked toward the ornate, mirrored room Frontenac had chosen for his office, Genevieve was sure she could feel the eyes of the staff watching her carefully. She clutched at Philippe's arm.

"What is it, my love?"

"I do not feel well. Mayhap I should go back to the rooms and lie down. You can talk with the Governor on your own."

"*Mignonne*, we are here. I promise I will not let the conversation drag on. We will conclude business and then go to lunch. If then you do not feel well, I will take you back."

She sighed and nodded, thinking how much different Philippe seemed dressed in his play uniform, as he called it.

The scene was almost as she'd suspected it would be. Walking into the office with Lancelot and Annette trailing behind, she saw the toad, Antoine Le Bera, dressed in a green velvet morning coat, seated next to the Governor.

Frontenac rose, full of charm and gaiety as he took Philippe's hand and smiled to acknowledge Genevieve and Annette.

"What does he do here?" Philippe's hand went to his sword handle.

"My friend," the governor said in his mellow, calming voice, "I believe, before you do anything else rash, you'd best hear Monsieur Le Bera out."

"Why?"

Frontenac shrugged and glanced toward Genevieve. "He has something quite interesting to say."

Genevieve took a deep breath and sank into the soft chair that had been provided for her. She clutched at the wooden arms, wishing that Alexandre was here to cuddle her and love her now, wishing that she were not even in this room. She felt Annette's hand on hers and nodded her appreciation for the other woman's support. But she feared support was not going to be enough in this case.

"Very well." Philippe took his seat, still wary, and glanced to the Governor. "Let us find out what this man has to say and then conclude our business. My wife does not feel well this morning."

"Indeed," Antoine's high-pitched voice agreed, "I can see why." He smiled at her, sending shivers down Genevieve's spine.

"Philippe, this is a matter of grave consequence." Frontenac looked from him to Genevieve to Antoine, then back to Genevieve. There was compassion on his face, but his voice was as stern as an angry father's. "Monsieur has produced this document."

He handed it over to Philippe, who slowly unfolded it.

"It is signed by Jean Colbert, our illustrious minister, and says that Genevieve Simon, the daughter of the Vicomte de Patin, is lawfully wed to the Marquis de Racine."

"No!" Genevieve bolted from her chair. "No, that is not true. I was never wed to the man!"

All in the room turned to look at her.

"What are you saying, *ma petite*?" Philippe's voice was as icy as his blue eyes. "Are you this Genevieve Simon?"

She looked to Annette and then to

Frontenac before facing Philippe's hostile gaze again. Taking a deep breath, she nodded. "*Oui*, I am. My father—" She swallowed hard, feeling the trembling within her, feeling the weakness in her knees and hearing it in her voice. "My father sold me to the Marquis as part of his gambling debt. The wedding was to have taken place the week after. But I fled before it could take place and—"

"And took the name of Bopar. Who is this Bopar?" Philippe's eyes were hard sapphires now.

Genevieve looked to her hands in her lap. "My former maid. 'Twas she who had the idea that I could flee to the colonies." She turned to Frontenac now, pleading. "Your excellency, I swear I was never married to the Marquis. I ran away before I could be married."

"That is not what this document says. Even so, if your father gave you as part of his gaming debt—" The governor shrugged.

"But I am wed here, to Philippe." She turned toward him, but he would not meet her eyes.

"*Non*, you are not." The fat little messenger delighted in the scene as he twirled his moustache. "The marriage documents here read Genevieve Claudine Bopar of Evreux and you are Genevieve Theresa Simon, daughter of the Vicomte de Patin, of Joigny. Therefore, your marriage is not legal here and you are mine to take back, since I have been employed by the Marquis to find you and return his property."

Stunned, Genevieve looked again to Philippe.

This time he met her eyes. "So that is where Joigny came in and why you mentioned it at the wedding." He paused, and she saw his anger building. "And why did you not tell me who you truly were? I am your husband, or so I thought. You said that you loved me and trusted me."

"I do love you, Philippe," Genevieve sobbed. "And I tried to tell you. Truly, I did, but I could not. Everytime I wanted to say something you would talk of the nobility and of dishonesty and of how you could not stand lies. And I feared your anger."

"You feared correctly, *ma petite*." His hard eyes seemed to look into her very soul and tear her apart. "It seems, as they say, that our marriage is not valid."

"But it is!" she protested. "I love you. I am your wife. I carry your child."

"*Non*, you are the wife of the Marquis. You are Genevieve Simon. 'Twas all lies. Every bit of it. The child you carry is a bastard." Philippe stood and started for the door. "You will excuse me, Your Excellency. *Adieu*, Mademoiselle Simon, 'twas a pleasure knowing you as I did."

"I am not married to Racine! I promise on the saints' holy book," she cried out. "I have never been wed to Racine!"

She tried to go after him and found her way blocked by the guards. Tearful, she turned to the Governor.

"I am sorry, Madame," he said, "but I can only rule as I see the circumstances. You will be publicly humiliated as an example for any other young woman who hides such a secret, and you will be sent back with Monsieur Le Bera to France and your lawful husband, the Marquis de Racine."

"Philippe St. Clair is my lawful husband." Her voice was barely audible as she looked to Annette and Lancelot. Both had pity on their faces, but there was nothing they could do to help her.

35

Because of who the Marquis de Racine was, and who her father was, and also partially because of her relationship with the St. Clairs, tenuous though it was, it was deemed politic to put Genevieve in more comfortable surroundings than ordinary prisoners might find themselves in. Indeed, Annette couldn't help but comment on how much nicer Genevieve's cell was than her own dirty bed of straw had been. Yet it was a jail all the same.

"Oh, Annette!" Genevieve cried, pushing away the beef and soup which she had been brought and which so far she had been unable to eat. "I do not know what to do. Philippe has not come to visit me and has sent no message. Does he hate me that much?" She continued to sob as she touched her stomach. "This is his child I carry and I am wed to him, not to Racine."

"Hush, sweetings." Annette tried to calm her friend, placing her arm about the distraught younger woman. "I know. And I believe you."

Genevieve sniffled. "But Philippe does not." She sank into the hard chair and stared forlornly out the window toward Lower Town, the harbor, and the boat which would soon be returning to France. She prayed she'd not be on it, but that had not yet been decided. "And Lancelot? Does he believe me?"

"He will not talk of it," Annette said. "He says it is not his affair."

"But he was my friend, too." Teary eyed, she asked, "Does he mention my name to Philippe?"

Annette touched Genevieve's shoulder lightly. "No one can mention your name to Philippe, for he goes into a rage and flies off to drink in the tavern. He has refused all messages from the Governor and the Intendant, both of whom have been to see him numerous times."

"About me?"

"I do not know. Philippe would not talk with them."

Her hands on her enlarging belly, Genevieve looked down. "I am to be publicly humiliated in the square on the morrow."

"*Oui*, I know. But surely, they would not flog you, being that you are in the family way?"

Genevieve looked up. "You forget, this child I carry is a bastard, or so Philippe says. Therefore I cannot think the church fathers would care overly much what happened to it, or to me."

"*Non*, that cannot be true. You have always been so good about mass and confession. Surely, you do not think God would forsake you now?"

Once again, Genevieve looked to the harbor. Her voice took on a faraway tone. "If He does not make Philippe see how I love him, if He sends me back to France, then He is no longer my god."

Antoine Le Bera came to visit Genevieve a number of times, encouraging her to eat, to keep up her spirits and telling her that it was all for the best. He described the estates of the Marquis and what Racine would be giving her, and how much the old man wanted her.

She realized that Antoine was still talking with her. His hand had reached out, close to hers, and she pulled back.

" 'Tis quite possible, Mademoiselle, that I could—" He looked around the room to make sure the guards were not within hearing. "I could forget that I found you, or tell the Marquis that you were taken by the savages and are believed to be dead."

Genevieve looked up as a glimmer of hope sparked in her.

"You would do that?"

"*Oui.*" He smiled at her. "In exchange for a few small favors." His tone, so hushed and reverent, made Genevieve look up at him, and it dawned upon her that he, too, wished to use her, as had so many men. Only Philippe had not used her. He had loved her as she loved him. It could not all be ending this way.

Her eyes narrowed as she stared at him. "*Non,* I am a married woman."

"Bah! Married to a ghost. The man will not even acknowledge you, will not even acknowledge the missives which the Governor and I both have sent asking him to come to talk. A deal could be made, if he were willing."

"I want no deal. I want nothing but Philippe." She felt the tears coming to her eyes and willed them back.

"If he would but talk to us, you would not have to be returned to France." His hand edged closer to hers. "If you would but consider my proposition, I could see that you were freed, and you could talk to Philippe yourself." He smiled at her, sending shivers up Genevieve's spine.

"Philippe does not want me any longer." Her voice was dull, like her hair, like her eyes, like her feelings. "I have no more reason to live. *Certainement*, I do not care if I return to France, or if the ship sinks on the way. Indeed, 'twould be better that way."

"Ma'mselle, you are making a dreadful mistake. I can tell you, floggings are not pleasant."

She turned abruptly. "They are to flog me?"

"*Oui*." His eyes twinkled. "What do you think public humiliation means?"

"Oh. I did not think." She stared at him a moment as if trying to see his truth, and she knew then that he was not just attempting to frighten her. "Well, they will flog me. Perhaps I shall die of my wounds and it will be done." She looked upward to heaven and thought of her sweet Alexandre. Mayhap he would play with her and the baby when they reached heaven, for that was the only salvation she could hope for. Or was she for her lies and duplicity to go to hell?

"I can escort you from here today, if you like. I can make sure that you never reach the scaffold. I can even let you stay here in the colonies if you like." He reached out now, this time touching her soiled gown. It was the same gown she had worn the day she had come to see the Governor, the day she had been accused. "We will make a wonderful life together, my Genevieve."

She looked beyond him, as if seeing her future. "*Non*, I do thank you for your consideration, Monsieur Le Bera, but I am at fault as you say. While I did not wed Racine, I have lied nonetheless and run from my destiny." She shrugged, her body already numb from the emotional pain. "I shall take whatever punishment they give me."

"Ma'mselle Simon—"

"I am Madame St. Clair!"

Antoine smiled. "You are not. Certainly, your husband, as you call him, has already publicity refuted you." He paused, letting his words sink in. "I do not think you know how painful floggings can be."

She turned away from him. "Whatever it is, it can be no greater than the pain I already feel."

It was only after Le Bera had gone that Genevieve recalled the witch, La Voisin. Had not the woman predicted that a man with dark hair would be the cause of her rue, would take away her happiness? In truth, it was happening just as the woman said. Tears in her eyes, Genevieve knelt by the statue of Christ and prayed that she would be given swift release from her earthly body, for if Philippe did not want her, she did not wish to live.

The morning of her public humiliation

came quicker than she'd expected, but then she learned that she was definitely being sent back to France and her punishment date had been moved up because the ship would shortly be leaving.

She had not bathed in the nearly two weeks since her imprisonment, and she wished she could be presentable out there. But would it matter? If Philippe was in the crowd watching her, then she would know of his hatred. Willing herself to die, she decided that it would not matter if she was washed or not.

The whole colony, all three settlements, it seemed, had gathered in front of the Governor's Chateau where the platform had been built. As she was led through the crowd, she saw faces familiar to her—the other women on the boat, the good Ursalines of the convent, and the men she had met. Annette and Lancelot stood near the front, but looking through the crowd she did not see Philippe. Did he even care?

Numbly, she ascended the wooden steps as the mob hushed and she could hear her name being whispered in small circles. She could see tears in Annette's eyes as her crime and punishment were read, but Genevieve herself was beyond crying. She had already done that, night after night. And being in the colonies, living with the Indians as she had, had taught her that she would get no mercy even from these supposedly civilized beings. She would not, she vowed, cry out. She would not let them see her pain.

Even as she was led to the pole and her arms lashed together, the back of her gown ripped from her, she said not a word. Philippe was there now, at the edge of the crowd. She looked toward him, hoping he would acknowledge her, but he did not met her eyes. It was probably just as well that way, she thought, for that meant he did not care anymore and she could allow herself to die without regrets. She thought of the infant she carried, and of how she had been reluctant because of her fear of childbirth to create a new life. Now it seemed that the baby would not live because she herself would not live.

The first lash came down upon her, kissing her back lightly. She closed her eyes, vowing not to cry out, vowing that she would be as stoic as the Indians Philippe so respected. With each stroke of the whip, she winced but said nothing. Tears came to her eyes, but she said nothing. She could see, through her own blurred vision, that Annette, too, was crying.

With a look of disgust, Philippe turned and left the watchers. She stared after him, wanting to cry out to him, wanting to go after him, but she could not.

The lash hit her again and she felt the blood running down her back.

Numbly she stood there, fainting only at the very last, scarely even aware of the blows that hit her after Philippe's departure. He was gone from her life and there was no more point in survival.

She dreamed about Philippe, about having his arms around her, about his tenderly touching her, but when she stirred and opened her eyes, Genevieve realized that she was still in prison and that it was Annette attending to her back and not Philippe.

"Where . . . where is he?"

Annette shrugged. "No one knows. He's not been seen since the flogging yesterday." She continued to rub the salve gently over the open wounds. "I could not believe how you stood there. 'Tis true, little Genny, you have become quite a heroine, for many of the women vowed they would have cried out and pleaded for release, but you did not. Even Lancelot was impressed with your courage."

" 'Tis not courage, but despair. The only release I wish now is to heaven," she said, still numb.

"Do not say that. As long as you are here, there is still hope."

Genevieve shook her head. "There is no more hope. I saw the way he looked at me when he left. He hates me and he always will. 'Tis over for me." Tears came down readily now.

Annette wanted to protest, to comfort her, but she could not touch her for fear of creating more pain, and could only lean down and chastely kiss her cheek. "Even in our most trying times, 'tis you who counselled me that it would be all right. Now you must take some of your own medicine."

"The only medicine I wish is the poison that Eugenia tried to give to—"her voice broke,—"to Papa St. Clair."

Annette's eyes were wide then. "Is that true?"

Genevieve shrugged, then winced. "She confessed her sins as I have confessed mine. Go. Leave me. I am leaving this land forevermore and you must forget me."

"Genevieve, do not talk like that. Even now Lancelot is with the Governor."

She shook her head. "He is an Indian. It will do no good."

As she had predicted, Lancelot's words had no effect on either Frontenac, Talon, or Antoine.

"You must go and talk to Philippe. You must bring him back here with you and have him talk to her, have him talk with the Governor. He can save her, if he likes."

"Love Dancer, I have done what I

can."

"But she is not wed to Racine. I know the story. I know the truth. She was sold as a slave might be, to pay her father's gaming debts. Is it right that she should suffer just because she is a woman? She escaped and came here."

He sighed. "She should have told Philippe."

" 'Tis easy for you to say, Lancelot, but you know how Philippe hates the nobility. Do you think his reaction would have been much different had he known earlier?"

Lancelot shook his head.

"Something must be done. Her ship leaves in a week's time."

"She is well enough to leave?"

"Well enough? I guess that is a relative matter." Annette put her arms around her husband, stroking his neck. "You call me Love Dancer and yet I tell you this, my darling, that I will do no more love dances for you unless you go to Philippe and bring him back here before she leaves."

Lancelot stared at his wife, unable to believe what he was hearing.

Annette's eyes narrowed. " 'Tis true. I will return to France with her."

"And risk the gallows?"

"If need be. I do not wish her to be alone. She is my friend, different though we are. Either you will fetch Philippe or you will lose me."

"And what of your house, your fortune?"

Annette shrugged. "I have not been able to start it because of a pig-headed Indian I have married. And anyway the priests and nuns of Ville-Marie were giving Papa St. Clair a most difficult time for allowing me to set up there. So, it is not to be."

" 'Tis blackmail, you know."

"*Oui.*" Annette stared at her husband. "But you are the only one who can talk with Philippe. Not even good Brother Emile has been able to get through."

"Very well, Love Dancer!" He hissed her name. "I will go and I will talk with my friend, but I promise nothing." He waved his fist at her as he left their rooms. "I do promise you, my wife, that you will dance love dances for me and me alone for many a day after this."

Annette nodded and, with a sad smile, watched her husband depart for the forests.

36

Despite Annette's brazen attempts, she
could not get passage on the ship back
with Genevieve, and Lancelot apparently
had not succeeded with Philippe, for he
had not returned. With desperate sadness,
Annette watched as Genevieve was led on
board, looking much thinner and more
haggard, despite her pregnancy.

"Oh, Annette." Genevieve sobbed
into the other woman's arms as the two
were allowed a few moments together. "I
will miss you so. You, and Lancelot."

"And not Philippe?"

"What am I to say about him? He
does not want me."

"No, I am sure that cannot be true.
Never have I seen a love so deep. He is but
confused. Once he knows the truth—"

"He will feel the same. The truth is that I lied to him." Genevieve's chin was high despite the pain in her back. "And I must face the consequences."

"But if you had told him in the beginning . . ."

"Then he never would have loved me. 'Tis no way around it, my friend. I am doomed, for without Philippe I do not care to live."

"I forbid you to talk so. You recall what I told you before—that if you wed Racine, he would probably die shortly and leave you a widow. Then you could return here."

Genevieve shook her head. "With my luck, Racine will outlive me, and even if I could return, Philippe does not want me. What would be the use?"

"He does, I tell you. I have seen it in his eyes. Give him time."

Genevieve shrugged as the first mate came to inform Annette that she had to leave.

As the women hugged, Annette once more whispered to her. " 'Tis strange I should be telling you to have faith, but it will work out. I know it will."

With eyes dulled from crying, Genevieve watched her friend walk down the gangplank. Her life in the colonies was over; indeed, her life was over altogether.

* * *

"Ah, so I have found you!" Lancelot said, as he came beside Philippe staring out at the stream where he and Genevieve had first touched, where he had asked her to be his wife. " 'Tis quite a distance you came."

The other man shrugged.

"Do you not want to talk?"

"I suppose that is why you have come. But you must see, Lance, 'tis no good. The woman lied to me." His fist clenched as he hit the rock at his side. "She was not who she said she was."

"And would you have wanted her, would it have made any difference to you, if you had known in the beginning?"

Philippe looked out over the waters churning like his emotions, but he remained silent.

"Tell me," Lancelot insisted.

"Why must you pursue this, my friend?"

Lancelot smiled slightly. "I must because my wife is concerned for her friend and has threatened to withdraw her affections from me if I do not do my best to persuade you to return."

"Ha! You, too, are under the spell of a woman. It is a damnable thing, is it not, my brother?"

Lancelot shrugged. *"Oui,* but I do believe what she says. Genevieve could not have been wed to Racine before she left."

"The document was signed by Colbert!" Philippe stood and stomped away from the river towards where he had made camp.

Hurriedly, Lancelot followed.

"Ye Gods, and I thought you French were wise! Even Indians have been known to forge promises. We are not quite as complex as you, but—"

"You are saying you think that marriage certificate was faked?"

"How else could it be? Think, man! She says she was not wed to the Marquis. Except for her name change, have you ever known Genevieve to be less than honorable?" Lancelot paused. "And did you not tell me she was a virgin when you took her? If she had been wed, would not the man have had his way with her?"

"If he could. From what I hear, the Marquis de Racine is quite elderly."

"But functional, nonetheless, I would guess."

Philippe sighed. "You are right. But what am I to do?"

"*Sang Dieu*! What are you to do? You come with me. You go to her. You tell her you love her. You discredit that toad of a man with his green velvet jacket. You fight for her. You talk with the Governor. Indeed, the Governor and the Intendant both came several times to our rooms seeking you, but you would not hear them out."

"I thought they were asking about the militia they wished me to lead and I could not talk about that then."

Lancelot shook his head. "Come. Now. We must hurry if we are to reach Quebec before the ship leaves."

Philippe looked toward the river once more and thought of her passion and his, of how she had cared for him during his illness, of how he had introduced her to the delights of love, of how she had saved the estate, of how she had bravely withstood the lash. And he thought of their child. "Very well. I will return with you and we will talk with this Le Bera and see what we can see. But if this claim is truly correct, then I wash my hands of her. I will have nothing to do with a woman who leaves her lawful husband."

"Not even if she loves you, not even if you are her lawful husband?"

Philippe grunted and picked up his belongings and the paddle to begin the journey up river toward the city.

Currents were against them, but even so, he and Lancelot paddled against the odds, returning to the city in half the time it had taken him to leave it. Yet, they had pushed themselves for nothing. It was all too late.

By the time they arrived at the

harbor, the ship had been gone a week or more.

Sadly, Annette welcomed her husband back into her arms as Philippe went off to talk with Frontenac and to look at the marriage document one more time.

"*Cor bleu*! This is indeed a fake!" Philippe cried out, angry not only at himself for not having looked closer at the parchment, but even more at the Governor for not having seen it earlier. "Did you not see this, man!" He thrust the certificate under Frontenac's longish nose. "Look at this date. Look at Colbert's signature! 'Tis written for the day when Genevieve was already on these shores."

The governor looked at the paper and shrugged. "Indeed, you are right, St. Clair, but even so, she was the property of Racine and, wed or not, he had a right to have her returned."

"*Non*, he has no right. 'Tis I who have the right. I am her lawful husband."

"Well, what's done is done."

"*Ma foi*! You expect me to stand here and hear you say that? After all the pain she and I have been through? *Non*, I will not take that answer, Your Excellency. I will leave on the first ship to France."

"And what will you do, St. Clair? Fight for your beloved's hand?"

"Indeed, I did once and I shall do so again. This time I must fight fire with fire.

My grandfather is a cousin of the King and we shall see what he knows of this Racine." With that he stormed out of the Chateau.

It was yet another month, during which Philippe impatiently paced the harbor walkway, before a second ship could be made ready. The captain had not planned a return voyage so soon, but a handful of ecus convinced him that it was worth his while.

"Do you come with me?" Philippe asked Lancelot and Annette.

Together they shook their heads.

"In faith, I have no desire to see France again."

"And from what I know, I have no wish to be there, either." Lancelot's arm went around his wife. "Love Dancer and I shall be awaiting your return in my village."

"You have given up the idea of a house, Annette?"

She smiled and turned toward her husband. "I have. 'Tis enough I have to do in satisfying my heart." Her eyes glowed with happiness. "I will do my love dances only for him."

Philippe felt a pang of jealousy as he saw the pair kiss.

"I promise you, Annette, I will find her and convince her of my love. I will return her here, for our children must grow up as brothers. 'Tis the only way this land will be righteous and free." He headed up the gangplank as the anchor was weighed.

Annette laughed. "You do not have to convince anyone of your love."

"Ah, but I do. I must make amends for my foolish notions, for I realize that Genevieve is the only woman who will ever be for me, and my heart is but half without her."

"Then godspeed," she called to him, waving as the sails billowed out and the ship moved into the waters, toward the Gaspé and the oceans beyond.

37

"What do you mean, we are leaving ship now?" Genevieve stared at the land and town surrounding her. "This is but Brest. We are in Brittany, not Normandy."

"Do as I say." Antoine nudged her out of the small stateroom that the Marquis' money had bought for her. "I am but following my orders."

Genevieve shrugged and picked up her small items.

Much to her sorrow, the ship had made amazingly good speed, crossing the Atlantic in less than four weeks. And while she had, once her back had healed, spent most of her days looking out at the water and wondering what it would be like to drown, she had never quite had the courage to go through with it. Perhaps it was the hope of the child who still lived within her and the knowledge that, even though she did not have Philippe, she would still, no matter what the Marquis did to her, have a part of him.

Touching her belly gently, she followed her captor out of the tiny room.

Several times during the voyage he had come to her room at night, but each time she had feigned sleep and he had turned and left. Genevieve did not know how much longer she could have held him off and was, in a way, thankful to have reached land. She did not know who was worse—Antoine or the Marquis.

Antoine planned, he told her, to head immediately for Racine's estates, but wishing to delay the inevitable as long as possible, Genevieve pleaded that she needed a day to rest, for her obviously pregnant body was now slowing her down.

Reluctantly, the messenger agreed, and directed his bags and her to the most comfortable tavern on the waterfront.

"Well, Antoine, you have made remarkable time. I salute you for your quick execution of my desires." The Marquis de Racine stood up, towering over the messenger as the pair walked into the common room of the tavern.

"Indeed, we did." The little man flushed, not knowing what to say. "I did not expect you to greet us at the port, Your Excellency. I would have brought her to you."

"Would you have? Delicate morsel that she is, I could not wait to feast my eyes upon her once more." Racine turned to eye his possession and felt his desire for her once more stirring, even though she was now as big as a house and as brown as a berry. 'Twould take a few months, perhaps, but her skin tone would soon return to the beautiful pale tints that she'd had when he'd first wet his lips over her, and no doubt the infant she carried, one of the savage's probably, would be dealt with quickly and efficiently by his staff.

"I would have thought you'd leave ship in LeHarve, my friend, for that is indeed closer to my estates."

"Oh, *non*, your lordship." Antoine bowed and scraped, knowing the reputation of the man. "There are a few short-cuts I know from here, and I could not wait to get her into your hands."

"Yes, yes." The Marquis nodded, rubbing his smooth palms together and wishing, just at the sight of her, that he could rub his treasures against her and release his love for her. Saliva drooled from his mouth, and his valet ran to dab it from his chin.

He moved towards his property and

studied her. It took all his effort to keep his hands away from his manhood as it inched up, delighted once more by her.

"You were very, very naughty, my Genevieve." His voice was soft, and almost soothing. "I shall have to spank you for that." He stepped forward, his hand on her cheek. "And I will soon have to show you the pleasures you have missed."

She tried to pull away, but his hand quickly reached around, grabbing her and giving her a light tap on her buttocks, then lingered for a moment near her cleft, his long fingers resting there as if he wanted to insert them. Even had she wanted to move now, she could not without feeling the obnoxious pressure of his touch.

Ignoring his entourage, he leaned over to kiss her, drawing her closer to him and slobbering all over her.

His kiss was not at all like Philippe's had been, and it disgusted her even more, but Philippe did not want her and so what choice of life did she have? His hand reached into her bodice to stroke and squeeze her breasts.

"My child—" she protested, feeling the pain here more than she had on the stake.

"Oh, yes." The Marquis made a face and pulled back. "You are right, my dove.

As much as I wish to bed you now and make you mine forevermore, I suppose it would be politic to wait. How long now?"

"A month or so."

He nodded. "Very well then, my Genevieve." He leaned over and slobbered his wet kiss over her again, his breath stinking of the snuff he had recently taken and his hands resting on her bosom. "I will give you time to prepare for me. I agree with your father. A man of my stature needs a proper ceremony. 'Twould not do to have only the marriage certificate, done by proxy as it was, to declare to the world that I see you as my wife." He stroked her belly so that she could feel the baby within jerking away as well, almost as if the infant sensed the danger he was in.

"Though mind you, this time there will be no convents, and no days of prayer." He grinned. "I'll warrant it was clever of you, but not clever enough, *non*." He snapped his fingers as several beefy guards appeared. "You will be carefully watched, and pampered too, I might add, as befits my wife. And when we are wed, you will see all you have missed and you will beg me, on your hands and knees, to love you and keep you." He leered and patted her bottom again. "Is that not right?"

Genevieve could only nod and pray

that the affliction which had taken her mother and aunt would also take her.

"Oh, Genevieve. Is it really my Genny?"

The Vicomte shook his head as he took her hands in his. "Why did you not tell me of your plans? Do you not realize how my heart ached when I realized you had gone?"

She turned to look at him for only a moment, then looked out the window. While the room was luxurious, it was a prison just as the room in the Chateau had been.

"My Genny, indeed, I was sorry for what I had to do, but I am your father. 'Tis my right to do as I see fit with your life."

"No!" She turned to him again now, fury in her eyes. "It is not your right! You are my father, that is true, but I am a person just as you are and have every intention of living my life as I desire—or not living it at all."

"Genevieve!"

"It is true, papa. I do love you, but in the colonies, when I lived among the savages, I saw there the Indians who were supposed to be less civilized than we. Do you know what they do with their daughters?"

The old Vicomte shook his head.

"They let them chose the man they want to wed. They give permission for their daughters to pick out whom they want."

"*Hélas*! They are a different breed than we. They do not know any better."

"Indeed, I think they know better than do we. I, for one, wish I were back there with them. I wish I were with my Philippe."

And for the first time since landing again on French soil, Genevieve began to cry. The tears washed over her, and nothing her father or maid could do would stop them.

Finally, exhausted, she calmed down.

"*Ma cherie*, I did what was best for you. If I had thought there was another way—"

"But there was," she told him, her eyes still moist. " 'Twas all right for you to dally with the servants and the peasant girls, but I could not."

"But I needed you a virgin. I could not sell you to the nobility if you were soiled."

"Ah, that is it, Papa. I am soiled. You see here—" she motioned toward her stomach, which indeed looked ready to deliver—" 'Tis my lawful husband's child I have here. You, my sweet father, are going against the laws of the church. 'Tis bigamy you are asking me to perform."

"*Non*, it is not, my Genevieve. You did not wed the man under your lawful name and therefore the ceremony does not stand. The child is a bastard and will be given to the servants to raise. And once you are somewhat healed, the marriage will take place. I have agreed, and it must be."

"Why? Because of your debts?"

He sighed. "*Oui*. Because of my debts."

She turned her head as he left the room and again sobbed into her pillows.

It was three days later that she was delivered of a healthy boy, his eyes blue as the sky and his dimpled chin looking much like his father's. Crying, Genevieve stroked the baby as she let him suckle her breast. Only God knew how long she would have him, or how long he would live. Only God knew if she would ever see him again.

The fever she had dreaded did not come upon her and within a week, the doctor, at the urging of the Marquis who had come daily to see her, pronounced her ready to become the Marquise de Racine.

She protested that she could not fit into the gown that he had originally given her, but her protests was immediately quelled by the presence of the dressmaker, who set to work altering the dress to Genevieve's new, fuller figure.

" 'Twill not take long before your size is back to what it was," Racine said, pawing her breasts as he again slobbered over her. "And you'll have no more worries about childbirth fever, my little dear, for I do not plan to ruin your beautiful little figure again."

Genevieve could only look over to her baby's crib and sigh as she tolerated the man's attention.

He gave her another wet kiss. "Until the morrow, my love, when we consummate our desire for each other."

Genevieve did not respond, but waited until he had left her prison. Going to the cradle, she picked up her son, her Philippe-Pierre, and cried as she hugged the infant to her.

She dreamed of Philippe the night before the wedding ceremony was to be held. With difficulty, she had tried to put him out of her mind, to realize that he was gone from her life, but every time she looked at the child, she knew that he was still as much a part of her as he could be and no time or distance would separate them. They were bonded by their love and by their passion, and no mtter what he said or what he thought, he was still her only love, and she was sure that no matter where he went he would never find someone to love him the way she did.

She moved the baby to her other

breast. What good did it do her to dwell on him now? The past was past and no amount of crying was going to change it.

Still, as she reluctantly allowed Claudine to help her dress for the ceremony, she couldn't help thinking of her wedding on the St. Clair estate. The gown had not been so jewel-encrusted, nor had it been so expensive, but she had worn it out of love for the man she was marrying.

Tears came to her eyes.

"Please, Madame Genevieve, do not cry." Claudine stared helplessly at her mistress. "Indeed, 'tis sorry I am that I told them where you were, but I had no choice. They were going to kill my Daniel."

Genevieve nodded. "It is all right, Claudine. I understand. I would not have wanted Daniel to be murdered on account of the Marquis' lust for me. And I know that even had your kept the secret, he would somehow have found me. It was God's way of punishing me."

"Oh, no! You must not say that."

"It is true," Genevieve said, laying the baby in the cradle and kissing his brow. "After today, I will not see my son."

"*Non*, did you not know? Daniel and I are to raise him."

Genevieve managed a smile. "Well, at least I know he will be in loving hands." The baby grabbed at his mother's finger and tears again came to her eyes. "You will not let him forget his mama, will you? Or his papa, for that matter. Perhaps one day, my son will go back to his homeland and see the house where he was conceived." She became tearful again and quickly took the linen from the maid. "I suppose it is time to get ready now."

"*Oui*." Claudine sighed. "It is."

The ornate chapel on the grounds of Racine's country estate was nearly as large as the church in the Ursaline convent. Shivering with the chill both from the stone walls and her thoughts of her future, a very subdued Genevieve walked down the aisle to her father, who waited to assist her, then with him the rest of the way to the altar.

Everyone noble in France, even the King himself, graced the wedding of the Marquis. But then they were blood-related and the Marquis had done many favors for His Majesty. She wondered how all the others could be so happy this day when she felt so miserable. Numb with the pain of living without Philippe these past months, she walked forward, wishing that she were already in her casket, wishing that she were being carried to her funeral, for in fact, this is what the ceremony was to her.

On her father's arm, she neared the altar.

The commotion outside the church startled everyone but Genevieve. She assumed it was someone arriving late, and she really didn't care who had come or not.

But as the yells and the curses grew louder, she too, turned.

The doors opened and her eyes went wide. Philippe! She couldn't believe it. Her heart pounded as she took a step forward. Quickly, the Marquis stepped into her path, blocking her way. "*Non*, my precious. You are going to be mine and I will not lose you again."

"You have already lost her, Racine!" Philippe shouted as he freed himself from the guards, his sword ready to challenge anyone. "She is mine and none of your faked documents can say otherwise."

"I do not know what you mean, boy." Racine's eyes narrowed as he looked to Colbert, then back to St. Clair. "Mademoiselle Simon is to be my wife this day. So go back to your forests and your savages."

"We will see about that!" Philippe stepped forward and was blocked by yet another guard.

"Let him go, Paul." The distinguished Duc St. Marc stepped inside the chapel. "We will let our cousin decide this matter. Leave my grandson alone." The Duc bowed to the King as he came forward, and the guards dropped their arms from

Philippe.

"Your grandson!" Genevieve exclaimed when she found her voice.

Philippe flushed for a moment.

"*Oui*, Genny. I am the Duc's grandson."

She could only stare at him then, as silence filled the air. The King rose from his chair and moved forward with the grace of someone who knew his due.

"Cousin." St. Marc addressed His Majesty.

"You have papers claiming that this woman is yours, St. Clair?"

Philippe glanced at the older man still at his side and then turned to the King. "*Oui*, Your Majesty, that I do." Philippe bowed low and kissed Louis' ring.

"Produce them."

From the pocket of his vest, Philippe produced the marriage certificate confirming the wedding of Genevieve and himself as it had been performed by Father Raoul of the Holy Society of Jesus.

The King read it and then at Racine. "What do you know of this, Paul?" He frowned and handed the Marquis the document.

"Nothing! I know nothing. It is true. The girl—"

"She is a woman, Racine. My woman."

Racine shot an evil look at Philippe. "The woman was already in the family way when she was discovered in the colonies and returned to her rightful place, but as you and I both know, that can easily happen without the blessing of marriage." He forced a laugh.

But the King did not laugh with him. He picked up the proxy document handed to him by his minister as he looked first at St. Clair, then at Racine.

"Well, Cousin?" St. Marc asked. "Does Genevieve come with us or not?"

Genevieve looked to the old man, not daring to look at Philippe, afraid that he would disappear in a moment.

"Tell me, my dear," Louis said, turning to the bride. "What is your story?"

"My story?" Her voice cracked but, quickly recalling her manners, she curtseyed to the King. "Your Majesty, I am wed to Philippe St. Clair."

"Indeed, than what do you do here?"

Her eyes lowered, Genevieve told the King of her father's gaming debts and of how she had fled to the colonies and married.

" 'Twas not a legal marriage, Cousin," Racine broke in. "She wed under the name of her servant. She is mine and I sent my messenger over to claim her."

"With a phony marriage document."

" 'Tis not phony!" Racine's voice reached a high pitch. "She is legally mine. And we were wed by proxy."

"Then why do you need another wedding?" Philippe asked.

"Indeed." The King nodded in agreement as Genevieve held her breath.

"Your Excellency," St. Marc said, couching his words in the most diplomatic terms, "is it not true that you sent the King's Daughters over to create new citizens for the colony?"

The King nodded.

"And Madame St. Clair, or rather Lady St. Marc, since my grandson will soon inherit my title, has already produced an heir to my fortunes and a good citizen of New France."

"That is true?"

Genevieve nodded at the King's question.

"Then I cannot allow the young man to be born on the wrong side of the blanket. Therefore, I do declare that your marriage is legal and binding."

Genevieve's mouth dropped open, as she still did not dare look at her love.

"That is not fair! That is not right!" Racine cried, in a tantrum. "I have paid good monies for her and I want what I paid for!"

"You will be fully compensated, Racine," St. Marc stated. "I will cover whatever debts the Vicomte has with you."

Anger shot from Racine's eyes, but he was forced to look on as Philippe stepped forward and took Genevieve's hand in his.

"My love, will you ever forgive me for doubting you?"

Through tears in her eyes, she nodded and swallowed hard as she smiled.

"Then kiss me to prove it."

"In front of—?"

He quelled her protest as his mouth met hers and it was obvious to everyone, even to Racine, that the pair belonged together. Lifting Genevieve into his arms, Philippe carried her down the aisle and out toward his grandfather's waiting carriage.

38

Once in the safety of St. Marc's chateau, the baby in her arms being fawned over by his adoring father, Genevieve relaxed. From the depths of despair to the height of happiness, she thought, stroking the cheek of her loving husband.

"It was unforgivable of me to leave you the way I did, *mignonne*. Lancelot was right. I should have known you better and I did know you, but my pride was hurt because you did not trust me enough to tell me the truth.

"And I suppose, in many ways, that is why I was attracted to you. I could see that you were not like the other women, but I did not know why."

"But now you know." She looked away towards the baby sucking at his fist, his tiny feet kicking in the air. "I love you, Philippe, only I was so afraid that I would lose you."

"It was my fault you almost did. Me and my stupid pride. But I swear I will never let you away from me again." He sat upright in the bed, staring out at the expanse of his grandfather's estate. "Even if it means staying here in France where your family is." He waited a moment. "Before you make a decision, there is something you must have."

"What?"

Her eyes opened wide as Philippe pulled a black fluff of hair from the box near the bed. Slowly the fluff ball moved and opened its eyes.

"A kitten!"

"To replace Alexandre. Though I know none can, I could not resist when I saw him."

"Oh, Philippe!" She kissed him, and her arms went around his neck as she kissed him again, stroking his rough cheek. "The only place for this kitten is in New France. 'Tis in the colony where I found my happiness, in the forest with you where we were free from the restrictions of civilized life. I would rather go back there with Philippe-Pierre. Besides, your father must want to see his grandchild."

Philippe nodded slowly. "You are sure, my love?"

"I do know that although you used your grandfather's influence to win me back, you need to be free as much as I do. And I would not be happy anywhere you were not."

"Oh, Genevieve!" He kissed her again, and again and again, as their passions mounted, spiraling to heights not yet dreamed of, and Genevieve knew that forever she would be with him because they were one.

BE SWEPT AWAY
ON A TIDE OF PASSION
BY LEISURE'S THRILLING
HISTORICAL ROMANCES!

Make the Most of Your Leisure Time with
LEISURE BOOKS